Marion Zimmer Bradley

Bradley

PRESENTS

DAW
No. 1152

SWORD AND SORCERESS

XVII

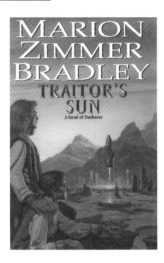

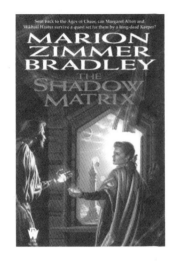

ISBN 0-88677-891-3

US $6.99 / CAN $9.99

50699

S EAN

"Tell me, Wise One, how fares my son!"

Bera waited for the vision to form . . . and saw nothing. Once more she called on her ally.

Still she could not hear him, but within her inner darkness, a spark began to glow. It grew, became a circle of fire. The flickering light showed hurdles of brushwood stacked around the hall, and men who stood with poised spears before the doors. Now the thatch was catching; bright flames surged toward the starry sky. In the midst of that radiance stood a woman, eyes blazing, her golden hair streaming toward the sky. As Bera drew closer, she saw that the woman was chained.

Unwilled, her lips began to move, giving voice to the goddess' reply—

"Enslaved I stand within your hall—three times you have burned me, three times speared me, yet I endure . . ."

Bera tried to block out the image of the burning woman, but found herself being drawn closer.

"While your chains bind me, I cannot see beyond the circle of fire . . ."

The flames grew brighter; heat seared her skin.

"Set me free!" Did those words come from without or within?

Fire exploded around her and she screamed.

From "Lady of Flame" by Diana L. Paxson

SWORD AND SORCERESS XVII

EDITED BY

Marion Zimmer Bradley

DAW BOOKS, INC.

DONALD A. WOLLHEIM, FOUNDER

375 Hudson Street, New York, NY 10014

ELIZABETH R. WOLLHEIM
SHEILA E. GILBERT
PUBLISHERS

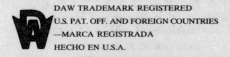

ACKNOWLEDGMENTS

Introduction © 2000 by Marion Zimmer Bradley
Memories of the Sea © 2000 by Dave Coleman-Reese
Free Passage © 2000 by Mary Catelli
The Conjuror's Light © 2000 by Lisa Campos
My Sister's Song © 2000 by T. Borregaard
The Summons © 2000 by Bunnie Bessell
Luz © 2000 by Patricia Duffy Novak
Caelqua's Spring © 2000 by Vera Nazarian
Deep as Rivers © 2000 by Cynthia McQuillin
Weapons at War © 2000 by Charles Laing
Hell Hath No Fury. . . . © 2000 by Lee Martindale
An Exchange of Favors © 2000 by Dorothy Heydt
Price of the Sword © 2000 by Kim Fryer
Demon Calling © 2000 by ElizaBeth Gilligan
Nor Iron Bars a Cage © 2000 by Deborah Wheeler
The Haunting of Princess Elizabeth © 2000 by Carrie Vaughn
Shadow Soul © 2000 by Laura J. Underwood
Memories Traced in Snow © 2000 by Dave Smeds
Valkyrie © 2000 by Jenn Reese
Soul Dance © 2000 by Lisa Silverthorne
Lady of Flame © 2000 by Diana Paxson
The Tears of the Moon © 2000 by Cythia Ward

CONTENTS

INTRODUCTION
by Marion Zimmer Bradley

Every year these anthologies seem to develop a unique theme, in addition to the elements required by my guidelines. The early ones had themes such as "a woman can do anything she really wants to do" (and that got old fast as new writers seemed to think that a story proving that a woman can too be a camel herder—or whatever—was all I was looking for) and "rape and revenge" (which was also something I did not want to do year after year). By last year's anthology, the theme had mutated to "a woman may be able to do *anything,* but she can't do *everything.*" This theme also had a strong note of exhaustion in it; I think my writers are getting tired of trying to be superhuman.

This year has been strange in the real world, and I suspect that the theme of many of this year's stories came from that. Even the most strenuous efforts to avoid television, newspapers, and news magazines could not insulate one from whatever it was President Clinton and Monica whatever-her-last-name-was were doing. Between people arguing over the technical definition of sex and/or adultery and one comment I heard to the effect that unless one considered the President, as Commander in Chief of the Armed Forces, to be subject to the Uniform Code of Military Justice, adultery was not criminal behavior for him and was therefore a matter between him, his wife, and

1

God—and neither his wife nor God needed Congress to help them deal with this matter . . . well, I could follow most of that, though I thought the impeachment was a complete waste of legislative energy and television broadcast time. (At least the O. J. Simpson trials were about a matter of life and death, not to mention whether the custody of two growing children should go to their mother's murderer.) But what really puzzled me was the media criticism of the First Lady; there actually seemed to be people who thought it was wrong for her to be keeping her marriage vows. An appalling number of people seemed to think that because her husband was behaving badly, she should as well.

I certainly do not believe that one should stay in a marriage at all and any costs, but I do feel that the dissolution of a marriage is a serious matter, not something you do automatically just because you are angry at your spouse. Some things cannot be tolerated, but surely that decision is up to the parties involved, not the media.

But the questions were out there: Do you keep the vows you made no matter what happens; or, if the situation has changed drastically, do you do what you feel to be right? How do you tell right from wrong, especially when other people are trying to make up your mind for you? And those questions made it into quite a few stories I got this year, as each writer tried to work out the answers. If I had to use one word to describe what this year's anthology is about, it would be "justice."

This year has been confusing and tiring in my personal life as well. The foundation of my house seems to have disintegrated—the grass and mushrooms growing through the downstairs floor were a strong indication that something was seriously wrong, so the entire bottom floor had to be removed and replaced. I've lost track of the number of times I've moved during the last year.

For a while I was in another city, which was particularly awkward, especially while I was in a hospital where many people didn't know me. The hospital spent five months trying to bill the wrong insurance company because they asked me for my insurance information in the emergency room while I was sick and confused and I gave them the name of the company I had four years ago instead of the one I have now. You'd think that when Emergency Room personal think you're having a stroke, they would check the billing information with someone who is thinking straight, like your next of kin. It took my secretary only a two-minute phone call to the billing office to straighten the mess out when they finally got around to writing to me about it. At the time I was hospitalized, she was still in Berkeley—someone had to stay home with the dog (a 115-pound Malamute), and she got the job. I think she'll be the happiest of all of us when the construction is over and we can all move back home; she's been staying on the construction site the whole time, enduring occasional loss of electricity and frequent loss of plumbing. ("Hey, guys, did you know that the water supply to the office building is turned off again?") But I'll certainly be glad to be in my own house again.

With all the confusion and moving around, and the fact that all of my manuscripts get picked up at the post office, taken to my office, logged in, brought to me wherever I happen to be at the moment, read, sent back to the office, and then rejected or bought, this seemed to be a reasonable time to change *Sword and Sorceress* from an open market to a "by invitation only" anthology. When we did the invitations for *Sword & Sorceress XVIII,* we discovered that over 500 people have sold stories to me over the years, so there's a large pool of talent to chose from. (In the spirit of last year's theme, I can read one slush pile, but two is a real stretch . . .)

Marion Zimmer Bradley's Fantasy Magazine remains an open market, but I don't want manuscripts from anyone who has not read my guidelines—and, believe me, I can tell. (So can the mailroom staff.) So don't send a story to S&S unless you get an invitation; and, if you want to submit a story to my magazine, either send a #10 SASE (Self-Addressed Stamped Envelope) to PO Box 249, Berkeley CA 94701–0249, or read the guidelines, including the manuscript format instructions, on my web site, www.mzbfm.com.

I'm looking forward to editing *Sword & Sorceress XVIII*. I wonder what sort of theme it will end up with.

MEMORIES OF THE SEA

by Dave Coleman-Reese

Dave Coleman-Reese is a part-time writer of fantasy and science fiction and a full-time software developer. He has worked in the computer field for twelve years, and expects to do so for some time to come. Dave lives in the Maryland suburbs of Washington DC with his wife, Jenn Reese, and their two cats. He enjoys movies, hiking, singing, and games of all kinds.

"Memories of the Sea" is Dave's first professionally published story, although he has another work pending publication in *Pulp Eternity*. That's how it goes—you batter the walls for ages, then they all fall down at once.

This story was inspired by the idea that the surest form of an afterlife is the impact that you have on others while you are alive.

A true midsummer storm threatened the harbor outside. Already Talgra could hear the raindrops on the tavern windows, scouting weaknesses to be exploited by the deluge to come. They found none in the walls of the Drowned Rat, as secure and dry an establishment as could be found within the waterside crescent of Reefhaven.

Talgra rearranged the four pearls before her once again. "You two started in storms, didn't you? You'll be free again in a storm tonight, you will." Her finger paused on the third—small, but near perfectly round, and white as milk. "A lady, I'll reckon. Or maybe a boy. But you had elegance before the sea took you."

The last pearl troubled her. It was irregular, ugly even. Misshapen and asymmetrical, but huge. There was a complex story here, but not a pretty one. That would come last, when those who sought drink more than tales of the dead had returned to their ships. "Yes, you will be last. But don't fear—you, too, will be free."

"And *you* will be locked up for a loiterer if you don't get out there soon!"

Talgra looked up, blinking away her close scrutiny of the last pearl. Darmin had swept through the curtain from the common room, carrying a hot mug wrapped in linen. Her young tanned face smiled broadly as she set the wine down on Talgra's small table. It smelled wonderful, but was masked by the odor of pipe smoke in Darmin's simple dress and long auburn hair.

Talgra wrinkled her nose in distaste. "How can they do that to themselves?" she said. There was nothing worse than smoke to the lungs of a diver, but stories must have their listeners. And sailors' habits were like the reef—built up over ages, and not likely to change soon.

"It reminds them of the land, Talgra. A bit of the green earth to take with them out to sea. You can't begrudge them that, can you? Besides, maybe I was a tobacco farmer myself, and now you're insulting my family's livelihood! How dare you!"

Her look of mock affront was just enough to make Talgra smile. "I still say you were a ship's cook, and you're just pretending not to remember any recipes so that Jakor doesn't stuff you back in the kitchen, where you can't flirt for tips." They laughed together, and for the thousandth time in six months Talgra marveled at how good it felt.

She scooped up the pearls on their velvet cloth, the wrapped mug in her other hand. Darmin dramatically pulled the curtain aside for her so that every sailor's view was upon her entrance. She reverently walked through the clouds of smoke to her table by the fire, breathing as shallowly as possible. Conversations quieted in her wake. By the time she sat and laid the pearls before her, only a single voice in the far corner droned on. He was silenced by a sharp elbow from his neighbor, and then only the sound of the steadily increasing rain remained.

Darmin immodestly sat cross-legged on the bar, high enough that her view of Talgra sailed over the heads of the gathered seamen.

"We have come to hear the stories of the dead. Their lives were lost in the sea, and are now found. I have wrested them from the depths. Listen, learn, and take their stories with you when you go, that they shall truly never die," said Talgra.

Every bench was filled, and most of the floor besides. Talgra lifted the first pearl, rolling it between her thumb and forefinger. She raised it high above her in the firelight, then gently held it up to her left ear. She listened to the pearl as only few could. She listened to her voice as all present strained to do.

"I'm a man, nobody special." *But you are,* Talgra thought. *Everyone is.*

"I served on the *White Gull.* I worked the rigging. I liked the high winds. I had a wife in Opalsgrove, and a son I never met. I hated the taste of fish. Once I won eighty bits in a single hand of poker, bluffing on a pair of sixes."

Talgra continued, her voice a litany of the trivial. In the back of her mind she sat and watched the audience as the pearl's story passed through her. Three sailors at one of the front tables had that spark of recognition that she looked for each time. They whispered among themselves. One turned away to rub his eyes where his fellows couldn't see.

The story was drawing to a close—the pearl was almost gone. "It was a storm." *I knew it,* she thought. "I was in the rigging, trying to loosen the mainsail lines. The wind caught me. It threw me to the deck, hard. I died."

The pearl was gone, leaving only a waxy feel on Talgra's fingertips and a tiny bit of grit. She swallowed dryly, then raised her cooling mug. "To the dead!"

"To the dead!" the sailors replied. "To Angris!" called the sailors from the front table. "We served with him, and he was the finest man you could hope to know!"

Their table became a cluster of voices as stories of Angris were traded. Talgra placed the bit of memory into a small glass vial. She then gratefully sipped her wine, free from attention for the moment. Darmin worked her way through the crowd with a steaming refill pitcher.

"You really have an ear for the pearls," said Darmin as she freshened Talgra's mug.

"Maybe. But it'll do me little good when my lungs finally give out. I was lucky to find these four as it is. Each dive gets a little harder." Talgra leaned back in her chair with an exaggerated sigh.

"So take an apprentice already, and spare us your complaining." Darmin's tone was mildly mocking. The sailors had begun to turn expectantly back to Talgra.

Talgra ignored them, looking questioningly at Darmin until the younger woman broke eye contact.

"Now don't start that again. You know that I'm just passing through." Darmin inspected the floorboards of the inn.

"It's been six months, Darmin. I don't care what the doctors say—you're as healed as you're going to get. Those memories aren't coming back," said Talgra.

"You have three more stories to tell." Darmin

turned on her heel and strode back to the bar. The sailors parted automatically before her.

The second story was typical—a passenger swept overboard in a storm. None seemed to recognize him, but Talgra knew that his story would radiate from here like ripples in a pond. It might one day reach the dead man's wife, or son, and bring them a bit of comfort.

Darmin sent another barmaid to refill her mug.

The third pearl was a woman. *Aha,* thought Talgra, *my eye is still sharp, even if my tongue has grown dull.* She had lived her life far from the sea. A schoolteacher, unmarried, her parents long gone as well. Her life was long, if solitary. She had touched many children. And one day the loneliness had become too much for her. A vacation to the seacliffs, taken on a whim. More wine than was good for her. A decision made in an instant. Sharp, sweet regret one second later, and then the sea claimed her forever.

Amazingly, one of the sailors had known her, had been taught by her as a child. He was awash with tears, and he was not alone.

After the toast, Talgra withdrew to the back room. She was crying. "That was not me. That was not me. I mourn her death, but that was not me."

"Talgra?"

Talgra turned her back to the curtain so that Darmin couldn't see her hastily wiping away her tears. "Yes, dear?"

Darmin walked in and sat across from the older woman. "Talgra, I'm sorry I was short with you. You've been great to me these past months, and— have you been crying?"

"It's nothing. Just a bit of sentiment in my eye. I'm sorry too, Darmin. You've got your own life—you don't need me hanging mine on you as well."

"But I *don't* have my own life," Darmin said. "If I did, I could choose. But I don't have any idea who I was—who I am. How can I move on when I don't have anywhere to move from?"

Talgra had no answer.

Jakor had removed those sailors who were too entranced with wine to appreciate Talgra's work, and barred the door against interruptions. He stood now in the shadows of the far corner, as serious as a deacon entrusted with the church keys on the night before high service. In short, he was as humorless and dependable as ever.

Talgra had pushed her problems, and Darmin's, to the back of her mind as she focused on the misshapen pearl. She turned it over and over between her finger and thumb. *You're stalling,* she thought.

Darmin sat in her usual position at the end of the bar. She and the sailors watched as Talgra raised the pearl, then placed it near her ear.

"I am a woman." *A surprise.* "I was the captain of many ships." *Extremely rare.* "I was young, but strong. My crews respected me. My cargo feared me. No revolt was ever attempted under my whip."

There were gasps from the crowd, hardened sailors all. Talgra heard the whispers, all reducing to one word: "Slaver."

Slavery was immoral, unthinkable, evil—and legal in several lands along the coast of the Middle Ocean. Talgra had heard all of the tales. Slavers had hearts of ice, veins that pumped money instead of blood. But she had never heard the story told from a slaver's lips. Her voice was faltering. She forced herself to listen, and speak. Even this one deserved to be remembered, to have her story known. Perhaps especially this one, so that none would follow in her footsteps.

"When I was twenty, I led a raid into the jungles

of Kaltrec. We killed thirty. We captured forty-one. I was wounded by a spear in the side, but I killed the boy who had done it. He was the son of their chief. He wore a jade necklace shaped like a tiger. He looked to be twelve.''

There was a disturbance back near the bar. But the story gripped Talgra too tightly. She could not spare the attention for whatever fight had broken out among the sailors. Her world was the pearl and its slaver's story.

"I needed to make an example. I collected the old and the children. They were useless as slaves. I put them in the huts and set them on fire. I burned them alive. They sounded almost human as they died. Some tried to escape. I—"

Suddenly the voice was gone. She looked up, dazed. Darmin was there. Her left hand pinioned Talgra's right against the table, the pearl still gripped in Talgra's fingers. "Stop!" she yelled. "For the love of the sea, stop! *I remember!*"

Talgra balanced on the edge of her trance, struggling to understand Darmin's words. The pearl whispered on, but she couldn't hear it, couldn't stop it. The story was being lost. "Darmin, let go. The pearl is speaking. It's good that you remember this woman— maybe she'll mention you."

Darmin's tears ran down her face, half-choking her reply. "She won't mention me. She *is* me. I was her. I remember—parts. The tiger. The children. I beg you, Talgra, stop. I don't want to know the rest!" She was fully crying now, but her grip was still iron on Talgra's wrist.

"Impossible," Talgra said. "The pearls are the stories of the dead. It has always been so." But yet, Darmin had been dead to the world. If her memories were taken by the ocean, could they not be captured as easily as the dead's? Talgra had read the pearls for all of her life, but still did not know how the memories came to be captured by the black oysters below.

The pearl continued to grow smaller in Talgra's fingers. Years were slipping away, memories which might never be known again. Did she have the right? She didn't know, but she had the duty to the dead. "Jakor! Help me—get her off of me." Then, in a gentler voice, "Sit, child. Listen."

Darmin was strong, and fast. It took Jakor and two other men to wrestle Darmin into a chair. But once seated the fight drained out of her. A sailor pointed to the pearl, fallen to the floor, but wouldn't touch it to hand it to Talgra. She bent and retrieved it herself.

Before placing it to her ear—precious years, memories, dissolving away—she spoke to Darmin. "I don't know if this is right, Darmin, but you must listen. Whoever you turn out to be."

Darmin sobbed, but listened.

Talgra put the pearl back up to her ear. It was the size of a raindrop, still wrinkled and ugly and shrinking quickly. She spoke.

"I was captain of the *Ivory Chain*. We sailed three weeks from Copperguard with an overloaded hold. There were seventy-eight cargo. The storms were a month early. I didn't expect them. I thought we could beat them to Gardenston. My crew was twenty-four."

"The storm hit us at night. The mainmast cracked. The hull split. We took on water. The hold was flooding. I heard the screams, the chains. Even above the thunder and rain, I heard the chains."

The tears had run free of Darmin, and she now sat watching Talgra with a look of blank horror. Jakor stood behind her with one heavy hand on her shoulder, a mixture of compassion and restraint.

"I sent my crew into the longboat. We took everything of value that would fit. No cargo. I was last into the boat."

"I didn't get into the boat. I don't know why. I heard the screams from below decks. Women. Children. A few spoke our language. They were crying for mercy. They sounded so . . . human."

"I cut the boat free. I went down into the hold."

Every eye in the room was on Talgra, but she looked only into Darmin's steady gaze. Each word was spoken directly to her.

"I climbed down into hell. The water was up to my waist. The hold will filled with screaming slaves, tearing their flesh to get free of the manacles. There was only one key. I gripped the ladder and just stared at them."

Darmin trembled. Her fingers gripped whitely at the arms of her chair. Talgra's voice continued, a dull monotone weighted with death and sorrow.

"The ship was going down, but I had to unlock them. They swam past me. I don't know if they made it. Most probably didn't. The water filled the hold. I unlocked every last one. The ship sank. It tumbled as it sank. I couldn't find my way out. I hit my head. I couldn't see. I tried to swim."

There was still too much pearl left for this to be the conclusion. But as Talgra wondered, the remains of the pearl melted away in her fingers. *Hollow.* The story, if not the life, was at an end. These were all of the memories that the sea had taken.

The tavern was silent, an expectant pause. Talgra continued to watch Darmin closely, not knowing what to expect.

Darmin's voice was a hoarse whisper. "To the dead, Talgra."

"Aye, Darmin," Talgra whispered back. Then in a louder voice, while raising her mug, "To the dead!"

The sailors' reply was automatic. "To the dead!" The tension was broken. But conversation was still whispered, and attention was on Darmin and Talgra both.

Jakor took charge, ushering them out into the gray streets, washed clean by the ending of the storm. Soon only Darmin and Talgra remained.

"What kind of monster am I?" Darmin's face was as open as a child's, looking to Talgra for answers that she didn't think she had.

"You're not a monster, dear." Talgra moved to kneel beside Darmin, holding the younger woman's torso in her arms. "You weren't a monster yesterday, and you're not one today."

"But those things that I did. And the ones you didn't hear—the ones I'm starting to remember—they're even worse. How could I?" Darmin grabbed Talgra's shoulders and turned her to look straight into her face. "How can I go on, knowing what I am? How can I *live*? I should have died. I should die now."

Talgra searched Darmin's tear-streaked face for an answer. She saw only the compassionate young woman who had kept her company for the past months, who had shared meals and stories with her, who had won the hearts of every patron of the Drowned Rat. The woman who had filled Talgra's life as no other ever had.

"Darmin, listen to me. I don't know all of what happened in your last life, but I know how it ended. And I know how your new life has begun. There is goodness in you, and I have seen it every day that I've known you. Maybe this new life is a gift, for what you tried to do for those people at the end. Maybe you shouldn't have ever learned of who you were back then. But you have. And now you have a choice." Talgra's voice was iron.

"A choice?" she said.

Talgra prayed that her own choice was as selfless as it seemed to her in that moment. "You can help me.

And I can help you. Those slaves—those people—the sea took many of them. And that means that they're out there. Maybe not on this reef, but somewhere," she said. *I do this for her, not me. And when she knows what I can teach, I will set her free.*

Comprehension dawned on Darmin's face. "And their stories deserve to be told," she said.

"If you die, you do nothing for them," said Talgra.

"Show me how," said Darmin.

"Of course I will, dear child."

FREE PASSAGE

by Mary Catelli

Mary Catelli lives in Connecticut, where she programs computers for a living and reads, writes, and collects rejection slips for fun. There seems to be a special relationship between fantasy and computers—I wonder what it is?

She has sold work to *Cricket,* various *Sword & Sorceress* anthologies, *Tomorrow, Marion Zimmer Bradley's Fantasy Magazine,* and *Absolute Magnitude.* She is currently working on short stories and a novel.

She got the original idea for "Free Passage" when she read, many years ago, a summary account of Hercules' Twelve Labors, and how fighting broke out between him and the Amazons. The idea of the fight with the Amazons went through several mutations, never really taking form, until she thought up Chloe; then it all fell into place.

Chloe perched by the prow of the ship and looked at the cliff ahead of them. The yellow sandstone, dotted here and there with grayish bushes, loomed over the narrowing strait. The warm wind tugged on her black hair and filled the sails behind her, bearing them through the narrow entrance to the sea beyond. The sun glinted off the sea and, up on the cliff, off metal.

Petros came up behind her. "So," he said, his voice unusually deep, "the Amazons have seen us."

Chloe looked over her shoulder at her brother. The black-haired man was staring at the cliff with dark eyes. "Did you think we could get by without their noticing?"

Her brother spread his hands. "Hoped." He grimaced. "The Amazons are an excellent guard for the herb."

Chloe's eyes darkened. They had no choice, she knew; only the herb could break the blight, and her father had no one else to fetch it whom he trusted not to hold it hostage. "I think, we've seen enough excellent guards already." She looked past him, to the men behind: several dozen young warriors of the Crimson Isles, their dark heads bent over their work; but when they had started out, they had had a couple dozen more. She scowled in thought.

"The Amazons are not mermecoleons, or that dreadful leopard," she said after a minute. "We could ask the Amazons for free passage."

Petros grimaced. "Their queen *might* grant it."

"What were you planning to do instead?" Chloe asked. "The Amazons outnumber us. Badly."

Light flashed from the cliff again, a pattern that could not be accidental. She swallowed. Petros nodded. "We'll try it." He stepped back and called, "Markos!"

Chloe ignored the renewed bustle behind her; they had brought her to find and harvest the magical herb, not to take care for the journey. The boat slowly advanced, and the cliff flowed by, sinking down to the level of the water. A narrow valley touched the shore; on each side of the beach, the stony slopes swarmed with the Amazons, sunlight glinting from their spears and shields. Chloe gulped. She could see a fortified city, deep in the valley, but her eyes kept coming back to the rocks.

Markos appeared beside her. "My lady, you should get back."

Petros' voice carried over the ship. "No, Markos,

she should stay." He strode forward. "The Amazons know that our women are not warriors; Chloe, you should ask the queen for passage."

Chloe flinched. Her eyes went back to the Amazons. They would know she was not a warrior, she reminded herself; Petros was right there.

Show them that you are a princess of the Crimson Isles, she thought fiercely. She rose to her feet, her hand smoothing out the skirt of her saffron chiton, and resisted the impulse to clench the fabric. The ship slowly approached the beach, until it came within a spear's cast.

Spears bristled from the rocks ahead of them. "Halt!" bellowed a voice. Behind Chloe, the men hurried about the sails, and the ship stopped. The waters lapped against the hull. The tall, dark-haired women watched them without moving.

"No outlander may come to the land of the Amazons," said the same harsh voice. "Go back!"

Chloe swallowed and raised her voice. "We are not coming to the land of the Amazons," she said, her voice lighter than she had hoped. She plowed on. "We are but passing by."

A stir went through the crowd—perhaps for her words, perhaps for her sex—but died quickly.

"We grant no passage," said the voice. Chloe picked out the woman, whose weathered face held the marks of years, and turned toward her.

"Your queen can," she said. "Let us ask her."

"Go back!" said another voice, younger and harsher. "Take your impudence with you!" Chloe looked toward that speaker and tried to marshal another argument when the Amazon spoke again. "Why should the queen listen to you?"

"Because the gods hate those who despise petitioners," said Chloe, formally, "who shed blood without reason and hate justice," She stopped, hoping she had not sounded glib.

The first woman to speak turned to the second and said something; her words did not carry over the water, but her angry tone did. The second retorted, but Chloe could only make out a few words, "The ogre of the north," and "candidate." The waves lapped against the boat. Chloe licked her lips.

A long time later, the first woman turned back to the water. "We will bring your petition to Queen Helen." The second woman looked at the boat with a malevolent expression. Chloe felt too relieved to care. The first woman said, "Pull your boat up on the beach and wait."

Petros called out the orders. Chloe sat, her heart pounding; she still had to speak to the queen. The boat lurched into movement. Chloe forced herself to take a deep breath. *You are a princess,* she reminded herself.

The city swarmed like an anthill as the ship drove into the shore, and as they waited. *We mean them no harm,* Chloe reminded herself; *why should they not let us pass?*

The sun inched higher. Out of the city came a party, and in its middle stood a woman on whose dark hair gold flashed. Chloe gulped and clambered out of the ship to stand on the sands. Petros came after her, with three other men, but Chloe looked only at the approaching queen.

The Amazons formed a line before them, a spear's cast away, and watched the outlanders with wary dark eyes. A tall woman of middle years, a golden circlet on her black hair, stood in their center and looked at Chloe.

"Who are you, who claim to be passing by our lands?" Queen Helen said, her voice ringing.

"I am Princess Chloe, of the Crimson Isles," Chloe

said, pleasantly surprising herself with the strength of her voice. "The crops of the isles are blighted, and to break the curse, we need a herb of Serpent Islands." She gestured up the strait. "In that sea." Queen Helen looked considering. Chloe lowered her arm. "We want nothing more than to go there, and to return by this strait. We mean you no harm; indeed, we will do nothing to you."

Queen Helen's mouth pursed. "And if I refuse you?"

Chloe felt her tongue freeze. Petros took a step forward. "My father the king told me to bear my sister on this quest." He met the queen's eyes. "It would be my duty to try to go on." He looked about. The queen's escort, Chloe noted, was larger than the ship's company, but not much.

Queen Helen smiled a little at this impudent half-threat. "Stay here," she said. Lowering her voice, she spoke to a woman beside her, and a dozen Amazons fell back to hold council.

A few grains of sand had worked their way into Chloe's sandal, where they ground against her foot as she waited; she wished she dared to pull off the sandal and shake them out. The Amazons on guard shifted a little. One of Petros' men eyed the nearest Amazon, and the woman looked back at him with bold eyes. Chloe remembered how the Amazons kept up their numbers, and looked sharply away.

Up on the rocks, more Amazons stood. The rocks half-hid them, but Chloe picked out two companies, one creeping slowly closer. Behind her, she heard the men on shipboard surreptitiously readying their weapons, but Petros stood like stone next to her. Chloe wondered how he managed it.

A woman sprang from the Amazons coming toward them and ran to the other group among the rocks. Chloe bit her lip. A messenger? she wondered.

Queen Helen's voice rose again. "I have decided!" The woman stalked like a lioness across the sands. She stepped past the band of warriors and spoke in a lower voice, her tone formal. "Princess Chloe, take your ship, and go onward. You may pass by our lands now, and you may return."

Chloe's shoulders slumped, and she let out a long breath.

A voice rang from the rocks: "Treachery!" An arrow whistled through the air within an inch of Petros.

"Your warriors!" Chloe called to the queen, panicking. The queen looked shocked but could do no more before a volley of arrows flew after the first one. Chloe fell back to huddle beside the boat. The Amazons swarmed out of the rocks—she had not realized how close they were—and Petros' men pushed by her, weapons in hand. Blood flowed, and the queen's guard moved to the defense of their comrades.

"Stop this!" Helen's voice barely carried over the din, and Chloe knew that she heard it only because she was not caught up in the battle. Crouched against the hull, she saw the queen rise up, gesturing with her weaponless hands. An arrow flew through the air, and into the queen's throat. Chloe could not move.

"You have murdered your queen!" shouted one of the Amazons. "Fall back!"

Some of the Amazons started to, and Petros shouted, "Men of the Crimson Isles, to the ship!"

In a minute, Chloe knew not how, the combatants had parted, and the beach lay empty except for the corpses—over a dozen of those. Chloe gulped. Near her feet lay the young man who had been eyeing the Amazon. Chloe's eyes drifted over the beach. Where the queen's guard had stood lay that Amazon, her eyes staring sightless at the sky. The air seemed suddenly darker, and Chloe, woozy, grabbed the hull and closed her eyes.

"Chloe!" said Petros. "Are you hurt?"

Chloe opened her eyes for a second and closed them again. She shook her head. "What happened?" she said, weakly.

"I wish I knew," Petros said grimly. He looked over the sands to the queen's body. "I do not think it safe to leave, whatever the queen said."

Chloe gulped, thinking that staying might be safer, but it was not safe. She opened her eyes. On the other side of the beach the Amazons gathered. Two of them disputed bitterly. Their words did not carry on the breeze, but she watched their angry gestures, and wondered what authority they held. Chloe licked her lips; one of them was the second woman who had ordered them off, who had argued that they could not petition the queen.

After a minute, the other woman made a gesture of concession, and stalked toward the ship, though not coming as near as Queen Helen had. "Outlanders!" she shouted. "Passage is in the hands of the queen! We have no queen! You may not pass!"

Chloe's mouth fell open.

"When we have elected our queen, you may petition her!"

Silence fell, broken only by the breeze and the lapping of the waves. Chloe's head sank. After a long minute, Petros roused himself. "Give us leave to honor our dead!"

Silence fell for a longer minute. The woman finally nodded her head. "And we will honor ours!"

The funeral pyres glowed sullen red in the evening gloom. The breeze flowed out from the land, bearing the scent of dried grass and a chill. Chloe shivered. *We meant them no harm,* she thought.

The Amazons stood guard on their pyres and gave the men the wary glances they had when they first gathered up their dead. Chloe turned away and walked to the ship. Petros looked up from talking with Markos as she approached.

"Any movement from the city?" he asked.

Chloe shook her head.

Markos swore. "How long does it take to elect their queen?"

"Weeks, with our luck." Petros rubbed his forehead.

Chloe crouched down by the men and lowered her voice. "If they're intent on choosing their queen, we might sneak by."

Petros' mouth twitched. "We would have to fight our way through on the way back."

"You thought of doing that both ways, or sneaking through." Chloe met his eyes. "Do you know why the Amazons attacked us?"

"They claimed," said Markos, "that we were preparing to attack and kill the queen."

"They would," replied Petros sourly. He looked over the beach and got to his feet. "First, we check for guards; they could slaughter us on the spot." He stepped out onto the shore, and Chloe scrambled after him.

A voice boomed over the sands. "What are you looking at, outlander?" A woman emerged from the darkness and loomed over the pyres.

"Lady Melantha," said one of the Amazons in fright. The uncommonly tall woman gestured her to immobility and glared at Petros.

Chloe pulled back, thinking this woman looked like the messenger between the two groups that had first attacked the ship, and wondering if she was imagining it. She peered at Melantha. The woman gestured again, reminding Chloe of the second woman who had ordered them off, and of the one who had argued over whether the ship could leave when there was no queen to give them leave. Chloe gulped: that would make Melantha a woman of importance among the Amazons.

Melantha smiled a little. "I have set guards. There is no queen to give you free passage, and you will not have it without a queen." Her eyes narrowed. "Olympe was a fool to let you wait to petition the new queen."

Chloe quailed. Fighting their way through was still folly, but asking had proven no less foolish.

Sunlight beat down on the plain between the city and the beach. The funeral pyres had burned down to ashes, and the Amazon guards, no longer keeping a watch on the fires, kept it on the ship. Chloe looked past them, at the two women being escorted out of the city.

One of the guards noticed her interest. "The games," she said, her tone belligerent. "They will show who is fit to be the queen of the Amazons." The Amazons took up positions across the plain.

"As if there were any question," another guard said, her voice heavy with contempt. "Olympe is a candidate only because her mother was queen."

Chloe looked at her. "They put her forth for the games for that?" she asked.

The guards looked at her with disdain for her ignorance. "She fought a monster—a little one, but a monster—and they named her candidate for that, seven years ago."

"If her mother had not been queen," grumbled the other, "that monster would never have been accepted. Melantha fought a true monster, an enormous ogre; she is the only fit candidate." The Amazon grinned. "Not only did she protect us from the ogre, Melantha saw what you were up to, preparing to attack."

"You were sneaking up on us," Chloe answered hotly.

"She saw your preparations," said the first, "so she got us close enough to mean something."

Chloe looked from one to the other. Her heart started to pound. The Amazon went on, saying, "Close enough to stop you in your tracks, and you could even deny intending . . ." Chloe barely heard her, as her thoughts formed: Melantha had gotten the Amazons to fight, and the queen had died, and now Melantha could become queen.

"Melantha saw us," Chloe said, her voice cutting through the Amazon's. "Or Melantha claimed to see us, and fomented the fight, and now she can claim a crown as her reward!" Chloe drew a deep breath. She had brought harm, no mater that she had not meant it, and the Amazons might be in danger of being ruled by a wicked queen, brought about by her arrival. Her hands clenched in rage.

The Amazons stepped back, looking aghast. "What did the outlander say?" said a woman further back. Chloe looked up to see Amazons all over the plain looking at her, and realized she had been shouting.

"She accused Melantha," shouted another as the rumors flew through the Amazon host, too numerous for Chloe to hear more than a buzz.

"What is this outlander doing?" Melantha shouted. "Fomenting trouble?" She raised a fist in the air. "You know our laws; no outlander is part of our counsels!"

"No outlander *man* is part of our counsels!" Olympe shouted. Melantha looked bitterly at her. Olympe drew a deep breath. "This is an outlander woman. Let her speak."

"You!" Melantha spat. "You who fought a snake and claimed yourself a candidate for the queen! Your mother killed a dragon! You are unworthy of her place!"

Olympe drew a deep breath. "My sisters! Let us hear the outlander woman! If you find her story pointless, I will withdraw my candidacy!"

Melantha stepped back, blinking. She collected herself as a murmur of assent went through the Amazons. "Let her tell her false tale, and you withdraw your candidacy!"

"Not if it is false," Olympe said, with dignity. "Only if it is pointless. We may grant her a mistake." Melantha started to speak, but Olympe cut her off. "If she is such a tale-bearer, why do you fear her?"

Melantha grimaced. Olympe turned to Chloe and gestured. "Come before us and speak."

Feeling every eye on the beach upon her, Chloe slowly walked before the two candidates. One way or another, she was about to decide the fate of the Amazons, she thought, since no one else had seen what she had, and felt cold. She raised her head. "We had spoken with Queen Helen, and she had decided to grant us passage, when Melantha called out treachery. It was Melantha who claimed to see my brother's men preparing to attack."

"Diotoma's women saw them!" shouted one woman. "Melantha came to tell us."

"We did not—you did! Melantha . . ." The Amazon's voice trailed off into silence. The wind whipped the grasses on the plain. Melantha's mouth worked.

Chloe drew a deep breath and added, quickly, before Melantha could devise a tale, "And now Melantha can become queen." Her thoughts jumped to the fight. "In fact, Queen Helen fell to an arrow shot from behind her. Perhaps Melantha made sure of the death."

"You wretched child!" Melantha's face contorted. She reached for her spear. Chloe took a faltering step

backward, and Olympe jumped to wrestle with the
other candidate for the spear. Several Amazons ran
up. Chloe took another step backward and collided
with someone. Petros' hand came down to seize her
elbow. "Come back," he said, grim-faced.

"Trying to run away?" shouted an Amazon.

Chloe remembered the pyres on the beach. "If you
want to speak to me," she snapped, "do it at the ship.
I did not attack one of you."

Olympe rose from the ground, her face stained with
blood and dirt. At her feet, four Amazons held down
the still struggling Melantha. "Let her go. We do not
need her testimony to convict Melantha." Her face set
in bitter lines, Olympe inclined her head to Chloe and
Petros. "Go back to your ship and wait. I do not think
it will be for long."

Melantha's face contorted with hatred; Chloe
gulped and walked away, feeling Melantha's gaze on
her back the entire walk back the ship.

At least it was over, she thought, as she reached it.

In the gray morning light, Chloe stood over the
ashes. Another day. She wondered if Melantha had
devised a story to cover for herself. Melantha was,
after all, a candidate for the throne, and her accuser
an outlander, not even a warrior.

"Hallo," shouted one of the men, waving toward
the city. Half a dozen Amazons walked across the
plain toward them. All about her, the men reached
for their spears and shields.

"Princess Chloe!" The leader raised her hand to
hail the boat. "Queen Olympe wishes you to attend
her in the city."

Chloe slowly got to her feet. "Alone?" she said.

The leader's eyes went over the men. "No," she
said, reluctantly. Chloe guessed that Olympe had or-

dered them to permit it only if she asked. "But six men—no more."

But they had to know she would ask, Chloe thought. She turned to Petros, who nodded and picked out the five. Wind blew in from the sea, hissing over the sands and grass. The men around her, Chloe followed the Amazons over the plain. The city slowly rose up ahead of them.

On the rocks outside the city wall, Melantha's broken body sprawled, staring blankly at the sky. Dried blood splattered the stone around her.

Chloe forced herself to her full height as she walked through the gate.

Within the gates, a straight road led up to the royal palace, and in the square before it the Amazons gathered. Olympe sat enthroned there, in robes of crimson with a golden crown.

The Amazons drew to one side as they reached the square, and Chloe stopped at its verge. "Queen Olympe."

"Princess Chloe." The queen smiled a little. "It appears in one thing you told my mother a lie." Chloe froze, her mind racing. Olympe's smile deepened. "You told her you would do nothing to the Amazons." A ripple of laughter ran through the assembly.

Olympe turned to one of her counselors and lifted up a box. "Queen Helen defeated a dragon who threatened this land, and so was named a candidate, and later the queen. It is only fitting that a piece of the dragon's treasure be bestowed on the one who saved the land from a greater peril." She lifted up a necklace of pure gold, sparkling in the light.

Chloe walked unsteadily forward to the throne. Olympe lowered the heavy, cool necklace around her neck. She straightened, feeling the burden on her shoulder blades.

"It is just as well for me that you are no Amazon,"

Olympe said, "or they would have named you a candidate after Melantha's trial, for dealing with the peril of *her,* and queen after."

Chloe drew a deep breath and met the queen's eyes. "Then it is just as well that I am not an Amazon, for I have my quest," she said, her voice steady. "It was for that that I spoke with your mother the queen." She smiled. If there were any other strange peoples along their journey, she would insist on speaking with them; they had lost fewer men here than anywhere else.

A ripple of laughter ran through the Amazons. Olympe smiled back. "So you did. Take your free passage, now and when you return."

THE CONJURER'S LIGHT

by Lisa Campos

Lisa Campos is a newcomer to our pages, and this was her initial reaction: "First of all, I want to thank you for the chance to discover what whooping for joy is really all about! I was thrilled to receive your acceptance letter for *Sword and Sorceress XVII*. This was one of my first attempts at short story writing, and it is wonderful to know that I succeeded in making it interesting! Contrary to the norm, I seem to have gone about my writing in a backwards fashion. With several novels already completed, I only recently decided to try my hand at short stories—a more daunting task, in many ways. This will be my first professional publication."

Lisa is 21 years old and has been writing stories for as long as she can remember. Sometimes you just have to keep on trying—that's what being a writer is all about. When she's not writing, she can be found curled up somewhere with a book. She is a passionate fan of fantasy and science fiction in all their forms, whether they be novel, art or movie. Outside of literary pursuits and pastimes, she plays harp and drum in a Celtic/Irish band, participates in historical recreation groups, and works a job in Medical Billing to make ends meet until she can finally get those novels sold.

She would like to dedicate this story to Heather, "because she has always kept my faith for me, and I will be forever thankful for her unwavering support."

I remember I was Conjuring butterflies when the King first asked me about the Warblade.

I have learned to Conjure thousands of images in

my life, and of them all, butterflies have always been my favorite. I have woven mirages of armies on the field to fool an enemy, of summer grass on the barren plains of winter. But there is something about the simple charm of the graceful butterfly that I have always loved. Maybe it's the colors. The secret to the Conjurer's magic is the use of light, for within light exists color. And on a sunny day, my butterflies are truly amazing.

That day, King Harad walked right through my fluttering rainbow of butterfly wings without a pause or a glance. I tried not to grimace. I couldn't tell if he recognized them as a mirage, or if he was simply so blind to beauty that he didn't even notice their brilliant colors. Whatever the reason, I couldn't show my irritation. This was the King, after all. And I had served the royal family long enough to recognize that the eager look on his face meant business.

It seemed my afternoon of relaxation was about to be brought to an early end.

King Harad was, as always, blunt and to the point. "Conjurer! Have you ever heard of the Warblade?"

I tried not to show my surprise. "Yes, your Majesty. In legends, only."

"And what do your legends say?"

I pushed a curl of red hair out of my eyes, and tried hard not to laugh as the King attempted to bat away a bright purple butterfly hovering right in front of his nose. His hand passed directly through the image, and his dark brows narrowed in irritation. Biting my lip against a smile, I waved my hand, dispelling the Conjuring. The garden seemed dimmer now, with the rainbow of wings gone. But I could tell the King was hard on about something, so I forced myself to concentrate. I could mourn my lost afternoon later.

"The legends of the Warblade," I said, "are very vague. It's an ancient story. The sword was supposedly crafted by sky spirits as a gift to a young knight. He was destined to become King and use the sword to lead his followers to victory."

"So I've heard." The King waved his hand impatiently. "I want it."

I blinked. "You *want* it?"

Harad frowned at my incredulous tone, but he didn't reprimand me. I served the royal family, but even Kings showed Conjurers their due respect. And I am a *very* good conjurer. It earns me some leeway. With my temper, I've always needed it.

"Yes." His tone was decisive. "I want it. My son will wield it in battle against our enemies, and create a kingdom even greater than the one I forged for him. With the Warblade, his victory is assured."

"Your Majesty . . ." I began, trying to curb the lecturing tone I felt creeping into my voice, "the story of the Warblade is, for all we know, nothing more than that. A story. And even if it is grounded in truth, according to legend, the sword was lost over a thousand years ago. There's no way—"

"Yes, yes." He interrupted. "I don't need it immediately, of course. Our campaign against Lesaran will not begin for another three months. You have until then to conduct your research. It should be plenty of time for you to find out where the Warblade is."

I felt my mouth fall open in disbelief. I closed it with some effort. "Majesty. Perhaps I haven't made myself clear. I—"

"See to it, Conjurer." Harad ordered curtly.

It was obvious my attempts at logic were going to fall on deaf ears. It would have been pointless, and unwise, to argue with him further. So I curtsied, sweeping my skirts, and the King stalked off as quickly as he'd come.

It took an enormous amount of willpower to refrain from cursing until he was out of earshot.

I stormed out of the garden, through the palace hallways, and into my suite of rooms, hissing colorful strains of invective all the while. Color was, after all, my specialty.

I spent a few minutes pacing the main room, venting my frustration at the ignorance of Kings, the ineptitude of the entire monarchical system, and at the ultimate futility of wishing to bring reason to either of these things before finally calming down enough to go into my library and begin studying.

Because in the end, the King's command was the King's command. No matter what my opinion on the matter might be. So I would have to grit my teeth and make the best of it.

But none of my books made more than passing references to the story of the Warblade. As I had expected. The most information I could find was in an illustrated book of children's stories that I sometimes read to put the youngest prince to sleep.

Maybe I should be reading it to the father instead, I thought with an ill-tempered sigh and tossed the book aside.

"I see I've come at a bad time." A soft voice observed.

I looked up to see Princess Coria, the King's only daughter, standing in the doorway of my library. Seeing her always made me smile. She had been a beautiful child, and had grown to be a beautiful woman, with pale wheat hair and piercing green eyes. She came into my library holding the long skirts of a green silk gown. And though she held the fabric delicately, I knew how much she hated it. She wore rich gowns in the palace because the King expected it of her. He had no idea that she spent her afternoons training in swordsmanship with the guard captain. I was still amazed that she had been able to keep her practices a secret from her father for so long, but King

Harad did not necessarily inspire great friendship from his retainers. The guard captain was willing to quietly train Coria because he saw great potential in her. And I was thoroughly convinced that the Captain was smitten with her, besides. It was easy to understand why.

"Let me guess." She said with a smile. "It has something to do with my father."

I snorted. "Perceptive girl."

Her smile broadened, and she picked up the children's book from where I'd dropped it on the table. One eyebrow arched eloquently. "Not your usual reading preference."

"The King," I said, speaking slowly to keep myself from ranting again, "wants me to *find* him the Warblade."

Coria's green eyes lit up with a sudden gleam of excitement she could not hide. "The Warblade?" I watched her right hand clench and unclench, as though the mere name of the ancient weapon made her itch for a sword hilt. "But . . . isn't that just an old legend?"

"That's what I told him!" I felt my ire rising again, and gave into it. Fighting it was always a fruitless venture.

"What does he want it for?

"He wants your brother to carry it into battle against Lesaran."

"Henry?" Coria's eyes sparked with sudden anger of her own. "Henry's an incompetent warrior, at best. How could he give such a sword to *him*?"

I felt pity overcome my anger, and I asked her gently, "Instead of you?"

"Yes!" she cried, hands in fists.

"Coria."

She sighed, shoulders slumping under the weight of an old defeat, all the anger drained instantly from her.

"I know." She said softly. "I am a woman. And women do not lead men into battle."

"At least not here in Verelis." I said sympathetically. "But I wouldn't worry. If the King thinks I can just produce an old legend out of thin air, then he's got another thing coming."

Coria smiled, her humor never subdued for long. "But that's exactly what you do, Aleah. You conjure things out of thin air. Why should this be any different?"

"Because," I said with exaggerated patience, "A mirage could never cut through melted butter, much less a man's skull. Henry cannot wield a Conjured sword into battle."

"Henry couldn't wield a butter knife into battle." Coria muttered.

"Yes, well, that's his problem, isn't it?" I replied testily. "Right now, my problem is finding this mythical Warblade. Or, more likely, finding proof that it doesn't exist. And I'm not going to find that in this library." I crossed my arms, tapping fingers on my elbows. "I need other resources. The King had better be willing to send to the city keeps. I'm going to need some help if he wants results by spring."

And the King *was* willing. Eager, in fact. He dispatched messengers to all the city keeps, ordering them to send any books or manuscripts they could find with information about the Warblade back to the palace, along with any scholars who may have known something of use to me. When we received word that a Conjurer from Elam was on his way to the capital with an ancient book of sorcery that might be of help, I actually found myself rather excited to meet with him. It would be nice to have another Conjurer to discuss with, and perhaps to work some magic with as well. But my excitement faded into instant dismay the moment the summoned Conjurer presented himself in my study several weeks later.

Of all the Conjurers in the Kingdom, it *would* have to be my old lover.

"Daryen." I glared. "What are *you* doing here?"

Daryen threw back his raven-haired head and laughed. Rather annoyingly, I thought.

"I see you're as courteous as ever, Aleah! I have missed you, you know." He smiled charmingly, and curse him for still looking so handsome.

"Well I haven't missed *you*."

"I'm glad to see the years haven't dimmed your spirit." He persisted, smile never faltering. "Or your hair. Still red and glorious without a hint of gray."

"And you're still arrogant and pompous without a hint of wit. Please tell me you aren't the Conjurer sent from Elam to meet with me."

"I am." Daryen sketched a little bow. "And I am at your service."

"Oh, good." I muttered. "Go jump off the balcony for me, then."

"Later, perhaps. If it will make you happy. But I think you might be interested in seeing what I have brought you first."

He pulled out from a satchel over his shoulder a leather-bound volume with an intricate pattern stamped on the cover, and fine yellowing pages. My breath caught, as Daryen had no doubt known it would. He had always known me too well. It made him intolerably smug.

He held the book up knowing it was an irresistible lure for me. Old books, old knowledge. After Conjuring, these things were what I loved most in life. As did Daryen. That had always been the attraction between us.

"How old is it?" I breathed.

"We can't be sure. But my best guess is that it's about nine hundred years old. Maybe more."

"Impossible! In this condition?"

"I believe it has some type of protection spell laid on it, to prevent decay."

"Protection spell? Then you think . . . this belonged to the old sorcerers?"

"Possibly. The content certainly seems to suggest it." That ingratiating smile of his returned, and he glanced pointedly to my study. "Shall we sit, then, and look it over?"

I hesitated, weighing the thought of having him in my private study against the desire to explore the old book in detail. Chances were that Daryen would be able to tell me a great deal about it, more than I could discover on my own with limited time.

The book won out.

At least he refrained from making a sarcastic comment about it.

That first night we didn't sleep or eat until dawn. The book was fascinating, written in an archaic and elegant script, and full of gloriously detailed drawings. Drawings of ancient castles, of old Kingdom maps, and diagrams of magical symbols and the proper arrangement of sorcerous tools to cast great spells. There were often notes scribbled into the margins on the success or failure of such spells.

"Have you tried any of these?" I asked Daryen.

"Some. But none of them worked. We think we may be doing something wrong. The book works on the assumption that you already have a basic knowledge of sorcery, and the old sorcerers took most of their secrets with them."

I frowned in disappointment. "It's likely that we may not even be capable of this kind of magic anymore. The power may have died out with them."

"That's what I believe. Though it depresses me to

admit it. But here . . . I haven't shown you the most
important thing yet. The reason why I brought this
book to you."

He carefully turned several pages, flipping toward
the end of the massive tome. And then he turned the
book toward me, spreading it flat with his palm, another of those smug looks on his face. But I didn't
even have time to be irritated by it, because as soon
as I saw those pages, I found I couldn't breathe.

Sketched across both pages in fine black ink was
the most intricately detailed drawing I had ever seen.
It was a sword. The crosspiece looked as though it
had been constructed of layered shards of crystal, and
at each end of the hand guard was a delicately faceted
gem, grasped by carved talons. The hilt itself was
wrapped in plain leather, but the pommel was crafted
in the shape of two wings, every strand of every
feather intricately carved. The wings swept back from
the hilt, cradling in between the crescent arches of
their feathers a star shaped stone. And even drawn in
plain black ink, on old and faded paper, it seemed
that the stone gleamed with an inner light.

"Daryen." I breathed, so struck by the beauty of
the drawing that I could hardly find my voice. "Is
this . . . ?"

"Yes," he said quietly. "This is the Warblade."

"How do you know?"

"There." He pointed to the bottom of the page,
where the artist, whoever that phenomenally talented
person had been, had written in the old language: *For
whosoever shall possess the Warblade, and be by it
possessed, will command the will and winds of war,
and be so commanded by them.*

"I don't understand." I said. "Be by it possessed?"

"I don't know. No one else does either. You're the
only other Conjurer I know who still knows how to
read the old language. The keep at Elam has dozens

of manuscripts written in the old tongue. I brought them with me, thinking we could work through them together."

I nodded. Even the thought of spending the next months in close company with Daryen wasn't enough to diminish my enthusiasm. How could I see that drawing and not want to know more?

Sometime near dawn Daryen left my quarters to find his own. I kept the book opened to the picture of the Warblade, and just sat staring at it. I couldn't seem to tear my eyes away. The sword was glorious. Riveting. And somehow terrifying.

I must have fallen asleep in my chair because sometime later, with the morning sun pouring in through the window, I opened my eyes to see Princess Coria leaning with both hands on the table, staring slack-jawed at the drawing of the Warblade.

"Coria . . ." I began, rubbing sleep from my eyes, but she cut me off.

"This is the Warblade, isn't it?" Her voice was a breathy whisper of awe.

"Yes. Yes, it is."

"Aleah . . ." Her hands were shaking, "Aleah, you must find this."

"Coria . . ."

"No. It exists. I know it does. You *must* find it."

There was something so passionate and so certain in her voice that I found I couldn't speak to contradict her. She had not taken her eyes from the drawing.

"We're still not sure . . ." I said uncertainly, "That is . . . there is still so much studying to do . . ."

"Let me help you." She looked up now, staring me straight in the eye, "Let me help you with your research. I can take notes for you. Find books. Run errands."

"Coria." I smiled wryly. "That is work for a scribe, not a princess."

"I don't care."

"And what about your lessons with the captain?"

A flicker of doubt crossed her face. Her green eyes narrowed as she weighed her love for her afternoons of sword practice against this new desire to aid me in my quest. Much to my surprise, the latter won out.

"I'll squeeze the lessons in somehow. The captain will understand. I have to help you."

I knew better than to argue with her once she had her mind set on something. She was much like her father the King in that regard, even though she would hate to have that pointed out to her.

Daryen made some complaint when he returned to my study and found Coria there, but I told him firmly that the princess would stay to help, and after a while he let the matter drop.

Coria made herself quite useful. True to her word, she took notes while Daryen and I discussed. She read through books written in the common tongue, in search of any reference to the Warblade. She was unobtrusive and silent when she perceived we wanted such, but eager to offer her own opinions when I asked for them. And she kept the book with the drawing of the Warblade always within her sight, as though she could not bear to have it hidden from her.

After a month of work we had all three fallen into familiar patterns. Daryen stood or paced by one side of the table while we discussed, and Coria sat quietly at the table's other side with parchment and quill, ready to document any finds or observations we might make. And I moved my personal desk near the large window in my study, so that I could always sit in the sunlight.

All Conjurers appreciate sunlight, or any kind of light for that matter. We must, for it is that light which makes our magic possible. But I have always had a love for the sun's fire that even other Conjurers do not share. Perhaps it is because my love of Conjuring is so great. I can't bear to be in shadows, for the darkness hinders me and prevents me from summoning the images that fill my life with color.

I was basking in the warm sunlight on one of those long days of study when Daryen launched into one of his tirades.

"This is impossible!"

I rolled my eyes and kept my face turned to the window and my view of the garden below. I could feel Coria hiding a smile.

"Impossible!" Daryen exclaimed again, in case we hadn't heard him the first time.

"No it's not." I said calmly. "What did you expect? That we would find a plainly written passage in some book, complete with a map and a big bold X marking where brave adventurers can find a real life children's legend?" I looked back to him, hearing my voice slip into its most acidic tones. "Maybe if we've lucky we'll find all the rest of the answers to life's mysteries written plainly on scrolls that scholars have been researching for hundreds of years, too. Like whether or not the world really ends in an eternal waterfall in the Eastern Ocean, where the people who disappear in the Shadow Mountains have gone to, whether or not you were truly dropped on your head as a child causing your most lamentable lack of anything resembling intelligence, or what—"

"Yes, you're very witty, Aleah." Daryen snapped. "But you know I'm right. If the Warblade does exist, we *should* have found more solid information about it by now."

However much I hated to agree with him on anything, he was right. We had received over a dozen shipments of books from the city keeps during our long month of study. They had nothing more to send us. It seemed that we had already exhausted our re-

sources, and still could find nothing useful. I cringed
inwardly to think of how the King would take it if I
were to report this lack of success to him.

But I was not about to voice my agreement to Daryen when he was going on like this. He began to rant
on about the Gods only knew what nonsense, throwing in a few snide remarks about me just to add some
spice to his raving. I was used to this, however. We
had, after all, been lovers for over three years. And
we were far too alike to get along peacefully.

I settled back in my chair to watch his tirade. He
was so wrapped up in shouting and waving his arms
about that he never noticed the little red dragon which
materialized and hovered behind his head, breathing
fire on his elegantly combed black hair.

Coria covered her mouth and stifled a laugh. Her
green eyes danced with glee as she watched my Conjured mirage.

On a whim, I set Daryen's hair on fire, and had
various disgusting insects flee the flame, emerging
from his glorious black hair to scamper down his neck.

Coria couldn't contain herself. She burst into
laughter.

Daryen turned to glare at her and caught a glimpse
of the little red arsonist flying just behind him. The
tiny dragon bared its teeth and spat another gout of
flame into his face.

To his credit, Daryen didn't even blink.

"Aleah!" He roared.

I dispelled the dragon. And the insects. I pondered
leaving his hair on fire for a while, but thought better
of it.

The rest of the day went rather poorly after that.

It was nearly a month later that Coria brought to
my attention the decaying book she had found in the
palace's library. By this time, Daryen and I were both
desperately anxious to find something useful. The

King was beginning to put pressure on us, and I felt hopeless to do anything but prepare to find a new home when he banished me for failure.

Coria found me with my head in my hands after having kicked Daryen out of my study for the day. And it was only an hour after breakfast.

She set the book down in front of me.

"I found something, Aleah," she said, and opened the book to a page so covered in scribbled writing that it looked more black than yellow. It was written in the old tongue.

"Coria, how did you find anything in this? You can't read the old tongue."

"I'm picking it up." She shrugged. "I've been studying with you both for two months."

I was impressed. More than impressed. The old tongue was hideously complex.

It was tragic that thick-witted Prince Henry would inherit the throne. Coria would have been a Queen to be reckoned with.

"I don't really know why I'm so sure about this." Coria said with a frown, "But I just know that this is important somehow. I saw the words for "sword" and "conjure" here. I couldn't quite make out the rest, but I think you should look at it."

I leaned over the book and began to read aloud. " 'For the gift of the sword is a double-edged one. Before the blade may be wielded, it must first be crafted. And the moon will only burn on one day of a thousand cycles. The conjure must be true. And the one chosen to bear the burden equally so.' "

That passage was the key. I knew it instantly. How Coria should have guessed that, I had no idea. I have since come to believe that it may have been destiny, but one can never be sure.

I sent for Daryen. As soon as he saw the book, all anger from our morning's argument vanished. We

were both giddy like children with a new toy. It took
hours to read the entire book, and it was a frustrating
task. The writing had no structure, and one topic
would abruptly end in the middle of a page to be
randomly picked up again forty pages later. But one
thing was for certain; the book was old, probably as
old as the volume of sorcery Daryen had brought with
him. And it contained unmistakable references to
magic long since lost in the world.

But it was that first passage which ultimately gave
us the answers we needed. I dissected it carefully. I
had scribes scour the library for every book on astronomy they could find. I had all the local blacksmiths
and craftsmen sent to me, and asked them how long
it would take them to make a sword like the drawing
of the Warblade. They alternately paled, reddened
with embarrassment, or simply stared in awe at the
truly magnificent drawing. But all of them agreed that
if it even lay within their ability to craft such a sword,
which they doubted, it would take even the finest
smith months of toil to create it. We did not have
months. The King's intended campaign against Lesaran would begin in just over one month's time.

But even the King's plans were ruined when, two
weeks after Coria's discovery, Lesaran suddenly in-
vaded. Verelis had been quietly preparing for war by
the King's order for a while now. Lesaran had always
been an aggressive neighbor, one we could well do
without. Yet in spite of the preparations, we were nowhere near ready to defend against such an unexpected and vicious attack.

Coria, Daryen, and I were all in my study working
when we heard about the invasion. The frantic serv-
ingman who gave us the news had no sooner run off
again, leaving us in a state of dumbfounded shock,
when the King himself stormed into my rooms.

"Conjurer!" he bellowed, throwing open the door.

Daryen and I both jumped to our feet and bowed. Coria rose slowly, a grim look on her face. Her father did not even notice her. Or perhaps he simply refused to acknowledge her.

"Conjurer!" Harad pointed at me. "I *must* have the Warblade! Those lice-infested dogs of Lesaran have dared to cross my border! Our defenses are not in place. The Warblade will win this battle for us. I *will* have it!"

I had never seen the King so livid. Even my famous temper could not stand against him. "Majesty, I—"

"You have a week, Conjurer. In one week my son will carry the Warblade into battle to save our kingdom, or you will be carrying your head!"

He spun and strode out, leaving only the echo of his words and a slamming door in his wake.

Daryen turned to look at me, his face pale. I could say nothing.

"He won't do it." Coria said confidently. "Don't worry, Aleah. He always rants when he is angry, but he does not have the strength or will to back up his threats. His campaign against Lesaran would have failed anyway. Our defenses *should* have been up. He is a poor general."

"Maybe." Daryen said. "But it does not change the fact that we do not have the Warblade."

I collapsed into my chair and put my head in my hands. Unruly red curls cascaded around my fingers. Coria and Daryen both remained blessedly silent. In spite of Coria's words, they knew that if there was a price to be paid for failure, I would pay it. I was the Royal Conjurer. The responsibility was mine.

And suddenly, in that moment of tension, I was struck by a revelation. "The Conjure must be true." I said, echoing the words written in the book. I lifted my head. "Daryen! Where is that astronomy book they brought in yesterday?"

It was Coria who acted. She picked up a large volume of bound parchment and brought it to me quickly and without comment.

I thumbed through the pages, all of them sketched with astrological charts and notations on stellar alignments. I finally came to the page I wanted, where several sketches of the moon and sun were depicted in their various cycles. The Waxing and Waning of the moon. Lunar eclipses. And solar eclipses.

"There." I breathed.

Daryen rushed over and he and Coria stared at the book over my shoulder.

"What?" Daryen asked.

I quoted the passage again. " 'And the moon will only burn on one day of a thousand cycles.' "

"But these are *eclipses*," Daryen protested.

"Look. Here." I tapped my finger on one of the sketches, and the notation beside it in the old tongue. "It says that on the Spring Equinox there will be a full solar eclipse."

Daryen corrected me, eyes scanning the notation, "It says that *one thousand years ago* on the Spring Equinox there was a full solar eclipse."

"No." I snapped, temper returning. "It says *every* thousand years there is a full eclipse."

"Aleah." He shook his head with a hint of his typical condescension. "How could these scholars have known that? There's no way to prove it."

"Does it matter?" I demanded. "We don't have very many options."

"*What* options? What does this have to do with anything?"

"Will you read the damn notation?" I nearly growled, then went ahead and read it aloud myself. " 'And when the moon passes over the sun, it is crowned by a ring of fire, where the flames of day and night mingle in the heavens.' "

Coria's green eyes were wide. "The moon will burn." She whispered.

"So the moon will burn!" Daryen tossed up his hands angrily. "So what?"

"Daryen." I tried to keep myself calm. "What do we use to Conjure? What is the necessary element to create our images?"

Coria answered for him. She had always wanted to know everything about Conjuring, and I had been happy to tell her. "Light."

"Light." I nodded. "And can you think of the one kind of light none of us have ever seen or used? I've used sunlight, candlelight, starlight, firelight. And moonlight, yes. But a burning moon?"

Daryen understood now. I could see it in his suddenly narrowed eyes. "You want to Conjure the Warblade. By the light of a burning moon on Spring Equinox. Very well. But what good will it do you?"

Coria gave a soft little sigh of defeat. "About as much good as a butter knife."

"Maybe." I stood up and paced to the open window. "But what if . . . what if on this one day, by this one light, a Conjuring could be more?"

"That's impossible!" Daryen shook his head. "A Conjuring is an illusion. A mirage. It's not a tangible thing!"

"Just listen to me for once, will you? The book said the sword must first be crafted. The conjure must be true. And only on the day when the moon burns. It all fits, improbable though it may be. You know as well as I do that we are not going to find the Warblade buried under a mossy boulder somewhere."

"Legend says," Daryen persisted stubbornly, "that it was a gift from the Sky Spirits."

"And who better," I retaliated, "To pluck something out of the air than a Conjurer? It's what we do."

And I smiled at Coria, remembering the conversation we had had on the day the King had first mentioned the Warblade to me.

Coria smiled in return, lighting up her lovely face, and she said, "Spring Equinox is in three days."

"Yes it is."

"Madness." Daryen mumbled.

"Perhaps." I acknowledged. "But as I said, we don't have many options."

He gave in, of course. There was nothing else to be done. And in spite of his doubts, he helped me all he could. I half expected him to demand that he be the one to attempt the Conjuring, but he surprised me by setting aside his usual arrogance and admitting that I was the more skilled of the two of us. I was Royal Conjurer for a reason, after all.

We spent those three days outside, always in the sunniest spot we could find. We took the book with the drawing of the Warblade with us everywhere. And I Conjured. All day long. I tried to weave the colors in the sunlight into an image of the Warblade. Nothing in my life had ever been so difficult.

Before creating an image, a Conjurer must have every detail of the mirage perfectly intact in the mind's eye. And the minute, intricate details of the Warblade seemed intent on eluding my grasp. After hundreds of failed attempts, I felt I knew every line and angle of the sword better than the beating of my own heart. But though my Conjurings came close to replicating the image of the Warblade, there was always one thing I could not do. I could not create the impression of light within the star-shaped stone set at the sword's pommel. There was a life, the feeling of a brilliant glow captured in that simple ink drawing that I could not recreate, no matter how I tried.

For that first day of Conjuring, Coria stayed with us. She said nothing, only watched, and sometimes held the book so that I could see it more clearly.

Every time I created an illusion of the sword, flawed though it may have been, the princess' eyes were riveted upon it. Her face was lit by such a fierce desire, it was almost painful to see. And it was evidently painful for her to watch, because after that day she left us and did not return to help anymore.

Sometime during the second day, when I wandered through the gardens during a much needed moment of stolen rest, I passed near the courtyard that led into the guards' barracks. The sound of blades clashing was clear and loud, and I followed it to see the guard captain in a training corral, sparring with Coria.

I had never seen her fight before, though I had long since known of these lessons. At that moment I regretted not having come to watch her earlier.

She was beautiful. Graceful and quick in all of her movements. It was obvious, even to me, that the captain was having a difficult time keeping her attack at bay. And this captain was renowned throughout the kingdom for his skill in battle.

I *had* seen Prince Henry fight, and he was an awkward incompetent beside his sister's skill. Alas that the King could not see the worth in his own daughter.

I sighed and left them behind, returning to my own battle with a far less tangible foe.

I told the King as much as I deemed prudent. Which was little more than half a truth, but all that I knew he could accept. I told him that on the equinox there would be a great celestial occurrence, and on that day when the sun was at its zenith, if I spoke the right words, the Sky Spirits would appear with the Warblade in hand.

The King was ecstatic. He planned a great ceremony for the occasion, and when the day came, I led the King and his retinue of courtiers to the top of a hill beyond the walls of the city. I wanted to be as close to heaven as I could manage.

I rode at the King's left hand, and Prince Henry rode at his right. The prince was dressed in full armor, girded as though for battle. But he looked ill at ease. Henry had a nervous manner, and a bad habit of darting his gaze around constantly, like a rabbit caught in a snare. It was evident he did not want to be there. His fingers anxiously rubbed the fine tabard he wore over his armor, emblazoned with the Royal sigil. A coronet shone on his head. But he carried no sword. Supplying the weapon was my task.

Coria rode behind us with the other high ranking nobles of the court. She sat astride her white horse, dressed in a riding gown of green and gold. She kept her gaze lowered, unwilling to look up at her brother.

We reached the crest of the hill, and the entire party dismounted with a rustle of fine silks and a clanging of armor. We were escorted by the King's Guard and all the kingdom's high nobles who would lead men into battle again Lesaran, all of them fully decked in war gear.

I walked several paces ahead of the party to stand alone on the hill's summit. Daryen moved as though to go with me, but I waved him back. He clutched the book tightly to his chest. Coria slipped her way to the front of the group to stand beside him.

I had been careful in my timing. I knew the King would not be willing to wait for long. So only a few minutes of tense silence passed before someone exclaimed and pointed up at the sky.

I mumbled a fervent prayer of thanks to all the Gods I could remember that the information in the book had been accurate.

A dark shadow began to creep its way across the sun. I squinted up at the sky until my neck ached, and brushed at my watering eyes. But I didn't move. I had a feeling there would only be a moment to do this, and I was not about to miss it.

As it happened, I couldn't have missed it if I'd tried. The land around us darkened with lengthening shadows as the eclipse progressed, and soon I could stare at the rapidly vanishing sun without shielding my eyes. On the instant that the last sliver of sun disappeared behind the dark orb of the moon, like a puzzle piece clicking into place, the golden glow of sunlight which encircled the moon like a halo burst into a brilliant crown of fire. To me, it seemed like the darkened moon had become a prism, and the sun's fire blazed through it, scattering rays of light and color all around. Seeing with a Conjurer's eyes, it was as though the sky were raining rainbows of fire.

My breath caught with the beauty of it, and I raised my hands to the sky, fingers splayed wide.

"The conjure must be true." I murmured under my breath, over and over, a mantra to guide me.

I felt the Conjuring in a way I can barely describe. The light coursed through me, and from me, like threads through a loom, weaving a thing of beauty in the sky. The Warblade began to shimmer into view, suspended in the air above my hands. And any Conjurer could have seen that the sword which manifested itself at my call was more than a mere mirage of light and color. It was a vision crafted from the ether, a tangible thing woven of filaments of light and magic. It felt for a moment that I was weaving my soul above me for all to see, so completely could I feel every detail of the Conjuring that I created. Every line and facet of the weapon gleamed in the unearthly light which bathed the land. The light of a burning moon.

But already I could sense that the brilliant fire was fading. It lasted for only a few moments, then the shadow of the moon moved inexorably on, unveiling the sun once more.

The glorious light melted away.

But the Warblade remained.

And I almost wept in terrible disappointment when I saw that the star stone set into the pommel of the sword was black, lifeless, and dead as any pebble in the dirt.

But still the Warblade remained. I turned my shaking hands so that my palms faced the sky, and the Warblade slowly descended to rest in my grip.

It was cold and heavy, and I could feel the blade's edge cutting into my left hand. It was real. Not a mirage.

I turned then to face the King. To face Daryen and Coria and all the nobles who had come to witness a miracle that I had somehow both succeeded and failed to give them. I *knew,* somehow I *knew* that as long as the stone in the hilt remained dark, the Warblade could not fulfill its purpose.

The King's eyes were wide with wonder. Prince Henry looked pale as a ghost, and utterly terrified. Daryen actually had tears in his eyes, and the smile he gave me was one of awe and undeniable love.

But it was Coria who caught my gaze.

She stepped forward, her movements graceful and confident, her green eyes were bright with wonder.

"Aleah." She spoke my name softly, almost a plea.

And at the sound of her voice the Warblade came to life in my hands.

Cold metal burst into searing heat, and the star-shaped stone at the pommel ignited in a blaze of white light. The carved wings which clasped the stone glinted as though ruffled by a breeze. The crystal shards which formed the crosspiece shimmered, and the jewels set at both ends of the hand guard lit with a vibrant green glow. A green which perfectly matched the shade of Coria's dress. Which perfectly matched the shade of her eyes.

And I understood it all then.

I extended my arms, holding the Warblade out to the Princess who would lead us all.

"The conjure must be true." I said, in a loud carrying voice. "And the one chosen to bear the burden equally so. For whosoever shall possess the Warblade, and be by it possessed, will command the will and winds of war, and be so commanded by them."

Coria stood frozen before me, our gazes locked.

"What?" the King exclaimed in unbelieving shock.

I looked to him without fear. "The Warblade has chosen. It is destined." I turned back to Coria. "Princes Coria, of the house of Sarenn, take this sword. As it was a thousand years ago, so shall it be again. For the power of the one who wields the Warblade cannot be disputed. We live under the grace of your protection."

Coria took the sword, her callused hand fitting to the hilt as though the weapon had been molded specifically for her. And I understood now that it had.

The exact moment she touched the sword, the moon completed its course, and the sun burst into full glory above us, setting Coria's golden hair afire with its light. She gleamed in the sunlight like a thing of gems herself, all gold and emerald and silver.

I sank to my knees. Daryen did so in almost the same instant. And because the miracle of what had happened could not be denied, all of the courtiers and warriors who had accompanied the King to this hill knelt also. I could see in their eyes, even in those of the most stubborn knight who would never before have suffered a woman to clean their armor, that they would follow this brilliant princess to the ends of the earth. The Warblade could not be denied.

Even Prince Henry fell to his knees, and he seemed effusively relieved to be freed from this burden.

Everyone knelt before Coria. Everyone save the King. She turned to look at him, and for a moment I feared that he would explode with rage, and even try to take the sword from her.

But I had misjudged him. Or perhaps he took himself by surprise as well when he nodded to his daughter, bowing his head in an acquiescence and acknowledgment which made Coria's eyes light up, more than the Warblade ever had.

And I knew then, as I had instinctively known so much about it all, that with Coria to lead us, and the Warblade in her hand, we would defeat the Lesarans. We would keep our kingdom safe. And with the blessing of the Sky Spirits, we would know a peace and prosperity that we had never known before.

I remember the brilliant colors of that day, especially how Coria shone in the light of the sun and the glow of the Warblade brought to life. I think of the green of her eyes, of the rainbows of fire that the eclipse had shown me, even the blue of Daryen's gaze as he smiled at me on that hill. I remember all these things when I think of the Warblade. And I remember butterflies. I was Conjuring butterflies the day the King first asked me about the Warblade. And that day on the hill, I felt my heart dancing with color, like a fluttering rainbow of butterfly wings.

MY SISTER'S SONG

by T. Borregaard

T. Borregaard is female, 23, and in hot pursuit of a MSc at Nottingham University in Archaeological Materials, focusing on "chemical analysis and comparative replication of pre-Dynastic Egyptian pottery fragments" (whatever that means). When she's not playing Robin Hood, she absorbs the sun, fruit, and thrift stores that bless those of us fortunate enough to live in the Bay Area.

Most of her writing has some sort of archaeological quirk to it. "My Sister's Song" is loosely based on historical fact (tribes around the Black Sea *did* repel Roman troops using this most ingenious, and toothsome, form of biological warfare). She was inspired by an article entitled "Mad Honey" by Adrienne Mayor, published in a 1995 issue of *Archaeology* magazine (Vol. 46, Num. 6—credit where it is due). This is one of those rare stories that sat in the back of the writer's head and then, suddenly, just "happened" without her input, as though something were working through her.

Arite has told me I must write this down, since nearly ten summers have passed and secrecy is no longer strictly necessary. I said to her, "My fingers are more used to knives than quills, and you are the singer in the family, not I." But Arite only smiled and hummed a little tune. I told her that she was the one who gave me the idea, so she has just as much right to tell of it as I. And she would tell it better. Arite shook her head, and said that the story was mine to tell. She is old enough now for me to listen to her.

55

Mind you, I won't do it often. I wasn't born the elder for nothing. In this case my sister may be correct (a grudging admission), the story should be told. But in truth, it was her song that started it all.

I was picking mushrooms from the mossy bank of the forest creek when I heard her singing. Bent over, I was plucking them carefully from the bottom of the stem so that they wouldn't bruise. Those little gray wiggly capped mushrooms hug the bases of the great forest trees like children hiding their faces in their mother's legs. The singing came to me, my sister's voice, wound into the low vibrating burr of a bee Charmer's song. I did not know until then that she had mastered the bee's song. At first I was delighted by the noise; it meant that the small flat cakes of bread Father cooked for evening meal would be sticky sweet. I have just as much a sweet tooth as the next person. Then I remembered the year time and the weather we had been having.

Judging by the sound she was about forty paces away, and yet the song was near its finish. I took off fast, dropping my mushroom basket in my haste so that its precious cargo scattered on the moss. The second I realized the danger I began to yell. Fear lent me the Deer-god's swiftness and I covered those forty paces in a heartbeat. I reached her just in time to see her gently lift, at the end of a forked stick, the first of the honey combs out of the hive. The combs were still green, capped with a thin covering of wax. Even so, I could see that the honey inside was faintly red in color.

Arite was bent over the hollowed stump, intent on her work and her song. Charmed by its vibrations, the bees did not protest her invasion, but they became slightly annoyed at my footsteps. She was touching a finger to the golden mass when I crashed into her.

As I tackled her, she stopped her song, dropped her honeycomb and began to yell. Without the song the bees became instantly alert to her invasion.

I took her with me in a roll, me yelling at her to stop, her yelling at me. She used several vulgar words I felt that a girl of ten summers ought not to know and resolved to have a talk with Father on the subject of her playfellows. The bees began to gather together, exchanged tactical maneuvers and plans of attack, and then turned in a body toward us. I lifted her up and, pushing her before me, charged us both toward the creek. Halfway there we began to flail our arms about our faces, batting away the stinging creatures. Arite hit the water first, still yelling at me, and submerged herself hurriedly. I followed suit, both of us rising only to breathe, briefly exposing our mouths before sinking back down. The water was as full and as cold as only wet spring waters can be.

Eventually the bees became bored hovering above the cold stream and returned to assess the damage. My sister and I hauled ourselves out of the stream, decidedly bedraggled. Instantly she began yelling again, calling me all kinds of a fool, telling me that she had been perfectly safe; many times while I was away, she had sung the bees into submission. Finally she settled into that type of deep seriousness and gravity that only the very young can achieve.

"Mithra, I know you have been fighting for the past year, but I have grown while you were away. The other singers have been training me, I have the voice to be a Charmer. I am not meant to be a warrior like you. And from what I have seen of your brilliant actions this day," she gestured to the welts already forming on her arm, "I certainly don't want to!"

Finally she wore herself out and collapsed dejectedly upon the bank. I sat next to her wringing out my long warrior's braid and looking not at all apologetic.

"Did you, by any remote chance, mark the type of spring we were having this year? If you intend to become a Charmer you will have to know your bees better than this. By the Deer-god's horns, Arite, you have lived your entire life in these parts, what possessed you to sing for honey after a wet spring? I barely stopped you before you took a taste, have you remembered nothing?"

She gave me a blank look. I plucked one of the deep pink rhododendron flowers from a bush near by and waved it in front of her face. "Do you see any other flowers blooming? Any amranta or oleander? No. Nothing but goatsbane throughout this wood, and all the surrounding countryside."

In sudden realization Arite lost her angered adulthood and lapsed into frightened childhood. Had I not reached her in time she might have eaten that honey. Both of us were raised on the stories, both of us learned by experience—do not eat honey after a wet spring. For when rains have continued longer than they should, flowers are knocked from other plants. Only the hearty rhododendron and her sister nerium survive to show glorious faces to the early sun. The bees are forced to chose between those two plants, dogsbane and goatsbane, each a deadly poison. The honey they produce is equally toxic, so strong that just a taste brings on dreams and sickness, to children— death. When I first reached my moon-time, the Melissai fed me a fingertip full so that I could see my future path. It was to be my only taste, unless of course my path was that of a seer, a Melissai. Arite, just five summers, had watched me writhe and scream through the morning, and held my head as I lost several past meals onto the grass.

In my dreams I saw a spider weaving a net of light, a glorious pattern of gold which melted into honey when I touched it. Then I saw the spider leap and turn into a black wish-seed, and I knew that if I caught it, I could have anything that I desired. So I chased it through the forest and over Inner Sea, its water black as coal, where the seed settled and was eaten by a silver fish.

The Melissai said that the spider wove a net of war, and that I chased a wish of freedom toward a weapon of black and silver. So my role among the Heptako-metes was told to me. My dreams made me a warrior, but then Melissai always twisted the dream toward the profession best suited to the dreamer. Arite, when she dreamed, would dream a song or something that could be interpreted as a song. No one ever doubted that I would be a warrior; from the moment I walked I ran, from the moment I spoke I yelled. Arite would be a Charmer, her walk had always been a dance, just as her words were always a song.

"Come, infant," I said, lifting her up from the bank and steering her back into the woods, "We have mush-rooms to pick."

Arite and I returned to the village just as the sky was darkening overhead. We had collected not only mushrooms but a few early fern fronds as well. Father was pleased with our provisions, and we kept our en-counter with the bees to ourselves. Joheri, my scout leader, raised her eyebrows at my stings, but asked no questions when I returned to camp. I shrugged at her, days of silent marching making words unnecessary among arms-mates.

Our warrior's training camp was situated two hills over from the village proper. This was, ostensibly, to keep the noise level down. We warriors were a rau-cous bunch. After too much barley ale we were prone to yelling songs rather than singing them, and the Charmers complained. Many summers ago we moved, two hills over. Far enough for the yelling to be a faint murmer in the village but close enough to run and aid—should it be needed. I often felt that there was something else, a way in which our very energy interfered with the practices of the Melissai and the Charmers. Whatever the case, it suited us all.

Melissai were to say that every step of that spring day was set for me to remember it in the days to come. Perhaps this was true. Had Arite not tampered with the bees I might never had thought to make warriors of them. But here I am getting ahead of myself. (That, too, is the mark of a warrior).

I was back in the forest three days later. A two-day march away from the place Arite and I found the bees, but the same forest. My scout group and I were on a routine search. The Council of Ten Tribes, in its doubtful wisdom, had allied with our neighbor and long-time enemy, King Mithridates. We both heard the growling stomach of Rome, who wished to devour us. We decided that together we might prove less digestible, shall we say? Rather like a rotten piece of meat. We would not kill her, of that we were certain, but we might make Rome unwilling to taste our particular region, and focus on another.

We knew it was like a bitter wine to Mithridates, having to ally with the Heptakometes. We had kept him out of the lush southeast region of the Inner Sea for our entire recorded history. Our mobile groups of warrior scouts harried his sluggish troops from the trees and then vanished. Unfamiliar with the terrain, unable to find food, and harassed by our warriors, Mithridates soldiers inevitably ran. It wounded his pride to ally with us—but even he recognized Rome for the hungry beast she was. It chewed our pride as well, until we saw the first squadron of Roman soldiers on our land. It was a bristling, impenetrable porcupine, with spines of spears and fur of chain-mail. During that spring of Arite's tenth year they were already beginning to harass our southern border. The villages to our west sent warriors with the news.

Three scout groups from our village, mine among them, were dispatched to help our southern neighbors. Thus we moved through the forest towards the borders of our area and into the unknown.

Joheri came into my tent and woke me well before dawn. "The other scout leaders and I have decided, Mithra, that you are to go ahead. You are the swiftest, the quietest and the most seasoned of my warriors. I want you off now; go south along the stream bank, we will follow. You are to report back by eventide. Not to worry, we will disassemble your tent and carry your pack."

So it was that I was the first Heptakomete to see Romans on our land. I actually heard them first. They walk loudly for the conquerors of the world. I wondered, as I climbed a convenient tree, how they could conquer when they announced their presence in such a way. They passed right under me, so close I could have spat upon the silly fringed helmets that they wore. As they passed, I realized the reason for the noise. The warriors in our village number thirty in all. But there are always scout groups out, even in the winter months, so all thirty are never together in one place. The most I've seen at any time is maybe sixty-five, the representatives who met with Mithridates, two summers before. All I knew was that below me there were many more than that. I had heard, but not believed, that the Romans traveled in squadrons one hundred strong. All male, these warriors were garbed in matching leathers and carried something called spears (very long knives) and shields, like great squares of tree bark, to protect themselves. Never had I truly believed the stories until I saw the squadron below me.

I did not move as I sat in my tree above them, I

hardly even breathed. All I did was count. And I counted one hundred and one men. As luck would have it, the leader called a halt just beneath my tree. I watched as they broke ranks and settled in the shade as far as I could see, leaning back against the bark or each other. They pulled out rations and began to eat, murmuring quietly in their peculiar tongue. They drank a blood-red wine from brown flasks and ate a bread which was fat and almost white in color, much different from our flat yellow cakes. I watched the leader closely. He sat a little apart from the others, surrounded by four men, whose helmet plumes appeared to be a little taller than the others. These, I surmised, were rather like scout leaders, only their scout groups would consist of twenty-four warriors, instead of six. They talked among themselves, but as I spoke no Latin, I watched their behavior and the movement of their bodies. Apparently they were dissatisfied with the bread. Its consumption was accompanied by much twisting of the lips and wrinkling of the noses in disgust. Finally the leader sighed and reached into his pack to produce a small ceramic jar wrapped in a linen cloth. This jar he opened. Its contents were greeted with cries of delight and much gratitude, which the leader accepted as his due. Immediately the four scout leaders began to dip their white bread into the jar. Only then did I realize what it contained, a familiar thick golden mass of syrupy sweetness.

They rested for only a brief time before their leader yelled a command and they reassembled the large, loudly stomping, porcupine. I dropped soundlessly (not that it mattered considering the racket they were making) from the tree, skirted around them to the west and ran to reach my companions. I estimated they were but two hours march behind me when I skidded to a halt at Joheri's side. As briefly as possible

I explained what I had seen, one hundred men, well armed and well protected from our arrows.

The scout leaders met and decided to take to the trees and launch a surprise attack from their branches, much as we did against Mithridates' squadrons. I lodged a formal protest; I felt the Roman's strange shields would protect them from such an assault. The leaders did not listen. What else could we do? We had no other way to deal with such a remarkable threat. Still, my protest was acknowledged and I was assigned the hilt position, to observe rather than lead the battle.

We would wait in the trees, just as I had done, until they were directly below us. We were to use all of our arrows from the trees, and then drop down to engage them at knife point. I was to provide back hilt. I had protested the attack plan, thus making it my duty to stay back and witness its success, or survive to report why it had failed. I was also the fastest of the runners, and should we be defeated someone would have to run the information home.

As it happened, the attack fared better than I had thought. Caught by surprise, the squadron, which clearly was made up of unseasoned fighters, was slow to realize that the attack came from above. A few of our best archers were able to pick off Romans through the eyes, or by way of one of their few unarmed spots. But by the time we dropped from the trees, they had regrouped. Our knives were little match against their longer spears. If we managed to get close enough to one warrior his neighbor picked us off. Even if he didn't, we could not get past those strange shields. The best thing, we found, was to roll under, or force our way between two warriors, like a wedge, so that we were in the center of the porcupine and could attack from inside. Joheri was the first to figure out this tactic and managed to claim four to her honor before she was killed. I hugged back hilt and watched. I picked off those who broke ranks and noted that in single combat, unprotected by his fellows, a Roman was no match for a Heptakomete. I also saw that the female warriors seemed to disconcert the Romans; apparently their women did not fight. I counted our losses to theirs and, though it was quite even, we hardly dented their number. By the time we had lost half our warriors, I had seen enough. As back hilt, it was my responsibility to whistle retreat. I whistled.

We melted back into the trees, our number halved, two of us wounded. I carried one atop my back and Sokar carried the other. We ran due east until dark; there I left them to tend to their injuries and ran north alone. All the scout leaders had been killed in the battle and I was the most seasoned warrior. By rights I should have stayed to lead those who survived. But I had also been back hilt, and first scout. I had observed everything, I was the one who should report. I left Sokar in charge; he had two seasons of fight in him and had struck well and true during the battle. He was also unharmed and well thought of, and so most able to lead.

I did the three days of travel in one day and two nights of running, stopping only to drink. I arrived back at the village at midday yelling warrior's rights to instant council assembly.

The village, accustomed to such meetings from the past battles with Mithridates, was quick to collect in the large central hut. There I told of the battle as quickly as possible. The remaining two scout groups, the Charmers, and the Melissai sat before me, silent. I emphasized the great number in the Roman squadron. I said that we were equally matched warrior to warrior, but that there were simply too many of them, and they were barely two days behind me. They were headed roughly in the direction of our village, though they might pass us by and head toward our neighbor to the east. A runner was immediately dispatched with this information, and finally I was silent.

So was everyone else. Finally my father spoke, "Mithra, are you quite certain of the number?"

I sighed, still panting slightly from my run. "Quite certain. I know the number seems amazing, but you must believe me."

A Melissai spoke. "We must consider all of our options, please offer suggestions. It seems that a full attack is impossible. Even those attacks we have used in the past against Mithridates are useless."

"We could send to Mithridates for aid."

"He would not get here in time."

"We could send to our neighbors to the north."

"They would not believe that the Romans came in such number."

"Then we must trick the Romans."

"Perhaps somehow we could convince them to enter the river. Their ranks would break, their armor would sink them, they would drop their shields in order to swim. The we could pick them off with arrows."

I sat slumped while they battered ideas back and forth. Nothing, I felt, could battle against such a menace. Rome was truly a mighty and hungry monster. I forced myself not to think of my lost scout members. It is a warrior's place to lose companions. None, I noted, had asked for the names of the dead. Parents wondered, but stayed silent; right now it was better to wonder. Grief would muddle the head, push anger into the soul where logic was needed. Grief and anger made for bad decisions and worse strategy.

Children were not meant to sit in a war council, but somehow Arite wiggled into the hut. I should not have been surprised, Arite tends to turn up where least expected. She went unnoticed, or at last unremarked upon, by the rest of the council. Arite looked at me, my clothing soaked with other people's blood, and her eyes went wide and her face white. In that instant I remembered, less than a week ago, picking mushrooms, hearing her singing. Her face had looked the same as we sat in the stream and I reminded her of the danger in the honey. Into my head flashed another image, the Roman leader as he produced a ceramic pot from his satchel and the delight on the faces of his comrades at the unexpected treat.

"Honey!" I spoke the thought aloud and into silence. The council had quieted, thoughtful and sobered.

My statement seemed to startle them.

"Honey." I said again, more to myself this time. "They love honey. I watched them eat it at their midday meal. You should have seen their enjoyment. We should give it to them."

"Child, our stores are nearly empty. What nonsense you talk. You think a little honey would make them treat us well? Don't be silly."

"No, the dreaming honey of the wet spring. Arite nearly ate some just the other day. It is a curse of just our lands; the Romans wouldn't know. If we could get them to eat it—even if we could get only half of them to eat it, we would have a fair chance."

The council looked thoughtful. The Melissai grumbled a bit at the use of their sacred seer honey for war purposes.

I ignored them. "Allow the Romans to get close to the village, pretend to lead them accidentally to our store of honey. Perhaps a secret cache in the woods. They would stop to eat it, I know they would."

So it was that dressed in skirts (a peculiar garment worn by the wives of Mithridates and other women south of our lands), I waited for the Romans at the edge of the village. I carried a dripping honey comb strategically peaking out of the top of a ceramic jar. I pretended not to see them or hear them (rabbit thumpers that they were) as I passed quite near. They set a scout to follow me, believing I would lead him to the village, unsuspecting. Instead I led him to a huge pile of honey, all the honey we could find from the many hives we knew of and a few new ones. Every Charmer in our village was hoarse from singing, even Arite. Every beehive in the forest was deprived of its loot. The honey, slightly watery and reddish, had made our palms tingle as we collected it. Now it sat, inviting and innocent-looking, before me. The Roman scout who followed let forth a glad cry at the sight. I pretended startlement and was quickly bound, gagged and tumbled aside. He ran to collect his comrades and the whole swarm—I counted ninety of them now—descended upon the honey. They ate it greedily, apparently unused to such wealth, licking it off of fingers, hands, and each other. They were too eager to notice the slightly acidic taste.

It took nearly an hour for the toxins to take effect. By then they were almost upon the village. Apprehensively the twelve remaining warriors stood at the front of the village and watched them come. The porcupine of warriors seemed undefeatable, until it began to wobble.

I knew how the Romans felt. First a strange tingling sensation all over, then an empty dizzy feeling in the head and that horrible sickness in the stomach. Then the loss of hands and feet, limbs that would not obey commands—like unruly children. They looked quite drunk, all ninety of them. Stumbling toward the village, the porcupine seemed to wiggle slightly, weaving from side to side. Bits kept falling out, meandering aside on their own. The watchers in the village began to laugh, almost hysterically, at the approaching menace. Their spears carved arches through the air, so that it looked as though the porcupine were shivering its quills. It began to lose momentum, and some of the Romans fell to the ground. Apparently not one Roman of the group disliked the taste of honey, all had eaten at least a mouthful or two. A few made it to the waiting warriors, but sick as they were, they were easily killed. The rest collapsed, breathing slowly, stiff as boards or jerking slightly. Before our village they lay, stretched out, the tassels on their helmets waving in a breeze. Some died from their overindulgence. Most we stabbed, quickly and painlessly. By that time, stomachs cramped, loosing their midday meal on the grass, feeling as though they were being clawed from the inside, our knives were like a blessing, a release from the whirling lights, the grueling sickness. Even from my small dose I remembered seeking death.

Of course, the real problem was the ninety bodies we then had to dispose of. Our warrior survivors from the first battle arrived that evening, in time to help us strip the Romans of their armor and their strange weaponry. Their mail and their clothing would prove useful in trade. We eventually decided to drag them to the meadow where we burned as much of them as we could, and buried the rest.

I was given my own scout group. Arite made a song about the whole thing, and every spring we began to collect the poison honey—not just for the Melissai to dream with.

The Romans named it *meli maenomenon,* mad honey. My people used it to kill three squadrons over then next eight summers. The Heptakometes kept the Inner Sea from the yearning maw of Rome and her allies for all the time of that great Empire. Each time they marched toward our sea they could not resist the honey laid before them, and its golden sweetness inevitably lured them into death.

THE SUMMONS

by Bunnie Bessell

The last time our paths merged, after Bunnie Bessell admitted to being a "dedicated hugger," I hoped she would continue to "hug and write." She thinks the two are bound one to the other. When she received my latest acceptance letter, she hugged the letter, her dog, her cat, a live oak tree, her other dog, various inanimate objects between the mailbox and the house, and culminated with a hug with her husband, Steve. Without her saying a word, he knew she had sold another story. She doesn't think it is possible ever to lose the incredible joy of knowing your story will be read and others will come to know your characters as you know them.

A lot remains the same since she last sold a story to me, and a lot is different. She still lives in Arlington, Texas, is still married to a wonderful friend (25 years now), and is still "frolicking through the forties." On the other hand, she has changed jobs (twice), has acquired a second horse, four new nieces and nephews (for a total of fifteen), and has raised two new puppies. For the past few years she has been happily busy training said puppies, and finishing a novel.

She is learning that novels are quite different from short stories; she complains that they take on a life of their own and become somewhat difficult to get to end. That's for sure.

Not too many stories deal literally with swordswomen. This one does.

Blaze pulled the prince from the brothel, ignoring the protests of the scantily clad pleasure girls at the doorway.

"You're supposed to be a bodyguard," Dorn complained, still pulling the last of his clothing into place, "not a nursemaid."

Blaze refused to let him bait her into an argument. Instead she scanned the dark streets around them. Doors were closed and windows shuttered tight. Blaze trusted nothing when it came to Prince Valadorn's safety. She couldn't afford to ease her guard, even at this early morning hour when the city looked deserted.

"God's feet, Blaze," Dorn continued to complain. "It took a month to arrange that appointment. You dragged me out of the most exclusive pleasure house in the city before anything happened. Couldn't you have waited another quarter hour?"

Still ignoring him, Blaze touched the token nestled within the folds of her amber sash. A servant had brought it to her yesterday. After three years of silence, the Temple had summoned her.

She had not expected a call, at least not yet, and she should already have reported to the Temple. The priest would not appreciate her delay. Even if she'd spent the night searching brothels for Dorn.

Normally, she would have made him regret such a stunt, but tonight she found it hard to discipline the youth. The summons meant her time with Dorn was over. She wasn't exactly sure how she felt about that. Could she truly trust anyone else to keep the wayward prince out of danger?

"You're just angry because I slipped away from you," he told her. "You didn't think I could do it." He flashed her a quick, teasing grin.

He was right, of course, but she wasn't about to let him gloat over his achievement. She stopped and faced him. "How safe were you," she asked, "with your pants and sword on the other side of the room? Do you believe that assassins never frequent exclusive houses?"

"Assassins?" he scoffed. "You've guarded me since I was thirteen. No one has ever tried to kill me. They wouldn't dare."

Blaze bit back a retort. Something must have shown in her expression, though. Dorn's eyes narrowed.

"Someone *has* tried?" he asked. "When?"

She shook her head and turned back down the street.

"Have there been attempts on my life?" he demanded, stepping in front of her.

Blaze sighed. She knew he wouldn't let it go. Stubborn was his middle name. She looked up tilting her head to meet his eyes. When had he grown so tall? she wondered. She kept seeing the boy she'd first met, instead of the young man he had become. For a moment, she took in his dark, curly hair and even darker eyes. She noticed for the first time the fuzz of a beard along his chin. "Yes," she said softly. "There have been attempts."

He rocked back a second. "When?"

Reluctantly she said, "The last attempt was a week ago—"

"Last?" he interrupted. "How many have there been?

"Three in the last month," she told him. Perhaps it was time he recognized the dangers. In a matter of weeks, he would be confirmed as Heir. She wouldn't be around to protect him after that.

A frown tugged at his lips. "The sugared fruit delivered last week. You took it away. Poison?"

She nodded.

"And the ride we took to Zarl. We turned back suddenly."

She felt a glimmer of pride that he noticed these things. Her teachings had not gone without gain. "An ambush. I refused to allow them to shoot barbs at you from behind the trees."

"Instead, you took us across the valley. If they had followed, they would have exposed themselves," he added.

"And faced my bow," she said. A tone of menace laced her voice.

"Not a choice I would have made," he assured her with a laugh. Then more seriously, he asked, "And the third time?"

"A Festin Slayer breached the walls. I stopped him at your door."

"Who is trying to kill me?" he asked.

Half the country, Blaze thought grimly, the half that didn't support his succession. "You have brothers," she reminded him softly.

He shook his head, but Blaze knew he wasn't that naive. He just didn't want to accept the obvious. King F'atrelle had six wives who each kept separate households. Among them were fifteen sons. By law, the king could name any of these male children Heir if the child survived to manhood. But until he actually named and confirmed an Heir, the king could provide no protection or assistance to his sons. Unfortunately, the system fostered a bitter and dangerous rivalry among brothers, or more specifically among their uncles. Each wanted his nephew to assume the throne. Each was willing to go to extreme lengths to assure the success of his candidate.

When F'atrelle announced his intent to confirm Valadorn as Heir, he passed over two older sons, and left twelve younger ones without prospects. The attempts on Dorn's life had intensified immediately.

"They haven't managed to kill me," Dorn told her, his voice tight. "Thanks to you. And they won't." Then his familiar, quirky smile touched his lips. "I guess it would be prudent of me not to slip away again."

"Most prudent," she agreed. She turned and motioned him to follow. "Let's go."

"Where are we going?" he asked.

"To the Temple."

He laughed, his eyes glinting with delight. "Well, why didn't you say so? The Temple's pleasure girls are far superior to any establishment."

"You will hardly have the opportunity to compare," she told him stiffly. "I have been summoned."

His sudden silence told her he understood the importance of such a call.

Again, she felt a twinge of concern. Dorn had been in her charge for three years. She had resisted the assignment when it began, but now she found herself reluctant to turn his care over to anyone else.

Eventually, the narrow streets opened onto a square. In the center stood the Temple. The immense stone building rose like a beacon in front of Blaze. She had spent a good part of her life here. Mixed feelings washed through her, worry over Dorn and uneasy anticipation about her own future. Where would the Temple send her next?

She paused to check the area before entering the square. A few dozen people were scattered around the perimeter. Vendors were busy setting up tents to sell their wars. Nothing looked threatening.

Behind her, Dorn shifted impatiently and she waved him forward. They walked across the square together, but he hesitated when they reached the first step.

Blaze stopped beside him, peering up the steep stairs. As a child she had counted each one, one hundred and one steps to the top, a sacred number. Now she found herself counting again as she began to climb, and memories rushed back to her.

At the age of nine, she left her home, climbed these

steps, and knelt before the first priest she'd found, touching her head to the stones. "I come to serve," she'd whispered in a voice filled with hope and fear.

To her surprise the old man knelt beside her. He had said nothing, just waited, until finally she found the courage to look up at him. His face, lined with wrinkles, showed neither welcome nor rejections, only patience. "What is your name?" he asked.

"Blaze," she told him without hesitation, rejecting forever the name her parents had given her.

She saw one of his eyebrows lift slightly. "Who is your family?"

Reluctantly, she told him and saw his eyebrow rise even higher as she named one of the more powerful families of the city. "I won't go back to them," she told him. "I want to be a Sword of the Temple."

She saw no surprise in his expression. "Why?"

The question baffled her. She thought everyone wanted to be a Sword. They were heroes. Ballads were written about their deeds. Swords changed lives, they even changed nations.

All her life, she had watched them stroll the streets of the city. Lean and dangerous looking, they moved with confidence and authority. The Temple Swords represented bravery and glory, and everything good and right about the world.

But as Blaze looked at the old priest, she could not find the words to explain. Instead she said simply, "I want to do something important."

He looked at her with dark, knowing eyes, "I am Iothe," he said, motioning her to her feet. "Come with me."

Blaze let out a breath she didn't know she'd been holding. "I will be a Sword?"

He glanced at her, as if weighing her in his mind. "If you survive."

It had been no idle warning. She spent the next ten

years in grueling training. She was challenged up to and beyond her limits. Slowly, painfully, her body and her mind were honed, chiseled into something stronger than steel. When Blaze finally tied the amber sash around her waist, she was one of only eight remaining from the fifty in her original group.

She'd been proud of her achievement, and acted like a fool, strutting around the city. She took to tying her sash with an extra twist so it that curled dramatically down her leg. She winced now as she recalled her actions those first days.

She had expected her initial assignment to be something exceptional—a challenge to her talent and a deed that would earn her a reputation.

Instead Iothe assigned her to guard Valadorn.

"You can't mean it!" she had sputtered.

He'd looked at her impassively.

"I thought you would send me to fight at the Becertherian Walls, or to search for the Basil-Stone. This, this is menial!"

His eyebrow pricked up. "Perhaps it will teach you humility."

She blushed as his point hit home. "I worked too hard to nursemaid a child, Iothe. A mercenary could do that. You don't need a Sword."

"Not every assignment is filled with glory," Iothe said tiredly. "I picked you to protect this prince."

"Why?" she demanded.

"This may help you learn who you are."

"I know who I am. I am a Sword."

"That is a title," he said. "You are more than a title."

"I am a Sword," she repeated, "That is all I ever wanted to be. Now you've made me a laughing stock. A Sword sent out to wipe the nose of a sniffling child."

"He is a prince," Iothe reminded her. "The king's son."

She snorted. "The king has fifteen sons."

"He wants *this* son protected," Iothe said.

"I will not do this," she said firmly.

"As you wish," he said. "You may choose. Your life is shaped by the choices you make."

His words hung between them. She had no doubt of their meaning. Accept the assignment or leave the Temple.

"He is important," Iothe told her softly.

Scowling with frustration, she had stomped out of the Temple and gone straight to the palace, demanding an audience with the king. In the back of her mind, she hoped rudeness might lose her the assignment.

She was led to the F'atrelle's practice yard to find the king waiting with a long blade balanced expertly in his hands. Before she could speak, he attacked.

Blaze's training saved her. She managed to get her blade up in a parry and launch a defense. In an instant she realized this was no simple test of her ability, she was fighting for her life.

F'atrelle was fast and clever, and employed moves she'd never seen. He was not her equal, but she was hindered by the fact that she could not kill or even dare to wound him. They fought until both dripped with sweat and Blaze's muscles screamed for her to end it.

Then as abruptly as he'd begun, the king dropped his blade.

"You'll do," he said simply and summoned a servant. "Take her to the household of my second wife. Introduce her to Prince Sol Valadorn."

As she turned to go, the king called over his shoulder, "Keep him alive. He is the best of my children."

That was the first and last time Blaze had been with

the king. On meeting Dorn, she discovered a boy no happier at being saddled with a female protector than she was at the task of protecting a child. Their first words had not been polite.

That was a long time ago, she thought wryly as she reached the top of the Temple steps. Three years and a lot of arguments ago. Now, it seemed to have passed all too quickly.

Dorn stepped up beside her, his face a tight mask. "This summons means you'll be leaving me?"

"You'll be confirmed Heir next month," she reminded him gently. "My contract was to protect you until that time."

He hesitated, then said, "My father would extend the contract, if I asked him."

She had always known their time together would be limited, and so did he. "We both have paths to follow, Dorn. You will be king and I must be a Sword. My next assignment awaits."

She realized how much Iothe would have appreciated her statement. Except he'd died last year. As old as the priest had been, it had never occurred to Blaze that Iothe might not be there when she returned to the Temple. She had learned of his death when the callers carried the news. Now, entering the familiar Temple foyer, she found it hard to believe that she would not see him.

Immediately, two Temple girls slipped from an alcove and came forward to greet them. Blaze nodded toward Dorn. "My companion will need someplace to stay for a while," Blaze told them. "Give him refreshment."

They bowed and, tossing flirtatious smiles at Dorn, motioned him to follow.

He barely glanced at them, "Blaze, I—"

"You'll be safe here," she told him, and headed toward the sanctuary within the Temple. Nervously, she straightened her sash, retying it neatly around her waist.

She nudged open the ornate bronze doors to the inner sanctum and slipped inside. Instantly, her years in training rushed back and she felt like a child again. The room stretched in front of her, dim and serene. At the far end, she saw three priests sitting on a dais. Fire baskets burned in a circle around them, casting their saffron robes and inscrutable faces in an ethereal glow.

Blaze straightened her shoulders and strode forward. A few steps from the dais, she knelt and touched her head to the marble floor. "I come to serve."

Their eyes drilled into her, and she immediately wished she'd taken the time to change into a formal tunic. She saw only censure in their stares.

Finally, the center priest spoke. "Your assignment with Prince Valadorn is ended."

Blaze nodded. "He will be confirmed next month."

One of the priests hissed. Blaze gritted her teeth and chided herself internally. Her relationship with Iothe had been one where she could speak freely. She knew better than to attempt the same familiarity with other priests.

"Your assignment is ended," the middle priest repeated sternly. "The Temple has another task for you." He waved and a servant slipped from the shadows. He laid a small bundle wrapped in silken cloth in front of Blaze and then retreated on silent feet.

"Unwrap it," the priest told her.

Blaze bent forward and folded back the smooth material. Within lay five gold krucoins and a small blade.

Whatever the assignment, it was costly. The coins represented more gold than she had ever handled. But the blade drew her attention.

"Take them," the priest said.

She gathered the coins, slipping them within the folds of her sash. Then she carefully lifted the blade.

It was delicate and barely longer than her hand, but felt neatly balanced within her palm. The ornate handle was made of bronze and silver woven in an intricate pattern. Writings that Blaze did not recognize ran along the side of the pommel.

She slipped it within the folds of her sash next to the coins, and looked up at the priests. "My sword is yours."

The priest nodded. "Before today's last bell," he said, and a humorless smile stretched across his lips, "you will use that blade to kill Prince Valadorn."

His words slammed into her. Blaze shot to her feet, "No!"

"How dare you!" one of the side priests shouted. "Kneel down!"

She sank to her knees, immediately regretting her outburst. But still she couldn't hold her tongue. "You must be mistaken," she insisted.

All three glared at her.

"My task was to protect the Prince until he was confirmed."

"That assignment has ended."

"But it isn't complete," she argued, trying to sound reasonable. "I must see him confirmed." Their scowls told her they did not agree.

"I told you this was useless," the side priest muttered. The center priest raised a hand to silence him.

"I am Carthier," he said. "I knew your master." He paused, his eyes burning into hers. "Iothe told me that he believed you were the best Sword he ever trained."

The praise wrenched at Blaze.

"He also said that frequently your tongue got ahead of your good sense."

The comment sounded so much like Iothe that she

struggled against a lump in her throat. "He assigned me to protect Valadorn."

"Yes," Carthier agreed. "And Iothe would give you this assignment, if he were here. He is not. I am." There was a warning in his tone. She knew she could not push his patience much further.

Still Blaze could not accept this order. "You want me to assassinate a—"

"Assassination has been used for generations," he reminded her. "Emeralde assassinated King Fredreen and Bandaal took out Lord Helstoan. Temple Swords have done what is necessary."

Blaze stared at him, realizing that he had deliberately named two female Swords. Women whose stories she had admired.

"They killed old men who had slaughtered thousands," Blaze reminded him. "You want me to murder a boy."

The priests on the side grumbled, and Carthier silenced them again. "We have looked into the future. It is best for the country that Valadorn never take the throne."

"Why?" Blaze asked. "He will be a good man."

"Do you question the wisdom of the Temple?" Carthier demanded coldly. "This one death may save thousands of others." He paused and added. "What would Iothe have you do?"

Not this, she wanted to scream. But she held her tongue. Iothe had said assignments were seldom pleasant. But this. This felt dishonorable. Would he really approve of something so treacherous? She didn't know, she couldn't be sure.

"You are a Sword of the Temple," Carthier said. "Do you accept your assignment?"

It always came back to that. If she was a Sword, she had to accept. The thought of refusing—giving up the sash—left her breathless.

She looked up at Carthier bleakly. "The king will know I did this. The Temple will be blamed."

"We will deal with that," Carthier assured her.

Reluctantly, she said, "I come to serve." The words felt like old leather on her tongue.

He nodded in satisfaction. "Once the deed is done, go to the wharf. Purchase passage on the first ship to Galindor. The gold should pay for passage and lodging when you arrive. Report to the Temple in Galindor for your next assignment."

Her next assignment, she thought with revulsion. She didn't know if she could face another assignment.

"Make sure to leave the blade with the boy's body," Carthier told her.

Numbly she climbed to her feet, and left without bowing. She shoved open one of the doors and stepped outside to find Dorn leaning against a column, his arms crossed, waiting for her.

He looked up at her, worry written across his features. His expression turned to alarm at the sight of her, "What's wrong?" he asked immediately.

She walked past him. "Come on."

He caught up as she started down the steps. "Has someone else died?"

His question stopped her. "What do you mean 'someone else'?" she snarled.

Hesitantly, he said, "You looked like this before. Last year. I went to my father. He said the priest, Iothe, had died."

Blaze was surprised that Dorn and F'atrelle had discussed her. "What did the king tell you?"

"To leave you alone, and you would get over it in time," Dorn replied.

Blaze started down the steps and Dorn walked beside her, adding, "He said Iothe was a good man. Too good. Father said the Temple destroyed him."

Blaze's steps faltered at his words. Iothe died of a

fever. Or at least, that's what she'd heard. Was there something more to it? She glanced sharply at Dorn. "What did he mean?"

"Who knows?" He shrugged. "Father doesn't like the Temple very much."

No, Blaze agreed mentally. The arguments between the king and the Temple had divided the city more than once.

Was that the real motive behind the assignment? The Temple did not want to deal with Valadorn because he would surely follow in his father's footsteps? Did they hope to find a more amenable heir among the king's other sons?

She weighed that thought. If it were true, did it change anything? She was still a Sword of the Temple. She still had an assignment. Did the motive matter?

More out of habit than thought, she paused and looked around the plaza as she reached the bottom of the steps. The area was crowded. Vendors and merchants displayed their wares. People wandered through the tents.

Too many people, Blaze thought immediately. Dorn would not be safe here. The irony hit her at once. Dorn wasn't safe with her either. Her stomach knotted at the thought. "Pull up your cloak," she snapped and as he did, she led him across the square.

"Where are we going?" he asked.

"To the wharf," she told him. She wanted away from the Temple and she wasn't ready to return to Dorn's household. The wharf was the one place the prince would not argue about visiting. He'd always been fascinated with ships. He spent days looking at vessels and talking with sailors.

He fell in eagerly beside her and shortly they stepped onto the wide stone docks. Weathered warehouses stood on one side, and the other opened to the sea.

The area teemed with people and activity. Immediately, Blaze took Dorn to the seaward side. They walked along the waist-high stone wall that held back the waves.

Ahead of them half a dozen ships were tied off in the deep bay.

"Look," Dorn called at the sight of the nearest ship. "It's the *Silver Hawk*. I told you about her. Look at those lines. She's the fastest ship on the water."

Blaze eyed the ship with little interest. It appeared to be preparing to depart. The sails were partially unfurled. Only one gangplank still balanced between ship and dock. A few sailors carried bundles of cargo aboard.

"She can sail to Bitrian in seven days," Dorn went on. "Nothing on the sea can catch her."

He paused and watched the ship with glowing eyes. "When I am king, I'll have a fleet made just like her."

The words twisted in Blaze's gut.

"I wish I were sailing today," he said wistfully, then glanced back at Blaze. "Are you going to tell me why you are in such a foul mood?"

She glared at him.

"Well, are you?" he demanded.

"I've been given an assignment I find unappealing," she snarled.

"Less appealing than watching over me?" he asked with a grin.

At another time, she might have laughed. Today, she continued to glare.

"That bad?" He shrugged. "Don't do it, then. Refuse."

"I've been given the assignment," she told him tiredly.

"And you don't have the right to refuse?" he questioned.

"I am a Sword of the Temple, I have to—"

"That's a title," Dorn scoffed. "Not *who* you are."

His words rang so close to Iothe's that they took Blaze's breath away. "It is all I know how to be."

"No," Dorn said firmly. "You are more." He added in a whisper, "You are my friend."

His words rattled her. She looked out to sea. No one had ever called her friend.

Everything muddled in her mind. Iothe had sent her to protect Valadorn. Would he truly approve of her killing him now? What was it he had said four years ago. *I picked you to protect this prince. He is important.*

Another of her master's statement drifted back to her. *You may choose, Blaze. Your life is shaped by the choices you make.*

"Tell me about this assignment," Dorn urged. "Perhaps there is something we can do about it." He spoke with the voice of a boy who would be king, someone who thought he could solve all problems.

Blaze looked toward him without really seeing him.

What path would she choose, the prince or the Temple? Her life spun out in front of her. All she'd ever wanted was to be a Sword, to have people respect her, recognize her on the street. Now would they remember only that she assassinated a child? She clenched her jaw at the thought.

Why had she told Iothe she wanted to be a Sword? *To do something important.* So what was important, her promises to the Temple where she spent most of her life, or to this boy who called her friend? She considered the two and found suddenly that the decision was not hard at all.

Reaching within her sash, she drew the knife.

She turned to face Prince Valadorn. "This is the problem," she told him, laying the blade on the wall.

His eyes widened at the sight of the blade. "What are you doing with that?" he demanded. "That's a

Kilavanne family blade. No one except members of the family may carry one."

Another piece of the puzzle clicked into placed. Kalandra Kilavanne was fourth wife to the king, and had a son only a few weeks younger than Dorn. The Temple did not aim to remove one heir—but two. One dead and the other accused of his murder.

Blaze, the bodyguard, wouldn't be around to report differently. She would disappear on the first ship out of the city. Would the Temple suggest that Blaze had been killed defending Dorn and her body thrown into the sea? That would mean she could never return to Ashram. But it would hardly matter. There would be plenty of assignments elsewhere. As an outlaw, she might be even more valuable to the Temple.

"No," Dorn said suddenly beside her, snapping her out of her thoughts. "You can't do it." He looked at her intensely. "If your assignment is to kill Kestorin," he named his younger brother, "I forbid it." He paused and added sincerely, "He is no threat to me, Blaze."

She met his eyes. "Do you trust me?"

"I don't want you to kill Kestorin," he replied.

"Do you trust me?" she repeated.

He wavered, struggling, she could tell. If he agreed to trust her, he might be signing his brother's death sentence. Finally, he straightened his shoulders and said, "Yes."

Without emotion she told him, "My assignment is not to kill Kestorin." She paused and saw the relief in his eyes. "I am ordered to kill *you,* with his blade."

Dorn lost his breath for a moment, then snorted. "That's crazy! You'd never do it." There was no doubt in his tone.

Blaze held his eye and let him think about it a moment. She saw a flicker of worry slip into his gaze. He glanced toward the knife and then back up at her. "You wouldn't do it."

She wondered how this boy had come to know her better than she knew herself. She shook herself slightly, and asked, "The girl last night, did you pay her?"

Dorn blinked at her, confused by the question.

"Last night," she repeated. "Did you pay for the girl?"

"No," he said, finally understanding her. "You don't pay until after, and you didn't let me—"

"Do you have the coins?" she asked and held out her hand.

He pulled krucoins from his own sash and dropped them into her palm. Two silvers.

"This girl *was* expensive." Blaze mocked him with a slight smile and slipped the coins into her sash. She picked up the Kilavanne blade.

Dorn eyed her suspiciously.

With a flick of her wrist she sent it spinning into the sea. "Let's go," she told him.

"Where?"

"To make your wish come true."

"I don't want the girl now, I—"

"We're sailing on the *Silver Hawk*."

His eyes lit up. "We are? But when? I can't go before the confirmation, and after—"

"Today. Now."

Her comment stopped him.

"If you aren't dead in the morning, the Temple will send its best Swords to kill you," she explained. "I'm not sure I can keep you safe here. But they can't kill you if they can't find you. We'll get on that ship and sail out this morning. Even if someone sees us board, it won't matter. You said yourself nothing could catch us on the seas.

"We'll sail to the first port, then book passage on

the first ship back. We should return several days before your confirmation. I can keep you alive for that long."

"But no one will know where we are," he protested.

"That's the idea," she agreed.

"My father," Dorn reminded her. "He won't know either."

"He'll know you are with me," she replied.

"We could go to him," Dorn told her. "He would help."

Blaze shook her head. "You know the tradition. He can't protect you until you are officially Heir. He's already pushed it as far as he dares by hiring me."

She saw him waver, weighing his options. She waited patiently, knowing her own life hung in the balance of his decision.

Then suddenly he flashed her his familiar grin. "Nice day for a sail, I'd say."

He turned away from Blaze, and called out to a nearby sailor, "You there, where is the ship's master? We need a word with him."

As Blaze followed him, her hand dropped to the amber sash wrapped around her waist. For a moment, she considered flinging it into the sea as they set sail.

Then she paused. No. Let them take it from her, if they could. She might not bow to the Temple any longer, but she was still a Sword.

LUZ

by Patricia Duffy Novak

Patricia Duffy Novak lives in Opelika, Alabama, with her husband, Jim, her daughter, Sylvia, four cats with attitudes, and two overly eager-to-please dogs. She has sold a number of short stories to MZB, for this anthology series, for *Marion Zimmer Bradley's Fantasy Magazine,* and for the Darkover anthology series. She's also sold to *Realms of Fantasy* and *Adventures of Sword and Sorcery.*

Part of the inspiration for "Luz" came while making Christmas ornaments with her Girl Scout troop. She wants to thank her husband, Jim, and her friend Lisa Silverthorne, for their helpful comments on earlier versions of this story.

> *She will speak to those she favors. Although the whole world turn against them, they will receive the sign of her love.*
>
> —*The Book of Truth.*

The Goddess didn't speak to Luz. Luz lay on the stone floor of the temple, facedown, arms outstretched and legs together. Behind her closed eyelids, she saw the light wax and wane, and then wax and wane and wax once more. The sea wind whistled through the temple windows and the distant cry of birds carried on the breeze. Closer to her ear came the occasional rustle of the priests' robes and the slap of their leather sandals going past. Sunlight warmed her back, followed by night's chill, and then the whole pattern once more. Her stomach growled, her bones ached, and her bladder screamed its torment.

All this she saw, and heard, and felt. But nothing more. No vision came. Luz would have stayed, waiting for Iridan's sign, until her death; her mind willed it so, but her body rebelled. She rose on trembling legs and staggered from the temple to face the ruin of her dreams.

The sun lay low on the horizon, and the wind had died. A saffron-robed priest in the courtyard smiled at her. "Three days and two nights. Longest vigil in temple history. You'll have a good vision to report to Simeon, I'll wager. Did the Goddess kiss your hand?"

Luz said nothing, her throat too dry for speech and her grief too raw to share with this man. Her soul lay crushed within her, like a moth battered against stone.

She returned to her quarters, took care of her body's needs, and dressed herself in a clean, white robe. Then she walked along a cobbled passage to the spare, stone chamber of Father Simeon, High Priest of the Star.

The High Priest sat in a simple, armless chair, his muscular hands quiet in his lap. Through the window behind him, Luz saw the setting sun striping the clouds with shades of red. Simeon's angular face lay in shadows, but the star upon his brow glowed lightly silver, the special mark of Iridan's love. Among all the priests at the Seawind Temple, only Simeon bore such a sign.

"What did you see, my child?" he said to Luz.

She lowered her head, refusing to let the hot tears emerge from behind her eyes. "I saw the darkness and the light."

"What did you hear?"

"I heard the wind and the rustle of robes."

"What did you feel?"

"I felt the stone, cold beneath me, and the sun, warm upon my back."

"That was all?"

Simeon's deep voice echoed in her ears. She wanted to lie, to claim for herself the mark of Iridan's love, but to lie to a starbrow was to lie to the Goddess herself. "Yes, Father. That was all."

"Ah." In that single syllable, Simeon put a wealth of feeling. Luz heard sorrow and pity and something else she could not name. She raised her head. Dusk had fallen. Simeon waved his hand and the room filled with a soft silver light. His sea-blue eyes were unreadable, like a page written in a language Luz didn't know.

"You understand what must follow."

Luz nodded. When she'd pledged herself three years ago, she knew there was no going back. Before coming to the temple at eighteen, she had been a nobleman's child. To pledge herself to Iridan, she had renounced family and friends and fortune. Now that the Goddess had rejected her, she had nothing. She would be marked as a failure, with an X branded upon her brow. Everywhere she went, people would know that some secret sin had kept her from Iridan's embrace. Yet Luz didn't know what that sin might be.

In her three years at the temple, she had witnessed a dozen other postulants receive their visions. Each one had emerged joyous from the temple, with a story of Iridan's radiant presence, a kiss bestowed, a word of favor.

Her sorrow gave way to bitterness. She had been devout. She had never spoken ill of anyone. Of all the postulants she had known, she had believed herself the most worthy.

Perhaps, she realized with a surge of guilt, that was her secret sin. Pride. Regret mingled with her anger. All for nothing, she had given up her home and fortune. For nothing, she had striven to perfection in Iridan's Way, if pride had doomed her every effort.

Simeon stepped forward. With his finger, he traced upon her brow the X of shame. Her flesh burned, but she didn't cry out.

"You are marked now," Simeon said. "Wherever you go in the Kingdom of Orath, the hearts of men will turn against you, as one rejected by the church. If you stay in this land, you will beg for your living or perform the lowest labor. No proper home will admit you. But they will not kill you or seriously harm you. Your fate is in Iridan's hands. To take your life from her is worse than blasphemy."

"I understand." Luz's voice came back to her, as if from far away. She felt disconnected from her body. The burning on her brow seemed only a distant irritation, something that didn't belong to her.

"At first light, you must leave the temple. Take only a robe to cover your body. And these." He reached into his pocket and pulled forth three silver coins. Each one was stamped with the image of the Goddess. Luz shoved them in her pocket, not wanting to see that serene countenance, which seemed to mock her now. Three silvers would buy her food for about six months, or passage out of the city, to a place where no one knew her. There was some mercy in the judgment of Iridan after all.

"My heart will go with you," Simeon said. "The Goddess grant you peace." Luz almost retorted that the Goddess had already taken any hope of peace from her, but she had no quarrel with the priest. It was the Goddess who had rejected her, not he.

On the trading vessel *Seahope,* she took passage to the island nation of Iloria, sleeping in the cargo hold, among the barrels of spices and bolts of cloth. When she showed her face above deck, the crew openly displayed their contempt, with words, with sneers, and sometimes with shoves and kicks. Luz bore their treatment silently, staying out of their way as much as possible, although the stuffy air of the cargo hold made her ill.

After three days, the ship made port in the city of Dormin, and, with the crew's curses following her, she walked down the dock. The harbor smelled of brine and of cooking cabbage and of too many people pressing close. The language was a babble of foreign words, but she could see the puzzlement in the people's eyes as she passed by them in her white robe, with long, unbound hair and an X upon her brow.

She had a dozen coppers to her name. Using gestures to make herself understood, she spent three of them at a dockside bazaar to purchase men's clothing: often-mended breeches and an ink-stained shirt. With five more, she bought a cheap dagger and used it to hack off her hair, cutting bangs in front to cover the mark of her shame. Tall and thin as she was, she was certain she no longer looked like a woman at all.

For five yeas, she stayed in Dormin, sleeping in the alleys of the slums, taking odd jobs where she found them. She learned the language enough to get by. They knew her along the docks as Crazy Lu, and the contempt people displayed for her was of a general kind—inspired by her raggedness—not the personal hatred she would have known in her native land.

She who had been sheltered all her life, first by her parents and then by the church, now emptied chamber pots or swept the filth out of cellars. Sometimes, when luck was with her, she was chosen to haul cargo from the quays. A desperate, hard life she made for herself, but better than what might have befallen her in Orath. At least she never needed to resort to begging.

Her heart hardened to the sights of the slums, to the starveling children and the pock-marked whores. She witnessed drunkenness and debauchery, saw a man killed for a handful of coppers, and another blinded for ogling someone's wife. Several times she had used her dagger to defend herself, twice drawing blood.

The scar upon her brow faded from vivid red to dull white. If the Ilorians caught a glimpse of it, when her bangs lifted in the wind, they made no comment, probably taking the mark as the work of a knife. Iridan, the Desert Queen, was not worshiped here. Iloria had other, stranger Gods.

Luz thought often of her failure. Of the other postulants who had gone before her, none were perfect. Some of them were vain, some lazy, others spiteful and domineering. One drank too much wine, despite his vow of temperance. Another was deliberately cruel to the temple servants. A third was sloppy in his work. And yet the Goddess had sent signs to them, chosen them as her priests.

In herself, she found nothing to blame, except her sense of pride. In judging her fellow postulants she must have condemned herself. If so, there was irony. After five years in the slums of Dormin, she believed she had no pride left at all.

Other times a voice, like that of a demon, whispered in her mind that she done nothing wrong at all, that the Goddess was capricious and unjust. She refused to dwell on that thought, instead sifting her memories for each small imperfection, each lapse of charity, teasing out a pattern that must have brought her doom.

One night in late winter, as she lay in an alley, wrapped in a tattered blanket, curled up for warmth near the chimney of a bar with some wooden boxes to shield her from the wind, she heard two men talking in her native tongue. They spoke of their business dealings, and as Luz listened, the blood drained from

her heart. They were buying children in the slums of
Dormin, to send to Orath for rich men's pleasure.

It was not her affair, she told herself. If the Ilorians
were willing to sell their children, there was nothing
she could do. By trading in flesh, these merchants
from Orath broke their Goddess' commandments, but
that, too, was not Luz's affair. The Goddess had rejected her. Let the Goddess find someone more worthy to enforce her laws. She closed her eyes and willed
herself not to listen, as the men's voices droned on.

That night she dreamed of the children, battered
and crying. When she woke, cold and stiff and tired,
she knew what she must do. In the last five years Luz
had endured hunger, cold, misery, and deprivation.
But never had she experienced a pain like these children would know.

She rose and went to the docks, cursing Iridan with
every step. It would not be enough to free the children, for their parents would simply sell them to the
next buyer. She must hire out to get passage on the
merchants' ship and unmask the network involved in
this trade. From her work along the quays she knew
the trading vessels from Orath were often un-
dermanned—the people of Orath were leery of the
sea. They could use her help, but whether they would
take her or not, she couldn't guess. If not, she would
find some other way abroad.

Her mind told her she was crazy to take on this
trouble, but her heart wouldn't let her rest if she refused its call. She was doing this for the children, she
told herself. Not for Iridan, who had scorned her.

She stood on the deck of the *Seamidge,* the cold
wind blowing the ragged hair from her face. In her
men's clothing, with her dagger strapped to her belt,
she should have passed unrecognized. But the Orathan
captain stared at her brow, clearly knowing her for

what she was. He wore an amber amulet about his neck, a token of luck, and Luz hoped he was a superstitious man.

"I must go home," Luz said, her gaze meeting his full on. "I will work for you. Any job, no matter how menial. It is the penance the Goddess marked for me, to live in Orath and feel the scorn of my own people. Refuse, and you may earn her enmity. The sea is treacherous in winter."

"All right." He spat into the water. "We could use a hand in the kitchen. But you dwell apart and speak to no one, hear? You will not contaminate us with your taint."

Luz nodded. Then she went in the direction he pointed, below decks. She had succeeded in gaining access to the vessel, and yet her heart felt heavy as lead.

By dawn of the first day, she had found the children, ten little boys, crowded together in an empty crewman's room. As she walked in, they stared at her, silent with terror. She coaxed their stories from them, but they knew nearly nothing of their fate, only that they had been thrust into the hands of strangers and put aboard this ship. Where they were going, they didn't know. She told them not to speak of her visit and promised them, if they did not, all would yet be well. Then she whispered to them what they must do.

The ship docked in Uraz, a city some small distance from the Seawind Temple. As Luz walked along the dock, the wind blew her hair from her brow. People spat at her and shoved her, but she bore it with silence, knowing they would not kill her or seriously harm her. To do so would take vengeance from the Goddess' hands, as Simeon had said.

She ducked into an alley, then into another, and waited there until dusk. No city guard, Luz was cer-

tain, would take the word of a cursed one that the
trading ship held illicit cargo. And so she must wait
until the proof couldn't be denied. She'd had nothing
to eat since morning, and her stomach felt tight against
her ribs, but she didn't stir abroad to beg. She wanted
no part of these people, or their money. Later, when
starvation loomed, she would swallow the last remnant
of her pride, but for now, she could wait.

At nightfall, she returned to the dock, grateful for
the darkness, which hid her mark of shame. By the
side of the *Seamidge,* a man stood silently. Luz slipped
into the shadows behind a piling and took her dagger
into her hand. Hours passed and the dock slipped into
silence. Her muscles grew weary with lack of motion.
The cold wind from the water cut through her tattered
garments, into her flesh. Finally, another man approached the ship, just as she'd heard them plan. Luz's
heart quickened its beat, and she no longer felt the
cold.

They came from the hold, tiny, shuffling shadows,
and the man started to lead them down the dock.
Luz tensed.

As they passed her, she sprang, taking the man
down in a roll. She held her dagger to his throat and
let out a wild yell. Startled, he lay silent beneath her,
his breath hard, his back warm beneath her frigid
chest. "Run, children!" she screamed in Ilorian, and
the children, bound together with ropes, ran forward
as best they could.

The man at the boat came running toward Luz. The
captain, she saw as he neared. He carried a dagger,
much newer and sharper than her own. "You!" His
blade quivered. To kill her would be to invite the
wrath of Iridan. But he had already broken one of
Iridan's laws. The man beneath Luz grunted. The moment stretched taut, like a wire.

And then came the footsteps, and the lanterns. Her

scream had done its work. The dock guards ran forward, three of them. Luz stood.

"This mad woman," the captain said, pointing at Luz, "attacked my companion without reason. Look at her brow. She's cursed by Iridan."

A guard raised his lantern. Luz pushed back her hair. The guard made the sign against evil.

"They are trading in flesh," Luz said. She pointed down the dock, where the children had run. "Children from Iloria, to satisfy rich men's perversions."

"You, a cursed one, accuse me so?" The captain let out a laugh.

"The children are here. Ilorian children, bound with ropes." She let out another cry, her signal to the children, and in minutes, they came shuffling back and stood in the lantern light. Black-haired, green-eyed children, with the fair island skin.

They drove her out anyway, the people of the city, pelting her with garbage and small stones.

She had done what she set out to do. The captain and the merchant had been arrested, and the guards had taken the children to the temple. All of this Luz had witnessed, dogging the guards' steps. The High Priest of the Uraz temple, a woman named Noreen, who bore Iridan's star, came to the temple wall and looked out at Luz, who stood below in the dust, demanding to know if the children were safe. "They are safe," the High Priestess said. "Thanks to you. What's your name?"

"Luz."

The High Priestess nodded; then she turned and walked away, saying nothing more.

Luz had saved the children, but the street people of Uraz blamed her for the shame. Her presence had contaminated, they said; her evil had permeated the vessel, leaking into the captain and the merchants.

Never mind that the plans to sell the children were made before she took passage. Never mind that she had set the children free. The word turned against her, and the crowd drove her forth.

She stumbled through the streets of the city, filth clinging to her garments and hair, her back bruised by stones. She passed the temple, where the High Priestess Noreen stood silent on the rampart, eyes bright as lakes of fire. Out into the desert Luz went, weeping now, as she had never wept before, in all the years she had dwelt in squalor and despair.

Alone in the desert, miles from the city of Uraz, she put her head upon a rock. The sun stood at zenith. The ground was warm, and the wind quiet. Her tears ran into the dry earth. She had done the Goddess' work, and again the Goddess had rejected her. Her heart broke, and she knew then that in all those years of exile she had clung to the hope that Iridan was just, that her own devotion had not been given in vain. But Iridan was cruel and arbitrary. A Goddess who returned evil for good.

The wind rose, sending sand to sting Luz's face. Clouds came across the sky, thick clouds, heavy with rain. A storm from heaven broke like waves on an endless sea.

Luz sat on her rock as the strange storm pounded her, the cold rain soaking the filth from her hair and clothes. And then as suddenly as it came, the storm passed.

The clouds vanished so completely, Luz would have thought she'd dreamed the storm, except that everything around her shimmered with damp. Wet and shivering, she sat in the sun.

She heard a cry, like a long whistle. The air glowed gold, then tore like a curtain. A woman walked through the rift. Her hair gleamed like silver starlight, her eyes black as the winter nights. She wore a robe of shimmering colors, like sunset across the sands. Luz recognized her face from a thousand images. Iridan, the Desert Queen.

Heart empty, she stared at the Goddess who had destroyed her; she, who had sent no sign when a sign was so badly needed, mocked her by coming now. Iridan reached forward and touched Luz's brow. Luz waited for death, but felt nothing, not even a tickle along her skin.

"Go to the Seawind Temple," the Goddess said. "Simeon will explain everything to you there."

Before Luz could react, the Goddess vanished.

Luz rose. She had no reason to obey the Goddess, and yet she burned to hear what words Simeon might offer.

In her four-day trek to the temple, she was treated like a queen. When she feared she would die from lack of food and water, she stopped at a small village. Expecting only grudging charity of millet and water, she was startled when the villagers brought her roasted goat and camel milk. In the next village, the same thing. Gone was the contempt, replaced by something approaching reverence. Were the desert people renegades, Luz wondered, who had spurned Iridan's laws? She didn't ask, fearing that her questions would drive them to revile her, as the coastal people had done.

At last, she approached the Seawind Temple. Along the way to Simeon's office, postulants and priests bowed their heads to her. So changed was she in appearance, she was certain they wouldn't recognize her as the postulant who was expelled long ago. What then, did they think she was? Luz looked down at her ragged clothing, at her work-hardened hands, wondering what they saw in her.

Simeon sat in his office, small and sinewy as she

remembered him, with hands as tough as ropes. He rose to meet her. She saw in his eyes that he, at least, knew who she was. "Luz."

She nodded. "I saw Iridan in the dessert. The Goddess said I should come to you."

Simeon gave a small smile. "You don't yet know, do you?" He went to a shelf and retrieved a hand mirror, then held it up to Luz.

She gasped as she saw her brow. The X remained, but now it formed the center of a five-pointed star. A star that glowed with silver fire.

She stared at the man before her, at the star that marked him. "You, too, once wore the mark of shame?"

He nodded. "Seven years it took me to return. In those years I learned what it means to be despised, to be lower than the lowest slave. I told you my heart would go with you. And so it did."

"But why?"

"The Goddess never sends visions to postulants in the temple," Simeon said. "But only a handful will tell the truth. That is the first test. If you keep your faith and do Iridan's work, that is the second."

Luz stood in silence, reflecting on all that had happened. On her bitterness, and her hate. "I didn't keep my faith," Luz said. "I cursed the Goddess."

"Faith is more than words," Simeon said. "Noreen of Uraz sent me word of what you'd done. You risked your life for Iridan's law."

"I did it for the children," Luz said. "Only for them."

"It is through each other that we serve the Goddess. It was her work you did."

"And all the ones who came from the temple and lied? How do they serve?"

Simeon spread his hands. "They are priests in name only. We—" He touched his brow. "We, the true priests, watch them, direct them. They are less of a danger to the faith under our eyes. If we expelled them, they would seek power in another way. The Goddess is wise."

Luz bowed her head. All those years she had searched for her secret sin. All those years she had lived at the edge of death, with bitterness in her soul. Was it necessary, all that misery? She didn't know. In time, perhaps, she would understand it all, but for now her heart ached with the pain of double betrayal. For Simeon, too, had his part in what had taken place. As she herself would someday have a part in the same deception.

They would give her robes and honors, a place in a temple such as Simeon had. And she would watch the greater number of her postulants lie and be received into a world of comfort and acclaim, and the few honest souls sent away to a life that not even a dog would envy. All of this she would do in Iridian's name.

The Goddess might be wise, but was she just? Luz's lips opened as if she might speak, but no sound came forth. She could think of nothing to say.

CAELQUA'S SPRING

by Vera Nazarian

Vera Nazarian was very young when she began writing for me, and an absolute beginner. Now we've both grown a lot—neither of us is as young as we once were. But then, that's the human condition.

Since last year she has sold stories to the new SFF Net Anthology, *The Age Of Reason,* and magazines such as *Talebones, Pulp Eternity, Maelstrom SF,* and the Dutch magazine *Visionair SF.* She is currently working on a couple of novels.

This story is dedicated to James D. Macdonald, also known as Yog Sysop at SFF Net, who gave her the idea for "Caelqua's Spring."

The desert spring drew the threads of her subterranean waters to her, picked herself up from the sands, and became a woman.

It had been a long time.

Her name was Caelqua. Rather, it was hers once, a human name.

The woman stood considering, while water-memories surged into her mind, and time flickered in eddies of cool liquidity.

She had once been a young girl with persimmon hair, a garish flame. And now there was only the sand ocean in her tresses, skin taut with wind, and colorless eyes.

She was a husk. As though she didn't exist . . . and yet, she was something more.

Caelqua walked slowly through the scalding sands, while the sky poured the anger of the sun upon her unprotected flesh. There was no sensation at the soles of her feet, and she felt no thirst.

She knew there was something she had to do.

But first, she had to find it.

The North-bound caravan came to a stop before an oasis of several palm trees, and a small ancient well that was now almost dry. This was once called Golden Livais, after a miracle of destruction had taken place here, and a whole town had been transformed overnight into solid gold.

It had been a miracle wrought of ignorance and tainted with greed. Legend said they had tried to buy the favor of the gods with the bright clamor of gold in exchange for a replenishing of the water supply in a dwindling well.

But the gods only give you back more of what you offer up.

The gold had long since gone; fortune scavengers from all points of the Compass Rose had taken care of that. Not even ruins here. Only a new growth of trees remained, and the oasis persisted somehow.

But now a woman stood there having come out of nowhere, with transparent eyes and hair like sand.

The caravan driver saw Caelqua from afar, or rather, saw for a moment a bit of sun dislocated, a shadow of a candle flame.

Upon approach, it was no longer there. But observing her up-close, there came a blurring in his vision, a moment of times mixing.

"Who are you?" he whispered hoarsely, for his throat was dry and he had not yet quenched his thirst by drinking from the well.

But as he looked at her, cool water stood before his

eyes. And it occurred to him that this woman might be one of the supposed immortals.

"Are you Ris?" he asked carefully.

Ris. Bringer of Stillness and Water, the Bright-Eyed Liberator, the Mad Sovereign of Wisdom.

That name stirred something within Caelqua, another ancient memory.

"No," she replied, "But I have been touched by Ris and given a blessing of Water."

And saying thus, Caelqua came forward and lifted her palms toward him, cupped together.

The air shimmered and her flesh became transparent, flowing.

He blinked, and now observed liquid, dancing in the sun.

"Drink," she said, "and take me with you."

The caravan took Caelqua through the desert. She came with them wordlessly, and they shrank away in awe, knowing from the first instant that she was different, one of the divine.

The journey involved a number of days that all blended into one day of sun-spilled monotony, silence, and the low hissing of the wind.

Eventually, a great city showed itself on the Northern horizon, and a road emerged from the sands.

They approached, blended with other rabble, and entered the gates of iron, past stone-faced guards, into a place of living frenzy.

Here, the caravan and Caelqua parted ways, for they would stop in the city only for two nights and then head farther North. She, meanwhile, knew that her destination ended here.

Caelqua walked several hours through the urban chaos of agoraphobic marketplaces and claustrophobic alleyways. The city air was an astringent stew of garlic, human excrement, and the perfume of roses.

But Caelqua's senses ignored the olfactory clamor, and focused on one single scent.

She smelled water.

And thus she moved like a shade toward the heart of the city where stood a grand palace of white stone and garish gold.

Water was within.

And there was something very wrong.

The tired queen with anemic skin looked down from her divan-throne, past the barrier of veils and silk pillows, at the woman with dull sand hair.

Caelqua stood before her like a stilled fountain.

"Who are you?" said the queen. "They told me you can help me. But I know that no one can."

"I am no one. And I am the only one who can redeem you."

The queen sat up with great difficulty, and pulled the golden veils from her forehead. Her lips were white with approaching death.

"You bleed," said Caelqua. "Your woman's cycle has not ended for many moons now. Your womb is refusing to close up, and thus your life is running out of you in rivulets of darkness."

"Yes . . . how did you know?"

But Caelqua said nothing. Instead, she stepped forward, and touched the queen on her brow.

And the queen felt a rhythm of blood begin in her temples.

Guards tensed forward, but the queen stopped then with one weakly upraised palm. She stilled, and remained thus for a long span of moments, beneath Caelqua's touch.

"I feel you . . . An ocean . . ." whispered the queen in vampiric ecstasy.

And Caelqua released her hold.

"I require a sharp knife," she said.

"Do as she says!" ordered the queen. "You, give her your dagger!"

A guard stepped forward with suspicious eyes and slowly drew forth his ornate weapon.

There was a moment of impossible silence.

Then Caelqua took the knife from him. And with it, she slit her own wrist.

A spurting fountain of hueless water began to pulse from her vein, and she offered it to the queen.

"Take my Water and drink, for even Ris has drunk once from my wrist. For that act of quenching, Ris has given me Water in exchange for my mortal Blood."

The queen fell upon her hand in mindless hunger, and pulled at the open vein with her pale lips. She drank for a long span, while the court watched in terrible wonder.

Finally, she tore herself away, satiated, and there was a new manic energy in her eyes.

"You have given me my existence, the one thing that was no longer mine," said the queen, "I feel it now, this new strength! My womb is closing even now, and my flow has ceased. What miracle are you? I have everything, and will give you anything you ask!"

And then Caelqua looked into her eyes, and for the first time a smile appeared on her face.

"I ask," she said, "for the Past."

There was an old place of stones and sand outside the city, a place where they buried their dead. The queen had given Caelqua a fine litter and servants to attend her, and a robe of ivory silk. That, in addition to the consultation with the temple Oracle whose Voice directed Caelqua here in her mysterious search.

Caelqua walked past the ancient monuments and gravestones, looking for a unique one.

The Past was buried here, the Oracle had said, and it is what you seek.

And Caelqua looked for it now, her vision blurring with many waters, and mindlessly taking in the sunlit expanse of white stone and sand.

She moved, drifting over the earth, and came upon a large antique tomb structure that was mostly below ground. Here, at the entrance, obelisks of cypress had sprung, reaching for the sky.

And here stood a man, his back turned to her, but his skin showing him to be of a dark race, and his hair tight and coiled like snakes of midnight.

Something started to beat wildly in Caelqua's heart at the sight of him.

"Nadir!" she pronounced, her still voice cracking with emotion for the first time, "Nadir, it is you. How you've grown!"

The man turned to face her, tall and muscular, like an ebony god, with warm eyes and skin like dates.

"Yes," he replied. "I am Nadir."

In response, Caelqua drew forward with a wildness, her whole form wavering for an instant from flesh to a column of water, and then back again. With one raggedly expelled breath she moved into his arms.

"I am Caelqua!" she said, trembling against his chest, "Do you remember me, little brother? Remember how Grandmother—who was Ris—used to call you a little demon? Remember how we wandered together, and how we suffered, and how you promised that you would grow up strong and fight injustice—and I can see that you have—"

The man called Nadir held her close in silence, allowing the torrent of her words to flow over him, and then whispered gently, "Yes . . . I remember. I know you now, my sister. Only—what happened to your bright fiery hair?"

"Ah," she breathed ragged bitter sobs, "It matters no longer. My hair is now like the desert, for I have been one with it for many summers now, as many as it took you to grow up from a child into the handsome man that you are now."

"How many summers has it been indeed?" he said, his lips forming the sounds over her brow, while she could hear the rhythm of his strong southern heart.

She felt the flow of blood, the subterranean currents of it moving through his flesh, and her own waters responded in sympathy, surging within her and over-flowing with intensity, bringing the excess of moisture to her eyes.

He turned her face to him gently, and noticed the tears brimming. "Why, Caelqua!" he said, stricken by the sight of the water, "You weep for your foolish younger brother?"

"Yes!" she cried, "Oh, yes! I weep for the moments of your life that I had missed, for your growth and the changing of your voice, for the strengthening of your arms, and the endless cycles of sunlit days that deepened the color of your skin, for the coming of force into your eyes . . ."

He looked at her, taking her in, all of her. She was stamped like an indelible afterimage of the sun in his mind's eye. His mouth curved now, easily, with the receptiveness of love. "But you have missed nothing much, sister!" he said, "For I am all here, every day and moment that comprises me, every compounded breath that has marked the passing of time. You see the years before you rolled into one. Now, rejoice, for the Past is no longer a fleeting thing, and you have caught up with it at last. . . ."

And then he laughed, and once again drew her into his arms, saying, "Oh, there is so much I have to tell you! Come, you must meet my children, and their mother, the woman who is the joy of my heart! You must see the house in the city where we live—"

But as he spoke these things, Caelqua freed herself from his embrace very suddenly, growing still. She continued to look at him, while the wind blew her desert-sand hair into a frenzy, and the heedless sun scalded them both.

"Nadir," she whispered, "little demon, apple of my eye . . . Nadir. I cannot come with you, and both you and I know it. This is but a Moment. A Moment has been granted to me, wherein I may reclaim a bit of my only love which is yourself, and see in you the years made transparent and formed into one thing of flesh and blood."

"Sister . . ." he began.

But she interrupted him violently, like a drowning one grasping for a bit of flotsam, floundering. "Don't!" she said, "This brief meeting has been a gift given to me, and maybe it has been a moment of equal wonder for you. But it must now come to an end. For—I now travel outside the normal flow of Time, and even now feel the beginning urge, the pull to return to my own state of being. While you—beloved brother of mine forever—must now live out the rest of your life, and your children will grow, and their children, and the sands of the desert will move in, and this city itself will fold in upon itself and buckle under the weight of centuries. And maybe then, some day I will once again be compelled to step into Time, and maybe your great-grandson or -daughter will come forward also to greet me before proceeding with their own flow of personal eternity."

"Caelqua. . . ."

"I am now a being of Ris, and in me run her waters."

"Caelqua!" he cried now, and for the first time his own dark eyes were filled with moisture.

But she drew her hand forward in an odd powerless farewell, and took a weak step backward, all the while her form shimmering, and beginning to transform into a pillar of liquid.

It was dissolving already.

Nadir reached forward, grabbing hold of transparency, crying out one last time, as he watched the pillar start to sink softly into the incandescent bleached sands. And all around the place where she stood, the sands discolored with darkness born of moisture, discolored with life.

The wind stood still, and there was silence.

Nadir stood like a bereaved child or a very old man, and watched white powder cover the last trace of her, the very ghost. . . .

"You have done well," came a woman's voice, as the queen herself stepped forth from the shadows of an ancient sepulcher to watch him. "You gave her what I promised."

Nadir started, then immediately lowered his face in obeisance and hung his head before the queen of this city.

"I have done as you asked . . ." he replied faintly. "The goddess of the spring mistook me for her ancient brother, my holy ancestor, the first man to bear our name. And as a result your promise to her has been fulfilled. Now, the curse is lifted from your womb, my queen. I am happy to have served you so . . . well."

The queen only nodded to him with tired eyes, and motioned for servants to bring forward a heavy purse.

"Receive your payment," she said, turning away, glittering with golden veils in the sun.

Nadir bowed, and took the weight of metal coins covered by silk. He could feel it, the weight of gold.

Gold for water.

And suddenly a memory came to him, one not his own. . . .

They had tried to make water from gold, but only gold comes from gold.

And now, he must always have water, to remember her by.

Nadir turned to the receding form of the queen and

her retinue. He was still clutching the moneybag, and he could feel it clanking inside, solid smooth metal.

The voices of his ancestors clamored in his mind, crying to him. The wind of the desert started to arise once again, blowing the ever present white dust of desolation.

You did not even see my children, ancient sister. Now that you've moved on from the Past into the Future, how will they remember you? Indeed, who will remember you?

But as he stood in the silence of the desert, Nadir heard within himself a rhythmic heartbeat, a pounding at the temples.

Internal waters rushing though his veins. Through him. They would always be thus within him.

And he thought he heard Caelqua's laughter in his very veins, with each pulse. *You think you have given me a false gift, brother of my heart?* the waters sang. *Don't you know that while you gave me the Past, I also gave you the Future? They are one and the same, with no end and no beginning, only a line of waters running through it all, binding us.*

The Spring of waters is Time.

And you and I will meet again and again, simply when one of us chooses to Remember.

The purse of gold fell on the desert sand, slipped from his fingers with a sound of bells. It lay there, and the wind immediately carried fine grains to sprinkle the fabric.

Nadir walked slowly, his sandals sinking lightly in the powdery whiteness. Ahead of him was the distant mirage city. Behind, stretched the desert.

Within him was Caelqua's Spring.

DEEP AS RIVERS

by Cynthia McQuillin

Cynthia McQuillin is one of the most multitalented people I know. In addition to her writing, she also sings, and she makes beautiful jewelry—those of you who attend science-fiction conventions may have heard her songs and seen her jewelry. She also does most of the cooking for our household, a gift for which we are all very thankful (even if I do gripe about the low-fat diet I'm stuck with, that's no reflection on Cindy's ability to do miraculous things within its limits).

She is currently working on a novel and has the obligatory two cats. I've often thought that I ought to write a book about why so many fantasy writers have cats. Maybe manuscripts would catch cold without cats sitting on them!

Thule came upon the elf not so much by chance as by fate. She had come to the river seeking food as she often did these days. The harsh breath of winter had driven many of the animals she normally fed upon to warmer climes or into hibernation, so she had to content herself mostly with fish through the long dark months. She usually avoided this stretch of the river, however, for it was near the human settlement of Calesh; but that night something seemed to draw her there.

She traveled warily. Long years of experience had taught her to avoid humankind; they were quick and clever and took delight in tormenting those who were unlike themselves. What Thule learned, she learned well, if slowly; and she remembered for a long time. What she felt, she felt deeply and long. She changed, yes, but as the earth itself changed, over long ages. Stone weathers slowly.

Keeping to the trees wherever she could, she loped to the bank, slipping a little as she came down the side, to what would have been the water's brink in warmer weather. The ice coat lay thick on its surface, but the tremendous strength in her thick, twisted arms and broad shoulders allowed her to break through with ease. Even in the dead of winter she did well enough, making up for her lack of speed and mobility with strength and persistence.

Again and again she plunged her arms into the icy water. The cold never bothered Thule, for she was herself a cold creature, with flesh and bones the stuff of the earth. Her mind, too, was like stone—slow and cold, reasoning in ways no creature of warmth and sunlight could fathom. Because of this, her kind were hunted and feared, not only by humankind, but also by the children of starlight, as the elves were called in the trollish tongue.

Some sound, perhaps, or a sense of warmth called Thule's attention from her fishing to the crumpled figure which lay several lengths upstream. She paused for a moment, deciding whether to investigate her discovery or flee. If the body were bait in a trap, she would be at a potentially fatal disadvantage, caught between the steep bank and the slick and treacherous ice. In the end, curiosity won.

Moving with ponderous caution, she approached the prone man shape. At first she thought him an unlucky villager who had strayed from the other side of the river to hers. The boundary between herself and the village—as well as their uneasy truce—had been achieved over the years more through experience than negotiation. But as Calesh continued to grow, young men sometimes dared to cross the river, scoffing at legends or seeking to prove their manhood by killing the monster.

Thule had no taste for man-flesh in particular, but meat was meat and it had been nearly three weeks since she had tasted the sweetness of warm flesh. Anticipation hurried her clumsy steps.

Meat be warm, please, she silently entreated the elemental gods who had molded her stony flesh and heart.

But as she leaned down to touch the slender form, he turned to meet her hopeful gaze without fear, peering at her with night-dark eyes that held a kind of detached curiosity. The elemental purity of their jet-like gleam fascinated Thule, as did his smooth pale skin, which was surprisingly warm to the touch. She had expected it to be as hard and cold as her own, though it was translucent and smooth in appearance where her flesh was the dull rugged gray of weathered granite.

Thule had never been so close to one of the elven breed before, and as she gazed upon his strange lovely features, vague memories stirred, slowly crystallizing into recollection. Again she experienced the raid that had destroyed her peaceful mountain home and sent her, a mere child of three centuries, into exile in these hated lowlands, the last surviving member of her clan.

Since then, she had only glimpsed their banners from afar or heard the thunder of their mighty steeds as they rode in moonlight to the wild hunt. Then she would scuttle back to hide in the deep safety of the cavern she had found in the nearby foothills and made her home.

Now that one of the hated tormentors lay helpless at her feet, she didn't know what to do. She should strike him down, she thought. He was the ancient enemy, possibly even one of those who had slain her family. Why did she not act? His poison flesh would be useless to her as meat and her kind did not kill wantonly as humankind believed, but there would be some rightness in hurting this one, for all the hurts she and hers had suffered. Still, she could not move, mesmerized by the deep longing his beauty stirred within her. She had been alone for so very long.

"Come, troll, be about your business," he demanded at length, using the human word for her kind as an epithet. Elf and troll were both words of the common tongue which they had learned from humans. Seeming disconcerted, almost irritated by Thule's dull, placid gaze he sneered, "Here I am helpless and dying, why don't you strike me down, you doltish horror?"

Even in anger his voice held beauty, as soft and liquid as the deep-running river that flowed through Thule's cavern home, etching its way persistently through time and stone.

"Why do you hesitate?" the elf cried, when she continued to stand there only looking at him. "Gods of Light deliver me from stone-bound brains! No wonder your kind are all but extinct. Do you not understand? I am dying and no threat to you."

"Dying?" Thule muttered at last, a slow grating sound like rock cracking in the frost. Though her thought process was slow, she was very old and knew the common tongue well enough, even if it was hard for her to speak, but his words made no sense.

To die, this she understood—for both animal and humankind it was to become meat. For Thule's kind it meant to move no more, forever. But the children of starlight could not die. Their magic was too strong; they would live forever. Even the sun, whose light would turn Thule's flesh to empty stone, could not harm them. Yet as she looked into his eyes, she knew that he *was* dying, and this disturbed her deeply, though she could not say why.

"What are you doing?" he demanded in a startled tone as she bent to gather him carefully into her arms.

"You need warmth, food," Thule replied as though it were the most obvious thing in the world, as she tramped doggedly across the snowfield toward the safety of her cavern.

Bringing the elf to her cavern was a foolhardy thing to do; every instinct she possessed told her this. He was the enemy. It was near certain death for her if any others of his kind were to discover where she laired; yet she could not kill him, nor could she leave him to die.

By the time she laid him on the cavern floor beside her favorite pool, he had fallen into a kind of trance-like silence, though his breath came evenly and his heartbeat was strong. He would need fire, she knew. She, being a creature of the earth and stone, was comfortable in the cold and dark and could see well enough by the dim phosphorescence of the stone, but he was a creature of light and warmth. Thule did not possess fire nor the secret of making it. If he were to be saved, she knew she would need help.

There was a woman in the village, Thule knew from having observed her with some curiosity over the years, who sometimes came out at night to gather plants and bark when the moon was full, even braving the troll's side of the river upon occasion. Thule had also observed her visiting households where sickness had taken hold, and had gathered from the odd bit of speech she sometimes overheard that the woman was a healer of some sort, though the villagers called her a witch. Her name was Saelim.

Having made up her mind, Thule took herself off to the village as fast as she could go, for half the night was already gone and she dared not be caught in sunlight.

*　　*　　*

Startled from sleep by the ungodly loud pounding at her cottage door, Saelim dragged herself from the warmth of her bed, wrapping herself in a quilt against the bitter chill of the night air. The knock sounded again, this time with enough force to rattle the hinges.

"What is it, for the gods' sake?" she muttered as she drew back the bar and pulled the door open. Startled, she stood staring at the massive creature which hunched before her. It was too broad and tall to pass the lintel, thank goodness, but looked powerful enough to smash in the wall if it decided to enter.

There was no doubt in her mind that this was the troll who haunted the foothills across the river. She had glimpsed it on more than one occasion during her nighttime peregrinations, though it had never offered her any threat or interference—before this.

"What do you want?" she breathed, gazing up into the deceptively dull and placid countenance.

"Come," it said, in common speech. "Need help."

Its gravelly voice held an almost frantic note. What could a troll possibly need with her, except to serve as an entree on a cold winter's night? No, she couldn't believe that was the case; the creature had never exhibited any aggressive behavior in the many years she had observed it. And if a local lad, usually a foolhardy braggart or bully went missing, she could hardly fault the creature for defending itself.

"What kind of help do you need?" she said at last. The troll seemed neither to mind nor to have noticed the length of time it had taken her to reply, but then they were reputed to be very slow-thinking creatures.

"Come, need healer, bring fire." Its speech was stilted but clear.

"Someone is hurt?" Saelim demanded in a no-nonsense tone, instantly transforming from a startled, somewhat frightened woman into the healer-witch she was.

"Dies." The troll nodded earnestly, motioning for her to come.

"Just a minute, I have to dress and get my bag," Saelim replied, making up her mind. This was just too strange not to be true.

"And fire," the troll reminded her, then added, looking nervously toward the eastern sky, "Go soon."

"Yes, yes, and fire, too. I'll hurry," she promised, but paused to ask, "Do you have a name?"

"Thule."

"Wait for me, Thule," she said. Taking a good long look at the creature for the first time, she realized with a start that Thule was female. Somehow one never thought of trolls as anything but "it." *Well, this is a night for surprises,* she thought, closing the door.

When she had dressed and packed everything she thought might come in handy, Saelim directed the troll to the woodpile, instructing her to take as much as she could carry. Thule simply nodded, lifting the entire rack with ease and lumbering off in the direction of the river. Saelim slogged along in her wake.

"Here," Thule's deep voice rumbled out of the darkness as she came to a halt, causing Saelim, who followed close behind, to bump into her. The echo sent a cascade of strange whispers through the vastness of the cavern.

There was a groan like stone folding under stress and the solid thud and rustle of shifting wood as Thule set the rack firmly on the floor, then guided Saelim to it, carefully taking the witch's hand and laying it on the top of the stack. It had never occurred to Saelim that trolls could be capable of such gentleness.

"Make fire," Thule urged, then moved away to examine the elf. He didn't stir when she touched him, but he still breathed and his heart was as strong as ever. *What could be wrong?* she wondered yet again.

Fumbling in the dark, Saelim took several pieces of wood and built a cone with them on the driest, flattest space she could find on the cavern floor. It was easier to work, she found, if she closed her eyes and tried to visualize what she was doing. After a few false starts a cheery blaze lit the immediate space, illuminating a fantastic tableau of natural rock formations.

"Magnificent!" Saelim gasped, glancing from a delicately fluted limestone curtain to pillar after pillar of translucent limestone and fantastically shaped icicles and mounds of stone. But that was nothing compared to the amazement she felt when she turned to see the elf clasped almost lovingly in Thule's massive rough-hewn arms.

"Help, now," Thule murmured, holding the pale, slender body out for Saelim to see.

"Gods above! What am I to do with you?" Saelim murmured in disbelief, as she recognized the elf for what he was. "What happened?"

"Found at river." Thule shrugged, seemingly at a loss to explain further.

"Lay him down on this rock shelf so I can take a look at him," Saelim directed, spreading her cloak on the cold hard surface. The troll did as she bade, stepping back to watch anxiously from the edges of the firelight as Saelim began her examination.

There were no external injuries that Saelim could see, and she ascertained by gently but firmly manipulating his limbs and body that there were no broken bones.

Fumbling quickly through her bag, Saelim brought out the crystal pendant she used for scrying, passing it over every inch of his body. But again she found no indication that there was anything wrong. Somewhat vexed, she closed her eyes and let herself slip into a light trance, lowering her defenses so that she could taste the pattern and flow of his life-force. This was something she was loath to do even with other people, let alone a creature born of magic; but she had no choice if she was to discover what was wrong.

"There is something very strange here," she muttered, when she had withdrawn once more into her own body. Her inner sight had revealed nothing out of the ordinary. As far as she could tell, never having examined an elf before, he was perfectly healthy and uninjured—unless he was under some kind of spell.

Reaching once more into her bag, Saelim brought out a blue glass vial whose contents smelled strongly of cinnamon, carnation, and spellbane when she uncapped it. She dabbed the spelled tincture on the elf's forehead, over his heart and on the palms of both hands, muttering the clearing spell quickly under her breath as she did so. But there was nothing, no reaction of any kind, other than the faintest whiff of residual magic. But he was an elf after all.

"I don't know what to say," she said, meeting the troll's anxious gaze. She was at a complete loss for the first time in her career. "He seems perfectly fine."

"Fine?" the delicately fluted voice murmured indignantly. "I'm dying, you foolish woman. Can't you see that?"

"No, I can't," Saelim replied, turning her attention once more to the elegant, dark-haired male who had arranged himself in a graceful if rather tragic pose upon her woolen cloak.

"Well, perhaps not this very minute," he admitted, still looking put upon, "but all too soon, I assure you."

"Very well, then," she replied, rising to the bait, "suppose you tell me, exactly what is it you are dying from?"

"Mortality, of course!" he exclaimed, sitting up to gaze at her with mournful jet-dark eyes.

"But you can't be mortal if you're an elf, any more than your trollish friend over there can."

"Ah, you've hit upon the point at last!" he exclaimed. "I have fallen from grace, cut off from my kind and doomed to walk the world in mortal bondage until death comes to claim me. I prayed it would be sooner rather than later, but that obstinate clumsy creature refuses to end my misery."

"Somehow I'm not surprised," Saelim murmured to herself, thinking that Thule was as smitten with this silly elf as any village maiden had ever been with a beau, and wondering how he could be so dense as not to see it.

"Is it so terrible to be mortal?" she asked him. "I am mortal and find it no great burden. In fact, I believe that time's brevity adds a certain sweetness and excitement to living that must be lost to your kind."

"You only say this because you do not know all that I have seen and done." He sighed. "All that I had hoped to be. But as you say, I must make the best of things." Then he sat up, looking curiously about the cavern. "Is there no food? I'm famished!"

"No food," Thule solemnly said, shambling once more into the circle of light cast by Saelim's fire. "Bring tonight."

"I could go to my cottage now and bring some back," Saelim offered.

"No!" Thule said, stepping toward her in a slightly menacing posture, which made Saelim suddenly and painfully conscious of her predicament. The troll had seemed harmless enough so far, but that was no guarantee she would continue to be so; and Saelim didn't altogether trust the elf either, now that she came to think of it.

"I only meant to be helpful," she assured the troll in a soothing tone. "It's not far and I would come right back."

"Not safe," Thule insisted, stepping even closer as if to bar any attempt on Saelim's part to bolt. A pointless precaution, since Saelim was certain she would never find her way out of the cavern without Thule's help. The tunnels and caves that riddled these hills were reputed to run for miles.

"She doesn't trust you, witch," the elf said, with a smirk. "And why should she? Your kind have treated her as badly as mine, no doubt."

"Is that it, Thule?" she said, ignoring his last comment. "Do you not trust me after I trusted you enough to come here alone?"

Thule could not answer. Instinct spoke to her of threat and survival, but what the witch said rang true where the elf's words rang false. She looked uneasily away, too far out of her cognitive and emotional depth to argue. For lack of anything better to do, she stooped to add wood to the fire which was beginning to die down a little. The flicker of the flame both fascinated and frightened her.

"Rest. Eat tomorrow," she said at last, retreating once more into the comfort and familiarity of the deep shadows.

"I wonder what she means by *that*?" the elf quipped in an extremely bright and annoying tone.

Too agitated to rest, Thule sat watching the elf and the witch as they huddled together on the rock shelf, sharing Saelim's woolen cloak for warmth. Something about the way they had conversed so easily—the casual way they touched—had disturbed her, but it was too far beyond her understanding to fathom.

"So do you have a name?" she heard Saelim asked the elf after a long silence. Apparently Thule was not the only one who could not rest.

"Oh, no!" the elf replied, eyes wide. "You'll not get my name, witch. Names have power, as you well know."

"Well, I must call you something if we're to spend

so much time together," she said, pulling her share of
cloak closer.

"Why not call me beauty; that's what you think of
me." He smiled at his own conceit.

"I'm beginning to notice your looks less and your
attitude more," she returned sharply, arching one
brow. "You had best beware, or I might turn you into
something unpleasant."

"So-o-o, you're a *spell-casting* witch after all, not
just a jumped-up country herb woman? There *is* a
spell to restore what has been taken from me, you
know." He gave her a hard searching look. "If you
have the skill and courage to use it."

"No doubt," she replied, eyeing him with an equally
hard and discerning gaze. "But in magic as in life,
you don't get something for nothing; and, as I'm sure
you know, Death bargains dear. So what exactly did you
have in mind to trade?"

"Don't twit me, witch!" He glared. "I know the
price well enough. It's a human soul that buys what I
wish back."

"A commodity which your kind is sorely lacking,
unless I'm mistaken; for by the laws of balance no
creature may possess both an immortal soul and immortal flesh. Or do you think to trade mine?"

"I have my own to trade," he quietly said.

Of course! Saelim thought, *I should have realized.*
But she simply asked, "How so?"

Unseen in the shadows, Thule leaned closer to hear
his reply which was very soft and a long time in
coming.

"I traded my immortality for love," he said at last.
"For the love of a mortal woman, so that we might
share the joys and passion of human love, which is
denied to my kind. But she was a witch like you and
she tricked me. For, as I found to my sorrow, it was
not my love she truly craved, but what I could give

her. And now I am bereft of everything, even the love I sought, and left with the unbearable burden of human sentiment," he bitterly said, sinking once more into brooding silence.

The cloak slipped from Saelim's shoulders when he drew away from her in his misery, causing her to shiver suddenly.

"Oh, dear, you're chilled to the bone," he said, focusing on something besides his own misery. "Come lie beside me for warmth. Perhaps we can sleep. You must be tired after such an adventure," he added, not unkindly.

A little sound almost like a whimper died unheard in Thule's throat as Saelim allowed herself to be drawn into his arms, and that strange unhappy feeling stirred once again within her. It was more intense this time, almost like a yearning. Unable to watch any more she turned away, and it suddenly occurred to her that she was hungrier than she had been in a long time. What a miserable day this was turning out to be.

Not wanting to dwell on hunger with human flesh so near, she considered what she had heard. Was it possible that the witch *could* restore the elf? A price had been mentioned, but one she did not comprehend. And what if Saelim could not restore his immortality?

Thule could not bear to think of the elf's bright perfection gone forever from the world. An emptiness opened deep in her breast, as if sunlight had somehow touched her there, and she felt she must do something, but didn't know what.

Unable to remain still, she rose and shuffled unhappily to the underground river that flowed deep and swift through her cavern. She loved the river, whose presence had been her only solace and joy through all the long years. The river was her only companion, ceaselessly singing to Thule of all the places it had passed through on its long journey to her cavern; but today the bright quickness of the water only made her sad, for it passed by so quickly, then was gone.

When Saelim woke, the fire had died to embers and the chill was nearly unbearable. She rose quickly to feed it from the diminishing stack of wood, wondering why Thule had let it burn down. But when she looked around, the troll was nowhere to be seen.

"We've been abandoned, it would seem," the elf said, stretching as he sat up. "Do come back to bed, it's freezing. It will do no good to fret about our hostess. I'm sure she'll be back soon enough, to delight us with her scintillating conversation."

"Don't be so cold," Saelim snapped, truly offended on Thule's behalf. "Can't you see that everything she has done, she has done for you."

"Surely you're not implying that that grotesquerie is in love with me!" he sputtered, looking aghast at the suggestion. "You *must* be mistaken, my dear. Trolls are not like you and me, after all; they have no tender feelings. How could they as slow-witted and brutish as they are?"

A sound disturbingly like a sob echoing from the bottom of a well filled the silence that followed, and Saelim turned to see Thule standing just inside the ring of the firelight. The body of a small deer was clutched to her chest the way a hurt child might clutch a favorite toy.

"Thule," Saelim said, starting toward her. Thule backed awkwardly away from her, but not before Saelim saw tears like bits of gravel slipping from her cavernous eyes.

"Food," the troll said in a dull empty voice, dropping the deer before she stumbled into the overwhelming darkness which lay beyond their tiny oasis of light. Saelim's first instinct was to follow the heartsick troll and comfort her, but she knew there was no chance of finding Thule if she wished to remain hidden, so she turned back to the thoughtless elf.

"I hope you're happy," she snapped, glaring at him.

"Gods of Earth and Air!" he whispered, staring into the darkness with a stricken look on his face. "You were right. I didn't mean to hurt her, I swear it!"

"Too late now," Saelim returned, sighing as she took the knife from the sheath she wore on her belt and went to work on the deer carcass. "At least we'll eat tonight. That's something."

Thule stumbled once more into the moonlit, snow-covered valley that stretched before the mouth of her cavern, gasping for air as she paused. She had never even noticed that she breathed before; now it seemed she couldn't get enough air.

What can be wrong? she wondered, staring numbly at her chest, unable to believe it could hurt so much when there was no mark upon it. Surely there should be a wound there the size of her fist, at least.

She had felt something like this before, when her family was slaughtered. The pain was so bad she thought she would die then, but after a while the pain lessened, and finally went away. Or maybe she just got used to it. But this she would never get over; that fact burned through every fiber of her being like molten rock.

She had been alone for so very long with no way to comprehend her loneliness until *he* had fallen across her path, and now she simply could not bear it.

Suddenly she was running toward the woods and the river which lay beyond, stumbling and slipping as she went, not knowing what she would do or why. But before she could reach the line of snow-laden trees, she caught a flash of firelight between the trunks, then another and another. Instinct stopped her headlong rush. She stared for a moment in frightened confusion at the advancing swarm of lights before she realized that the villagers were coming. They had followed her from Saelim's cottage—followed the wide, clearly visible trail she had left in the snow.

She would die now. Thule knew that. There was no way out; the certainty of it ran through her as strong and deep as the river that etched its timeless course through the stone of her cavern floor—as strong and deep as the love that had etched itself into the stone of her heart. But it was all right, she could see that now. It was better this way, but there was one last thing she must do.

"They're coming!" Thule bellowed as she stumbled into the chamber where Saelim and the elf sat gnawing half-cooked chunks of venison.

"Who?" Saelim demanded.

"Humans," Thule gasped out. "Found my trail."

"Of course," Saelim cried, swearing under her breath as she jumped to her feet. "I should have thought of that. Someone must have come to my cottage seeking aid and thought you had carried me off in the night. Quickly, take me out to them. I can explain what happened, send them away."

"No," Thule said, wearily shaking her massive head. "Better this way. Help me now."

"Help with what?" Saelim asked, a tight, sick feeling beginning in the pit of her stomach.

"Help trade soul," the troll said, sitting down on the floor next to the fire to pick up a piece of raw deer meat and swallow it whole. "Fresh meat. Good."

"You can't mean what you're saying," Saelim murmured after a long moment's stunned silence.

"Can you?" the elf whispered stepping between the two. His expression was something between hope, shame, and desperation.

"Long time alone," Thule said, in a matter of fact

tone. "Not good alone. Trade, please." She held out her hand to Saelim in a very human gesture.

"No, I can't let her do this," the elf suddenly said, conscience winning over self-interest at the last. "Not after . . . It's my fault she wants to die, isn't it?"

"It doesn't really matter now," Saelim said, siding with the troll because her gut instinct told her that Thule's answer was the right one, but not for the reason Thule thought. "It's what she wants and there may not be much time. Make up your mind, or everything she has done goes to waste."

"Please," Thule said, holding out her hands to him. "Love hurt you, love hurt me. Take gift, please. Be happy."

"Thank you," he whispered after another moment's hesitation. With a tear in his eye, he took her broad, rough hands into his and kissed them with something akin to reverence. "I am so sorry, Thule. I truly did *not* understand, and I struck out blindly in my pain and anger."

"Quickly, dammit!" Saelim snapped, turning him abruptly around. "Tell me your true name and how to work the damn spell!"

Oddly, Thule hardly felt any different when the spell was done, though it seemed the elf, Eloran, had changed completely. He stood tall and proud, carrying himself with strength and grace as he stepped forward to take her hands once more and thank her with the grace and eloquence that only true nobility of thought can provide. Surprisingly, when he was gone, she felt better than she had expected.

"Now what?" Saelim asked, giving her a measuring glance.

"Your people wait," Thule said with a shrug, turning toward the way to the cavern's entrance.

"Think what you are doing, Thule," Saelim admonished. "You have so much yet to experience with your new mortality. A human soul may offer gifts and abilities that Eloran's elfish intellect was too shallow to appreciate. He chose to wallow in self-pity and spite rather than discover the finer emotions he was capable of experiencing with a human soul. Even before the transference you had somehow found those qualities within yourself. Now, Thule, you could be so much more, experience so much more. Please, please, do not throw it all away for the sake of your grief."

Thule paused for a long moment to consider the witch's words. It did seem that she had a broader scope of understanding now, perhaps even what humankind called vision. And something else had changed as well. The pain she had felt so keenly before was still there, but it was less of a burden somehow. And when she remembered how happy and strong Eloran had become because of her sacrifice, the answering flush of warmth nearly wiped the pain away.

"Still alone," she said, struggling to master the conflicting emotions that welled without warning at every new thought or memory. "It hurts."

"You don't have to be alone," Saelim said, cocking her head to one side and giving her an encouraging smile.

"I don't?" Thule's face seemed to crumple on the verge of tears for just a moment, as if she didn't dare believe what she was hearing.

"No, you don't," Saelim said, smiling up at the troll woman as she laid a reassuring hand on her arm. "Not unless you want to be."

"I don't!" Thule said decisively, returning the witch's smile as she laid an equally gentle, though somewhat rougher hand over top of Saelim's, then allowed her new friend to lead her from the darkness of her past into the bright, torchlit future.

WEAPONS AT WAR

by Charles Richard Laing

Charles Richard Laing is a 37-year-old New Jersey resident; in fact, he still lives in the house he was born in. his life revolves around reading, writing, watching baseball games, and writing. He has about 40 stories published, mostly in small press magazines, but "Weapons at War" will be his first national (and probably international—most of these volumes sell overseas sooner or later) publication. He is a member of a special elite minority: writers who have sold stories to me and are *not* working on a novel.

I don't think I want to kill for you anymore, my sword abruptly announced.

It wasn't a good time. It had been a rocky couple of days. Our company had the tragic misfortune of running into an entire clan of well-armed Juggian bandits out for trophies. We were caught in an ambush like a bunch of green farm kids with the ink still wet on their enlistment papers. We'd started the morning with twenty fighters. Only six survived the trap. We retreated, and they pursued. Now, we were pinned down in an abandoned fort that had been falling down for at least two hundred years. We were surrounded, and we were outnumbered by a conservative count of at least thirteen to one.

Juggians attached great religious significance to long red hair. My head would make a lovely trophy, hanging from a Juggian saddle. Now, the only thing keeping it attached to my neck was a temperamental enchanted sword.

Lovely.

"Why now?" I growled. There was some activity to my left about five hundred yards away. A dozen raiders were bunched together, with their weapons drawn. They were extremely animated, motioning wildly, smacking each other, psyching themselves up. Occasionally, they would point at me and make crude, unfriendly gestures that made the hair on the back of my neck stand up. It was easy to see another charge was imminent. I nocked an arrow and took careful aim. Fortunately, I was still on good terms with my bow.

Why did you pick him? one of my arrows whined. *I'm a much better arrow. Look at how he's feathered. Mark my word, he'll pull to the left. Use me. I'll fly straight to the target.*

"You'll get your chance," I promised. "You all will."

The arrows let out a group cheer. I couldn't help but smile. They were a spirited bunch. They would serve me well.

"Why can't you be more like the arrows?" I asked the sword.

It's easy for them, he explained. *They're arrows. They're used to working with women. I'm a sword. I'm a man's weapon. Hacking and slashing, that's my game. It's degrading for me to have to work with a female.*

"That's a rather sexist point of view, don't you think?" I asked.

I am what I am, the sword sighed.

"I'll make you a deal. If you get us through this battle, I promise you the next town we hit, I'll trade you to the biggest, hairiest barbarian I can find."

I could feel the sword thinking.

Do you really mean it? he finally asked. *This isn't another one of your empty promises?*

"I swear by the Fire of Siksik Sabella!" I solemnly vowed.

Make the sacred sign, the sword demanded.

I frowned. Making the sacred sign would make my oath binding, and I had no intention of actually following through. Still, it was the only way I was going to live to see another day.

Reluctantly, I made the sacred sign.

"Satisfied?" I spat.

Extremely satisfied, the sword said smugly. There is nothing I hate more than a smug sword. Oh, I'd trade him to a man, all right. I'd find the dumbest, crudest barbarian—one fresh off the icefields. Somebody who wouldn't know the first thing about how to treat a first class sword. See how he'd like it when his edge was gone, and rust started to crawl all over his pretty body. It would serve him right.

I was too good to him. That was the problem.

I was pulled out of my funk by the sound of the raiders charging. I could never figure out why they screamed when they attacked. It seemed like a lot of wasted energy to me.

I let them get a little closer before I fired.

The first arrow did pull a little to the left. Instead of hitting the target squarely in the chest and killing him instantly, it caught him in the shoulder. It slowed him down, but it didn't stop him. He struggled to his feet and staggered on.

Told you so, the smarmy arrow jeered.

"Do you think you can do any better?" I asked.

Try me!

I did. He did a beautiful job, flying straight and true. I could hear the raider gasp as the arrow buried itself in his delicate heart.

"Nicely done!" I cheered. I took aim with another

arrow, but before I could let loose I was struck in the head by a lucky shot from a sling. The stone crashed against my helmet, almost knocking me off my feet. When the ringing stopped, I took inventory. I was dizzy, but I was still conscious.

"Thank you very much," I said to my helmet.

Just doing my job, the helmet said proudly.

Time to go to work, the sword said. About half a dozen of the dirty buggers had made it to the wall, and were now scrambling up rickety makeshift ladders. I kicked two of them down, and chuckled at the curses the raiders uttered when they crashed to the ground. I couldn't understand a word of the language, but I could interpret the sentiment. I could have pushed off a couple of more ladders, but I knew that would only tick them off. There was only one way to stop them. I took a step back and unsheathed the sword.

"Ready?" I asked.

Ready! he said. I could feel him vibrate in my hand. As the first raider pulled himself up over the edge, I pulled back my arm and attacked. . . .

Much later, after he was cleaned and polished, the sword said to me, *You know, you fight pretty well for a girl.*

"Stop it; you'll make me blush," I said sarcastically.

No, I really mean it. I think we make a pretty good team.

"Thank you:" I said. "You know, I'm really going to miss you when you're gone."

Let's not be too hasty, the sword said. *I think I've changed my mind. Chalk it up to prefight jitters. Things said in the heat of battle that we later come to regret. Why don't we just forget the whole thing?*

"I made a sacred vow," I pointed out.

You know, I'm pretty sick of him. Why don't we let

him go. Good riddance! the armor said. Everyone else agreed with her. I had a mutiny on my hands.

I took a deep breath. It was a long way back to civilization. Plenty of time to mend fences.

We don't need them, the sword snarled. *We can get along fine without them.*

Oh, yeah. Plenty of time.

HELL HATH NO FURY . . .

by Lee Martindale

Since we last "met" Lee Martindale, some things have changed while others remain happily the same. She's still unabashedly female, still unapologetically fat, and now unashamedly 50. She's moved to Plano, TX, where she still publishes *Rump Parliament Magazine,* and she's still a size rights activist, songwriter, performer, SCA bard and merchant, filker, paraplegic and access advocate. Her husband has more reason than ever to call her his redheaded "Hell on Wheels," and it's been "quite a marriage" for ten years now.

Her genre credits now include a tape of original filk ("The Ladies of Trade Town"), and story sales to the anthologies *Snows Of Darkover* and *Sword and Sorceress XIV* and the magazines *Zone 9, Marion Zimmer Bradley's Fantasy Magazine, Pulp Eternity,* and *XOddity.* Her story "Neighborhood Watch," which appeared in *MZBFM #40,* was included on *Tangent's* 1998 Recommended Reading List.

Lee has also joined the ranks of anthology editors with *Such A Pretty Face: Tales Of Power & Abundance,* due out Summer 2000.

By all accounts, the Baroness Muirean was held in high regard by those who looked to her. They spoke of her in glowing terms, counted themselves fortunate to live in her lands, commented often on her great beauty, and even more often on her wise rule and generous treatment of all. Except bards. For reasons either unknown or unvoiced, the noble lady loathed the craft and those who plied it.

Too sound a ruler to violate the ancient right of free passage or to deny her people occasional pleasant distractions, she didn't blatantly discourage bards from visiting her barony. She merely ignored them, particularly with regard to the custom of inviting an evening's entertainment for herself and household. Those who attempted to pay traditional respects did so to the seneschal, the baroness herself being "unavailable to itinerant minstrels."

All this Llyra knew, both from the reports of her brother bards and from the gleanings of two nights in the common room of the FireFall Tavern. So when a messenger in baronial black and red arrived with a stiffly formal summons for the Bard of the Copperwood Harp to attend Her Excellency, Llyra answered it with equal portion of surprise and curiosity. And, she admitted to herself under Muirean's chill examination, a faint trace of apprehension.

The baroness signaled to one of her guardsmen, and a low stool was carried in and placed behind Llyra. "Play," she ordered curtly before turning her attentions elsewhere.

Llyra took her seat and pulled Copperwood out of its carrysack and onto her lap. After a quick check to make sure of the tuning, she leaned the harp against her shoulder and began to run through a variety of instrumental pieces from stately march through spirited dance to traditional lament. No one seemed to pay the least bit of attention, which afforded Llyra the opportunity to engage in another bardic duty— observation.

The baroness was every bit the beauty that all accounts and her subjects praised her as being, and in all the details so described: the graceful neck, the porcelain skin, the cloud of blue-black hair unbound and unadorned except for a red-gold coronet. The illusion was as perfect as illusion can be and sound enough

to almost mask those things illusion could not hide.
Cheekbones too high and sharp for a human face, lips
too red for anything human save the color of human
blood. And the eyes, more at home in feline fur or
reptile's scales than under delicately curved eyebrows.

The accounts all agreed that the Baroness Muirean
was either demon or demon-fathered. The accounts,
it seemed, were true.

"Actually," Muirean said, as she turned her attentions back to the young bard, "my father was human.
It was my mother who was demonbreed." Llyra acknowledged the correction with a respectful nod and
no more. As if the bard's reaction—or lack of one—
was something for which Muirean had been watching,
she signaled for refreshments to be placed beside each
before the two were left alone.

"Do you sing, bard?"

"Aye, Your Excellency."

"Sing for me, then. The saddest song you know."

Llyra considered the request for a moment, then
gently placed Copperwood on the floor beside her. In
form, the song was a lullaby set in a minor key, and
she sang the first two verses softly and without embel-
lishment, letting the simple melody establish itself. On
the third, she increased tempo and volume slightly,
adding slips and turns that matched the increased urgency of the words. The final verse she sang slowly,
hesitating between phrases to convey the anguish of a
mother who knows she sings her babe into final and
permanent sleep. The last note she drew out and held
until it dissipated into silence.

Llyra opened her eyes to find Muirean watching her
intently. "How came you by that piece?"

"A few years ago, on Second Journey, I rather foolishly wandered into a siege. One night not long before
the town fell, I happened on a woman singing the tune
to the infant in her arms." Llyra paused for a moment

as she recalled the memory. "One of the bardic duties is to chronicle the times."

Muirean lifted one eyebrow slightly. "And the death of one babe is worthy of a bard's remembering?"

Llyra met her eyes evenly. "I consider it so."

The blood-red lips lifted in a slight smile before the graceful hand invited Llyra to drink from the goblet at her side. "I'm told that bards learn many songs during their training, and gather more in their wanderings."

"It is so, lady."

"And is your repertoire extensive?"

"For one of my rank, I believe it to be."

"There is a song," the baroness continued as she reached for her own goblet, "an old one, I'm told, widely sung. I wonder if you might know it."

"The title?"

"Hell hath no fury like a demon lover scorned." She spoke lightly, but Llyra's ear caught a barely audible harmonic in the voice that stirred the hairs on the back of her neck. "Do you know it?"

Llyra swallowed, the trace of apprehension she'd felt earlier returning. "Aye, Your Excellency, I learned it many years ago."

"And do you sing it often?"

Llyra shook her head. "Only as often as someone calls for it and I cannot distract him to something else."

"Why is that?"

"In all honesty, madam, I've never cared for it, and have never been able to do it without unease. The tune is not a pretty one, for all that it was meant to be simple enough for a tavern crowd to join in on the chorus. And the words have always struck me as . . ."

"Go on."

"Mean-spirited, Your Excellency."

"Then why sing it at all?"

"Because I have no choice in the matter," Llyra replied. "Among the oaths we take is one to perform when, where, and whatever requested. A rather pointed portion of the oath addresses songs and tales we would, by personal preference, avoid."

Muirean leaned back. "So if I were to request it . . ."

"I would, most respectfully, remind Your Excellency that it is a piece more suited to common room than noble lady's chamber."

"And if I were to insist?"

Llyra inclined her head and settled Copperwood into place, playing the introduction that always struck her as sounding like derisive laughter. Then she began to sing, shaping her voice to a delivery meant to suggest what the words indicated—a man as the teller of the "tale." Verse followed verse to build the story: a handsome young bard seeking shelter for the night in what he is deceived into thinking is a noble's castle. The resident demon's equally demonic daughter, overcome with the bard's comeliness, offering him numerous and progressively more tempting inducements to forsake his Journey and stay with her as husband. Incorruptible bard forthrightly rejecting the various temptations and the "lady" herself, hence incurring the titular wrath. Several verses devoted to said bard's tribulations in making his narrow but heroic escape. A final verse revisiting the rejected "lover," whose sorrow reduces the number of demons in the world by one.

The last chord melted into uncomfortable and lengthy silence, broken only by a sound that reminded Llyra of claws tap-scraping on stone. "A pity my father's gift for satire," Muirean said at last, "so far outstripped his dedication to veracity."

"And a pity your mother's memory has been so ill-used," Llyra ventured quietly.

"Oh, Mother doesn't mind," came the reply with a chuckle. "In truth, aside from my begetting, she considers it about as important, and no more annoying, as you might consider the buzz of a passing insect. Having a human half, I am cursed with the unfortunate disadvantage of actually *caring* about such things as truth and falsehood."

"Inasmuch as this touches bardic honor," Llyra said after a moment, "would you do me the great favor of giving me the true tale? I should like very much to hear it."

"Does it matter to you?"

"It does, Your Excellency."

"And you will believe it as it comes from my lips? Despite what I am, and against the word of one of your own?"

"Lady, until I actually hear it, I cannot say for a certainty. But," and Llyra met the odd eyes again, "I have already told you the original piece made me uncomfortable. I think, perhaps, that was my own sense telling me that I sang a lie."

"Very well, bard. Let us begin with my father.

"His name was Gavris and, as my mother tells it, he was a thin, sallow, ill-kempt young man with bad teeth and breath foul enough to wrinkle the nose of a cess-swimmer. My mother's brother noticed him first, standing in a torrent of rain at the entrance to Below, singing at the top of a not-very-pleasing voice and demanding the bardic right of free passage into Demonkeep. It was decided that, if he were ignored, he would go away. Three days later, he had not, although the howling was considerably lessened in volume and he coughed more than he sang. My mother, whose near-to-only fault is being tenderhearted when it comes to strays and the stupid, hauled him Below the next time he passed out."

Llyra hid a smile behind her goblet.

"A little warmth, a surprisingly large quantity of food and, in fairly short order, Gavris was his former self. And a wretchedly unpleasant self it was. He whined, he threatened, he stuck his nose in places and business where it decidedly did not belong. And, according to my grandfather, he stole . . . just about anything that was not secured. I gather that there was serious consideration given to granting his frequent requests for a personal tour of The Pit."

The young bard chuckled. "A one-way tour?"

Muirean rumbled a chuckle of her own. "So I've been told. Then, as if all this was not bad enough, the vile creature decided that he was in love with my mother. She could hardly turn around without bumping her nose into his bony chest. He followed her more closely than did her own tail. To call him a nuisance is to liken the Plague to a spring cold.

"And then it got worse. He convinced himself that she was in love with him, could not live without him and would, if he asked, follow him anywhere. Bringing with her, of course, a dowry of riches from Below worthy of his reputation as Premier Bard of DemonKeep. It was then that my mother decided that she'd had enough and was more than willing to throw this stray back into the rain from which she had, so foolishly, rescued him."

"Am I correct in guessing that he wasn't nearly as easily ejected as he was acquired?"

"You could wager your harpstrings on it in safety. All manner of bribes were offered, all manner of threats made, the full demonic anger of a goodly portion of Below was waged against him . . . and the silly twit refused to go. Finally, my mother asked him what it would take to dislodge him."

"And . . . ?"

One baronial eyebrow lifted expressively. "A night spent in my mother's arms. Mother was so overjoyed by the prospect of his speedy departure that she nearly broke her neck—and his—complying. I have it from her own lips that she took the greatest pleasure of her long and wicked life bodily tossing him out the following morning."

"I will say this for Gravis," Llyra said as soon as she could recover from her laughter, "to have crafted that song from those events shows more imagination than I hope I ever possess in my entire lifetime. Unfortunately, the situation has done a grave injustice to you, and sullied the name and reputation of bardcraft in your sight. And for that, amends must be made."

Muirean regarded Llyra for a long while. "Are you offering to wipe that wretched song from out the memory of man? Remove it, perhaps, from the knowledge of your brother and sister bards?"

"Would that I could, Your Excellency, but what one bard has crafted, another cannot destroy. But I do have an idea."

If the patrons of FireFall Tavern had been surprised at Llyra's initial summons to the baronial keep, the sight of her returning safely some hours later was beyond their belief. When, the following evening, an honor guard arrived to escort her to the Baroness again, they were shocked speechless. And when the tavern, and the town itself, was rocked by a demonic howl long and loud enough to shatter crockery, they had shaken their heads and muttered about some things being "bound to happen." Some even explained the sight of the bardlady gliding through the common room later that night as a ghost.

So when Llyra took her place beside the hearth the following evening and began to play, the tavern filled to overflowing with townsfolk more than a trifle curious. Not a few remarked on the black-and-red brooch she wore at her shoulder. And when one bold fellow asked about it, Llyra smiled and explained it was a token of appreciation from their good baroness for a bardic service done. Would they like to hear the song that prompted the gift?

AN EXCHANGE OF FAVORS

by Dorothy J. Heydt

Dorothy J. Heydt is one of our local, much-valued writers. Since she began selling to me, she has moved once, to another house in the same city, and both her children have grown up. (I can't believe how fast children grow up—while I'm delighted to have grandchildren, it still seems strange to me that my "baby" is old enough to have a husband and two children.)

In addition to her many wonderful short stories, Dorothy has two novels: *The Interior Life,* and *A Point Of Honor.*

Samos was a dark shape in their wake, flattening into a shadow on the horizon. Forward, the whole sky was an unblemished brilliant blue as far as anyone could see. Cynthia had a length of black wool and a length of rust-colored linen to make two new gowns with, bought in the Samian market, and she was basting the black sleeves to the shoulder-seams in the bright sunlight when she saw the man approaching.

No, not a man. He cast no shadow, for one thing, and the busy Punic sailors never raised a head as he walked past them to ask who in Hades he was. What's more, he had never come on board at Samos. He was quite close before she saw the clinching argument, the little golden wings on his heels that opened and closed slowly like the wings of butterflies.

She bowed where she sat, over her lapful of woolen goods. "My lord Hermes: or, I should say, Mercury."

"You've called me by both names," the god said. "You *can* see me? That's a relief. They can't."

"I don't think you have a name in Punic, my lord," Cynthia said.

He considered this. "I don't, now that you mention it," he said. "I need to talk to you."

"Then we'd better go inside, before the sailors think I've gone mad and am talking to myself." She got up and led the way to her cabin.

The rough wooden door stuck in its frame, as it always did. A bronzed arm reached over her shoulder and touched it, and it swung open. Cynthia stepped inside, trying not to wonder what was afoot. Gods had always interfered with luscious young mortals, there were a thousand tales; but she was twenty-three, no longer young, and never luscious—

"Oh, nothing like that," Mercury said. "Getting entangled with mortals is more trouble than it's worth; I learned that a long time ago. And I could wish—" and cut himself off sharply. "Have a seat."

Two benches had appeared in the cabin, and a low table, and now the god brought out from nowhere in particular two trays and set them down. One held bread and olives and smoked fish, and a jar and cup of fine Samian ware.

The other held a jar and cup that must be of glass, finely patterned with swirls of blue and green. The liquid inside was as clear as water. In the dish lay things she had no words for, little round things bright green as emeralds—but they quivered as Mercury set them down. Another, the size and shape of a roll of bread, but translucent as mist, its wisps drifting slowly about a common center. And strips of things that looked like beaten gold. Ambrosia and nectar, the food and drink of gods. Homer had implied that it was greatly different from the food of mortals; he must have known something.

Mercury poured dark-red wine into her cup. "Your wine is called 'The Tears of Tireisias,' " he said. "Let me know if it's all right."

Obediently, she raised the cup. (If he had wanted to poison her, he could have blasted her where she stood and saved himself trouble.) "Your health, my lord," she said, and drank. "It's very good."

"Good." He poured colorless nectar into his own cup, and the room filled with its fragrance—roses, maybe, or the fresh wind of spring. She took a deep breath and let it out again. The young goddess Aretë had warned her she mustn't try to taste the food of immortals, and she had been right about everything else.

"You remember about Tireisias?" Mercury asked.

"Well, yes; the twining snakes, and how he changed his sex twice—"

"And after that, Zeus and Hera asked him, as one who'd know, which enjoyed bed-sport more? Men or women? And he said, Women, and Zeus had a great laugh at his consort's expense, and Hera was so angry she struck Tireisias blind. And Zeus said, I'm sorry, but I can't help you; what one god has done another god cannot undo; instead, I'll give you the power of prophecy—"

"Is that the truth?" Cynthia said. "I always wondered—Oh, forgive me, I interrupted."

"No, no, please: ask."

"I always wondered whether it was true, that what one god has done another can't undo. How can the immortal gods be bound to such restraints on their powers? Or is it simply that if they were not bound, all the stories would fall to the ground? If the character in your play gets into terrible trouble and then immediately the god out of the Machine comes down and makes it all right, you've got no plot, and you'll never win the Drama Festival award."

Mercury laughed, and tossed one of the green things (wobbling between one shape and another like a droplet of water flung into the air) into his mouth. "That's almost right," he said. "It's a matter of honor. It's not 'what a god has done, no one can undo;' it's 'what one god has done, another god is bound in honor not to undo.' You'll remember how Hera turned Io into a cow, because she'd lain with Zeus. Zeus couldn't undo that; but she wandered into Egypt where she not only regained a woman's shape, but rose to godhead as Isis. But if that hadn't happened, she might have wandered into some mortal's farmyard and been slaughtered—or put in the stockpen to bear calves for the rest of her life. It happens all the time. It's tricky, for a god to circumvent another's actions without breaking honor. Sometimes the shortest distance between two points is around three sides of a square." He drank again, and sighed.

"Well, my lord, maybe it's just the wine, but I am beginning to think you want me to do something."

The god smiled.

"And you can't tell me what it is, because that would be interfering."

The god smiled wider (the room was becoming warmer), and made beckoning motions, as if to say "Go on, go on."

"Then how am I to find out what to do? Never mind that. What *can* you tell me?"

"I can tell you," the god said, "that if you go to Mytilene, on Lesbos, you will presently see and recognize what needs doing. And if you'll agree to do it, I'll teach you a fine charm for undoing enchantments."

"I thought I already had one," Cynthia said, looking at the iron ring of Arethousa, dark on her finger. "Though it doesn't seem to have done anything of late."

"Arethousa has fallen into deep sleep," Mercury

said. "I can tell you that, you see; it hasn't anything
to do with this other matter. In fact, it would be a
good deed if you gave the ring back to Arethousa; I
mean, drop it into her spring. If you get the chance."

"All right."

"And when you get to Mytilene—"

"We're not going there. We're bound for Athens,
not even making landfall anywhere between."

"Oh, that's no trouble. *That* I can handle. If you
agree."

"And you're sure that when I get to Mytilene, I'll
know the task when I see it?"

"Certain sure."

"Oh, very well. *Most* of the gods I've met, and I've
met entirely too many, have told me the truth eventually. I'll have to take you on trust."

"As I do you." Mercury's face and body were shining with delight, like the sun thinly veiled in cloud.
"Give me your hand." He took it and shook it firmly,
like a merchant sealing a bargain. "Now we're in my
part of the world and I can do anything. Quickly, let
me teach you the charm." He recited a pair of hexam-
eters in Ionian dialect:

*"Kourë stood in her garden, deep in the shadow
asleep there;*

*Out of the shadow, Kourë, rise up anew to the
lightlands."*

And when Cynthia had repeated it over thrice, the
god vanished and the cabin was very dark.

She stumbled toward the window—the table and
benches were still there—and opened the hatch to let
some light in. But there was not much light to let in:
the sky had clouded over and the sea had gone
choppy—but there seemed to be no wind. Maybe it
was from a different quarter? She opened her cabin
door (it opened silently at a touch) and stepped out
onto the deck. Banks of thunderclouds were building

up toward the west, and a stiff breeze blew across the deck, scattering rope-fibers and dust, and struck her in the face. The sailors were running about reefing the sails and getting loose bundles under cover. "Better get below, lady," one of them called as he hurried by; and Cynthia did so. She barred her door and looked around the cabin to see if all was secure. The window hatch was banging in the side-gusts of wind, and the ship was beginning to roll. The god had taken away his own tray but left hers; she had better finish the jar of Tears of Tireisias before it fell and broke. Then she dogged the hatch, fell into her bunk, and spent the next several hours in a borderland between dreaming and waking, while the wind howled and the ship tossed and the furniture whispered back and forth across the floor.

"Curse it," the captain said the next morning, glaring under the rain-washed sun. "What good does this do me?"

The citadel of Mytilene, like many others, had been built on a rocky spit of land connected to the island itself by a low isthmus. Long and patient digging had cut a wide passage through the isthmus, protecting the acropolis against attack by land and providing safe passage for ships between the northern and southern harbors when the sea was rough outside their sheltered waters.

A fine harbor, but not the Piraeus of Athens. They had been blown north by east instead of west by north, and the captain was not pleased.

"Well, none of us is drowned," Cynthia pointed out. "That's an advantage right there. Your hold's practically empty of cargo, is it not, Captain? It looks as if they've had a good harvest; maybe you can pick up a load on the cheap and sell it dear somewhere else."

"When they've had a good year, which I grant you," the captain said, "Lesbos exports wine. Sometimes olive oil. Athens is an exporter of both wine and olive oil. It would be like hauling copper to Cyprus, or tin to the Northern Isles. And it's still Athens we've got to go to next; my only cargo is a letter to be delivered there. Barring that load of Samian pottery I picked up at a venture—if it hasn't all got smashed to shards in the storm.''

"I will bet you a dinner ashore," Cynthia said, "that there's been no breakage whatever. Go take a look."

The captain looked at her, not quite dubious, but cautious. The witch of Syracuse had never done him any harm, and some good, and she had paid her passage with gold. It wouldn't do to cross her. "Some time today, I will. We'll be here for hours, looks like, with the repairs we've got to make. I thank the gods the mast didn't break.''

"The gods will appreciate your gratitude. I'll go ashore and keep out of your way." And surely a mostly honest tradesman like the Punic captain would be pleasing to Hermes, now called Mercury, patron of roads, bargains, trade, the newly dead, and thieves.

Mytilene's waterfront was like every other in Greater Greece: piles of reasonably fresh fish for sale, nets to mend, sails to dry, sailors looking for amusement, amusement looking for sailors. Further away from the harbor, the market street was lined with booths: bread, grilled fish, fruit, and wine all offered for sale, as well as yard goods and squid's ink and baskets and pottery and eggs, and chickens with their legs tied together; and the smells of charcoal and frying oil drifting out of the doorways of alehouses. Children ran to and fro underfoot, some begging, some offering to carry small packages, some with an eye out for purses to cut. Chickens squawked, flutes twittered, voices quarreled. And the rattle of a sistrum, and voices raised in song, and (when they paused for breath) the soft bleat of a sheep. A sacrifice bound for the altar.

Fresh mutton: Cynthia hadn't tasted it since before leaving Alexandria. And if she joined the procession, made a witness to the sacrifice, then after the blood had been spilled and certain bits offered to the gods in the fire (fat and bones mostly, the parts the human worshipers couldn't eat anyway), the meat would be shared out among all the participants. She drew her stole a trifle closer about her head, lest anyone happen to ask, "Who are you?" and followed.

The procession moved on, along the Broad Street lined with the freshly whitewashed houses of the rich. A manservant was washing the steps of one of the houses with mop and bucket, and chatting to a maid-servant leaning out an upper window. A peddler went by with a handcart, crying autumn flowers for sale, and somewhere a child cried in infantile rage, and shouted "NO!" and cried again.

They turned right onto Temple Street and headed eastward, between the houses of little gods and greater gods, with the scent of incense going stale around their porticoes, all the way up to the great Temple of Zeus, with its golden pillars, at the far end.

The sacrificial sheep seemed to be nervous, which was not the kind of behavior one would expect from a sheep. It was a young ewe, a year or so past its lambhood: its wool washed white, its head garlanded with flowers, its hooves polished. And its eyes rolled from side to side, and it shied if anyone came close to it. If it hadn't had a beribboned cord around its neck, held by a pock-faced young acolyte, it would probably have vanished into the crowd by now. Twice it had tossed the garland off its head into the dust; twice someone had replaced the wreath (slightly the worse for wear) on the fleecy head.

They passed through the golden pillars (gold leaf

over wood, of course, and beginning to wear away) into the cool semidarkness of the temple. Under a tall statue of Zeus All-Father, bright in new paint, a shaft of sunlight fell through the smoke-hole onto the altar of sacrifice, dusty with ashes. The sheep set its hooves and tried to back away, but the floor was paved with smooth tiles and the acolyte easily dragged it along, click-click-click.

The sheep bleated again, and jerked frantically against its cord, as if it knew what was ahead of it. Sheep generally didn't; for however many thousands of years the clever sheep that looked out for themselves had wandered off and been eaten by wolves, while the stupid sheep that allowed the shepherd to look after them had stayed at home and been eaten by shepherds. Perhaps a wild ram had wandered down out of the mountains and mounted this one's mother?

Cynthia moved up through the crowd to take a closer look. The head of the family offering the sacrifice had stepped to the fore, taken a little knife and cut off a lock of wool. He gave this to the priest, who laid it on the altar. Atop the wool he laid tinder, and a few sticks of kindling, and struck two stones together till sparks fell and set it alight. The sheep reared, and the acolyte with the cord leaped to grab hold of the fleece atop its head, and wrestle it to the ground.

The ritual continued. The singers sang, the acolytes waved incense in elaborate patterns all round the altar, the priest brandished the sacrificial knife—

And the sheep, its head pulled upward to offer its throat, looked up at Cynthia with human terror and despair in its eyes.

This was what Mercury had meant.

"Kourë stood in her garden, deep in the shadow asleep there;

Out of the shadow, Kourë, rise up anew to the lightlands."

The fire flared up, casting blinding smoke in every direction except where Cynthia stood, and the sheep vanished. A naked woman lay on the floor. Somewhere outside, thunder rolled. The acolyte with the cord—but the cord seemed to have fallen away—let go his grip on her hair and rubbed his eyes as if they stung. Cynthia whipped off her stole and covered her, hauled her to her feet and half-dragged her away. Nobody seemed to notice till they had reached the edge of the crowd.

The acolyte took his fists from his eyes and seemed to notice only now that they were empty. The priest lowered the knife. Thunder rumbled again. The worshipers looked around, and cried, "Where's the sheep?" and looked around again. But they saw nothing. A sleek-looking old man with a neatly trimmed beard was staring directly at Cynthia, not seeing her.

Cynthia leaned forward and murmured into his ear, "Zeus took the beast entire for himself," and the man repeated it. Soon the words were going through the crowd, to general approval. *But nobody gets any mutton chops,* Cynthia thought, and led the woman out of the temple before the glamour should break.

She was young, no more than fifteen, with tumbled fair hair and a delicate face. Her shudders were beginning to turn into sobs. Cynthia turned about looking for a hiding place, somewhere the girl could cry and recover herself unseen.

Nothing offered itself. No dark alleys on Temple Street, only bold-faced temple fronts, bright and airy with colonnades that promised holy things within. Overhead it was growing dark. Winds howled between the columns; what in Hades was happening to the weather? There to the right of the Temple of Zeus, in the place of honor, stood the temple of Hera his sister-wife, and from in it came an ominous rumbling, like thunder far-off or drums close to. The story fell together, the same as all the other stories, a poet's formula: *Zeus tumbled Whoever-it-was, and jealous Hera turned her into*—in this case, a sheep, and in an excess of clever cruelty arranged for her to be sacrificed in her lover's own temple. That frustrated, now she would rise up in wrath—

Cynthia turned her head. On the left side of Zeus' temple stood that of Hermes, the son of his left hand, whom Hera, no doubt, never had liked. Cynthia lifted the girl by the elbows and dragged her inside.

It was quiet here, and a pair of small fires burned on either side of the statue. The sculpted Hermes hadn't the grace of the living Mercury, but the symbolic power was the same. The wrath of Hera could not get in. They sat on the steps and Cynthia waited while the girl cried. Presently she dried her tears, and looked around, and looked up. Over their heads something was glittering, like a swarm of shining bees, pouring out of the Hermes-image's hand. Cynthia had just time to remember, *Zeus came to Danaë in a shower of gold,* and then golden rain fell all around them and was gone, and Cynthia's stole fell empty to the floor, leaving only the fragrance of roses.

She looked up into the statue's sightless eyes. "All right," she said. "I'm not sure you owe me for this; it's what I would have done myself, given the opportunity. Good day to you, my lord."

The storm must have passed over, outside; sunlight was pouring in the temple door. Cynthia wrapped her stole around her head again and left the Temple of Hermes for the waterfront while the getting was good.

The Punic captain was waiting for her on the dock. "Dinner is on me," he said. "Not a cup broken. How did you do it? The Red Horse serves good shellfish."

The Red Horse also had dark corners, sturdy tables, very good wine, and music from a girl who twanged a lyre and sang in a Theban dialect. The captain seemed known here, and the waiters kept their cups filled.

A bronzed hand reached over the captain's shoulder with a plate of grilled shrimp. Cynthia looked up: the man's face was unfamiliar but Cynthia recognized the smile. "Buy wine," he said, and vanished into the darkness.

"Eh?" the captain said. "What'd that fellow say?"

"He said, 'Buy wine,'" she answered. "Perhaps I will. What are your rates for freight, Captain?"

"Woman, have you gone mad? We're finished with the repair work and at dawn we sail for Athens. Athens *exports* wine."

"So you said. But I think I'll take it on trust, and buy wine. Ah, here comes the crab in sour sauce."

When they left the Red Horse, the sun was sinking, but the merchants were still open for business. She found a factor for a rich farmer inland, who was selling off his surplus to any that would buy it, and she bought enough amphorae to fill half the hold. The captain sighed, and said, "But you *know* things," and bought enough to fill the other half.

Over the next few days, as they cruised past island after island, stopping only to take on water and look at the damage Mercury's sudden storm had done to every waterfront, Cynthia had time to rethink her decision a thousand times. She had entrusted such savings as she had to the promise of a god: the god of bargains, yes, but the god who spoke out of both sides of his mouth. And who seemed not to care whose waterfront got wrecked, for example, just as long as one Cynthia daughter of Euelpides got washed up to the shores of Lesbos to run an errand for the father of gods and men. And who might not care about her either, not afterward.

But he had said *he* had to take *her* on trust. As if
it were difficult, and as though he feared disaster if
she didn't keep her half of the bargain. Well, she had.
But he had never said what his half would be. Maybe
he had taken her at her word, and there wasn't any
other half—

They came to the Piraeus, the harbor-town of Athens, just as the sun went down; the captain ordered
the anchor dropped in midharbor rather than try to
dock in the dark.

At dawn they put out oars and entered the great
Kantharos harbor. The early sun shone on the white
marble of the five great stoai, pillared courts full of
warehouses and factors' offices, between the docks
and the great marketplace called the Emporion. A
little later, pulling into the slips, they could see that
the divine storm had done damage here, too. Ware-
house roofs had fallen in, walls buckled; workmen
were hauling away broken timbers and picking up
shards of tile, or what looked like them.

"By the gods," said the first mate as he slipped
the docking-rope over the bollard. "That's my brother
Hanno. Captain, by your leave?" And he leaped to
the dock and ran to greet the other dark-bearded
sailor. They talked, and they waved their arms, and
pointed to the demolished warehouses. Then they
turned and walked back to the ship. "Hanno was here
when the storm hit," the mate remarked.

"Captain," the other sailor said politely. "It was like
the end of the world, only it was merely the end of a
good many warehouses. Blew the tiles up off the roofs,
and sucked the walls in like grapeskins, and then the
tiles fell in again on the amphorae. It was like that
old song, the one where the rivers ran with wine.
Funny, isn't it? For the Piraeus to run short of wine?
They'll have more coming in by the cartload, ten or
fifteen days; but right now there's a lot of dry throats

in the Piraeus, and an amphora of good wine is worth its weight in—well, copper, anyway."

"Like hauling copper to Cyprus, or tin to the Northern Isles," the mate said with a grin (he knew what was in the hold); and the captain looked slantwise at Cynthia, who merely smiled.

PRICE OF THE SWORD
by Kim Fryer

Kim Fryer has had stories published in *Marion Zimmer Bradley's Fantasy Magazine*, *Tomorrow* Magazine, DC comics' *Justice League Quarterly,* and a variety of small press magazines. A misplaced Midwesterner, she lives in Washington with her husband Bob and their house rabbit, Scwooey Wabbit. You can visit them at http://aol.members.com/kkfryer/flotsam.htm.

It's always struck me as strange that otherwise normal people write comics. When I was a kid, no one over twelve would be caught dead reading one. Evidently either times have changed, comics have changed—or perhaps both.

The door to her cottage swung open suddenly, arcing into the adjacent wall and rebounding slightly. Nadia, who was in the midst of bringing the soup spoon to her mouth, paused in mid-motion. In the doorway stood a tall figure with broad shoulders, backed by the setting sun.

The spoon fell from her fingers. "Marcus?"

Then Nadia remembered anew that her son had died in battle three years ago. It was a fact she still had difficulty accepting, although she had buried Marcus beneath the high rock behind the cottage.

Slamming the door shut, the figure strode to the table where Nadia sat.

Now that the sun was out of her eyes, Nadia could plainly see that this was not her son. The hair was reddish-brown, like clay, while her son's had been black. Judging from the oval face and long neck, Nadia suspected this was a woman rather than a man, although she was larger than any woman Nadia had ever seen, and her arms were well muscled. The young woman wore shabby but clean leather armor, which bore the battle crest of King Macedon.

"The war has been over for two years," Nadia said, not rising to meet her visitor. "How does a king's soldier come to be wandering in battle armament?"

"I'm Tamath of the Brook-and-Stone Glen. I seek the village witch woman," the soldier replied. The voice was a husky alto, unmistakably female. She was young, no more than twenty, about the same age as Marcus would have been. Her face had a fierce, almost proud look.

Nadia pushed her soup bowl away, into the clutter on top of the small wooden table. "For what reason?"

The soldier drew her sword faster than Nadia thought a person could move. "Are you or are you not the witch woman?" the young woman growled, looming over Nadia.

"Which will cause my death?" Nadia asked, eyeing the blade.

"I need a spell. If you can cast it, I spare your life. If not, I kill you."

Nadia reflected on that a moment and said, "I suppose I must be a witch woman, then."

The young woman brandished the sword in Nadia's face. "If you lie, I'll stab you through the heart."

"I can see you're no stranger to killing," Nadia said mildly. Having served in the war, she was used to calming the fierce bravado of young soldiers. "What magic do you seek?"

"A curse must be removed." Tamath lowered her sword, looking at it rather than Nadia. Her voice dropped in volume, almost as if she were sharing a secret. "The blade wants death."

"Isn't that the nature of swords?"

Grimacing, Tamath said, "It speaks to me. A multitude of voices that starts as a whisper, but gets louder as the days pass, until I can hear nothing but the sword's shout. It's been this way since the war ended."

Nadia looked at the sword. It looked no different than any other used by the king's army. "Is it speaking now?"

Tamath nodded. "The whisper has turned to a murmuring. By the rising of the moon tomorrow night, I'll hear only my sword."

Nadia frowned, wondering if the voices Tamath heard were real or battle fatigue left over from the long war. She had seen how killing affected some—the price of using the sword. "What do the voices tell you?"

"I don't know," Tamath said, starting to pace across the width of the small cottage—from the cooking hearth, black with soot, to the unmade cot on the other side. "There are too many voices, anguished ones, and screams—I can't make out what's being said. It doesn't stop until the sword takes a life. Then I know peace for a few days, until it begins once more."

"Haven't you tried to destroy the blade?"

"Yes," Tamath spat. "It won't break. The hottest blaze won't melt it. And if I abandon the sword, it still calls to me, no matter how deep I bury it or how far I ride." Towering over Nadia, she waved the sword. "No one has been able to lift the curse, and so I've killed many a witch woman. If you can't lift it either, I'll kill you to satisfy the blade. Then I'll go to the next village, to the next witch."

Nadia drew back slightly, although her face betrayed nothing. She'd heard tales of witches across the river who'd disappeared, leaving many villages without one. She thought of her sister, the witch woman in the next town, and her sister's two young children. A midwife, Nadia's sister had a bit of magic that aided healing, but it wasn't good for dispelling a curse. Nadia wasn't sure she could handle this either.

Still, she rose and said firmly, "I will help you."

Relief flashed across Tamath's face and was just as quickly replaced by the fierce look.

Nadia pointed to the cluttered table, heaped with dishes and bits and pieces of old metal and broken gardening tools. "We must clear it so you can lay down the sword."

Tamath frowned.

Nadia said patiently, "You may hold the sword, but it must be down, flat, for my spells to work."

The frown deepened into a scowl. The soldier did not move.

Nadia reached under the table, to grab an empty grain sack lying on the floor. "I'm not a threat, am I? I have no weapons. And I'm older and slower than you."

"What of your magic?"

Nadia sighed. "Have you heard of magic that can kill?"

Tamath shook her head as she sheathed the sword. "Magic is strange."

"It varies from witch to witch." Nadia started gathering the bits of metal and old tools on the table. "Stack the bowls and put them on the floor for now."

"Why are there so many?" Tamath asked. Her hand hovered over the hilt of her sword. "Are others here?"

"No, I'm alone," Nadia said, as she put the tools into the grain sack. "I haven't cleaned for days. See the old food in the bowls?"

"This only makes the cleaning that much harder," Tamath scolded, suddenly sounding very young. "You shouldn't let them sit."

Nadia shrugged. "I have much work. The dishes don't seem important in comparison."

Tamath gingerly picked up one of the bowls. "This was one of my duties when I was with my family, before the war," she confided. "I washed the dishes every day."

"Oh?" Nadia asked, sweeping the last bit of rusty metal into the burgeoning sack. "What of your family now?"

"Gone," Tamath said, frowning at the bowls, her husky voice flattening to a monotone. "My father and my brothers fought for the king, as did my uncles and cousins. All died in the war. Our farms were close to the fighting, and they were overrun by invaders. My mother and aunts were killed, our livestock butchered, our fields destroyed. I'm alone."

Nadia stole a look at the soldier. Tamath's head was bent low over the table, but she could see the heavy sadness etched in the young woman's face. Nadia turned away. Going to the cupboard by the hearth, she pulled out a couple of small jars. "My husband was killed in battle, as was my son, my only child. The war took much from all of us."

Tamath nodded, as she slowly stacked the bowls. "I didn't choose to fight for King Macedon, but because of my size, I was forced to join his army with my brothers. There were few women in battle, save for the witches."

"It's said it was witches who turned the course of the war," Nadia remarked. She set the jars on the table. "Our abilities are small when we're apart, but together we can accomplish much."

"It was a witch who made my blade magic," Tamath said. "She saw the wounds I took in my first battle and cast a spell upon a sword to aid my swing. Each time the blade bit into an enemy, it would sing with the purest notes." Tamath put the bowls on the floor in neat towers. "Were you in the war?"

"Yes, I can speak to objects and help broken ones to mend," Nadia said, opening the jars. "Then I worked on weapons. Now it's plows and tools." She looked up at Tamath. "Put the sword on the table."

Tamath drew it from the scabbard and laid it down, holding the hilt.

Nadia dipped her fingers into one of the jars, half full of thyme-scented oil. She traced a small circle upon her own forehead. She dipped the fingers of her other hand into a jar of faint blue liquid and traced a line of moisture down the center of the blade. Keeping her hand lightly upon the sword, she silently spoke a few words in her mind.

The room darkened around Nadia, everything freezing in place, including herself. Without words, she asked the sword, *Are you cursed?*

No, the sword replied in many voices. *We only hunger.*

Nadia realized that the voices were not natural to the sword, but a symptom of the magic laid upon it. *Hasn't your purpose been served?* Nadia asked silently. *Isn't it time to rest?*

We kill for Tamath of the Brook-and-Stone Glen, the voices told Nadia. *We cannot stop.*

Will not, you mean, Nadia said somewhat angrily. *You've taken innocent lives, the lives of witches.*

Innocent or not, blood tastes the same.

Nadia ended her spell and looked at Tamath. "The spell on the sword spoke to me. Did you hear it?"

Her eyes wide, Tamath shook her head.

"The voices will end when it's broken."

"I've tried," Tamath cried. "The spell protects the blade."

"The opposite of mending is breaking," Nadia said. "I can break this spell." She gestured at the sword.

"Destroy it," Tamath said quietly, "and I swear I'll never take another life."

Nadia thought she saw tears filming Tamath's eyes. She looked away from the soldier, picking up the jar of blue liquid from the table. "We must go outside."

She led Tamath out of the cottage and around it, to the high rock in the weeds, the marker for Marcus' grave. The soil was reddish-brown with clay, and still moist from the rain that fell earlier. The sun, which was nearly gone from the sky, cast a rosy glow across the field.

Nadia gathered a fistful of clay-filled soil and put it in one of Tamath's hands. Tamath looked at her questioningly.

"Draw a line upon the stone at shoulder-height," Nadia said. "I am too small to reach that high."

Tamath rubbed the clay across the rock face.

"You'll hit that line with your sword using all your strength," Nadia said. "But first I must cast a spell. Lay your sword upon the ground."

Drawing her sword, Tamath put it down at Nadia's feet. She stepped back.

Nadia knelt. Dipping her fingers into the small jar, she lightly stroked the center of the blade.

Do you see? Nadia asked the sword. *Do you understand what will happen here?*

Our hunger grows, the sword replied.

I will end this. The war is over.

What is war? We know only blood at the hand of Tamath of the Brook-and-Stone Glen. To draw it is our only purpose.

With your assent, I can give you another purpose, Nadia told the sword. *You are fine and strong; it would be a shame for this to be your end.*

It will be yours, the sword said. *You cannot destroy this blade.*

Nadia ended the spell. "It's well made," she told Tamath. "This'll cost me more than you know."

Tamath looked at her without speaking, her face proud but her eyes pleading. Nadia noticed the deep, dark shadows under the young woman's eyes and the sallow skin on her face and long neck above the leather armor.

Nadia positioned Tamath a short distance from the rock, just far enough that the soldier could swing the sword. Nadia pointed to the clay line Tamath had drawn. "Remember, swing as hard as you can." Nadia stepped back several paces.

"You're like my mother," Tamath said. "You're giving me a new life."

Closing her eyes, Nadia said, "Do it now."

Nadia heard a whish of air, a clang as the sword hit stone and rebounded, and then an anguished cry. She opened her eyes to see Tamath kneeling, blood spurting from her neck.

She looked up at Nadia, her mouth forming silent words.

Nadia folded her arms tightly across her body. "I couldn't break the sword, but the sword's spell—and the killing of witches—dies with you." Her lips trembled slightly as she said, "I'm sorry."

Tamath fell forward, upon her face. Nadia watched the still form for a few long moments, then slowly walked over.

The soldier was not breathing, blood pooling around her head like a halo. The sword lay beside her. It seemed duller to Nadia, the edge of the blade not as sharp.

Feeling very old, Nadia rubbed her eyes. As she turned away from the body, she thought she heard a faint whisper. Nadia whirled around, but she saw that Tamath's body was still and she was alone in the dusk.

She turned away once more, and the whisper came

again, saying something that Nadia couldn't make out. She stepped back and touched the sword, but it was as dead as Tamath.

She knew then. Shivering, Nadia walked to the cottage, the whisper of a husky voice rising around her, a snake about her heart. This was the way it would be, then; this was the way it should be. The sword always had a price, Nadia knew, and so she would carry Tamath's voice until the end of her days.

DEMON CALLING

by ElizaBeth Gilligan

ElizaBeth "Lace" Gilligan is an award-winning journalist who dedicates most of her writing efforts to fantasy and science fiction these days. Growing up, ElizaBeth traveled the world as a military brat and so is now content to remain in the San Francisco Bay Area. She is happily married and homeschools her children (Brianna and Patrick).

She just completed her fantasy novel *Vendetta in Silk*—first in a series about Sicilian Romani set in the late 17th century to be called "The Gypsy Silk Books"—and is now working on its sequel, *The Silken Shroud,* and designing the Gypsy Silk Tarot Deck.

Sounds like a lot of fun to me. On a scholarly tour I made of Britain we had a young Gypsy girl who lent us a lot of youthful light and zeal, so I'm predisposed to like the Romany.

ElizaBeth is an herbalist, a fiend for crafts and, most importantly, a research maven. With all the spare time on her hands, she adopts rescue animals such as the five cats—Katrina (The Hunter of Miscellaneous Things), Jabberwocky (Empress of the Universe and a jewelry-stealing dragon in disguise), Pyewackett (The Cat Without a Clue), Chovahani (The Other Womyn), and Maggia Chavi (The Feline Pit Bull)—and a border collie named Gypsy. The menagerie also includes guinea pigs Chocolate and Dulcinea, and tanks of fire-bellied newts, miniature crabs, and fish.

She invites you to come visit her web-page http://www.geocities.com/area51/portal/3628.

Covered in dust and weary from another day's long walk, I followed the witch. She had grown quieter and more fierce as time passed. The sun lay ahead of us on the westerly road, radiating amber ripples over the fields of grain. A one-eyed tom padded at her side, sometimes hidden beneath the sway of her indigo skirts. He was a reclusive beast, like our mistress.

"Come along, girl," Zorya called. She stopped and turned, waiting for me. I wished, for the hundredth time, that I was as beautiful as this woman. Perhaps the air of magic and mystery about her made her seem beautiful for she certainly met no standards of loveliness . . . at least, not like the girls from home. Strange tiny braids woven with bells and feathers adorned both her hair and the dark clothes she always wore. In the end, none of this truly mattered. Zorya was my mistress. I knew by the set of her mouth that she must be frustrated, perhaps, even angry.

I hitched my pack and hurried to catch up. I had followed her for three months now, ever since she destroyed the demon that hunted my neighbors in my home village.

"I'm sorry, Zorya," I said. I owed her so much . . . the life of my father and my friends . . . and now she tried to teach me magic, only I was too dull to understand her lessons. I feared she tired of my stupidity and might send me back to my father in shame.

Zorya shook her head and stared off over the fields on either side of the road. "Valeska, do you know what you are?"

I shook my head, confused by the question.

She poked her finger in the spot beneath my breasts, between my ribs. The inner fire I sometimes felt stirred. "Here, child. Answer from here." She pressed her hand flat. "What are you?"

I shook my head again, feeling like a simpleton

when the magic fire within me cooled. "I don't understand!" I swallowed back tears of frustration.

Zorya walked away from me, but I heard her voice soft and clear. "Valeska, you must learn to name what you are and what you do. Until then, I cannot help you."

Help me? She could help me by explaining the question, but that seemed to be half the point of her asking. How this had anything to do with the fire inside me or the subtle magics she worked escaped me.

The cat bounded ahead of us, suddenly sniffing and flicking his tail, mrowing like he did when we hunted the demon who devastated my home village. I shifted my pack on my shoulders.

I ached all over. The tom returned to twine around my feet. He didn't do that often, so I knelt and scratched his chin, stealing a moment to ease my muscles. Purring, he rolled onto his back and batted at my hand like a kitten. I rubbed his belly and called out to Zorya, glancing up expectantly.

The road appeared ominously empty. I stood and shouted for my mistress, shielding my eyes from the sun. On this hillock, I saw in all directions. The fields lay empty. None of them showed signs of being passed through. No broken stalks of wheat, no crease in the solid wall of grain to give a hint where Zorya might be. Except for the tom, I was suddenly alone.

Desperate that he not desert me as well, I snatched the cat up and cradled him close, ignoring his indignant howls as I turned indecisively. I knew no spells to help me find my mistress and possessed only those things in my pack which I had collected along the way or brought with me from home. I was alone.

Of all the wonders Zorya introduced me to, I liked this one least . . . even less than facing the evil, because at least then someone stood at my side. Neither my rural village upbringing nor my few months with Zorya had prepared me for this.

The tom's gouging claws brought me out of my self-pitying reverie. Though he did not like it, I looped a long leather thong around his neck to make sure I did not lose him, too. While he twisted, clawed, bit, and hissed at the cord, I sucked at the bloodiest of my wounds and tried to decide what to do next.

The sun hung lower than ever, staining the sky a raspberry hue. Habit dictated I make camp or find shelter. In the far distance, I saw smoke rising from a cottage chimney.

I boosted the pack up and set off, tugging at the one-eyed tom who struggled, hissed, and spat at every step. I found a crooked little path through the wheat fields and took it. All the time, I watched for signs that my mistress had passed this way before me. I wondered how she could have left me like this . . . and why she would leave the tom?

As I rounded the corner, I came upon a disorderly farm yard. While it is the nature of farm yards to be disorderly, I did not think I had traveled so far from my home that farmers' habits differed so much. The yard stank with the smell of rotted eggs. The vegetable patch near the house lay in a sorry state; fruit molded on the vine, the plants shriveled from lack of water, and weeds threatened to strangle the life out of what few plants survived such inattention. Nowhere did I see any sign of life, except . . . the little farmhouse.

A gust of wind blew blonde hair into my eyes and made the barn door creak and bang. The one-eyed tom yowled and bristled at my feet. I felt lonely on the road, but here loomed desolation.

I crossed my arms over my chest, suddenly feeling very cold. The farmhouse glowed with a welcoming light. The smell of cooking meat wafted from the open door. Reluctantly, I approached the house. I peered around me. Perhaps some blight had driven the farmer and his family away and they'd just returned? Or, better still, perhaps I had actually found my errant mistress!

"Zorya?"

The cat growled and hunched into a tight ball of animosity.

"Hello?" I started forward, but stopped short when the cat refused to move. I backtracked and bent to pick him up. The miserable beast lashed out and left ribbon trails of blood tracking down the length of my wrist. Without thinking, I hissed back at him and clutched my hand to my chest. I felt the heartfire glimmer within.

I heard a noise behind me and turned. The unsteady light of a cook fire outlined a figure in the doorway. The tom growled again, the sound rumbling up from his center. His tail lashed back and forth. I shushed the cat and shivered against the sudden cold which mysteriously returned.

With my foot firmly planted on the makeshift leash, I rose politely. "I—I have come from the road." Like a village idiot, I pointed back the way I came. I hid the gesture by burying my hands in the folds of my gray skirts and rubbed them clean. "My—My name is—" I bit my lip and swallowed. What harm was there in giving my name? And yet, deep within, it felt like a terrible mistake. "I came from the road," I said lamely.

The cat coiled silently around my left foot beneath my dust-stained skirts.

The figure pushed the lower half of the door open and backed away.

I started forward, but hesitated. I looked around again for Zorya. The tom on my foot was all I needed to tell me she was nowhere near, but I looked just the same. After confirming the obvious, I squared my shoulders and summoned what little courage I possessed. The heartfire flickered. I crossed the threshold with the one-eyed tom hidden beneath my skirts.

I bobbed my head and murmured my thanks as I shrugged out of the pack. Steely fingers roughly pulled the pack from my shoulders, spinning me around. I caught a glimpse of my host as he recoiled to the darker corners of the hearth. He was a fat little man, built rather like a frog with his mass around his middle, seemingly neckless, with scrawny long limbs. Strands of colorless hair sprouted around his turnip-shaped head. He smelled greasy and fetid. His clothes hung in filthy tatters, and he wore no shoes.

My manners failed me. I could not hide my distaste as I withdrew from him and drew a pentagram over my heart. I felt immediately shamed at my behavior. This poor fellow deserved my pity. I carefully composed myself, determined to present a soothing presence. I smothered my wild fears about whatever cursed this poor fellow and had taken his family from him.

In the hope that I might repay my host's kindness for a night's shelter and to keep from further ill-mannered displays, I turned and took stock of the farmhouse. The home, such as it was, consisted of one small room and a sleeping loft, much like the home I was raised in—except for the mess. Bones from half-eaten animals lay strewn on the table and floor. Piles of filthy cloth filled the corners. I swallowed back my disgust. I grew up taking care of Father. Cleaning and tending I managed well enough, and if I intended to stay here even one night, then I must do something about the house.

My host hardly stirred from his corner as I began to clean the grease-stained table, sweeping the leavings of countless meals into a scrap bucket I found upturned near the hearth. He never left his corner, though I felt him loom briefly as I headed for the door. Uncertain what to do in the face of his continued silence, I motioned to the bucket. "I will just go outside, I—I will return shortly."

The tom moved with me, his dainty paws shadowing my steps as he remained hidden beneath my skirts. I clucked at him as we stepped outside. I breathed deeply of the night air, only now aware of the constriction in my chest. I rubbed the point between my breasts and tried to soothe my own unease. As I rubbed, my wayward mistress and her confusing questions came to mind. Almost as soon as I grasped upon a rather startling idea—that in some way perhaps I might be as magical as my mistress—I doubted it and the thought slipped away like the hauntings of a wraith. Shaking my head, I tossed the bones in the refuse pile behind the house and went to the well.

Heavy rocks weighed down the sturdy boards which covered the well. Odd. Resigning myself to the chore, I dusted my hands and began to drag the rocks away, wondering what kind of madness had struck this place that a well would not be left available to passersby. No markers warned that the well had gone dry or that the water turned bad.

I rolled the first of the rocks to the ground beside the stone wall of the well. Darkness settled, and the gloom of early evening clutched at me. Anxious to return to the relative safety of the house, I hurried, pulling at the board. I could hear water splashing as pebbles dropped into the water waiting below. I sniffed. The well smelled clear. I spied my host in the doorway watching me. I muttered mean-spiritedly to myself. Why didn't he come to help? Why hadn't he done this already?

As I began to drag the boards away, I heard a groan from the house. Light from the cook fire silhouetted

my host as he shifted from one bare foot to the other.
Clearly, this addled fellow feared the night even more
than I. I resolved to be more tolerant. Until I found
my mistress or decided what to do with myself, I
needed to rely upon his kindness for shelter.

The gap between the boards was large enough to
wedge the bucket through so I untangled the pull
rope, attached the hook to the bucket's hemp handle
and dropped it into the well. The man made a keening
noise and his dancing became more agitated as the
bucket banged its way down the rocky walls and
splashed into the water.

An icy evening wind whipped up, snapping my
skirts. I gathered my shawl closer against the night.
The sun's last rays of rosy gold hovered on the distant
horizon, beyond the deep forest to the west. The complete silence of the farmyard chilled me even more
than the wind. What was there about the dark that
made one feel hunted? I shivered and began to haul
up the bucket.

The one-eyed tom's sudden growl made me jerk
around as I pulled the bucket over the lip of the well.
At first I saw only darkness, in a large shapeless blot,
and then I realized that my host had left the house
and approached me. He moved with a surprising sense
of purpose to his uneven gait. I gagged at the sudden
smell of rotted eggs.

Not so very manlike as he seemed earlier, my host
mumbled and hissed as he lurched toward me. The
tom's growl turned into a back-arching yowl. His claws
tore into my ankles as my host reached for me. I
leaped back, away from the cat and the man-thing.
Water sloshed my skirts, the spitting cat, and the feet
of my host. A greenish fog erupted from the twisted
man's feet as he screamed.

The sound of pain and anger thundered in my ears.
I responded with an instinctive snarl of my own. A

fiery fury bloomed and burned hot and bright in my chest.

Bony fingers reached through the oddly glowing green fumes and snatched at me. I knocked the hand away with the bucket, the last of the water splashing out. A jabbering howl rewarded my ineffective strike, but I, for the life of me, could not tell if the sound came from my attacker, the cat, or my own throat. Not knowing completely why or how I knew, I understand that water hurt this fiend. In a frenzy, I flung the bucket back into the well and leaped onto the remaining board to avoid grasping hands.

Away from the man-beast, I could not mistake the stink of evil. It sickened me . . . like the evil that had haunted my village before Zorya took me. I retched at the smell.

Fire roiled within me, making it impossible to think. Anger smothered my fear and fueled my arms as I pulled the bucket once more from the depths of the well before the evil thing could recover.

I flung the contents of the bucket into the foggy plumes where the shrieks seemed loudest, then plunged the bucket back into the well intent upon continuing my watery defense. I nearly fell into the well when a cool hand gripped my own. Prepared to throw yet another bucket of water at my tormentor, I pivoted on the balls of my feet, still hunched, ready to strike this new opponent. Zorya's fierce gaze pierced my madness. I caught my breath.

"No time to stop, girl! That will only work for a short time and then what will you do?"

I shook my head and the fire within flickered at the sudden doubt. My mistress struck me across the cheek.

Angrily, I jumped down from the well and seized the broken handle of a pitchfork leaning against the wall. I turned to the witch still unsure what to do next.

The fiend's claws raked through my hair and tore

the shawl and blouse from my shoulders. Without thought, I lashed back with the shattered staff.

"It must be contained, girl! You cannot fight it that way!"

I spat furiously, jabbing at the mottled face with the staff. I glared at my teacher standing by the well. She raised not a single finger to aid me. She only told me what *not* to do! Damn her eyes!

Then I remembered. In these months she had taught me the sign, I used it sometimes without thought. How could I have forgotten now? I stabbed the earth near the fumes and carved a deep line. Dodging the clutching talons and flailing feet of the fiend, I cut an intersecting line. With each rut drawn in the dirt, the fire inside me sang. I drew the fifth line of my furrowed pentagram in the earth deep, dragging the shaft of the pitchfork between my legs, foolishly leaving one leg inside the containing symbol and the demon seized upon it.

I screamed, the cry drawn from me by the agony and smell of my own flesh being burned by the strange green flames and torn by the thing's claws. I kicked and lunged for the bucket, but the demon held me fast, the water just out of my reach. Green flames burst along the hem of my skirts and licked at me. I screamed and clawed at the bucket, cursing as my fingers grasped the edge and tipped it.

Water spilled out and flowed free and clean, spreading like a great wet blanket across the soil. It cascaded in a slowly seeping tide into my furrow and ran down first one line then into another and another. The beast howled as my pentagram was sealed by clear running water and as he twisted, searching for an escape, I plunged the jagged end of the handle upward into its eyes and rolled clear. It fell back screaming. Water flowed down the final line while I beat the foul-smell-

ing flames that consumed me. Shrieking filled my eras
as the darkness swallowed me.

I awoke to pain and a great weight upon my chest.
It took all of my strength to force open my eyes to
find the unblinking tom staring at me. He moved from
my chest and circled down into a comfortable ball in
the middle of my stomach.

A chair scraped across the rough-hewn dirt floor.
The witch sat, the beads and bells woven into her hair
jangled with her movements. With strong and steady
hands, she tipped my head and raised a cup of gruel
to my lips. When I was done, she set the cup aside.

Anger filled my first conscious thoughts. Her tender
care now seemed like a mockery. I waited, wondering
what words of apology she might offer.

"Do you know what you are, Valeska?"

My anger bloomed like a fire. "I suppose you do not
seek the obvious reply that I am a girl?" I snapped.

The shadow of a smile creased Zorya's nut brown
face. "What are you, girl?"

"Half-dead." I closed my eyes.

Her hand settled in the hollow beneath my breasts.
"Do you remember the battle?"

I grimaced. My legs and back ached with burns and
claw marks, but even without them . . . "I cannot
forget."

She seemed unconcerned by my tone. "You battled
bravely. Name what you fought."

"A demon." It came to me then, this lesson so long
in coming.

"And you?" she asked.

"I?" I swiveled my head, curious and scared. "Mistress, am I demon, too?"

She shrugged slightly. "They say that there is some
demon in those of us with the calling."

I struggled to keep my eyes open as a strange sense

of peace settled through me, banking that inner fire. It all seemed so simple suddenly. My questions faded . . . at least for now. "I am a demon hunter."

For once, my mistress seemed pleased as she pulled the blankets up to my chin. "With some training, girl, with some training."

NOR IRON BARS A CAGE

by Deborah Wheeler

Deborah says: "This story owes a special debt of gratitude to Charles Dickens and James Mason, who wrote and narrated an audio tape book of *A Tale Of Two Cities,* which I listened to on the long commute to work. As usual, once I started writing, the characters spoke to me about healing, friendship, courage, and the enduring human spirit, so I let them tell their own story."

Deborah Wheeler has written two science fiction novels, *Jaydium* and *Northlight,* both from DAW, as well as many short stories, which have appeared in most of the volumes of *Sword and Sorceress,* Darkover anthologies, *Star Wars: Tales From Jabba's Palace, MZB's Fantasy Magazine, The Magazine of Fantasy and Science Fiction,* and *Isaac Asimov's Science Fiction Magazine.* Her background includes over 20 years in kung fu san soo, being "fairy godmother" to a local elementary school library, and raising two remarkable and talented daughters. As we go to press, she is in the process of relocating from Los Angeles to Boulder Creek, CA, along with her younger daughter, since she much prefers redwood trees to freeways. Who doesn't?

Tax collection day dawned clear and bright over the walled city of Ghillensa. Farmers arrived even as the first light softened the ancient battlements; wooden gates swung open to admit a procession of ox-carts creaking under late summer's bounty, sacks of wheat and barley, tubs of pale-gold butter, sheaves of clover grass to keep cattle fat over the winter, bushels of carrots and cabbages, kegs of country ale. A market had set up in the shadow of the gray-walled Affliction Tower where it was said kings had gone in and never seen the sun again, until their ghosts wandered the endless corridors, so confused they did not know they had died. Others said there were no ghosts, only the endless, weary sighs of common criminals.

Tax collection day it was today, and Alaina bent over the slop pit behind her father's cloth shop, retching dryly. Nothing came up but acid. She knew better than to try even a mouthful of dry bread. Wiping her mouth on the back of one sleeve, she tucked the folds of her shawl into her wide belt, adjusted the money purse, and went back into the shop. The shop smelled of cedar incense, used to keep away moths. In the light from the mullioned front windows, bolts of blue and crimson cloth shone like jewels. As a child, she loved to bury her face in the fine wool, velvet, even brocade from far Eastern lands. How safe she had felt then, hidden.

A movement from the front of the shop startled her alert. A familiar shape stepped away from the shadows and became distinct.

"Come on then, my dearling."

Her father's teeth glinted, although the light came from behind him. He held the book of records close to his belly and pulled the door open for her. Walking past him into the bright, dusty street, she drew in a quick breath. The heat of the morning struck her in the face.

"You are too warmly dressed," her father said, as if he had forced her to display his wares and thus increase their value.

The tax collector and his scrawny assistant had, as usual, set up at a table in the market square, so that everyone could see that the King's law knew no favorites and all their neighbors paid their due. This early, the line was short; many were still abed or about their morning marketing. The plain wood table was covered only by a runner bearing the tax collector's sigil: a double-headed ax. Here Alaina's father set his record book and a common clay token used by even those who could not read or write. The book with its tiny looped inscriptions was proof of his own stature, his learning.

The tax collector, a squat, grizzled man in his age-stained tunic, glanced past the book as if it were no more than a speck of dust. He picked up the token, studied it with lower lip outthrust and eyes squinted. "Miles the Cloth Trader. Fourteen princes of silver."

Exactly, Alaina thought, the same as it had been for the past ten years, since her mother died and she had been the one to accompany him to the market square on tax days. Behind her, a piglet squealed in its cage. Someone hawked turnips in a loud, hoarse voice.

The collector placed a ten-prince weight on the scales, then added four singles. The weights were soft lead, grimed from much handling, but not so much that the stamp of the King's own treasurer, the likeness of a prince long dead, could not be clearly seen.

At her father's signal, Alaina took out the coin purse, double-layered leather carefully stitched in compartments, holding their hard-earned silver. Like traders' coins everywhere, some were small, some large, some round, some oval, even a few Markoni squares. One or two were not coins at all, but silver buttons, and the collector let those pass. Silver was silver.

As she placed the silver pieces, one by one, on the balance pan, Alaina rested her gaze on the weights, lowering her lids so that the image blurred. She felt the familiar, sickening sensation of moving closer and closer until she was inside the metal, she was the metal. Cold . . . Hard . . . Heavy . . .

She moved among the tiny metal-demons, felt them crowding in on her, throngs so many she could not count them, dancing to their silent music, whirling fast and faster . . .

Dance with us! Dance with us!

Yes, she thought, and felt the cold metal bubble of their delight. *Dance . . . Lighter . . .* She nudged the demons with that special sense, the one she must never let anyone know she had. Dancing faster now, and lighter, as if she were Earth itself longing for Heaven . . .

Lighter . . .

The pan bearing the weights lifted, swung up and down. The collector signaled her father to stop, plucked a small coin from the tray and handed it back, holding it between forefinger and thumb as if it might bite him. With his free hand, he waved them on.

For an instant, Alaina could not move. The feeling of oneness with the metal-demons ripped from her, leaving her senses raw and reeling. She swayed on her feet. Dimly, she felt her father's hand, hard as the lead and as cold, close around her arm. The tax collector might have glanced her way as they hurried past, although she could not be sure.

"What's wrong with you?" her father hissed, as soon as they were out of easy hearing. "Do you want to get caught? Do you know what they will do if they find out about you?"

Hanging, hair and nails pulled out by the roots, molten lead on her eyelids, skin flayed in strips and salt rubbed in . . . She could recite the words in her sleep, her father had said them so often.

Alaina didn't bother with an answer. She knew better. She steadied, but the old familiar feeling had wrapped her stomach in its viselike grip, as unrelenting as her father's grasp of her arm. *Don't be sick again,* she pleaded with herself.

He let her rest for a while in the back of the shop. She drank the thin, sour beer because she knew she must. Weakness would not spare her, would only make things worse. Finally, warmth spread from her belly and loosened her muscles. She could breathe again.

That afternoon, a lady and her retinue came in, not a real lady but a spice trader's wife, newly rich, but with ready money to spare and a taste for colorful gowns. The price of the fabrics would go far to replenish the coffers drained this morning. Yet Alaina knew it would not be enough to please her father.

For a while, Alaina lost herself in the choosing of the cloth for the lady's undergarments, chemises of smooth, tightly woven linen to lie against tender skin. She brought out bands of colorful embroidery, stiff with patterning of grapevine and peacock feathers, and tatted lace brought by barge and caravan from the far mountain kingdoms. Time stood still as the beautiful edging strips and fine cloth moved through her hands. At last, the lady sighed with contentment, looked toward the bustling street, and turned to go.

Her father bolted the door behind her, signaling that the day's business was done.

"You fool! You simpering, fainting fool! You could have given yourself away! And then where would I be without you?" He rubbed his hands together, soft merchant's hands. Alaina could not take her eyes off his hands. She wished she could cry, but found no tears waiting.

"Yet," his voice softened, crooning. "You did well. I'll wager your curse saved us five solid princes. I might not have to beat you after all."

She kept her eyes lowered, so he would not see the hope which always flared up when he said those words. Flared and died, this time like every other. Her vision went white and she sank to her knees, knowing there was no escape.

Pounding woke her, not the throbbing pain from her back and thighs, but waves of sound. She started to swing her legs over the side of the narrow trestle bed. A cry tightened around her throat. She quashed it, forced herself to move slowly. It was past dawn, so she must have slept, finally. She heard her father's snoring from the other side of the thin wall that marked off her tiny room.

"I'm on my way!" she called out.

She'd slept in her clothes last night, full skirt and long-sleeved blouse gathered high around the neck despite the day's heat. She knew from experience that was easier than having to put them on the next morning. Now she eased herself to sitting, shifted her weight forward, straightened up. The stairs were the hardest part. They always were.

"I'm coming!" she yelled as the pounding redoubled.

"We know you're in there! Open for the King's men!"

She flung open the shop door and let her face twist into a scowl, part genuine pain at the day's brightness. Two guards stood there, alike in blue-and-silver tunics, nondescript breeches, scuffed boots. One had a sword scar across one cheek.

"My father's still abed. What do you want?"

"You are Mistress Alaina, that stood with him at the tax collector yesterday."

"Yes, of course." Her impatience now gave way to dawning fear.

"Then it's you we want."

They took her, manacled her wrists together as if she were a common thief, would not let her stop to put on her boots so that she had only time to slip her feet into the wooden sandals she saved for muddy days. "Father!" she called, but before he could shuffle downstairs, cursing, the King's men had dragged her through the door and on to the street.

"What's going on? Where are you taking me?" She stumbled. Her neighbors stared. "I haven't done anything!"

Streets and facades blurred by, the faces of the curious, carts and strings of pennants above, smells of fresh-baked bread and overripe fruit, wet wool hanging to dry, boiled cabbage. The guards half-carried her the rest of the way to the King's Voice, court of the western part of the city. She had been to this building with its carved frontel once or twice before, always in her father's shadow.

Spectators jammed the courtroom, eager for amusement. The two King's men pushed Alaina forward. She looked around wildly, recognizing no one. A clerk bent over his desk with a stack of curling foolscap paper to one side, his pen scratching furiously. The tax collector's assistant stood to the side, along with a priest barely old enough to grow a beard. The Voice herself was an old woman with beetle-bright eyes and a mouth like a dried prune. She got up from her dark-wood chair, carved all around with bound demons and the saints who had bound them, and peered into Alaina's face.

Please, Alaina prayed, closing her eyes, *let me not go back.*

The Voice made a *h'rumping* sound as she lowered herself back into her chair. "Explain to me again how this child managed to cheat on her taxes."

My father's taxes. Her mouth would not move. Her throat closed up.

The tax collector's assistant said ponderously, as if that were the only speed he knew, "The cloth merchant was to have paid fourteen princes in silver. After he and his daughter left, I reweighed their portion and it came to only nine princes. She was the one who carried the purse and placed the silver on the scales."

The Voice peered at Alaina with those too-bright eyes for a moment before asking, "Is this true? Come on, girl. Speak up! Do you have anything to say for yourself before I sentence you?"

Words rushed to Alaina's mind, excuses, pleas for mercy—her father was poor, it had been a hard year, the prices of wool were so high, she hadn't meant to do wrong, she would never do it again—

Let me not go back . . .

They took her away with a word from the Voice and the pounding of the staff that sealed her fate to the King's word. To the Tower of Affliction they took her, in whose shadow she had lived her whole eighteen years.

In whose shadow, she thought as the doors clanged shut and the other prisoners, a wave of stinking, starving womanflesh, drew nigh to drown her, she would die.

That night, Alaina lay curled on the mat of straw in the farthest corner from the door, wishing she did not have to wake up ever again. *Let her sleep, poor child,* said the crone with more gaps than teeth and a welter of festering sores across her chest and back, and gestured to herself. *Soon enough she will come to this.*

But it was not day, not yet. Around her, sleepers sniffed and whimpered, coughed and snored, shifted on their thin pallets. Alaina pushed herself to sitting. Her wrists smarted where the manacles had torn her skin, and it would be several nights before she could lie on her back.

She thought of praying that she might die here, this night and in this place. But her prayers, said by moonlight or not, had never been answered before. There was no reason to think they would be now.

Without thinking, she let her senses wander until she touched the metal-demons in the lock. It was iron, not lead, and she liked its subtle liveliness. With her mind, she followed the shape of the lock. How easy it would be to slide this piece here, to lift this other one.

And where would she go, even if she passed this locked door and the next and the next? Back to her father? To starve on the street?

She stared at the beam of moonshine coming through the single narrow window. No light-demon dancing here, but only a silent song, waves of movement and delight. Exhaustion weighed her eyelids, leaving them heavier than any tax collector's weights. The light grew, reached for her, luminous and piercing like an angel's song. . . .

She awoke again to the clamor of her cellmates rising, complaining to themselves and each other about the hardness of the floor, the body lice, things she didn't understand. Thirst rasped along her throat, but her legs and back were less sore than the day before. Somehow, she found herself near the front of the throng as the guard passed a basket of bread and a bucket through the door and locked it fast. Alaina gathered up two chunks of bread, one in each hand, then backed off as the other women pressed forward, scrabbling for their share. She looked around, wondering how she was to drink.

"Here you are, dearie." The crone appeared at her elbow, holding out a battered tin cup. Alaina dropped one of the pieces of bread into the crone's hand and took the cup. "That's the way, that's the way."

Alaina realized as she scooped up the brackish water that without the exchange, the crone might have gotten only the hard crusts at the bottom of the basket. With friends, one might survive a long time here.

Alaina turned to find a place to sit and eat. She bumped into an older woman, a good head taller than she, with heavy shoulders and cropped pale-red hair jutting at all angles. The woman's face and most particularly her nose bore a ruddy tint.

"Give that here. I'm hungry."

Alaina handed over her chunk of bread without a blink; she had no appetite for the dry, musty stuff. But she hesitated to surrender the cup. She was so thirsty. The smell of the water rose and filled her head like perfume. She licked her lips. Then, without thinking, she lifted the cup and drank deeply. She heard gasps around her as she gulped. Someone jostled her, breaking her balance. She lowered the cup. Red-hair glowered at her and Alaina realized how much bigger and more powerful the other woman was. Strangely, she didn't care. What could the woman do to her that had not already been done?

Water had dribbled around the sides of the cup as Alaina drank, wetting her chin. Now she wiped the back of her free hand across her face.

"What's wrong with you, girl?" came a voice behind her. "That's Maryam The Sword! She'll beat the stuffing out of you!"

Maryam's eyes narrowed. Alaina could well believe the older woman had been a pirate, a soldier, a berserker. But still there was no fear in her; it had all been used up.

"You want water? Here it is!" She downed the rest of the cup over Maryam's head. A gasp rippled through the cell.

"Fight!" someone shrieked.

"Call the guards! She'll kill the child!"

Maryam shook her head, scattering droplets. Her

pale-red hair stood up in spikes, like a dozen devil's horns.

Do it, Alaina silently urged her. *End it.*

Somebody by the door was taking bets on how long the fight would last. A clatter down the corridor indicated the approach of the guards. Yet it seemed to Alaina that the cell, that all the world, held its breath.

Maryam leaned forward, scowling down at her. Alaina could feel the heat from the other woman's body on her own face. Suddenly, Maryam threw her head back and laughed.

"Ho ho, ho jo! A fearless one, this!" Still laughing, she turned away to her own pallet by the front wall. The others shrank back from her. She stretched out her legs and gestured at Alaina. "Come here, Little Dragon, and tell The Sword how you came to be in this vile place and who it is that beat you so."

Alaina, who had no idea what to do now that she was going to live, crouched beside Maryam. "How did you know . . ." she asked timidly. *About the beating?*

One glance at Maryam's eyes told her. *She knows what it feels like inside her own body. She knows how it is to wake the next morning, to be afraid to move, even to breathe. She knows the footsteps that come in the night.*

The gates to a flood she did not know existed opened inside Alaina. If she could have thrown herself into Maryam's arms and sobbed like a baby, she would have, but she sat, back straight and eyes level, as if they were the only two in the world, and told her story from the beginning, all except for her witch-sense and how her father forced her to use it. Her father's warnings still echoed in her heart, what became of witches.

When she got to the morning and the tax-collector, Maryam stopped her.

"In and out of these places I have been, more times than I can count, Little Dragon, and only one rule

have I ever kept. Whatever brought you here, or me,
or any of us, that we leave behind."

"Oh." Alaina saw that it didn't matter to this squat
ugly woman what she had done, what demons she
danced with or why, only who she was right now.

In the nights that followed, as she lay in her pallet
that was now next to Maryam's, Alaina sometimes
heard the swordswoman cry out in her sleep. A soft
cry, not enough to waken anyone else, yet it penetrated into the very marrow of Alaina's bones, where
her deepest nightmares hid. At first, Alaina covered
her ears with her hands and shivered until she sank
back into her own uneasy dreams.

One night, she could not shut out the sound, and
she could not bear to hear it. Demons not of metal
or of light but of pain, of wordless, endless pain, called
out to her. Their voices tore at her soul. Her vision
went white and she sank down among the demons,
opening herself to their claws and fangs, knowing
there was no escape.

Numb endurance was the best she could hope
for . . . or was it? Little demons they might be, little
motes of memory, edged like the sharpest knife, but
she had some power over demons. Did she dare use
it on another person and take the awful risk of being
recognized and called out for a witch? Yet did she
have a choice? Was it so wrong, so evil to want to
ease such terrible pain?

She reached out for them with her unnamable sense,
deep into the mind of her sleeping friend. They did
not dance, like Earth, nor did they sing, like light.
They collided with each other, swirling, tumbling,
shrieking in their own language.·

Alaina seemed now to be floating in their midst,
surrounded by the chaotic frenzy. They took no notice

of her, and she realized that the moment she feared them, they would rise up to drown her. She nudged them as lightly as she dared.

Dance. . . ?

The agitation intensified, whirling, twisting even more frantically now. She could almost see waves, ripples of something which was neither demon nor space between them. She saw it, in a moment's clear vision, like a river in which they struggled, lashed out as if shadow-boxing. Their passion whipped the waters into a foam, dark and poisonous. No, no dancing.

Alaina heard the whimpering again, somewhere beyond the raging, frothing seas of demons. She knew that sound, knew what it was like to long for sleep that never came, knew the pain that had no words. Gently, she reached out to the child beyond the demons, imagined pulling her into strong, safe arms.

"Rest now, my small one, my treasure." In her mind, she said the words she wished to hear a hundred times. She heard them in her mother's voice. *"Quietly, gently, rest . . ."*

As she spoke, the waves seethed less powerfully, as if calming slightly under her words.

"Quietly now . . . Gently now . . ."

She went on speaking in her mind, cradling the invisible child. Slowly, in groups and patches, the demons slowed their terrible whirling. The waters between them grew clear, waves becoming ripples, ripples becoming stillness. The voices of the demons faded, except where they blended into a rhythm which built and faded as smoothly as a song.

"Quietly now . . . Gently now . . . Rest now . . ."

She fell asleep, rocked in the comfort of her own words.

Movement woke her shortly before dawn. The slit of a window through which she had seen the moonlight on her first night in Affliction Tower now admitted the creamy glow of dawn. She sat up, rubbing tear-grimed eyes. Around her, sleepers lay in dreamless sleep. Maryam stood, facing the window, one hand clenched tight in a fist, the other covering it. She turned, bowed slightly to Alaina, and lowered her hands.

Pale eyes bored into Alaina's so that she wanted to look away, hide, but something in that searching gaze held her fast. Then Maryam nodded, as if satisfied, and the moment faded.

The guards came tramping down the corridor, four in formation and not one or two as usually came. In their footsteps, Alaina heard their numbers and their fear. The other women felt it, too, for they froze in their games of knucklebones and chance. Tin cups and dice disappeared. A few scuttled to the corners. Maryam, who had been standing in the exact center of the cell on one foot while breathing noisily and waving her arms in a complicated pattern, came to attention and turned to face the bars.

"Oh—ho—ho—" the crone cackled. "There'll be a hangin' sure enough this day."

"Quiet, old woman," Alaina snapped, and received an injured glare in return.

The guards arranged themselves, two on either side of the barred door, the other two a pace behind them. They looked more frightened than grim to Alaina, and it came to her, watching with curiosity as one guard took out a scroll and proceeded to read it, that these were no different from the two who had dragged her here. It was she who had changed.

"Maryam The Sword, accused mayhem and berserker, leman to the dead pirate Caribe, late of the King's Fifth Company of Swords, graced with the Rib-

bon of Fortitude and since disgraced by crimes against
God and His Majesty, stand forth!"

Maryam did not move. The guard looked up from
his text and squinted in her direction. "That *is* you,
isn't it?"

"All but the leman part," she answered equably.
"*That* I never was."

"You are to come with us," he said, still reading.
His comrade fumbled with the keys and finally got the
door open.

Alaina stood and watched, open-mouthed, as Maryam strode through without a backward glance. Behind her, one of the women muttered a prayer for the
dying and the lost. Alaina turned, eyes half-blind, to
find the crone holding out her hands.

"Ah, dearie, don't weep for that one. It's a better
world she's goin' to than she's ever known on this
side."

She's to be hanged—

"The only way out of here," some other woman
said. "Ten years and more I been, and never saw no
one walk to the gallows like that one."

"Aye and a raw lump she was, too," another
replied.

"You could see the death in her eyes, that one,
when she looked at you."

"She was kind enough to the child—"

"After she near to eaten her for breakfast!"

The voices went on, but the words brought Alaina
no more comfort than the bony arms around her
shoulders. The prison cell, which had become a sanctuary, in an instant turned desolate.

She cried herself to sleep that night, not caring who
heard, her fellow prisoners or the guards or her father
for all she cared, that night and the next and the next.
The demons whirled and the waters frothed, but they

could not touch her. Never again would they touch her.

I will die here, she thought numbly. *I will die alone.*

They came for her a fortnight later.

Down one corridor and then another, up a flight of stairs, a landing, then two, through more twists and turnings than a badly snarled loom, Alaina followed the pair of guards. They'd manacled her, the way she'd come here, and the chain jangled with her steps. She wished she'd had the courage to witch the locks, that first night in Affliction Tower, though that might have brought her a quicker death.

She found herself wishing that Maryam had said good-bye, even a turning of the head, a word or two.

Alaina had only a vague notion of where she was in the tower. By now, she could not have retraced her steps for any amount of princely silver. She assumed they would take her to the battlements, where she had seen the bodies of traitors swaying in the wind. Yet after ascending a flight of stone steps and then another, their path wound on the same level. Her eyes stung with the brightness of the day, crossing a courtyard where a pair of well-dressed ladies, probably noble prisoners, sat beneath a long-dead tree, bent over their needlework. Something within her stirred as the guards paused to unlock a barred gate and then a heavy wooden door.

A public flogging before they hanged her? She shivered with outrage. For the first time, she believed in her own innocence, knew in the very marrow of her bones that she had done nothing to deserve such a punishment.

There was no flogging pole, no stocks, no barrel for dousing. No gallows. Alaina saw only a few ordinary people looking curiously, not at her but at the guards, and a knot of fighting men in swords and leather vests.

Their loud, percussive voices rose above the noise of the street.

The guards removed Alaina's manacles. She wondered if she ought to be afraid. She could not understand what was happening. Was this some new form of torture? Her native wit urged silence.

They retreated through the open door, leaving her alone. A heavy hand gripped one shoulder from behind. She closed her eyes, steeling herself for the worst.

"Little Dragon!" Strong arms enveloped her, almost lifting her from her feet. She smelled newly polished leather, soap, steel oil.

Maryam set Alaina down, grinning. Alaina had mistaken her for one of the men with her pale-red hair hidden beneath a helmet that flourished a wildly crimson plume.

"What are you doing here?" Alaina blurted out. "You're dead!"

That brought a fresh round of laughter. "It matters not what Mar has done—"

"—merely opened up the bag of a windbag for the wind to come in!"

"—compared to what we might refuse to do the next time his Royal Backside gets himself in a mess," one of the men said.

"Blaw, now they're saying it was all a mistake!" the second of the three men said.

"And what are two less mouths to feed?" Maryam said, keeping one arm around Alaina's shoulders. "What think you of her, my mates?"

"Little Dragon indeed, to naysay you, hung over!" laughed the third.

"And you," Maryam turned to Alaina, "will you take the freedom of the streets or go with us to far Kurestan, where there is a king's son needs rescuing and many locks to be picked?"

Two thoughts warred for Alaina's attention, the first that Maryam had somehow contrived her release, that she was not to be executed after all, and the second—

She knows! She knows and she does not care!

"Little Dragon," Maryam said in a lowered voice. "Think you I would not know the touch of a healer's mind, I who have seen fields run red with blood, and darker things done when there is no moon? Think you I would not know the value of that gift, wedded to courage such as yours?"

For answer, Alaina slipped her thin small hand into Maryam's callused one and followed her into the bright, unforeseen day.

THE HAUNTING OF PRINCESS ELIZABETH

by Carrie Vaughn

Carrie is living *la vie bohème* in Boulder, Colorado, where she is pursuing a master's degree in English Literature at the University of Colorado. Her primary interests in that regard include Tudor poetry, Victorian literature, and cyberpunk. Someday, she will write a story containing all three topics.

In 1998, Carrie graduated from the Odyssey Writing Workshop, where she was known as the Queen of Copies and the Xena of Xerox. She won the 1994 *Military Lifestyle Magazine* fiction contest and has published several short stories and poems in small press magazines.

All her spare time and money go to her Appaloosa mare, Rosie.

Finally, Elizabeth's captors allowed her to walk from her chambers. Seventy feet along the leads to Beauchamp Tower. Turn. Seventy feet back to Bell Tower, and the whole time a guard walked in front of her, a guard walked behind, walking and turning. Not much of a walk, but at least there was a breeze outside.

Why did she need guards? She fumed quietly while her exterior displayed only gentility. Did they think she might fight her way free? A sickly thing like herself? Or that she might jump off the battlements and to her death in an effort to avoid the ax? They should know her better.

Seventy feet, only thirty paces, turn. This direction brought her in sight of the Green. The awful, bloody Green. She could make herself not look at the Green. Instead, she looked at the three figures standing with their backs to St. Peter's chapel, facing her.

No one else saw them; they were her visions alone. There was no doubt either that they were visions. One had joined her the first night in the Tower, having only died a fortnight before. Elizabeth knew Jane's form well; death had not changed her cousin's quiet, pensive mood. The middle figure, Katherine, had been with her for much longer, over ten years now, attempting to regard death with the carefree amusement with which she had approached life. She took it upon herself to make Elizabeth laugh when she was unhappy, which was often of late, and Katherine was finding it difficult to succeed in her self-appointed task.

Elizabeth could not remember when the first of the three had arrived, or the details of the manner of her death, although she heard tales and guessed much from the particulars of Katherine's end. Elizabeth remembered a woman's voice whispering lullabies to her after the nurse had snuffed the candles and gone to sleep. As a child she sat up in her bed and tried to touch the apparition. The figure of a slim woman, around thirty years of age, with rich brown hair and dark eyes, stepped away and put a finger over her lips. Silence, the ghost indicated. Even then Elizabeth was old enough to know that if she told anyone of the ghost, no one would believe her. Elizabeth remained silent through all the years when first Anne, then Katherine and finally Jane came to watch over her.

At the age of eight, Elizabeth saw Katherine alive for the last time. A great commotion, the result of some intrigue which Elizabeth did not pay attention to because there was always some intrigue or another in her father's court, rocked Hampton Court while her father attended chapel. Elizabeth was with him when screaming in the gallery outside disturbed the proceedings. The doors at the back of the chapel stood open. She could see into the gallery; Katherine ran toward the chapel, followed by guards.

"My lord! Let me speak, I beg you. He will hear me if you only let me pass!" Two more guards, previously hidden, stepped into the doorway to block her. Katherine pulled up to avoid capture, but they were already reaching for her, and she was surrounded. "Hear me, my lord Henry!"

She screamed again, forcing the priest to stop his sermon.

"No! Let go! Let me speak to him!"

Her desperation punctuated each word, the brocade of her gown swished and rustled around the guards' legs as they reached over the skirt's spread to grab hold of her arms. Katherine struggled with all her might—her very small might—to free herself and make for the chapel doors. All the while the guards drew her away, dragging her down the gallery.

Henry stared for a moment, after the hall was empty but while Katherine's sobs were still audible. The ruddy beard on his chin moved slightly as he pressed his lips into a frown. The screams became more distant, then disappeared.

A mass rustle broke the silence; the members of the congregation shifted as one entity, turning back to the priest, straightening and arranging themselves to appear normal, desperate to prove to their king that nothing at all was amiss. Henry also turned to the front and raised a finger to the priest, who resumed his recitation at the exact verse where he had left off, and his voice for the most part remained steady.

Only Elizabeth still craned her head over her shoulder, staring down the gallery where Katherine had been arrested and carried away. She also stole a glance at her father, Katherine's husband, who led everyone in behaving as though nothing had happened. Kat, Elizabeth's governess, put her hand on her shoulder and squeezed, reminding her to be respectful in God's house. Kat's hand trembled just a bit.

That was when Elizabeth first had the thought.

"I shall never marry," she mouthed the words, and if someone saw, she looked as though she prayed. The words became something of a prayer, a litany she repeated to herself over and over through the years as she thought of Katherine in the gallery, then saw the shade of Katherine standing beside Anne's spirit.

Insult followed insult. She was a traitor in the eyes of Gardiner, brought to the Tower by Traitors' Gate, guarded like a common thief, and interrogated. The "interviews" with Gardiner were frequent and useless. He and his Council asked the same questions, she gave them the same answers, and they still could not prove a link between her and Wyatt.

"You say, my lady, that you did not ever agree to marry his lordship Edward Courtenay?"

The very idea. "No, my lord," she answered calmly.

"You should know, my lady, that Thomas Wyatt has named you both as conspirators in his rebellion."

What was she to say to that? That she knew Wyatt by reputation only? That she had been careful to separate herself from him and his like to prevent this very misunderstanding. But their parents, his father and her mother, were rumored to have been lovers, so could they be any different? Supposedly Wyatt had written her letters about his march on London, asking for the support of her and Courtenay, but Gardiner had intercepted them all.

The true conspiracy lay far beyond Gardiner's reach, for the true conspiracy was Anne's. Her will kept her here beyond death, her will bent toward a single goal: to see Elizabeth named queen.

"You made plans to move your household to your estate at Donnington Castle. Was this in response to Wyatt's urgings, as exposed in this letter addressed to your ladyship?"

"I received no such letter."

"Then how do you explain the coincidence? My lady."

He was insufferable. "Might I not, my lords, go to my own houses at all times?" The lords' nervous shuffling as they ducked away from her glare gratified her. She knew what they saw in her: old King Harry's temper.

Lord Chancellor Gardiner looked imposing only because of the thick chains of office he wore over his ermine-trimmed robes. A determined set to his dark eyes gave no doubt that he was the grand manipulator, that he whispered into Mary's ears and those whispers became policy. Again and again he demanded that Elizabeth confess, beg the Queen for mercy, and Her Majesty would no doubt be merciful. No doubt, as merciful as she was to any proclaimed Protestant. Then his plans could continue unhindered, with his major barrier eradicated. Mary's hold on the throne was in danger as long as Elizabeth lived. But if there were no Elizabeth, another usurper would rise to take her place. She and Jane had other cousins.

Gardiner made his demands, but Elizabeth could not confess to what was not true. And if no one but God believed her, then God would be her final judge. A strength of determination that surprised even her made standing by her convictions easy.

Wyatt was executed. Courtenay was released and fled . . . to Belgium? Bavaria? No matter. Gardiner and the lords could find nothing to implicate her. Indeed, she was innocent, but it took months to convince them. Finally, they released her to the custody of Sir Henry Bedingfield, who carried her off to his estate in Oxfordshire. She left the Tower alive.

That pleased her ghosts immensely. "That would have been too much to bear, to have your body lodged next to mine in the floor of that accursed chapel," Anne muttered the night before their departure. "I'd have had to haunt this place until Judgment Day."

"Then why could you not do more for me? You have the power to appear before me after death, you claim to be here to protect me, but you could not keep me from that wretched place, from Gardiner's filthy claws!"

"You don't think the strength to withstand Gardiner came from my blood? My will?"

That fierce resolve that had flooded her spirit at Gardiner's accusations—Elizabeth had thought it was her father's blood. The implication of what Anne said unsettled her, made her rebel angrily. "Your blood has rotted away, and what good is your will!"

Elizabeth did not have to wonder what it would have been like to have a mother watching over her; the arguments she and Anne engaged in surpassed anything they might have experienced had she lived. Anne, a translucent form wearing a brown velvet dress twenty years out of fashion, stood calmly by the door, watching Elizabeth pace around the chamber like a caged cat; her escape from here could not come too soon. But during these debates Katherine and Jane disappeared, waiting until a more amenable atmosphere returned.

"There are limits, daughter. I cannot force your accession. It must look as though the natural sweep of history takes its course or I would not be allowed to protect you at all. There are enough voices clamoring for your death that to keep you from the Tower would make Mary look even more a fool than she already is. We tread a fine line between protecting you from suspicions of treason and raising suspicions of—sorcery."

Elizabeth's sharp mind took to task the middle of the statement. "Allowed to protect me—by whom?"

Anne smiled, lighting her dark eyes. The expression gave a hint as to the humor, the joy Anne must have showed in younger, happier days. "Ah, some mysteries must remain that, or you might lose your religion." It was a bad jest.

"So. The mysteries that lie beyond death would shake my faith."

"They might. Jane came with me, to help you keep your faith."

"And Katherine?"

"To help you keep hope."

Strange, Elizabeth thought, to have three failed queens as guardians, to ensure her own rise to the throne.

The journey to Oxfordshire taught Elizabeth something: the people did not like Mary. They did, however, like Elizabeth. Traveling by barge up the Thames, she was astounded by the crowds lining the shores of the river, cheering for their beloved Henry's daughter, the good daughter, not the Papist Mary. Elizabeth understood Gardiner's worries, then. There were those who would risk treason and the ax to pull Mary off the throne and place Elizabeth there instead. A great deal lay in having the affection of the people. Mary forgot or ignored that. Mary was her mother's daughter more than her father's. Unlike Elizabeth.

"You look so much like him it makes me ill." A year had passed since the time in the Tower; Elizabeth was deep into her captivity at Woodstock.

The house arrest frustrated Anne as much as it did Elizabeth; for the moment, they could do nothing but wait, wait for the next conspiracy to rise, the next tide of royal favor to turn. Anne could only use her powers of protection when she had an attack to defend against. For now, she could only keep Elizabeth company. Poor company, sometimes.

Ghosts had moods, Elizabeth discovered. She had a keen mind which, when it moved beyond the absurdity of actually seeing ghosts at all, studied them with a feline curiosity. Anne could have terrible moods, and Elizabeth almost sympathized with her father.

"Your hair, your nose, your very spirit, all his," Anne ranted in a steady, icy voice, pacing back and forth across the chamber. The movement annoyed Elizabeth, who in the end had as much of Anne's temper as Henry's.

"Do you see my father often? Might he also haunt the halls of Hampton?" she said conversationally, pushing her voice into the honeyed tenor used at Court for superficial conversation.

"He may be in Hell for all I care," Anne hissed.

"So, there is a Hell?" Elizabeth returned, slipping into yet another tone of voice, the one she would use when speaking Latin with her tutor, Roger Ascham. "Some Protestant philosophers have raised doubts."

Anne knew she was being teased, and by one of the few souls in the universe who could out-heckle her. "I'll not argue theology with you. Even in my position I know less of it than you would expect. Although we are both dead, I have not seen your cursed father. But why would I want to when I can look on you and see him?"

"My hands are yours, I think. I'm always told how very fine and graceful they are." Elizabeth set down her quill and raised her famous, lithe hands for the ghost to see.

Anne looked and gave a little huff. "Very graceful, indeed. Fine, indeed, for wielding a pen. What do you write now?"

Elizabeth sighed. Anne scoffed at books and pens. "A letter to the Queen."

"Another? May it do more good than the last. It couldn't do worse, I'm sure."

Anne taunted her, saying the letters never got to Mary, that Bedingfield carried them all to Gardiner and Mary never saw them. Bedingfield read them all, must as he provided the paper on which they were written. Anne's tongue, however insubstantial, had barbs to it.

"Mary is too old to have children and she knows it. She'll have no heirs, and this country will not suffer her ghastly Philip to stay on these shores once she's dead. Mary is sickly. She'll die soon, with no children. You will be queen, Bess, and that will be my revenge on Harry. On everyone who still calls me a witch."

Elizabeth had heard the stories for as long as she could remember, though she could not believe them and still hold any affection for Anne. But she wondered.

"Stories tell of witches coming back from the dead to seek revenge," she said, carefully watching Anne's response.

Anne laughed. "If you believe that, my dear, then you will have to live with the belief that you came to your throne by the powers of witchcraft." Elizabeth blushed, waiting for more of Anne's acid teasing. But her voice turned soft. "There are other powers than those of witches, Bess. Think of what is right, here."

Elizabeth thought of the throngs who wanted her as queen and was almost ashamed of the pride their adoration kindled in her. Shame, because it was not right to want to be queen, not when Mary legally preceded her in the succession, and it was surely wrong to wish Mary dead. Even if Elizabeth knew she would be a better queen than Mary.

"She is my sister," Elizabeth said. "Despite all, she is my sister."

"Half sister, mind you, by that cow of Aragon. No wonder she sympathizes with the Spaniards."

Elizabeth set down her pen again, then set her expression. "I am a loyal subject to my sister the Queen, and it is right I should beseech her for my freedom." It sounded haughty and false. Elizabeth herself did not believe the words.

"Such a fine queen she is, too, using her own subjects as firewood. You know the temperature of the air in some parts has risen perceptibly since she took the throne?"

Elizabeth felt an illness coming on. She thought she had finished with sickness, between the Tower and her implication in conspiracy after conspiracy, the suggestive accusations involving Tom Seymour, her brother Edward's death, Jane's execution, threats of assassins, the play-acting at court, the masks she put on and changed with alarming swiftness: chaste scholar, playful courtesan, dutiful subject, Protestant rebel. She lost herself in the politics of it.

The candle on her writing table hissed and died, extinguished by a draft. Lost in sudden darkness, she stopped writing. Her slim hands looked white as bone in the moonlight shining through the window. She'd been awake too long, late into the night. A hand, even paler than her own, reached over her shoulder and touched the wick. A spark flared from Anne's finger and the candle burned again.

Anne could light fires with a touch, but could not turn Mary's heart to forgiveness, could not dissipate the conspiracies Elizabeth aroused. Could not, because the legal heir to the throne always attracted schemes and plots. If it were otherwise, *that* would raise suspicions. *When I am queen, I will not name an heir.*

"You are deep in thought," Anne said, her voice calm, at odds with her earlier hostility. "Learning more lessons of politics?"

Elizabeth turned on her mother, glaring. "Can ghosts read minds as well?"

"Why? Are you trying to hide something from me?" She turned a sly smile. Elizabeth ducked her head, an uncharacteristic show of shyness. Anne continued, speaking a rare confession. "Can I read minds? Can I see into your heart? Can I see the future? Are there really fairies and have I seen them? What philosophers' questions have I found answers to since my death? Well. I can walk through walls and sink through floors. I can travel from here to Paris in the blink of an eye. I can light a candle. I can feed you the strength of my will, I can advise you, I can guard you from loneliness and despair, and if you have any doubt as to how powerful those enemies can be, watch your sister in a year or two, when her husband and all her friends have left her. If need be, I can keep poison from your food and knives from your heart. I have many powers as a ghost. But your mind is your own, Bess."

Elizabeth spoke, so softly she barely heard herself. "Sometimes I think that is all I have."

A small presence slipped beside the princess. Jane had been pale, ethereal in life. Death had not changed the complexion of her spirit. Wearing white, she knelt beside Elizabeth and gazed at her with washed-out eyes. The only color to her was her hair, reddish-gold, like Elizabeth's.

"Trust in God, cousin," Jane whispered. "Trust, and all will be well." Jane smiled thinly, mouselike, still a timid child though the light of heaven shone in her.

The pounding of Elizabeth's heart slowed, the pinched nerves in her body loosened. Perhaps ghosts could read minds. Or only some of them, like watchful

Jane. No matter. Elizabeth smiled at both spirits. She was grateful for the company.

Years passed. Captivity at Woodstock became captivity at Hampton. Then the captivity ended, officially, but a governor appointed by Mary and her Council kept watch. Bedingfield was replaced by Pope, she removed from Hampton to Hatfield. More conspiracies, and Elizabeth did not know which was worse, that Courtenay's name was again connected to her or that Philip of Spain turned his roving attention to her—under his wife Mary's very nose. Elizabeth weathered it all, only weakening to the point of utter despair once. Anne saved her.

Elizabeth's followers developed a plan for her to flee to France. England had become too dangerous, the voices calling for Elizabeth's death had not stilled. Perhaps she could find allies, backing in France, perhaps even from King Henry II himself. The French ambassador, De Noailles, had always believed that France would benefit by having Elizabeth on the throne, allied with them against Spain.

As if she could truly escape the conspiracies by simply fleeing across the Channel. But it was a thought. Perhaps even a good thought. Elizabeth had begun to believe that Philip would not give up the English crown, even if Mary died. He would make England a province of the Spanish Empire, and would not suffer her to live except as wife to a man of his choosing—perhaps even himself.

Her friend the Countess of Sussex made inquiries, visited De Noailles more than once, and urged Elizabeth to take this path, to seek safety in France. It would be so easy.

Her sitting room at Hatfield became a prison, although now Elizabeth was jailed by her health rather than by Gardiner. A small comfort. The dampness of winter had weakened her. She sat near the fire, bundled in furs, too disconcerted to read or stare at needlework, waiting for word about her escape.

It came one evening after supper. One of the housemaids curtsied at the door and showed in the Countess. She had not even removed her fur cloak before coming to see Elizabeth, and her face was still flushed from travel.

"My lady," she said breathlessly, curtsying low to the floor. "A coach is ready for you and your attendants."

Elizabeth pushed away her blankets to nod a perfunctory greeting at the Countess. The lady's apprehension surprised her and made her nervous. "Must we leave so soon?"

"Tonight, my lady, if we are to take advantage of the river's tide."

Had something happened to prompt this anxious message? Had Mary finally resolved to do away with her? Perhaps a new rebellion was afoot. Perhaps assassins. Ah, how these times made her imagination wander.

"My health is not so well. I would have time to recover and regain my strength for such a journey. Must we depart this very night?"

"The ambassador was most urgent. Circumstances alter so quickly and unexpectedly of late that he fears for your safety if you remain here."

Such a vague anxiety. The ambassador so wanted her to leave for France, sure that gathering support and forces would be easier there, no matter that she had so much support here. If there were another plot against her brewing—the Countess seemed to believe it, the way she clutched her cloak and glanced from the door to the window and back again.

Elizabeth pushed the blanket fully away and rose.

"Help me pack my few necessities. I trust servants will be allowed to follow with the bulk of my belongings?"

"Yes, my lady."

She packed lightly, as though for a day out and not a grand escape. Her cloak, some jewels. She called a servant and sent the Countess to see after the coach. Elizabeth was set to follow her immediately, but she stopped at the door to her chambers.

There Anne stood, shimmering, her face shining with fury.

"You shall not leave here, daughter!"

Anne had taken on substance. Her color had deepened. The sparks that flared around the edges of her form were bright as embers.

"I must," Elizabeth said. She held herself tall, forced herself to look the ghost in the eyes, no matter that those eyes were angry. Anne stood with her arms spread wide, blocking the doorway.

"Why?" Anne fairly shouted. "Because some French twit tells you that you must? There was a time when the English did not obey the commands of the French. The ambassador serves his own purposes by digging his claws into you!"

Ghosts were not real. They were figments of a disturbed imagination. Though if that were true, Elizabeth's imagination was quite agitated indeed, and had been for most of her life. Ghosts were creatures made of charged air. They had no matter to them. Elizabeth reflected upon this briefly before attempting to walk through the doorway, Anne or no Anne.

She could not, although she could not rightly say why she could not. She took one step, and something blocked her. Anne. A force emanated from her, something more than charged air. Air made strong enough that a full-grown woman could not pass through it. Elizabeth raised her hand, brushed her fingers back and forth in front of her. Her fingertips skittered off the surface of . . . something. Something hard, impenetrable, and invisible. She stared through it to Anne, who glared with fierce brightness.

"You shall be Queen of England, Bess, and you cannot be that in France."

"My lady, why do you stare so?" The Countess stood in the next room, gripping the edges of her cloak and worriedly watching Elizabeth. She could not see Anne, no matter how much her form glowed or how solid she appeared to Elizabeth. She only saw Elizabeth standing frozen, staring at nothing as intently as she might stare at death.

"My Lady Sussex, I cannot travel. You must deliver my apologies to the ambassador." She said the words in a firm, clear voice, and let her vision clear and go soft for a moment. The Countess would think it was only her imagination that she saw the princess so stricken a moment ago.

"My lady?" The Countess' voice went to a slightly higher pitch.

"I am not well enough to travel," Elizabeth said simply, then returned to her seat by the fire, gathering her furs from the floor. How that excuse had served her well over the years. Behind the form of Anne, Elizabeth could see Lady Sussex curtsy and scamper away.

Anne remained standing at the doorway, still shimmering, still keeping her arms spread to block the door, but her brilliance had faded somewhat.

Elizabeth learned within the week that a new ambassador had arrived to replace De Noailles. The new ambassador, the Bishop of Acqs, immediately sent Elizabeth an earnest message: Do not leave England if you aspire to its crown. If she left England, she might never return.

Anne saved the Crown for her, though whether she

saved Elizabeth or rather the instrument of her revenge only, Elizabeth could not tell and preferred not to make a distinction.

Mary became very ill. Suddenly, Elizabeth was important. Not as a traitor, not as a point from which to launch rebellions, but because all knew that she would next wear the Crown of England. Suddenly everyone, all the lords and nobles and hangers-on that had clung to Mary's court, all of them denounced Catholicism and professed Protestant beliefs, vacillating as they had done so many times before when it was expedient, and now they were Elizabeth's friends. She wanted to ask them where they had been when she was held prisoner in the Tower.

Elizabeth gathered her resources, locating her true friends and calling them to her service. She had chosen one of them to bring her news and proof of Mary's death, which had not happened yet, but Elizabeth had already finished mourning it. Soon there would be no time.

All that remained was the waiting. The dead queens waited with her.

"Has it happened yet?" Katherine was like a child waiting for the return of the season's first hunt. She went to the window one evening, then ran to the sitting room where Elizabeth read and Anne and Jane stood somber watch, then ran back to the window. Ghosts were made of air, insubstantial and not bound by time or space. Elizabeth had seen them wink in and out of existence like candle flames when they chose. If Katherine truly wanted to know, she could transport herself to London in a flash, right to Mary's deathbed, and return in the next instant to bring them the news. But Katherine enjoyed Events. She enjoyed anticipation, suspense, drama. Elizabeth remembered the episode in the gallery at Hampton Court, seventeen years gone now; Katherine was, if nothing else, theatrical.

"Throckmorton will bring news, Katherine," Anne said curtly. "Be still before you drive us all mad."

Anne and Jane also did not fly to London and back for news. They preferred to keep watch over Elizabeth. Elizabeth herself was silent, lost in thoughts which she could not recognize clearly. She held a book in her lap, but she had not paid attention to its identity when she picked it up. She had merely wanted something to look at, and it was too dark for embroidery.

She studied it now, ignoring Katherine's fevered pacing and Anne's and Jane's lurking presences. It was a handwritten rather than a printed volume. Different hands had copied favorite poems in the pages as the book passed from person to person. They were courtly verses of love and heartbreak, composed in the Italian style, some of them direct translations of Petrarch and the like, a few in the original Italian or Latin. The scribes seldom recorded the names of the poems' authors, but on one page there was a name below a sonnet: Sir Th. Wyatt.

For a moment the name struck her cold. But then she remembered. This was the elder Thomas Wyatt, her father's courtier.

As though reading her mind—ah, but ghosts could not read minds—Anne appeared beside her chair and read the page over her shoulder.

Anne said, "Dear Thomas. I remember his verses, his rich, self-pitying verses. He courted me once, did dear old Tom."

"Whoso list to hunt, I know where is an hind, but as for me, alas, I may no more. The vain travail hath wearied me so sore I am of them that farthest cometh behind," Elizabeth read solemnly.

Anne smiled all the wider. "He never caught me."

"I think I see him! A rider up the way! Oh, see

how his mount's hooves fly! A rider, come from London!" The shade of Katherine rushed into the room,
grinning, as flushed as a being made of air may look.
The others stared at her, and she ran back to the
window. Elizabeth saw her shoulders slump. "Oh, it's
not him. I think it's one of Lord Cecil's men. Oh,
bother."

"She is truly maddening, isn't she?" Elizabeth said.

"Poor Kat. Too much excitement always set her off.
She played Harry's game even more poorly than I
did," Anne said wryly. "And I had thought it were
not possible."

Elizabeth thought of all the times she would have
been alone were it not for the ghosts: this time of
waiting, the Tower, the time after Edward was born
and she was forgotten by the Court. Many pitied her
because they thought she had grown up motherless.

The night wore on. Still no news. Elizabeth drifted
to sleep, her ghosts drifted away. She wished she
would dream. Dreams sometimes revealed omens,
which Elizabeth desperately wanted—no matter that
omens may be heretical. Her thoughts often lingered
on heretical bents, by both Catholic and Protestant
standards, of late. Like the thought that religion was
not all-important, that a monarch sometimes had more
consequential matters to dwell upon. Religion might
very well be the soul of a nation, but a soul did little
good without a healthy body in which to reside. When
one saw ghosts, lived with them for twenty years, what
was heretical and what was not became confused. She
could very well expect omens in her dreams.

Omens, or poetry. Anne's voice again, her ubiqui-
tous voice which spoke of revenge, of hate for Harry,
of the mysteries of the spirit world . . . or sometimes
her voice laden with affection: "A poet will write these
words someday, '*She shall be an aged princess; many
days shall see her, and yet no day without a deed to*

crown it.' And another poet will call you 'greatest Gloriana.' There, a small gift of prophecy from a dead witch. You shall be Queen, my Bess, and a better monarch than your father."

Elizabeth walked the next afternoon. Open air had always done her good, especially during these nervous times. She could walk and know that if nothing else, she had the power of her own two legs to support her. Her ghosts preferred candlelight in which to lurk—or perhaps they knew that this was her hour. Then Elizabeth realized they would not be with her forever; they'd leave her when their work was done. So they were not with her when the lords of Mary's Council arrived in the park on horseback in a grand procession. These men who had accused her of treason and held her in the Tower six years before, these men dismounted, knelt on the ground before her, and called her Queen. She scarcely knew what to say.

Less than two weeks later she arrived in London to take possession of the Tower. In all that time she had not seen Anne, Katherine, or Jane, but she felt their presences very strongly now, here, at the site of their deaths. The cheering, the salute of gunfire for her, had not stopped since she entered the city. But all fell quiet now, at least to her.

She went to the Bell Tower, flanked by attendants and lords who beseeched her to come with them to the royal chambers in the White Tower. But no, she wanted to see. She climbed the stairs and looked out the window of the room where she had been a prisoner. Opening the door, she stepped out onto the leads and took a short walk. Just enough to see the Green and the site of the executions.

The ghosts stood there, Anne, Katherine, and Jane, more clearly defined than she had ever seen them. Sunlight caught the auburn highlights in Anne's hair. Even Jane wore a smile on her lips.

One by one, they turned and made their way into St. Peter's chapel. Jane first, then Katherine. They faded from view as they crossed the threshold. Anne went last, and she turned back to Elizabeth, touching her hand to her mouth and raising it to wave good-bye before disappearing forever.

Elizabeth started to wave back, then remembered the attendants standing nearby, the ones who could not see the three women disappearing into the chapel. But Elizabeth could not hide the smile on her face. Those who noticed it said only that she was a gracious queen, often merry with those around her.

SHADOW SOUL

by Laura J. Underwood

Other than the fact that the number of short stories sold keeps growing (thirty to date) Laura J. Underwood's bio remains pretty much the same. Her work has been featured in such publications as *Marion Zimmer Bradley's Fantasy Magazine, Bonetree, New Millennium Writings, Vampire Dan's Story Emporium,* and a number of anthologies (to name a few). She's still a librarian, a hiker, an artist, and a fair harpist whose fields of interest range from history and archaeology to fencing and folklore, and an active member of the Science Fiction and Fantasy Writers of America (SFWA). While her beloved Cairn Terrier Rowdy Lass is no longer with her, she finds her work just as frequently disrupted by a cat of very little brain named Gato Bobo whose paws are reaching under the closed bedroom door even as she writes this.

I believe that "Gato Bobo" is Spanish for "stupid cat"—they all are, more or less. So why do writers want cats? I think there is a book there: *Fantasy Writers and the Cats Who Love/Hate Them*. Maybe somebody will write it.

"**Y**ou know, they say dogs can see ghosts and demons," Manus MacGreeley wind-whispered into Ginny Ni Cooley's ear.

Ginny ignored the mageborn spirit hovering over the bow, and kept her gaze fixed on the reluctant little oarsman who was rowing her across Loch Craddie to the ancient crannog at its misty heart. Malloch was his name, and Ginny had never met a surlier man. Oh, he had taken young Alan MacFarr's gold readily enough and offered to row her where she pleased, but as soon as he learned their actual destination, his manner quickly changed.

"I'll not go to the demon's den!" he argued straight away.

"Oh, then you'll be giving *back* Master MacFarr's gold sgillinns, will you?" she said with a pointed glower.

Malloch went sullen over the suggestion and took his place at the oars. And granted, Ginny had no more love of this quest than he, but after all, she had given her word to young Alan to set the matter right, and bring back the shadow soul of his bride.

A foolish gesture, she scolded herself.

"Then ye should not have gone to Conorscroft to trade eggs for milk," Manus teased. He made faces at the back of Malloch's head as he floated behind the little man whose arms were straining against the oars each time they dipped into the water.

Ginny bit her tongue. That was Thistle's fault. The Moor Terrier had seen a squirrel in her window and lunged for it with a mad spate of barking. Unfortunately, his wild path took him straight into the pail of milk from which Ginny had planned to skim the cream. The milk went everywhere, forcing her to vent her anger through a stream of unsavory words while she cleaned up the mess. She had no cow of her own, and was forced to gather eggs and take her bucket to the village in hopes of a trade.

What she found in progress was a wedding feast. Young Alan had recently inherited a croft of his own, and once he became a man of property, he began to look for a bride. Alas, most of the available lasses in Conorscroft were far too young for his fancy, so he sought a bride elsewhere, and found her in the likes of Mary Ni Bracken from Glen Craddie.

The shy bride looked beautiful, sitting on the marriage pavilion before the villagers who danced and drank in earnest to her health, long life, and blessed union. As soon as Ginny arrived, she sensed that something was amiss, and it wasn't long before that reason revealed itself. Among the guests was a lass Ginny had never seen before, and since she stayed around the dais and spoke frequently with Mary, Ginny assumed the two were old friends. Not quite so, she quickly noted when a ray of sunlight glinted off the silver face of a mirror the girl held in her hand . . . a mirror she raised slowly for Mary to see.

At once, screams broke the revels. Ginny turned toward the source of the commotion with a gasp. A dark cloud began to unfold in the midst of the guests and spread a shadow that blotted out the sun. Demon essence assailed Ginny's senses as the creature flitted straight over to the bridal platform. The second girl turned with a shriek and dropped the mirror, which the demon seized in one claw. Argent eyes glittered as brightly as the rows of fangs revealed by its malicious grin.

Ginny rushed toward the dais in vain. With so many bodies fleeing like sheep before a wolf, she could not get clear enough to throw a magebolt, and white fire would have hurt the bride who sat as still as stone. The demon quickly spun its dark self into nothing and magically gated away. And the girl on the dais started to run, so Ginny shouted, "Stop her!"

A merry chase ensued. Young Alan himself brought the lass down. He pinned her to the ground and screamed, "Why, Shona, why?"

"Because you were meant to be mine!" Shona wailed in reply. "And now that the demon has Mary's shadow soul, you are free to marry me!"

Ginny quickly pushed herself through the gathering crowd and knelt beside the pair. Already, she heard mutters from the locals. The mageborn had arrived and would deal with this matter. Ginny ignored them, touching the lass with mage senses. There was no hint of power in the girl who ceased her struggles at the sight of a mageborn.

"Where did you get that shadow mirror?" Ginny asked.

At first, Shona refused to respond, but when Ginny let it be known that she would do nothing to stop the hanging that the local villagers were shouting for now, Shona pondered the question more carefully. "From old Bothy of Craddie Wood," she said faintly.

"And what did you offer him in trade?"

Shona hesitated. "My first-born child," she whispered.

The villagers hauled her away to punish her after that, but Ginny needed to hear no more. Old Bothy was a bloodmage for whom the description "inept" was a kindness. He had managed to ruin more than one of his own spells before, and was more buffoon than master of magic. In fact, the only reason Ginny had not bothered to report him to the Council of Mageborn, who were determined to eliminate all his kind, was that Bothy presented very little danger to anyone other than himself . . . at least, until now. Ginny suspected he had come across the shadow mirror by sheer luck rather than skill. She had also heard of the shadow demon that once dwelled at the heart of Loch Craddie beyond Glen Craddie and the woods that Bothy called home, and before yesterday, she thought it little more than a granny tale she learned from her own mother. According to the story, it was imprisoned long before the Great Cataclysm and of no danger to anyone.

If Bothy had truly found the creature and set it free, Ginny would have to report him to the Council of Mageborn in Caer Keltora for causing such chaos, but first, she had to deal with the demon. Without a shadow soul, poor Mary would wither and die, and all the True Healers in Ard-Taebh couldn't stop that.

So, in spite of her better judgment, Ginny had offered young Alan her skills, which was why she was now risking death by drowning in the company of the cranky little oarsman who could have easily passed for a bogie, what with his outsized head, thick shoulders, and greasy mat of hair under a ragged tam.

Malloch shifted to capsize the boat, still determined to escape this chore. Ginny seized the sides and glowered.

"Try that again, and I'll burn you with mage fire and let little Thistle gnaw your blackened bones!" she said.

A lie, of course. She would never take the life of another except to defend herself. Only bloodmages like Bothy had no regard for life, and used its essence to feed their power. Of course, she would never have told Malloch this. If she could, she would have *gated* herself across to the crannog, for the small craft leaping through the choppy water was leaving her stomach a bit queasy. Unfortunately, Manus had died before he could teach her the spell, and it was one of such complexity, it could not be learned by merely reading its words from a book like some of the lesser spells. The frustration of it all made her hope there would be some opportunity for Thistle to bite Malloch, which would, in her opinion, serve the little man right.

Malloch muttered a litany under his breath with each stroke. "Fool quest," he said darkly. "The shadow demon will have all our souls, you mark my words."

Ginny ignored him, her gaze falling on the faint silhouette of the crannog now growing visible through the drapery of fog. Ruins greeted her gaze, tumbling walls and a crumbling tower all looking like broken

black teeth against the filmy gray-white. She stretched
mage senses, and was immediately burned by the raw
acid of the shadow demon's essence.

"It's there," she said, more to Manus than Malloch,
but the little man made warding signs. No hint of
Bothy, she noticed. She had stopped by his cottage,
intent upon dragging him along by one ear and forcing
him to undo the mess he'd caused. He had not been
home, and the folk in Glen Craddie admitted they
hadn't seen Bothy in at least a fortnight. Probably for
the better. If she met him now, she would be more
likely to feed *his* blackened bones to the Moor Terrier
sitting beside her wagging his tail and forcing her to
keep a tight hold on him lest he throw himself into
the water for sport.

"I'll go no closer!" the oarsman said sharply.

Ginny fixed him with a glower and raised her other
hand. *"Loisg,"* she said, white fire filling her palm.

Malloch's eyes widened and his strokes increased to
quickly pilot them toward the shore. There was but
one place to dock, steps and a platform carved into
the face of the crannog long before the Great Cataclysm left it in ruins. Malloch rowed straight at it as
though he'd been here many times. He seized the
ledge and steadied the craft, then with a cross look,
he ordered Ginny out.

Naturally, she suspected his plan was to desert her
the moment she was on shore, so as she scrambled
onto solid ground, she pulled essence from the water
to feed a spell and whispered the words of a binding in
the mageborn tongue. Her caution proved well placed.
Once she and the Moor Terrier were ashore, Malloch
seized up his oars and tried to push off. To his chagrin,
he quickly learned his little boat was stuck fast, for it
held its place against the stone and refused to budge.
Frantic eyes rose to meet Ginny's coy smile.

"I'll be back as soon as I'm done, and then we can

both go back to the mainland," she said. "You'd best stay put until I return. No telling what might be living wild on this island."

She heard him muttering all manner of curses at her back as she clambered up the stone stairs. Thistle had already made the top, and when Ginny reached the summit, she found Manus waiting there as well. The mageborn spirit scanned the horizon with a frown.

" 'Tis not a cheerful place," he quipped.

"Demon lairs never are," she said.

"Wonder how auld Bothy got that shadow mirror away from the beastie," Manus said.

"Who cares?" Ginny replied, starting toward an opening in the outer wall of the crannog and making for the tower at its center. "Let's find the shadow mirror and get out of here."

"Easier wanted than gained," he muttered and followed. "A shadow demon feeds on shadow souls. It's not likely to give up a tasty soul like poor Mary's without a fight."

Ginny nodded, stopping just at the edge of the square tower. A small number of steps led to the door at its base which stood open like a gaping hole. The wood and iron that once kept out the drafts had long ago disappeared. She approached it with ample caution, letting mage senses touch the opening.

"Did ye remember to bring the mirrors?" Manus asked.

Ginny reached into her belt pouch and drew forth two palm-sized ovals of silver glass. In life, Manus used them for scrying. At his suggestion, Ginny had marked them with glyphs of enchantment. She intended to capture the demon's essence between them, then bind them together and bury them in a safe place. At least, she hoped it would work.

"Whatever you do, don't look into its eyes," he said. "Otherwise, it's likely to claim your shadow soul."

Ginny took a glance at her own reflection in the little mirrors. Brown and small like a wren was how she had always described herself, with her darker locks and sparrow eyes set in fey features. Now she looked at her own shadow soul, the reflection that stared back from the glass and sighed. "I will remember," she assured him, putting the mirrors away. Calling *"Solus,"* she sent a ball of mage light rolling into the opening. So far, no sign of the shadow demon in that bright light. It did prefer corners akin to its name. She stepped into the gap herself and looked around at the decay.

At once, she was confronted by stairs going up and more going down. The latter was a likely place for the creature to lair. She pushed the orb of mage light in that direction and followed. Thistle, however, balked and growled, the hairs on his back going stiff.

"Oh, wheesht," Ginny said. "Stay behind, then."

The Moor Terrier backed away as Ginny started down the stairs. Then, he followed, apparently unwilling to leave her side. Questioning why he should show such loyalty at this moment, she caught a movement at the edge of her light and heard the chuckle of a stoat surprised as it hunted mice. The weasel-like creature turned and lunged down the stairs, and Thistle, with a grand bay, bolted after the fleeing beast. Before Ginny could catch him, he disappeared into the dark.

"Horns!" she hissed. So much for subtlety.

"Thistle! Wheesht!" Manus shouted for all the good it served. Thistle was on the hunt and far too excited by the close proximity of his prey to obey.

"Terriers," Ginny muttered as she pushed the light after him and rushed down the spiral of stairs.

As Ginny reached the last step, she saw Thistle plunge into a short corridor. She bolted its length, then froze as her mage light revealed a large storage chamber and the glitter of many mirrors scattered about her.

"By the Silver Wheel of the Lady," she whispered, sending mage senses scrying the world around her to see if there was a danger present. No sign of the demon, but then, its essence permeated so much of this place, she realized it was hard to be sure. Some of the mirrors caught her mage light and bounced back, but not all the mirrors reflected light. In fact, most of them had a sort of pitch to their depths as though they absorbed the light instead. Thistle sat scratching his ear. Of the stoat, there was no sign.

The Moor Terrier was the least of Ginny's interest. Across the chamber stood a mirror as tall as a man, wrought around with an ornate frame of dark wood. Behind its glassy surface, she saw the familiar figure of Bothy. He was sitting on a wooden stool beside a small table of stone. The feeble glimmer of mage light cast its greenish glow about him. His head was in his hands.

"Bothy?" Ginny said.

Her call got his immediate attention. A long, haggard face with more nose than was attractive came up out of the stringy hands. Wisps of faded gold hair fluttered about his face. His eyes were pale and watery, and from the deep rings under them, he looked as though he were being drained.

"Bothy, what in the name of Cernunnos are you doing in there?" she said.

"Ginny?" he said and rose, staggering weakly over to the glass. He put his hands against the surface. "I thought no one would ever find me. . . ."

"How long have you been in here?"

"Nearly a fortnight, I think . . . I've lost track of time."

"And just how did you get in there?"

"The shadow demon put me here," Bothy said. "That foul creature tricked me!"

"Then this is just your shadow soul?" she said.

"Oh, no, lass," Manus said and pointed to the runes decorating the wooden frame. Meticulous, they were, entwined in knotwork patterns of confusion. He followed them with the fascination of a child presented with a new toy. "This is no shadow mirror. This was wrought by mageborn hands."

"Oh, yes," Bothy said. "It's a very interesting tale, and I shall be delighted to share it with you once you get me out of here."

"And how am I supposed to do that?" she insisted.

"Well, if you touch each side of the frame and look into the glass and imagine that it is a door . . ."

"I wouldn't try that," Manus said with a sharp glance in her direction.

"Why not?" she asked.

"Because Bothy will be out here, and you'll be in there," Manus said.

"She will not!" Bothy retorted.

"Aye, she will. That's how the demon trapped you, isn't it, Bothy?" Manus said with a smile that twinkled with mischief.

Bothy heaved a long suffering sigh as Ginny crossed her arms. "You were going to let me take your place?" she said. "Trap me in this thing?"

"Well, I wouldn't be a proper bloodmage if I didn't try," he replied with a sniff.

"So just what are you doing in there?" Ginny insisted.

Bothy rolled his eyes and fetched his stool, sitting on it to face her. "About a fortnight ago, a lass came to me and asked for a curse to stop a wedding."

"Shona, by any chance?"

"Well, we never actually got introduced. Anyway, I've been in and out of these ruins for years, and I had found the shadow mirror just lying about . . . as you can see there are more than enough of them to spare, and I'd never actually seen anyone claim them. So I gave it to the girl and told her how it worked . . ."

"And in exchange, she promised you a first-born child?" Ginny said. "How could you?"

"She didn't have any gold to pay me, and it seemed a fair price. I knew that I could always find more mirrors, so after she left, I came back here to fetch another. This keep once belonged to a great mage back before the Great Cataclysm, a Dark One, I think by some of the things I found. Anyway, I came looking to collect a mirror, but when I picked it up, this voice whispered to me from the corner. Offered me riches if I would help it . . ."

Ginny shook her head.

"I found this mirror hidden by an illusion of shadows. Knew right away that it was more valuable than anything else in this place, for I could see the shadow demon in it. He told me his master imprisoned him there as punishment centuries ago, and that if I would set him free, he would obey me and tell me all the secrets of demon power. I would be invincible."

"And you fell for it," Manus said and shook his head. "Greed's been the waste of many a man."

Bothy sneered at the mageborn spirit. "The demon told me there was power in the mirror, and that all I had to do was lay my hands on the matched patterns to either side and close my eyes and imagine the door opening. The next thing I knew, I was in here, he was out there, and since that day, he's been feeding on my mage essence, slowly draining me as he does the shadow souls of those he captures in his mirrors. So what brought you two here?"

"Shona used the mirror to steal the shadow soul of Alan MacFarr's new bride, a lass named Mary, and I've come to fetch it back before she dies," Ginny said. "You wouldn't happen to know where he put it, would you?"

Bothy made a face. "Well, he did come back clutching a mirror, and I seem to recall that he placed it somewhere over there. If you get me out of here, I'll help you look for it."

"I think not," Ginny said and started for the corner, pushing mage light along. The tickle of the power she used to maintain it, along with the glare from various bits of glass, was starting to give her a slight headache, but she was determined to find Mary's shadow soul and leave this place.

But even as Ginny reached for the first bit of glass to examine it, she heard Thistle bark and Manus shout. The burn of demon essence suddenly swelled much sharper than before. Ginny turned with a gasp.

A shadow detached itself from those ranging above and glided into solid form just two arms' lengths from Ginny. She quickly reached for the two mirrors she had brought and drew them forth. Not daring to look up, she used one of them to watch the creature that reared over her, eyes glittering like broken glass in the sun.

"Who dares steal my shadow souls?" he hissed.

"I have come to retrieve the soul of Mary Ni Bracken," Ginny said, averting her gaze from those glittering eyes in the reflection of the glass and concentrating on watching the creature's lower limbs for a sign of its intentions. It stood between her and the mage light, casting a shadow over her. She would need more light if she were to trap it.

The shadow demon laughed, its voice the tinkle of glass chimes. "And what would you trade me for such a fine prize, mageborn?" it said.

"Your life," Ginny replied.

A dark claw raked at her. She ducked back, nearly tripping over the stacks of mirrors about her feet. "If

I were you, mageborn, I would fear for my own," it said.

The shadow demon spread itself like a blanket, threatening to fold over her and smother her. Ginny crouched, pulling essence from herself and throwing it out in the form of white fire as she shouted *"Loisg!"* The shadow demon screeched and jerked away, dissipating like a fog. Ginny quickly turned to glance at the shadow mirrors, seeking one with Mary Ni Bracken's reflection among those still bouncing light back at her. There were faces here, folks she did not know and who looked by her judgment beyond her skill to save. She turned over mirror after mirror in a frantic search. The white fire might have dissipated the shadow demon for the moment, but it would soon get itself back together. Even now, she could sense the gathering of that essence filling the air with its acrid burn.

A mirror that looked more familiar suddenly flashed into view. Ginny seized it up and looked into it. The frantic face of Alan MacFarr's young bride looked back. With a whisper of thanks to the Lady of the Silver Wheel who watched over all mageborn, Ginny tucked the bit of glass into her pouch.

"Ginny!" Manus shouted, and she sensed him rushing toward her from across the room. But she also felt the shadow demon regain its form, and knew it had succeeded when a talon seized her arm and jerked her around.

"It's not so simple as that, mageborn," the creature hissed, sounding like claws raking across a window pane. The noise alone was enough to still her breath with fear.

His other talon caught her chin and sought to draw her face up so she would have to look at him. Ginny closed her eyes, hands scrabbling in her pouch for the spare mirrors. She smelled the fetid breath and heard Manus shouting in rage. But he was spirit and could do nothing to assist her now. She was on her own. Even having little Thistle lunge at the demon and try to bite it would serve little purpose, for the creature was able to turn any part of itself to mist at will.

The talons deserted her chin and arm and seized her around the middle. She was hoisted into the air like a child's moppet. Ginny kept her eyes closed and hissed, *"Adhar buail!"* A wild gesture, she realized, since she could not aim with her eyes closed, but the strength of hardened air did buffet the demon well enough to knock it off balance. It let go of her, and she fell, landing on her feet only to stagger. Still, that was all she needed. She raced toward the mirror housing Bothy, desperate to end the threat.

"Not so fast!" the demon snapped and its form misted before her, blocking her from the large mirror. Ginny stopped and held forth the small mirrors, one in each hand. She kept her eyes open now, holding the twin glasses so they caught the demon's attention. It froze, fascinated with the glamourie calling it from the bits of glass. Reflected in each one was its own image, and that of the wood-frame mirror to its back. She glanced at Manus, hoping he saw her intentions and was rewarded with his smile.

"Down a little, lass," Manus whispered. She shifted her hands in response. The demon moved with the glass, caught in its own gaze.

"Take what is yours," she said softly.

Drawn to the bait, the demon reached for the magical bits of glass. Ginny felt the glyphs she had traced on each one grow warm. The demon touched the surfaces in an almost loving fashion, and Ginny imagined a door opening. . . .

There was a scream of outrage when the shadow demon suddenly realized it had been deceived into touching the reflection of the large mirror's magical binding runes, but it could not draw free of the mirrors in Ginny's hands. Though the noise of its cries ripped into her, she called a bright ball of mage fire between them. Then she pushed the creature with the flames she knew it could not bear to touch, forcing it back and following to maintain the contact, and, for just a moment, allowed herself a pointed glance at Bothy. He seemed to realize what she had done and with a grin, he touched the wooden frame from within the mirror that imprisoned him.

There was a flash of darkness as the demon was drawn into the surface of the large glass. It shrieked as the mirror absorbed its shape, drawing it into the prison just as Bothy fell through to his freedom. The demon's last wail tore at Ginny, but she had more important concerns—like the groping hands of the bloodmage who managed to tumble right into her arms. With a yelp, she jerked back, letting him drop to the floor where he landed with a resounding thwack. Bothy yelled and grabbed his nose.

Ginny sank to the ground, her strength nearly spent. If Bothy chose to attack her now and steal her essence, she would have been helpless to stop him.

Instead, he sat up, clutching his nose and struggling to find a bit of cloth to staunch the crimson flow that dribbled down his upper lip. "That was not necessary," he groused.

"Next time, ye'll watch where ye put yer hands," Manus said. "Ginny, we can't leave this here, ye know." He gestured toward the framed glass and the demon raging in its depths.

"I know," she said wearily.

"Then we're taking it with us?" Bothy said, sounding thoroughly delighted with the idea.

Ginny nodded. Once she had recovered, she covered the mirror, ignoring the ranting of the shadow demon now trapped within. Bothy helped her haul it out of the tower and down to the boat where Malloch looked surly as ever to be forced to help load it. Ginny insisted on placing it in the stern, and made Bothy sit between her and Malloch who started to row them back across the loch with even less enthusiasm for his heavy load. Bothy protested, not wanting to be so far way from what he considered his prize, but Ginny shrugged, petting Thistle who sat at her side and asked, "Can you swim?"

"No," Bothy replied, looking uneasy.

"Too bad," Ginny said.

When she thought the water deep enough, she pretended to lose her balance and knocked the demon in the mirror overboard. Bothy wailed in grief, and for the first time Ginny could recall this entire trip, she saw Malloch smile.

MEMORIES TRACED IN SNOW

by Dave Smeds

Dave Smeds, a Nebula Award finalist, is the author of several books, including the novels *The Sorcery Within, The Schemes of Dragons,* and *X-Men: The Law of the Jungle.* His high fantasy short fiction has appeared in five previous volumes of *Sword And Sorceress,* as well as in *Dragons of Light, Return To Avalon, The Shimmering Door, Enchanted Forests,* and *Realms of Fantasy.* Other fiction—sf, horror, contemporary fantasy—can be found in *Asimov's SF, F & SF, In the Field of Fire, Full Spectrum 4, Peter S. Beagle's Immortal Unicorn, David Copperfield's Tales of the Impossible, Warriors of Blood And Dream, The Best New Horror 7, Sirens and Other Daemon Lovers,* and *Prom Night.* His work, called "stylistically innovative, symbolically daring examples of craftsmanship at the highest level" by the *New York Times* Book Review, has seen print in over a dozen countries.

It's always nice to have your work appreciated by others, especially by your peers. But I feel the important thing is the work, that writing should be its own reward. Of course, I'm well-known for "iconoclasm"—literally the breaking of idols. I don't believe that we need awards; if I want a little statue that I have to dust all the time, I can buy one. I once asked a friend "What's a Hugo worth anyhow?" She replied literally, "About $10,000 a year." That's true enough, but it's Marketing—a field I regard as one of the Black Arts.

The important thing is to write and love what you are doing.

Communities were small in the loftiness of the Peaks. Flat land was scarce, the growing season short. In the hamlet of Cascade Dell, the chimney smoke of each homestead rose within sight of every neighbor. When snows grew deep, the families gathered to spend four and sometimes five months housed within the great lodge, their dogs at their feet, their livestock in the vast barn across the yard.

Of all the people of the Dell, only the Seekers of Truth lived apart. That bleak fact plagued Scholar Radiance as she emerged onto the balcony of the contemplation hall. A stone's throw to her right, the waterfalls for which Cascade Dell was named thundered into a great pool. The noise failed to drown out her thoughts. She gazed down the terraced slope. The distance from abbey to lodge never shrank. But today, the weather fair and her fortnight's quota of scrolls already copied, Radiance had dispensation to enjoy the refuge of those log-and-mud walls again, if only for a few hours.

Her feet collapsed newly fallen snow as she set out along a trench path deeper, in shady areas, than she was tall. The scholar inhaled the tang of the fresh powder, a rarified, scentless scent she doubted she would know again this spring. Much as she loved the white purity that cloaked the peaks, she welcomed the melt. The winter's storminess, sheer cold, and extended darkness often precluded visits such as this, even when her monastic duties did not.

Numbness was clutching at her toes by the time she raised the flap of the scullery entrance and descended upon her usual stool by the kitchen hearth. A cornucopia of aromas washed over her. Rising bread. Hot clay. Cooked bacon. Welcome smells of home—even the whiff of ripe swaddling clothes as Metirha suckled her new baby by the butter churn.

"Mulled cider for you, Scholar?" asked Metirha's older daughter. The eight-year-old, looking very pleased that she was no longer the youngest of her family, filled a dipper at the steaming pot.

"Thank you, child." Radiance let the first swallow percolate downward, quelling the residual shiver in her bones. She smacked her lips.

Metirha grinned. Shifting the baby to her other breast, she commented, "Your near-brother was asking if you had come down the mountain today."

"Where is he now?" the scholar asked.

"Splitting logs, I believe."

Radiance sipped more cider, fortifying herself against the renewed embrace of the snow.

She found the day already much milder. Perhaps it was that her stockings had been warmed by the fire. Probably it was the company.

Axil looked as handsome as ever as he swung his maul onto a wedge. His upper body was clothed in only a shirt, its laces undone. The hair curling out of his collar was going gray, but the chest itself was supple and toned, the battle scars no longer vivid.

In her young womanhood, his comeliness had made her ache in a way that could not be assuaged. He was the son of her mother's sister, as well as the son of her father's brother. A first cousin twice over, and therefore too intimate a relative to marry even by the standards of the Dell. All he could do was spoil her for any man less fine. At eighteen, she had sworn the oath of the Seekers. That same summer he had accepted the king's service and gone on to soldier for nine long years in the lowlands. For all that circumstances and choices had pulled them apart, still she could sit down on a log near him and be immediately at ease.

He tossed the firewood he had split onto the pile near the lodge wall. To her disappointment, he did not tender his usual smile of welcome.

"I need your help."

"You have it always," she replied.

At that, his smile flashed. Suddenly she was conscious of herself, wondering if he would note the new skein of gray in her hair, the ink smudges on her fingers.

He turned solemn again. "I do not ask you as my near-sister or as my friend. I ask you as a scholar."

She tilted her head. "Go on."

"I need the assistance of someone who can read and write."

"I see. What troubles you so?"

He set down the maul. In the distance, a hawk plunged toward some unseen prey behind the trees to the west. He paused to watch it. Stalling.

"This morning I went to fetch my wife a reed basket," he began. "When I pulled an old one from the north storeroom, my mind took a fey turn. I was sure I had seen the basket many times, with a woman's comb laid atop it."

"And?"

"And that is all. A memory of a comb on the basket lid, laid there by habit. It was not Vittra's comb, nor that of any woman I know. Wooden, one side adorned with a carving of a creek lily, the other side inlaid with a bit of polished mussel shell."

"A detailed impression."

"Yes. I would have dismissed it as a sunlight dream save that when I was milking the goat this dawn, I recalled a time when I had been milking that very doe and heard a child sing, 'The Girl Who Made the Avalanche.' But what girl, I don't know, even though I remember that the child altered the lyric so that the avalanche girl's mischief was ultimately the fault of her brother."

"Have you had such turns before?" Radiance asked with concern.

"No. Or so I thought." Axil gestured at the large stump he was using to brace the logs for splitting. "You see these marks here? I made them to start a tally of the recollections, see how often they might afflict me. As soon as I finished the cuts, I noticed these."

Radiance followed his finger a third of the way around the stump. Two other marks lay in the wood. The cuts had yellowed; they were perhaps a week old. Her mouth popped open.

Axil nodded. "After I dug away snow from the stump, I found these." He revealed yet another pair of marks, blackened by months of winter.

"Are you sure you made them?"

"See for yourself. They are identical. The extra pairs must mean I had unexplained recollections in days and months past. Were I to have two mere hours apart, it is in my nature to begin a tally. Yet now I have no memory of *having remembered*. To my knowledge, today was the first time I tapped the corner of my hatchet into this stump."

"Sorcery," Radiance murmured. "Is that your fear?"

At once she understood his earlier hesitation. "Surely there can be no enchantments afflicting the Dell," he said fervently. "Perhaps I should not have broached the matter with you."

"No, you are correct. It may be nothing, but we should take measures. What do you want me to do?"

"I may succumb to forgetfulness again. I need a record that mentions details. Will you write one?"

"Of course."

He sighed, but did not entirely relax. The poor man. She knew he fretted that he was acting too much the warrior here amid the peace of the Dell. His wife, Vittra, had once described how his swordhand would twitch in his dreams if he slept out of easy reach of the weapon. He must have been truly unsettled to have been willing to discuss his qualms. To do so was to reveal the stirring of the soldier within.

She rose from the log, touched his cheek. She let her hand linger, pleased that he allowed it. "I revere your trust in me. Take comfort. We *will* find the answer."

By sunrise, Radiance had completed her morning rituals—a bath in the hotsprings at the heart of the abbey, porridge with her novices in the dining hall, meditation in the contemplation hall, where the waterfall's roar was intended to overcome all distraction. Now that sufficient light poured in through glazed panes to make possible the meticulous copying of Old Empire records—the chief duty of all scholars of the Seekers of Truth—she stoked her workroom fire and, breathing on her hands to warm them, reached for her quills.

She stopped, puzzled by the layer of slate leaning against her spare bench.

She knelt beside the object. The surface of the slate gleamed. In a corner lay the mother slab, one layer thinner than she recalled. Someone had tapped loose a new piece—chalk on slate being the medium of choice for temporary, mundane writings, preserving ink and precious vellum for work meant for the ages. Had one of her novices chosen to leave her a message?

No. The glyphs inscribed on the slate were in her own hand!

Heart beginning to race, she pored over the sentences, recognizing her own diction and style. By the time she was done, she was shivering so badly she feared she must return to the hotspring and immerse herself head and all.

She stumbled in the direction of the abbess' sanctum, to beg dispensation to visit the hamlet again.

Axil was a changed man when he received the news. No longer a shepherd and mountaineer struggling to cast off a youth spent in war, he brimmed with a veteran's readiness to act. As soon as he had heard her recount what she had read, he marched from his family's alcove in the lodge hall outside to the woodpile. Radiance had to scamper to match the pace of his strides.

He halted on the woodchip-littered snow and regarded the stump. The tally marks were there, just as her journal entry had described.

"How many other times have I forgotten?" He nearly spat out the words. "Am I haunted by a memory every day, and fail to note them here because I only have one between each sleep?"

"Do not dwell on that," Radiance said. "It is vile enough to distill sorcery as the cause. Come, let us tell the others."

Axil did not step with her toward the lodge. Instead he rubbed the marks on the stump, frowning.

"You believe we should keep counsel between ourselves?" Radiance guessed.

He nodded. "For now. I cannot imagine that anyone within the clan is in league with an enchanter, but it is a fact that an enchantment stole our memories as we slept. It is best that we tell no one of our discovery, for fear the knowledge will reach the one who forged the spell."

"Does he or she not already know?"

"I think not, or my tally marks would be obscured, and your slate would have been wiped clean. If we act in secret, perhaps we can flank the enchanter. In the near term, it is the enchantment itself that is our foe."

"How do you suggest we defeat it?"

"First, we must ensure we do not lose the gains we have made. Sorcery that affects the mind must be borne by a living emissary, true?"

"So say the scrolls. A minor spell of persuasion can be carried by a gnat or a flea."

"And magic that makes one utterly forget?"

"That would something larger. At least a mouse, a bat, a bird. Perhaps one of the frogs that live in the well." Radiance pictured the well that ran into the earth from the main hall of the lodge, unfrozen even in the depths of winter. Many a night as a girl had she fallen asleep on her pallet, listening to the croaking beneath the wooden lid of the hole.

"Dogs? Livestock?"

"Possible. The owners would notice changes in their beasts' behavior. A mage would prefer not to leave such clues."

Axil pulled out his knife and began tossing it into the stump top, as if imagining the wood housed his enemy. "There is no way to make the lodge secure."

"I fear not."

Axil pointed his blade up the slope. "The abbey is not so vulnerable. Take me there."

"But—"

"Men can visit in daylight, with cause."

She did not disagree. She was merely startled by the idea. Her near-brother had been to the abbey once in his lifetime, and then only as a member of the funeral party come to collect the body of the old abbess to be given to the eagles. "Come, then."

Once Radiance heard Axil's plan, she saw its merit. The abbey had been built in the old tradition. It was warded from familiars who might carry spells. Such minions, be they ticks or bears, could not cross the building's thresholds of their own accord. They could only enter if assisted, wittingly or not. The lodge might be infested, but the abbey should be lean of invaders.

"This is manageable," Axil said, gazing about her cubicle. 'Surely we can root out any creature that may be hiding here."

Radiance burned with embarrassment to have him see her living quarters, much less inspect them. No male had been within its confines in her lifetime. She suppressed the urge to conceal the all-too-visible stack of women's rags on her shelf.

To his credit, he behaved as if blind to any feature save those he had come to seek. Though stripped of weapons and awash in the purification anointment the abbess had dabbed on his face in the main vestibule, he was fierce with the demeanor of combat.

"I don't know where it might lurk," she said. The cell contained little beyond the bed, a few neatly folded garments, and a manuscript she was reviewing. Axil raised her blankets and saw for himself that she had no straw tick in which a mouse might nest, only a frame laced with strap. But to have stolen her memories, something must have brushed her skin during the night.

He reached for the manuscript. She bit back an admonition to be careful. It was unnecessary. He caressed the leaves delicately, revealing to her what he had spied. She now perceived a minute gap amid the stacked sheets. Two pages did not quite rest upon one another.

He left it to her to nudge open the volume. She found a pressed flower, a meadow kiss.

"Easily explained," she said. "You know that Xivhia, Morzei's daughter, has been my novice these past three years?"

"Yes. I saw her at midsummer, when her brother Borto left for the king's army."

"Borto picked her a bouquet of these flowers. I

have found others preserved thus. I fear she will be long worrying over him. Fate allow that he will come back to the Dell, as you did."

Axil looked straight at her. Suddenly he seemed very near, though he had not moved. "Not a night will go by that he will not dream of that homecoming," he murmured.

He knelt down to examine her fireplace. That, she was proud to display. Her status as prioress had won her little luxury beyond a cell of her own and the ability to command novices, but the hearth was a marvel. Built generations past according to a design in a scroll now lost, it did not pilfer warm air from the room as did a normal fire. Doors of iron separated the room from the burning logs, letting in heat, but permitting no drafts to form. The air that fed the flames and vanished up the chimney originated outdoors, drawn through a duct in the stone walls.

Did Axil suspect the duct to be a means of entry for a familiar? The wards should prevent even such furtive access as that.

Axil turned his attention upon the small pile of unburned cordwood in the nearest corner. Opening the metal doors, he seized a log with a large amount of loose bark and placed it on the blaze.

The piece was wet and moss-flecked, the sort best used when retiring to bed, when one wants wood that will take all night to be consumed. It hissed and steamed. Axil waited, leaving the doors open. Firelight danced across his features.

Abruptly, a salamander burst from a crack and raced to the part of the log farthest from the flames. Axil's hand struck like a viper, catching the amphibian on the first attempt.

He held it up in a grip so snug Radiance blurted, "Remember the law." Residents and visitors alike were abjured from killing any living thing within the grounds of the abbey.

"Fear not," he said. Carefully he turned his hand over and began to study the small beast.

A salamander was a likely familiar. Radiance knew that sorcerer-healers used them to swallow the nightmares of people whose sleep was chronically troubled. For an enchantment requiring subterfuge, what better carrier than one that seldom needed to reveal itself in order to forage, one that could ride across warded thresholds concealed in ordinary firewood?

"I will need to take care," Radiance commented. "My novice might bring in another infested log."

"Best if you carry your own wood from now on, inspecting each piece before you come in."

The salamander wriggled. Axil ignored the movement. Its magic would not influence him while he was awake. He turned it this way and that. Abruptly, he grunted.

"See the way the red and black combine? Does it not appear as though a troop of ants were crossing its back?"

Radiance studied the pattern, imagining the black portions were insect silhouettes. "Yes."

"The markings tell me this is native to a particular stream over the pass to the east." Eyes narrowing, he rubbed his empty knife sheath. "We have done more today than secure your den. We have learned where our enemy can be found."

The snows melted, the wildflowers bloomed. Life in the Dell went on, the families dispersing to their homesteads to raise their annual crops of grain, hay, and flax. The summer closely resembled those of the previous few years, with no exceptions of any apparent consequence: Some rejoiced at the number of births after a barren spell, and wagging tongues commented upon the frequency of Scholar Radiance's visits to the home of her near-brother.

Radiance was sitting near the entrance of Axil's root cellar one afternoon when Axil returned from his tenth journey to the uninhabited valley to the east. As he approached, she sighed and set down the mallet she had been using to shell walnuts. She had been enjoying the warm, brink-of-autumn sunshine, but now the day was marred.

Axil was carrying a gutted-and-dressed deer over his shoulders. Hunting was the public reason why he had gone over the mountain pass. Her mood had soured because the arrows in his quiver were all feathers up. According to their code, if he retained his memory of the real reason for his trip, he would have left two or three arrows points up.

He had forgotten. Again.

Radiance gnawed her lip, busying herself with cleaning up walnut shells and storing the nuts in the cellar while Vittra and Axil's three boys, ages nine, seven, and one, greeted their father. Only when the returning hunter had indulged fully in the reunion did she approach him, finding a private moment while he was hanging the carcass from a pole.

His face clouded as she recounted to him the phenomenon of the missing memories. It was an oft-repeated tale. Nearly every morning in the lodge or his house he woke up as unaware as ever. Up in the abbey, she had thrice been ensorcelled, discovering what had occurred by reading her journal. Mice or salamanders had breached her cell a dozen times, but usually she found them before she went to sleep.

"Everyone has lost memories?" he asked.

"All who live in the Dell, it seems. Metirha or Vittra or Morzei will describe an odd recollection. The next day they will know nothing of it."

"And the nature of the glimpses is the same?"

"Yes. Just snatches of experience. They add up to nothing decipherable, except that many have to do with small children. I myself noticed the way Coiz's toddler's blond locks resemble the hair of some other, unremembered boy."

Axil studied the unturned arrows in his quiver. "On my other trips to the east, I kept my memories?"

"Usually," she confirmed. "You would sleep under the stars, and apparently the enchanter's familiars did not find you. This is the second time you have come home unknowing."

He paced restlessly around the suspended deer. "Some trap of the mage may have snared me."

"You expressed this fear the last time this happened, near midsummer."

"If I failed twice, I may fail again. We must do more."

"Should we enlist others?"

"Perhaps." He tugged his beard. "But as before, we know not who may be the ears of the magician. Let us try once more unaided. This time, you must accompany me."

Abbess Tranquillity gazed at Radiance with brows furrowed. They were sitting in the abbess' chamber, a room barely half again as large as Radiance's own and nearly as spare, save for the desk and visitor's chair. Radiance had just finished making her petition.

"The journey to the valley and back requires the larger part of a day," the abbess said. "Do you intend to be gone overnight?"

"Yes. Two nights, perhaps."

The older woman pursed her lips. Radiance was all too aware of what went unspoken. Couples who slipped away into the forest sometimes did so to engage in a dalliance. Radiance's official reason for the journey was believable. She would go in order to catalog wild medicinal plants, making maps of their locations, drawing them in their native terrain, gathering samples. Axil's knowledge of the mountains would speed her task, and he could also serve as her protector.

Still . . .

The abbess tapped her fingers on the desk. The calluses, thick from years of labor with stylus and quill, resounded loudly against the wood. Finally she spoke.

"If your near-brother's wife has no objection, then neither do I."

Radiance stumbled over her thanks.

"Child," the old woman added when her petitioner rose to go. "One day I expect you to succeed me. Now would be an unfortunate time to become entangled in the distractions of the hearthfires."

"Have no fear," Radiance replied, wishing she sounded more convincing.

Radiance hated lying to her superior. How much easier it would have been to take Tranquillity into her confidence. The same applied to Axil's wife.

Vittra listened silently to the request. Radiance had never been anything but kind to her, had tended Vittra as a child in the years before departing up the mountain to become a novice. Still, it came as a relief when Vittra agreed.

"Axil has been so unsettled lately," she said. "Perhaps the task will distract him."

Vittra gave her the same measured glance that Tranquillity had used. Both women trusted her, but both entertained the possibility that their faith might be shaken. Radiance left the cottage ill at ease with the price she had paid to make the excursion. Elsewhere in the Dell, gossip would flow. It was like the cascade. Once it poured down the mountain, it would not go back uphill.

*   *   *

One thing was certain: Had the sole purpose of the trek been to create the treatise on plants that Radiance was now obliged to compose, Axil would have been an ideal guide. By the time they reached the valley, he had already pointed out dozens of useful herbs, seeds, and fungi. He knew varieties of mushroom at a glance, and easily recited which were toxic, glorious to the palate, and/or capable of prompting visions. The latter were prized by the Seekers of Truth in certain rituals.

They came to a stream that tumbled over boulders and through pools toward a lake. The valley was starkly beautiful, the sort of place that would long have been settled had it contained flat land or were it closer to the trade routes.

"The salamanders can be found along this brook," Axil said.

They hiked up the gentle canyon until they came to an expanse of bracken grown thick and high over the summer. They tucked themselves into a bower of lacy fronds. A deer had smoothed a bed in the shadows. From this refuge Radiance and Axil could observe a long stretch upstream and down without being seen in return.

Radiance, her scholar's legs unused to long travel, was grateful for the respite, but Axil remained strung hunter-tight, eyes roving the land.

Twilight soon claimed the forest, for most of the first day had been devoted to the journey and the need to attend to the treatise. They ate dried meat and nutmealcakes. At last, when the darkness precluded any hope of glimpsing their prey, Axil lay back with a sigh.

He did not converse. Radiance had gown used to that these recent years, but here, alone, with no wife or kin or neighbor within sight, she thought of the times in their youth when, hidden behind a haystack or in a loft, they had talked·long into the night. At that age he had bubbled like a hotspring, chattering of dreams and new discoveries, his words weaving such a rapturous spell that she would have lain with him were it not for taboo and her younger self's smug faith that opportunities repeated themselves.

She would lie with him now, if it would cause him to open himself as he once had. She had never asked him what had happened in those long nine years in the king's army. There would never be a better time than this. All it required to broach the matter was that she rekindle the boldness that had led her to announce, long ago, that she would go up the mountain to learn and copy ancient lore rather than stay in lodge and homestead as her parents expected and be bred to a ram less worthy than her near-brother.

Her calves throbbed from the hiking. The thin air over the pass had left her throat raw and her mouth tasting of metal. The more she readied herself to speak, the more she felt like an old woman. Lying in the gloom a mere arm's reach from him, smelling his musk, united in a great task, only now with her excuses stripped away did she know the choice to alter her life's course to be a thing entirely surrendered to the past.

They spent the night in silence.

The deer had chosen its bed well; the overhang of bracken fronds fended off the dew. Radiance awoke without the stiffness that so often earmarked a night's exposure to the elements, though her legs had lost none of their ache.

Axil was wrapped around her, his front to her back. His warmth staved off the chill and prompted her to linger beneath the blanket, savoring this token intimacy. It did not change their roles, but it was a balm.

The moment lasted as long as her bladder would

allow. All too soon they were folding their packs, downing a cold breakfast, and resuming their station.

"Are you troubled?" Axil asked as the last of the dew evaporated.

"Some. It will pass," she replied. *All things do.*

They waited hours longer. Once, she suggested another location, but he shook his head. "I have hiked the length of this creek from lake to source on visits past. Our best chance is to remain hidden in one spot."

Waiting further tested her composure, but she could see the sense of it. Salamanders, magical or not, had limited lifespans. This day or another, the magician was sure to pass by while collecting new specimens.

"I cannot come here with you again," she said.

"No. Not without blighting your reputation, and that I will not ask of you."

Radiance was surprised to hear him state the case so succinctly. She hadn't been certain he perceived all she risked. After all, no one would dare accuse Axil to his face of impropriety. She had misjudged him. Strong as his limbs were, he could be wounded by the disapproval of the clan, even that which occurred behind his back. The Dell was not a place where any resident could hide from the judgment and opinion of the community.

As she contemplated that fact, a face briefly drifted into her mind's eye. She saw a narrow-chinned woman, her dark red hair streaked with one lock of white. The woman was thin in the shoulders and wide in the hips, with a pock mark beside the corner of her mouth. The pox had visited her as a child, that same winter that Radiance herself had been taken abed with it.

Radiance had possessed no memory of the woman's face until that moment.

Her breath caught. "Axil . . ." she murmured.

He motioned suddenly for silence.

A cloaked figure was meandering along the stream.

Radiance's pulse thundered in her temples. The stranger was thin, well wrapped even on this temperate day. Beneath her hood her face was deeply wrought with wrinkles.

Someone of her age had no good reason to be so far from the nearest hamlet with no younger person to escort her.

Every few steps, the newcomer bent down and turned over a stone. Despite her age she was nimble. At last a salamander scurried from a niche she had uncovered. She caught it deftly and thrust it into a moistened sack. The fabric rippled with the movement of other captives.

Axil strung his bow, but he left his arrows in his quiver. When the crone was on the verge of vanishing downstream, he began to follow. Radiance kept silently at his heels.

The need for quiet was perhaps unnecessary. When a woodpecker rattled in a tree, when a pine cone thudded to the earth just behind the cloaked stranger, she did not react. Deaf? In any case, she concentrated on harvesting salamanders, catching two more before she headed back upstream. Axil and Radiance hid themselves while she passed.

By midday, they reached a gently sloping meadow. The old woman abandoned the stream and set out across the treeless area. The pursuers had to hang back lest they be revealed.

Halfway across the meadow, the crone disappeared.

Radiance hissed softly. Axil grunted.

"Did you see her step down?" the scholar asked.

"No," her near-brother replied. "One instant she was walking; the next she was gone from our view."

They hesitated to emerge from the clump of doe-brush that concealed them, but they dared not let the trail grow cold. They crept to the verge of the meadow.

Axil scowled. "Do you feel it?"

"Yes. I am seized by an urge to skirt the meadow's edge to avoid the boggy places."

It was true the meadow appeared boggy, especially at the center where the stranger had vanished. Had they encountered the site by chance, they would surely have surrendered to the inclination to go around.

Instead, Axil strode forward with determination. The compulsion increased. Radiance found herself revolted by the cold, squishy clutch of the mud sucking at her feet. Only her high level of suspicion ensured that she recall that her feet were encased in fur-lined boots that would never be penetrated so quickly and thoroughly as they seemed to have been.

The compulsion vanished as if they had snapped a weaving of spiderweb. They found themselves on solid, grassy earth. Not a boggy meadow at all, but a pleasant sward gone yellow and firm with summer's end, and their feet quite untouched by mud.

In front of them stood a handsome cottage, its roof pitched sharp against the snow of this elevation, its walls of stone and log thick enough to withstand winters for generations.

"I have passed this way a dozen times in my life, and never saw this dwelling before," Axil murmured.

Radiance was still sloughing off the tremor that comes with confronting powerful magic when her near-brother glided up to the thick door, bent down, and peered into the crack where it was latched. He returned and whispered, "It is barred. We will have to create a welcome."

He quickly explained his plan. Setting down his bow, he boosted Radiance up the stacked stones that made up the chimney. The footholds proved worthy.

She reached the top and covered the smoke hole with her pack blanket.

Smoke soon began to trickle out the tops of the shutters. On the ground near the entrance, Axil unhooked his ax and raised it one-handed.

The sound of coughing grew louder. Next came the noise of a bar being raised. Axil stepped forward, slipping out of Radiance's view. He reappeared dragging the old woman into the open, holding his blade so that one stroke would end her life.

Radiance removed the blanket, tossed it to the ground, and clambered down without injury.

The old woman's wide eyes darted from Axil to Radiance and back. She crumpled to her knees.

"He will not harm you," Radiance said, hoping the woman was not, indeed, deaf. "As long as you supply answers."

The hand that held the ax twitched. Radiance swallowed hard. She had never seen Axil confronting an adversary before, except in play. He was not quick to step back, and then only two steps.

The woman's trembling lessened when she spied the tiny tattoo upon Radiance's cheek. "Seeker," she said.

"I am Radiance, prioress of Cascade Dell abbey."

The old woman reached to her own cheek and smoothed out the wrinkles beneath her eyes. Her skin was marked by an identical tattoo, its blue tint gone to gray.

Radiance gasped. "Who are you?"

"A scholar."

"And an enchantress."

The old woman blinked. "Yes. My studies include the lore of sorcery."

"Then why are you not in a city, serving the king or his governors?"

"I would be, should my interests have lain in the

areas of spying or war. I came here long ago, in order to pursue charms of a gentler sort."

Axil drew air through his teeth. "Gentler? You are the one who steals away the memories among my clan."

The mage looked down. "Yes."

"Why?"

"I could explain, but you will believe me only if I return your memories to you."

Axil lowered his weapon. Radiance knew he had not expected such a reply, nor had she.

"That is true," he said, "but how can I trust you to do so without teachery?"

"When last you came, you bound me in such a way that I could not escape without your help." She smiled humorlessly when she saw the reaction to her statement. "Since you have a companion this time, she can stand guard. The process is swift. Shielding a person from one's own spell is trivial compared to weaving the lace of it around him."

He studied her for five heartbeats. Radiance would have needed the rest of the day to decide, but her near-brother was not given to vacillation. He handed the ax to her.

Radiance hefted the weapon, hoping she projected the impression she could use it.

The old woman climbed to her feet and dusted off her skirt. "Come with me," she said. Her voice was overly loud, in the way of a crone with bad hearing, but her smooth tread as she reentered her abode demonstrated her profound health. Radiance no longer wondered how the woman had survived the wilderness alone.

The enchantress waved away the pall of smoke. She filled a small brazier with coals from her hearth and set it upon a worn table littered with earthenware bowls and beakers of glass and metal, including one of gold.

She tipped a splash of liquid from a pewter cup onto the coals, which shifted from orange to azure in color. She lifted the lid of a small barrel to reach inside. Axil stopped her long enough to inspect the contents. He nodded, and she withdrew a salamander.

She uttered a sentence in a language Radiance recognized from Old Empire writings. The scholar had never heard the tongue spoken aloud, and could not decipher the words on the spot.

To Radiance's shock, the old woman hefted the amphibian onto the coals. The creature did not burn. It huddled as if in confusion. When it had taken on a halo of the same color as the coals, the woman lifted it toward Axil.

"Breathe its breath, and your memory will be as if I had never cast my spell."

Axil leaned in, placed his nose a finger-width from the salamander's mouth, and inhaled forcefully.

His eyes widened. He cried out in anguish. "Take them away! Take them away again!"

"You recall now how it was when last you came here," the old woman said. "You know how many hours it will take to repair the weave. Do you wish to sleep?"

"Yes!" Axil cried. Radiance had never once heard him sound so plaintive, not even when he had broken his wrist when he was nine years old.

The enchantress uncorked a bottle and filled a thimble cup with a dark, odoriferous liquid. She waved it toward Radiance in explanation. The younger woman recognized the aroma as that of a powerful soporific. The amount she was offering Axil would make him sleep profoundly, but was not enough to endanger his life.

Axil seized the cup and quaffed the dose. Holding

his head and stifling whimpers, he tumbled onto the bed in the corner and closed his eyes. The potion took effect in moments, but even then his breathing snagged and sharpened unpredictably.

"By the time he awakens, I will have restored his forgetfulness," the crone said gently.

Radiance realized she was still holding the ax aloft. Her grip had grown slick with sweat.

The sorceress continued calmly, "So you are the reason he has come again. I feared he must have an accomplice, but he would tell me nothing."

"He has truly been here before?"

"Yes. I sent him home without his memory, hoping that would make an end."

"How can I be assured this is not some sort of trick?" Radiance asked.

"I can give you back your memories," the crone said.

"My escort is asleep. I fear to let down my guard."

"That is wise." The woman settled onto a stool. "How may I gain your trust?"

"Give me a reason for the enchantment upon Cascade Dell that I can believe."

"I wove the spell at the request of my closest friend, whom you knew as Insight, your late abbess. It settled a debt I owed her from the time we were novices at the Seeker's Retreat at High Cliff. But in truth, mercy alone demanded that I undertake the task. I have willingly maintained and refined it these past three years. It will be a few years more until I can leave it untended."

"Why did Insight ask this of you?"

"To forget an atrocity. To heal the Dell."

"What could have happened in the Dell that we would want to forget it had occurred?"

"You find it near impossible to conceive of it. That

is as it should be, according to my enchantment. Even the roots of the tragedy are obscured."

"You have not answered my question."

The crone reached down and picked up the salamander where it had fallen. It still gave off a slight blue radiance, and did not scurry away as would an untouched specimen. She set it gently in the barrel with its kin.

"Well?" Radiance insisted.

"You love the Dell, and see it through loving eyes. But consider its long winters. Imagine how they might be to someone who does not wish to be there, whose presence is looked upon as a blight."

"There is no one who—"

"Not anymore," the old woman said.

Radiance's throat tightened. She recalled the image of the red-headed woman with the pockmark. "She is dead?"

"Beyond dead. So dead that, until a moment ago, I was the only person in the world who recalled she had ever existed, and I had no occasion to meet her in life. The wolves took her bones, and should I live long enough, the pain and loss and guilt she caused will have vanished with them. It was Insight's wish, and I granted it."

Radiance shook her head, wishing not to believe, but feeling her resistance ebbing. "Surely there must be some sign left, one that enchantment cannot erase."

"Alas, yes." The magician wilted. "Tell me, Scholar, how many children are there in the Dell between the ages of three and seven?"

"Eight or so."

"Half as many as one would expect, save in a year of pox or the fevers."

"There was a barren time." Radiance choked on her words. "Oh, no . . ."

"I would spare you the recollection," the enchantress said solemnly.

Radiance set down the ax. "No. Now I must know. Answer me a final question or two, that I may be sure of you. If you truly knew my late abbess in her youth, you will recall her name before she became Scholar Insight."

"Yes. She was Ophille."

"Do you recall the name of the abbess' older sister?"

"You speak of the one who died young, inspiring Ophille to take the vows in place of her? That was Lireth."

Radiance nodded. "Restore the past to me," she said.

"As you wish." The sorceress drew a fresh salamander from the barrel and repeated the incantation. Radiance inhaled.

The images hurled into her. They cut her more deeply than had the original experiences by virtue of arriving all at once. The blood. The horror and sorrow and rage and vengefulness on faces she knew well—it all flared to the point of blinding her.

But she was blessed with a cushion Axil had not possessed—she had been in the abbey when the event occurred that winter night in the lodge. She had observed the aftermath, but she had not seen Axil strike, saving the remaining children from a kinswoman claimed by snow-madness. She had seen the bodies of the victims only after they had been covered.

The worst part, for her, had been to witness the broken spirit of her near-brother, bent over the shrouded remains of his only daughter.

"How could she? How could she?" Radiance moaned.

"You know the answer to that," the crone said.

The truth was bitter. No one in the Dell—aside,

ironically, from the youngest generation, the group
that had become the victims—was truly innocent. All
had done their part, in their own way, to create the
conditions that led to the tragedy. The Dell could
speak in one voice. In most matters, that was its greatest strength. But not when one kind word, one mitigat-
ing caress of approval, might have kept a lodge
dweller from the brink of insanity.

Radiance turned toward the bed. Axil was twitching
in his sleep. "After all the things he must have seen
in the wars. I know he had comrades die in his arms.
I know enemies died so near he smelled their last
breath. He weathered that."

The crone bowed her head. "He had a lodgepole.
He was able to endure what he endured because he
had faith he would one day retreat to a place untouched by such evils."

"What am I to do?" Radiance murmured.

She had spoken too quietly for the crone to hear,
but eventually the other said, "Peace, child. I will take
the pain from you again."

"No."

"Eh?"

"It won't work." Radiance explained how she and
Axil had solved the mystery of the enchantment.
"Even if the journal I have already made is destroyed,
the same inclinations will lead us to repeat our efforts.
Ultimately we would return here."

"No doubt you are correct. That is why Insight
chose to recall the past entire, so that she might keep
others from stumbling across it. Her death unraveled
that part of the scheme."

"I must take her place. When Axil is troubled by
minor remembrances, I will purchase the time to allow
him to forget his suspicions. I will erase his tallies, and
keep no record of my own."

"I could not ask this service, but if you offer it, I will accept. Are you certain?"

"I am a Seeker of Truth," Radiance replied. Never before had she suspected how much truth she would have to know.

A weight lifted from the old woman's shoulders. She went to a shelf on which sat a dozen books—the most Radiance had ever seen one person own—and opened a volume. She withdrew an eagle feather from between its pages.

"I wish you to take this. Do you know what it is?"

"It is from the funeral bower of the children," Radiance said. "A token left by one of the birds who ate their flesh and ferried their souls to the afterlife."

"Do you know why I ask you to hold it?"

"For the same reason I must stand outside the enchantment. Someone must remember the little ones, now that Insight is gone to the eagles." Someone had to remember her little cousin, who loved to sing of the Avalanche Girl.

"Indeed." The crone handed over the feather. "I can only imagine that this is why you were given the life path you took. You show by this demonstration of your character that you were always meant to be a Seeker."

Radiance frowned. It would take more time before she could believe this herself.

"Let us make our plans," the sorceress declared.

In Cascade Dell, harmony ruled. The long winters were treasured for their role in binding the families closer. Axil grew old raising fine sons and eventually daughters as well. The abbey absorbed those members of the community who craved to know the written mysteries, or who needed to retreat from other destinies. The edifice weathered the years on its perch beside the waterfall, apart. Radiance never spent another night outside its walls, but she was not contained.

VALKYRIE

by Jenn Reese

Jenn says that she has always read speculative fiction and has recently channeled her energies toward writing it. As a measure of her devotion, she quit her long-time programming position to attend the Clarion writing workshop in Michigan during the summer of 1999.

More of Jenn's stories appear in the anthology *Prom Night* and various issues of *Pulp Eternity*. Her web page can be found at www.sff.net/people/jenn—where she keeps a list of publications and an online journal.

Jenn says: "Regarding 'Valkyrie,' I've always been fascinated by different cultures and their mythologies, and with the aspects of the human spirit which appear in all of them. I'd like to dedicate this story to my mother, who has repeatedly found the strength to pick up her life and start it over again."

When I was seventeen, someone told me, "If you're writing science fiction, learn science; if you're writing fantasy, learn mythology." As Jenn has done, I did study mythology, and I found the advice to be sound. Go thou and do likewise.

Audun stood over her son's bleeding body and screamed her defiance. All around her, amidst the smoke and clash of sword and battle-ax, men fought.

Hauk Egilson and his kin had attacked in the middle of the night, while all of the men-folk swooned from their ale and flirted with each other's wives.

Audun's blood burned as she thought of all the women and children their weapons had slain in just the first few minutes.

A man staggered toward them, and Audun hefted her son's blade and waved it through the air.

"Take one more step, and I will kill you."

He ignored her and lurched closer, clutching at his side. Audun could see the blood dripping between his fingers as it glistened wetly in the moonlight. A light gut wound, at most, or he'd be lying in the street instead of looking for more sport. She menaced him with her sword, but he seemed oblivious to her threats.

"I am Audun, widow of Leidolf Eirikson, mother of Eirik the Swift. One more pace and it means your death." Audun leveled the sword at his throat, thankful that her many chores kept her arms strong enough to wield such a massive weapon.

The man, now only a dozen paces away, appeared to notice her for the first time. His eyes grew wide, and his jaw slipped open. A low whimper escaped him.

"Run," Audun said. "Now."

The man turned and fled. His right leg wouldn't bend, so he dragged it across the hard-packed dirt and groaned with each step. Audun smiled.

"Do not be so pleased with yourself, Audun Jorunn's Daughter," a woman's voice said from behind her. Audun spun around. The woman sat on the back of a silver-gray mare no more than five paces beyond the place where Audun's son lay in the dirt. Her blonde hair was bound in two tight braids along her head, and she wore chain armor that glinted in the darkness. "This warrior saw my threat more than he heard yours," the woman said. Audun saw the woman's sword, and raised her own in response.

"What do you want? How could I not hear you approach?"

The woman laughed. "Do you not recognize me? I am Gunhilde Grunna's Daughter, one of Odin's shield-maidens."

Audun sucked in her breath. "A Valkyrie?"

Gunhilde smiled and patted her horse's neck. "The same."

"Then you had better step away from my son," Audun said, pointing her sword at the woman and stepping closer. "He's not ready to die."

The Valkyrie's smile twisted into something crueler. "Not ready to die? Do you presume to know more than I about such things?"

Audun winced and lowered her sword. "No, but I— I thought—"

"Speak, woman," the Valkyrie said, her voice rolling across Audun's skin like a winter chill.

"My son," Audun said, "is not yet dead. He is not ready for Valhalla. He will live to fight many more battles." She feared the Valkyrie, but she could not keep the defiance from her voice.

"What if he lives for a long time, Audun? What if your son becomes old and gray, and dies in his bed, without a sword in his hand? Would he thank you for your mercy now?"

"My son will not die of old age," Audun said. How dare this creature insult Audun and her family in such a manner! Feuds had lasted generations over slander less vile than this.

Audun lifted her blade once again and moved forward to stand directly over her son's body. "My son is a warrior, and he will die a warrior," she said coldly, "but he will not die today."

The Valkyrie stood silently. Both her eyes and the eyes of her ghostly-white mare studied Audun with such intensity that Audun was tempted, if only for a single heartbeat, to lower her eyes in return.

Finally, the Valkyrie laughed.

Audun spat on the ground in font of the Valkyrie's horse. "You come to take the soul of my son, and now you laugh at my pain?"

"You have mistaken me, Audun Jorunn's Daughter," the Valkyrie said. "I have not come for your son."

"What?"

"Look over there," Gunhilde said, pointing to a dark patch of shadow, a dead body, lying against the side of Audun's house. "Tell me what you see."

Curiosity fought confusion in Audun's mind, and curiosity won. She lowered her blade and walked over to the body, careful not to disturb her son's unconscious slumber as she stepped over the broken timbers and smashed earthware covering the street.

Audun peered into the shadow, and soon a form emerged. It was an older woman, her gray hair long and loosely entwined in a single braid which now lay across her neck. Her face was lined and weathered, but also strong and open. Audun's gaze drifted down to the woman's hand, where a simple band of copper adorned the third finger.

The body was hers, and it lay in a wide pool of sticky blood.

"I did not come here for your son," the Valkyrie's voice called to her, "I came here for you."

Audun studied the corpse. She remembered the pain now, her surprise and anger to find Hauk Egilson's ax in her back—that man had hidden his cowardice behind his cruelty. Audun took one last look at the ring, her wedding band, then turned and strode back to the Valkyrie.

"Women cannot journey to Valhalla," Audun said. "It is a place for men and their battles."

"It is true," Gunhilde said, "that Valhalla has little to offer us. But there is always room in the Sisterhood of Valkyrie for a brave woman."

Audun frowned; everything had changed so quickly. "But I am old. I do not know how to use a sword."

"Then you will learn," the Valkyrie said. "A strong spirit is all that the Sisterhood requires, and your talents in that arena are abundant."

Audun smiled, but she was far too old to blush.

"You are more than just somebody's widow, or somebody's mother," Gunhilde continued. "You are the sum of these parts, and more. You are Audun, and you will be one of us."

Her bones used to feel used and tired, but now Audun felt a new strength growing from their marrows. She bent over and kissed her son on his forehead. Then she stood, walked over to Gunhilde, and mounted the mare behind her new sister.

SOUL DANCE

by Lisa Silverthorne

Lisa says:

"I have recently sold a story to the SFF-NET anthology, *The Age of Reason*. I still do computer technical support, and I still live in Indiana. Gosh, I think my bio gets more boring every year. Time goes by so fast. I remember six years ago when I submitted my first stories to your magazine and to this anthology. Took me 17 stories (I guess I'm just stubborn) to make that first sale. I'll never forget that day. That was my first professional sale, and every time I manage to sell another story, I remember that electric moment. Thank you for providing new writers with a magazine that has allowed us to learn about craft and an anthology that has allowed us to test that knowledge."

You're welcome, Lisa; that's exactly why I started *Marion Zimmer Bradley's Fantasy Magazine.*

I would not call your biography (or any of the others I get) "boring"—"nice and stable" would be a better description, with no nasty surprises. Several of my writers have endured some really nasty surprises (one of them developed writer's block literally overnight, hasn't recovered from it in over three years, and says she never wants to write again). Nobody needs that kind of grief, particularly not writers, who need what I call "emotional strength" in order to be able to write.

Silhouetted against the raging peace fire, the Soul Dancer danced. Drums pounded a steady pulse. Drisani watched the woman twirl and spin around the flickering blaze, remembering when she had once performed the dance. But that was long ago. She stooped to pick up bowls of half-eaten stew and crusts of bread scattered across plates. Her ankle chains clanked in the tense quiet of the camp. It was the only sound besides the drums and the rustle of the Soul Dancer's veils.

On the west side of the fire, in line with the setting sun, stood Kanago, her chieftain and leader of the mountain tribes—her tribe. His hand rested on his sword hilt, his narrow gaze darting from the Soul Dancer to the shadowy figures crouched on the east side of the fire. To Kanago's left stood Reggel, his second in command. Reggel's gaze scrutinized every face, every movement. The plains tribes were wary, and their chieftain, a thin, sullen-faced warrior woman, glared around the camp. The plains people wore tans and olives like the color of grasslands, unlike the thick, dark clothes of Drisani's people.

Drisani knew that only a soul dance would bring her people peace, but with both sides ready to attack each other, the soul dance might never be completed and the war would continue.

When Drisani had gathered all the dishes, she laid them in a reed basket. She would clean them tomorrow—if she and her people survived this night. She gazed at the thin gold line of sunlight slipping away on the horizon. It would be a long night.

The Soul Dancer leaped and turned, the drum beat louder. She seemed distracted at times, the thin, hard line of her mouth twisting into a grimace. Sweat beaded against her face, brow furrowing. She was working hard, Drisani knew.

Drisani took her place beside Kestra, another slave. It had taken Drisani a long while, but she had finally accepted her place here. She'd long ago given up hope of redeeming herself in her chieftain's eyes. To this tribe, Drisani had no name. It had been stricken from the warrior's book because of her cowardice in battle.

"How well does Cirra dance?" Kestra asked, settling herself on a reed mat. She bore the same thin ankle chains as Drisani. Slave chains. She had once fought beside this woman, but Kestra, too, had fallen from Kanago's favor. In the mountains, once a warrior's loyalty was questioned, running the gauntlet or becoming a slave were the only paths out of this camp.

Drisani watched the Soul Dancer twisting the silvery mana lines in her hands, summoning their magic. From here, Drisani felt the magic tingle in her hands and feet. Even her ankle chains gleamed with mana silver.

"She seems to be struggling now," Drisani whispered. Her stomach clenched. The dance was going badly.

"Why do your chains look silver?" Kestra asked, pointing. "Mine are tarnished and dull."

"It's the mana lines' magic. Since I possess the skill of soul dance, I can't help but summon a little of the magic when it's so near to me."

"Do you see what she sees right now?"

Drisani shook her head. "Only when I'm holding the lines can I see everything that she sees. I do see the mana lines, though."

"I wish I could see if the dance was going well," said Kestra with a sigh.

The Soul Dancer stumbled and for a moment, Drisani couldn't breathe. Her gaze darted to her chieftain's taut face. How hard Kanago's expression looked tonight. She remembered a time when laughter lit those hazel eyes, how they'd gleam when he told battle stories around the fire, bellies full, the mead warm. All she saw in his eyes tonight was anger and tension.

With a strangled cry, the Soul Dancer collapsed beside the fire.

Drisani and Kestra struggled to their feet.

"Reggel, go to her," Kanago ordered, motioning at him. Reggel, shorter and stockier than the chieftain, rushed forward, kneeling beside the dancer. Her veils fluttered around her in a gauzy cloud and she did not move.

The chieftain of the plains tribe stepped forward, a hand against her sword hilt. Her ruddy hair was wild like the fire and Drisani remembered how her own hair had once shone like that. The woman wore a swath of olive and butternut fabric across her left shoulder. It gathered at her hip, and hung loosely over her short, olive shift and iron breastplate.

"Why does she stop?" asked the plains chieftain. "The dance isn't finished!"

Finally, Kanago moved toward the Soul Dancer and the other chieftain, almost as if he'd put himself between them in protection.

"Reggel?" he asked, a hint of urgency beneath his forced calm. Drisani knew that false calm well. She'd seen it in battle dozens of times. "How is she?"

Reggel stood up slowly, his fingers splayed. Blood clung to his palms. "She is dead."

Kanago looked up, his gaze on the other chieftain as he clutched his sword hilt. The plains tribe murmured, restless and fearful now.

Drisani shuddered. This couldn't be happening.

"You trick us into coming here!" the plains chieftain's voice was a mixture of anger and fear. She stepped back into the safety of her warriors.

Blades snicked out of sheaths. Reggel swept his sword from its sheath and stood beside Kanago. The rest of the mountain tribe drew their swords. Only Kanago had not drawn his blade.

"Please," he said, holding a hand into the air as he turned to his own warriors and the plains warriors. "The Dance would have shown us the right path.

Don't do this now—not after we've finally come together."

"Lies!" shouted the plains chieftain. "It was a trap to lure us into your camp so you could slaughter us— like you've killed your own dancer."

Kanago tried to calm the plains tribe, but Reggel and the other warriors were seething with violence. Drisani saw the bloodlust beginning in their eyes as they advanced slowly around the fire. Kanago was trying to reason with them, but it seemed that only he wanted peace now. She had to do something to stop this.

Running as fast as her chains would allow, Drisani sprang into the fire circle, arms spread wide. As the plains tribe moved toward Kanago, she stepped in front of him.

"Stop! Listen to one more plea, I beg you."

The plains chieftain held her arm out, stopping her warriors from moving closer. Amusement shone in her eyes, the hint of a smile on her face.

"Tell us, little no-name, what wisdom do you bring all of us this night?"

Chuckles rippled through the plains tribe and Drisani felt her cheeks burn with embarrassment. Until tonight, she had accepted her station without argument, but here she was standing before two chieftains and offering suggestions. She would be beaten for this, but she didn't care if it stopped this war.

Reggel glared at her and tried to jerk her backward, but Kanago's hand fell to her arm.

"The slave will speak," he said, his voice sharp. "But only with words carefully chosen."

He would only warn her once to be careful. Long ago, she had been careless and led her warriors into ambush. Again, carelessly, she had gone for help, only to return to a massacre and murmurs that she'd run like a coward. And she *had* been a coward because she chose slavery over the gauntlet. It was time that she finally faced that gauntlet.

"Only a soul dance can save both our tribes from wiping each other out," said Drisani, her gaze daring to meet the plains chieftain's gaze. She would show this woman strength, even if she were only a slave. "It is never an easy thing to reveal a black soul and expel it. Sometimes, a soul dancer loses her own soul and her life in this dance, but it is the only way to save ourselves."

"The dancer is dead," said the plains chieftain. "Why do you bother us with meaningless drivel?" Her gaze moved to Kanago. "Why do you allow this no-name to waste our time?"

He pointed to the silvery gleam of her ankle chains. "She has the skill of the dance," he said. "Listen to her."

"I once danced this dance and with my chieftain's permission, I will perform it again. I am the only other person in both tribes able to dance the soul dance." She pointed at the dancer's lifeless body. "Like this dancer, the skill was passed down to me by my mother. Please, let me perform the dance, before all of us are killed and there is nothing but ashes to pass down to our children."

To her surprise, Kanago gently squeezed her arm.

Again, the plains chieftain stared at her in amusement, but there was no malice in her eyes.

"I am willing, Kanago, if it will avoid bloodshed. What say you?"

"It will be done. Return to us in an hour."

With a nod, the plains chieftain backed away from the fire, blade still drawn, until finally the fireside was empty of plains people.

Reggel grabbed Drisani's arm and jerked her to the ground. "You insolent little grub, I'll lay your back open!" He unfurled the whip in his belt and Drisani braced herself for the pain.

"Step down immediately, Reggel!"

Kanago's voice halted Reggel in mid-swing.

"But, my chieftain, she asserts herself where that privilege was lost along with ten warrior's lives. She deserves to be put in her place."

Again, Kanago stayed the whip. "You will not strike her. She knows the risk she took, but she took that risk for all of us, not for herself." He smiled at her as he helped her to her feet. "You offer your life in the dance, Drisani, for that we are all grateful."

Tears welled in her eyes at the sound of her name on his lips. It had been several years since anyone had spoken her name. "Thank you, my chieftain. I give you my word I will not stop unless I succeed or die in the effort."

"Go prepare," he said with a nod and left her.

She rushed toward Kestra, grabbed her arm, and ran toward the slaves' hut to prepare for the soul dance.

In a short while, Drisani had unfolded the carefully packed dress with its layer upon layer of white-and-black veils. It was a tight-fitting dress, but the gauzy layers of veils gave it an almost ethereal feel. She felt free in the dress as she tested pirouettes and plies. She was in good enough shape to perform the steps of the dance, but what of the rest? Could she summon enough of the mana lines' magic to bring forth a black soul among the rest? The draining of her soul during the dance might kill her or worse, the black soul summoned forward might destroy her, too. She had to succeed—the fate of her people rested on her shoulders again. This time, she wouldn't fail them.

She gazed over at Kestra and found the slave kowtowing on the floor. With a gasp, she turned to see

Kanago standing in the doorframe. She fell to her knees and bowed her head.

"Forgive me, my chieftain, I did not see you."

"Rise, both of you," he said, his voice sharp. "Drisani, are you ready? Can you do this?"

He took her by the shoulders and his gaze almost seemed to plead with her.

"We risk so much tonight," he continued. "There must be a black soul among us. I would prefer otherwise, but I know that is what killed Cirra. If she had not found one present, the dance would have concluded and we'd have been feasting in celebration with the plains warriors. Can you do this?"

He didn't trust her, she finally realized. Again, that night so many seasons ago haunted her. Why hadn't she stayed and died with her troops? "I know you do not trust me, but know that my loyalty can never be questioned. This is my home. I will do what's asked of me." This was her gauntlet at last.

Kanago stared at her for a moment, and then he bent slowly to unfasten the slave chain at her ankle. The jangle of the chains left her, and she wanted to cry in relief.

"They have returned. Dance what will be, Drisani."

He held out his hand to her and reluctantly, she laid hers in his. Then he led her out to the fire.

She stood before the plains chieftain. "With your consent, may I dance the soul dance for your people? I pledge that, regardless of who carries it, I will reveal the black soul among us, the one halting peace between our tribes."

The plains chieftain offered a gruff nod and glanced at her warriors. They seemed tenser than they had an hour ago, but perhaps that was because she had been farther away. She turned, at last, to Kanago and bowed her head, awaiting him to grant his consent as well, out of respect.

"The mountain tribes consent to the dance."

The tribal drummer sat down in the sand near the fire, the brightly colored drum wedged between his crossed legs. He began a slow rhythm that always began the dance. And with that, Drisani danced in the fire glow.

Letting the drumbeat fill her senses, she whirled in a tight circle and then swayed in rhythmic steps until the veils fluttered around her frame. Her pulse pounded with the drum's rhythm and she beat out a harmony with her feet. She twirled faster until, at last, the silver threads of mana lines coiled around her feet. She kicked them up and whirled like a top, gathering the strands around her waist. When she felt their snug presence against the veils, she felt the energy spreading through her arms and into her hands.

Her mother had always told her that a Soul Dancer's soul must attract other souls into the dance. When she danced, she must share her soul with all who watched, for only then could she take up the mana lines' magic and draw out other souls. It was a hunger, her mother had warned her, a hunger that could swallow up a dancer, but it was the only way to draw out the blackest of souls who sought to devour her magic.

Slowing her rhythm, she concentrated on the veils' gentle movements, trying to mimic their graceful flutters. She imagined a butterfly as she dipped from side to side, her arms undulating. The silvery strands of magic slithered out from her hands, purling through the clusters of warriors and summoning their souls into the dance.

One by one, their silvery forms joined Drisani around the fire as she turned and leaped, leading them along with the silvery magic. She swayed past each one as she whirled and moved in the other direction around the fire. Kanago and Reggel were close now.

For an instant, Drisani's gaze met Kanago's, but it

was enough to make her cry as the black soul trickled into the firelight.

She gasped, missing a step, but she tapped out a new rhythm with her feet and swayed into it again. No, it couldn't be Kanago—but the dance never lied.

Quickly, in gentle, rhythmic motions, she traced the mana lines that had woven a glittering pattern around the fire. She grabbed hold of the one connecting her to the black soul and followed it, moving closer to the hungry, dark thing as it leaped wildly around the fire.

At last, she swayed before Kanago again. His confused gaze seemed almost panicked that she would single him out. His warriors stepped back from him, including Reggel, his second. She danced around Kanago and whispered into his ear.

"Trust me."

Sighing, he closed his eyes and nodded.

She held onto his arms as she leaped into the air and turned, one hand gripping the mana line that bound the black soul to him. As she landed, she saw the silvery line disappear into the earth. The black soul wasn't Kanago's. Breath rushed out of her lungs and she froze for a moment.

Someone else among them possessed a Soul Dancer's skill.

Turning softly, she stared out at the circle of warriors. There grinning at her from across the firelight was Reggel. It was him. But how would she prove it?

"It's Kanago, isn't it?" Reggel shouted, drawing his sword.

"That isn't certain yet," Drisani replied, breathless, and launched herself into a mad dance around the fire again.

As long as she danced, Reggel could do nothing to Kanago. A chill brushed past her, Reggel's black soul touching her arm. Her body went limp, the magic draining away for a moment. She stumbled back from it, fell into the sand, but picked herself up and into a spin. Swaying from side to side, she moved farther away from the black soul.

"It stands before me," she replied, her voice nearly a whisper.

"It's Kanago's black soul!" Reggel shouted. "Restrain him!"

The mountain tribe warriors swarmed over Kanago who did not fight them.

Reggel grinned. "You'll run the gauntlet before the moon is full, Kanago," he said. Then he held up ankle chains. "Unless you succumb to the chains."

His wicked laughter cut through Drisani. She glared at him. Reggel would destroy her people. Somehow, she had to stop him.

Moving around the fire, she danced before Reggel, a seductive smile on her face. She laid her hands on his shoulders.

"You have the skill to touch the lines," she said in a soft voice as she moved behind him, leaning against him so that her lips pressed against his ear. "But you cannot call the magic, can you? That's why you hide the skill, because it's only partly within you."

"You're perceptive, no-name grub, but I'm merely out of practice." He laid a hand to her chestnut hair and whispered sharply. "You'll not live to tell anyone though. You'll follow your chieftain into the gauntlet. That, I will promise you—if you survive the dance."

"You hunger for the magic, don't you, Reggel," she said, her voice calm and enticing. "Call it now, through me. Taste what you'll lose when I'm gone."

He grabbed her hands and spun her around in front of him. She swayed back and forth, her veils fluttering. His grip hurt, but she pretended it didn't. Then she saw the black soul turn away from the fire and gyrate toward her. He would hold her here and allow it to consume her soul. She would die, and Kanago would be ruined. She had to make the others see what she saw.

Inhaling sharply, she turned her gaze back to Reggel. He seemed to be fighting the urge to sip from her magic. He ached for it.

"Drink of it, Reggel, taste its raw flavor on your tongue."

She kept up some semblance of dance until finally she saw the hunger burn in his eyes. The black soul moved closer now. It, too, was starving. It would move toward the greatest concentration of magic.

"Drink the mana magic, Reggel. Drink it!"

Only then did Reggel take hold of the magic entwining her soul. Magic drained from her and she nearly collapsed. The mana lines rippled and turned black for a moment, then the electric flash of silver cascaded toward Reggel from all the mana lines. Famished, the black soul rushed past Drisani and returned to its source. Reggel.

He shoved her away and she fell. The slave chains in his hands lit with an eerie, silver sheen. At last, the drum beat stopped.

"See the chains!" she shouted. "See how they glow in his hands. The black soul has returned to him. That's why they gleam with magic."

The sated look on Reggel's face slipped into a mask of shock as he stared at the chains and then at Drisani.

"He summoned the lines and crossed them to make Kanago look guilty, but it is Reggel who wants war."

Reggel backed away from the fire, but Kanago's warriors rushed at him, the plains warriors joining them. Once more, his gaze met Drisani's and he raised his hand, magic building.

Struggling to rise, Drisani reached for the lines, but she was drained. The flash of silver struck her in the chest, but she managed to take hold of one mana line—Reggel's soul line.

The magic slammed through her body and arced, surging down the silver cord back at Reggel. The magic slammed against him, knocking him off his feet. He collapsed dead on the ground.

Kanago was beside her now, helping her to her feet. She was too weak to stand, so he carried her over to a reed mat near the fire.

"You saved us all, Drisani," he said, his hazel eyes bright. "You have earned back your name."

"And peace with us," said the plains chieftain. "There will be no more fighting between our tribes."

The plains chieftain reached out her hand to Kanago who shook it, and then she held out her hand to Drisani. Surprised, Drisani hesitated, but then shook the plains chieftain's hand.

"We will return tomorrow evening to a true peace fire, Kanago." She started to leave, but turned back for a moment. "And perhaps by tomorrow, Reggel will be replaced by a more loyal second?"

Kanago nodded and rose from the ground. He left Drisani for a moment. Kestra hurried over with a flask of water, which Drisani drained.

Then Kanago was back. He extended a sword and sheath to her. She stared at the red-and-blue hawk crest on the hilt. Her sword. Taken from her the night she had become a slave.

"From this night forward, I'll expect you to stand as my second, Drisani."

She accepted the sword and the new station. At last, she, too, had her soul back.

LADY OF FLAME

by Diana L. Paxson

Diana L. Paxson is the first writer I asked to submit a story for my first anthology, *Greyhaven,* and she's been with us ever since. Her stories are always good reading.

Diana's most recent work is *Hallowed Isle,* an Arthurian novel in four volumes: *The Book of the Sword, The Book of the Spear, The Book of the Cauldron,* and *The Book of the Stone.* She is also working with me on the next book about Avalon.

Many Irish captives were brought back to Scandinavia by Viking raiders. In "Lady Of Flame," Diana looks at what might happen when Norse and Celtic magic collide.

Diana still lives at Greyhaven with her son Ian, her daughter-in-law Elizabeth, and her three grandchildren. This puts her one ahead of me in the grandchildren department, but she has an unfair advantage: two of hers are twins.

In the valley below, a farmhouse was burning. Billows of black smoke rose to stain the sky. The men who had set that fire were coming up the road, laden with plunder. Bera eased back behind the pine tree, motioning to Haki to drive the horse and wagon farther into the trees. Through the screening branches she watched the file of warriors pass by, laughing as they took the road back toward the sea.

"Danes . . ." breathed Bera, placing the accent as they disappeared down the road. She sketched a protective bindrune in the air. "The sons of Eric Bloodax have got an army from King Harald at last. Trolls take them all! Hakon has been a good king, for all he is a Christian. Eric's cubs would as soon destroy as rule the land!"

Haki grunted and spat into the grass. He had grown old in the service of the Voelva who had been Bera's teacher in the art of prophecy, and thrall though he might be, he was the closest she had to a kinsman and friend.

"Makes no difference," he grunted, "we'll get no welcome down there."

"Hakon will defeat them," she whispered, willing herself to believe it. "But the coasts will be unsafe for a while. We've no choice but to go farther into the hills."

Haki gazed at the jagged line of the ridge, shading his eyes beneath one gnarled hand. "The last fork in the road leads to Ormsdale. In times past, they gave the Voelva a good welcome."

Bera nodded. "We'll give the reivers a bit of a start, and then we will go there."

Haki grimaced and stifled a cough. In the light that filtered through the pine boughs he looked every year of his age. But until the Ericssons were defeated, there would be little safety anywhere.

The shifting wind brought them the reek of smoldering thatch. Bera sniffed. Gods, she hated that smell!

They came to the farmstead at dusk, when the smoke that curled from the rooftops was heavy with the scent of cooking food. Their news won them a swift welcome.

"And where were the beacons?" asked the master of the place, a big man called Olvir who had fought for Hakon when the king first came to Norway. He was old now, with a bad hip that kept him close to

home, but still hale. "Five years we have been paying
ship-tax for protection and warning!"

"And a fine for false alarms—" added another man.
"Maybe by the time the southern folk knew for sure
who was coming, the Danes had got past them—"

Bera held out her horn cup to the woman who was
bearing the ale pitcher around the table to be refilled.
She was even shorter than Bera herself, with black
hair and a milk-white skin that had never been bred
in these northern lands. *Irish,* she thought, *captured
on some raid. Like my mother . . .*

She gazed after the thrall with some sympathy, hoping to catch her eye, but the woman continued around
the table with a serene disdain that refused to acknowledge the drinkers even as she served them.

"They must be lying off Ulvasund, to come raiding
this way—" said Olvir's son Asmund. "And the king
is at his farm on Birkestrand, I hear, with only his
household around him."

"Nay, by now he will be sending round the war-
arrow," said the chieftain.

"Maybe Havard Arnasson will join him, spoiling for
a fight as he always is!" anther man exclaimed.

"Hah!" Olvir grimaced. "He's more likely to offer
his sword to the sons of Eric!"

"Let him go then, and may they have joy of him—"
said the housecarl.

"So long as he no longer troubles us here! But *we*
will not shirk our duty—go sharpen your sword, Asmund, for I want you and every fighting man we have
off to Hakon's aid with tomorrow's dawn!"

The talk went on from there to tales of other wars
and warriors. The Arnassons, it appeared, had been
enemies to Olvir's family since before King Harald's
time. Bera could not tell whether the men were glad
or sorry the blood feud lay in the past.

When she had finished eating, she picked up the

carved staff that leaned against the wall and made her way to the high seat where Olvir sat with his ale horn in his hand. His wife was dead and his daughters married, she had heard. Bera wondered who kept the keys in his hall.

"I have to thank you for your hospitality," she said softly. "I am a Voelva, heir to Groa who came here during King Harald's time. If you have need for a healer or a seeress, I will be happy to serve you."

"I remember her—" Olvir drained his horn and set it down. "And for her sake you are welcome to stay till the fighting is finished, though I've no need for your services. I have my own wisewoman now." He peered through the confusion of light and shadow beyond the long hearth and beckoned. "Achtlan! Come here, woman, and see to our guest!"

Bera watched the Irishwoman move among the housecarls and this time noticed the keys hanging from one of the round brooches that pinned her apron to the top of her hanging skirt. Olvir squeezed her shoulder with a heavy hand.

"Find a place for our guest to sleep, and make sure she has all she needs."

Bera smiled, opening her awareness to the other woman as she would have done to greet Groa—and felt the current of energy rebound as if it had hit a wall. She blinked in surprise and tried again, but she could feel nothing at all.

Achtlan's face had not changed when Olvir gripped her, and she betrayed no relief when he let go. She surveyed Bera with the same lack of expression, and motioned to her to follow.

She seems to understand Norse— wondered Bera. *Does she say nothing because she cannot, or because she does not think us worthy of her words?*

They moved down the hall. "In there—" Achtlan pointed to a curtained box-bed built between the houseposts and the wall. "I put clean blankets on when you come." The words were oddly accented, but clear.

Bera nodded. "And what about my man, Haki?"

"He sleeps there, by the fire," the woman answered. Hearing his name, Haki looked up and grinned. He was sitting on his roll of bedding, and clearly had made friends with the other servants here.

"I thank you—" said Bera, but the Irishwoman was already walking away.

Having offered his hospitality, Olvir paid his guest no further attention. Bera thought it best to wait until the Danes had been dealt with before she tried to leave. She had hoped that with time the Irishwoman would be willing to talk to her, but Achtlan's speech barely sufficed for communication, much less courtesy, even, Bera suspected, when Olvir required his thrall to share his bed. She might accept her master's right to her labor, but her soul remained her own.

Only when they brought in a thrall who had broken a leg did Achtlan show any softening, murmuring to the man in soft Irish as she straightened the limb and wrapped it in sheepskin before binding on a splint of willow slats. Bera watched with interest. She knew a spell or two for healing such ills, but the only word she recognized was the repeated name, "Brigid," and though she tried, she could sense no use of power.

Still, the woman seemed to know her herblore. When the injured man at last lay sleeping, Bera followed her back into the hall.

"What herbs did you add to the willowbark infusion?" she asked.

Achtlan kept walking, and Bera began to wonder if she had heard. "There are other herbs in the drink— what did you give him?" she said more loudly.

"Chamomile . . ." the Irishwoman replied unwillingly, "and comfrey."

"To help him sleep, and to knit the bone." Bera nodded. "And what spells did you use?"

Achtlan turned away, and Bera felt herself flushing. "Olvir calls you a wisewoman!" she exclaimed. "Are you a seidhkona, or are you simply taking advantage of his superstition? Do you think I would not understand? Even the goddess Gullveig stood in the hall of the Aesir in chains!"

But Achtlan was already beyond earshot, solitary in the midst of the crowd.

Bera stared after her, fuming. Was Achtlan some royal woman of Ireland, silent in captivity? She had enough pride, but though Norse queens were said to be skilled in magic, Bera did not think it was so in Christian lands. She had rarely met anyone who presented such a neutral surface—she could not tell if the woman was warding, or trading on the common Norse belief that all Irish slavewomen, as if in compensation for their captivity, possessed magic powers.

My mother could have told me what this woman is, thought Bera, wondering if the attraction she felt for Achtlan were simply some long suppressed longing for her own mother's love. But if the Irish thrall was a woman of power, how had she been taken captive? Bera's own powers gave her no clue—though she had no symptoms of illness, she felt as locked into her own skull as if she had been ill.

Still, Achtlan was a minor mystery. As the days passed with no word, the folk at Olvirsstead spoke more often of the war. The countryside was full of rumor. Some said that the sons of Eric had twenty ships and were hunting King Hakon all around the coastal islands, while others had heard that the king had set up the hazel wands at Rastarkalf and summoned his enemy to battle there. But no word had come yet from Asmund Olvirsson, from which they concluded that the warring was not yet done. Bera slept badly, her dreams haunted by images of blood and fire that she could never remember when morning came.

When Asmund had been gone half a moon with no word, Olvir asked Bera to use her arts to get news of him. She watched Achtlan to see if the Irishwoman resented her intrusion into an area that was, according to Olvir, her own, but the thrall showed not even the common curiosity with which the rest of the household viewed her preparations. She directed the women to prepare the dish of heart-meat and the goat's milk gruel, and found a cushion filled with goosedown to set atop the seidh platform Haki was lashing together from saplings, as unmoved as if she were setting up a new loom.

It was as if she denied the very possibility of magic, and Bera, failing to find within her own belly the anxious anticipation with which she usually approached such workings, began to wonder if she was right. Still wondering, she set her foot in Haki's linked hands and let him boost her to the seidh seat. All the folk of the farm had gathered, enjoying this break in the routine of the farm, eager to hear what she would say.

Perhaps I will say nothing . . . she thought, waiting for them to grow still. *Perhaps the spirits will not come to me, and I will see nothing at all.* But she had such fears every time she sat here, waiting for the sacred song, and always, once it began, she would find herself whirling away to soar between the worlds. She sent out a prayer to Brunbjorn, the spirit bear who was her ally, yet even as she did so, she found herself unable to remember how long it had been since she had felt him near.

Then Haki began singing, and as the others joined

in, she felt the familiar lift and drop, and the world of humankind disappeared. She waited for the spirits to begin their whispering, but there was nothing. She floated in a well of darkness.

Brunbjorn! Straining, she could sense his familiar presence, but it was muted, as if they were separated by a thick veil. Haki's singing was the only reality in her world.

Then it ended. She heard Olvir clear his throat.

"Tell me, Wise One, how fares my son, and whether King Hakon will win this war!"

Bera waited for the vision to form . . . and saw nothing. Someone coughed. She could feel the weight of expectation in the room. Panic mounted, and she fought to control it. Despite her earlier anxieties, after so many years she had not really believed she could fail. Once more she called on her ally.

Still she could not hear him, but within her inner darkness, a spark began to glow. It grew, became a circle of fire. The flickering light showed hurdles of brushwood stacked around the hall, and men who stood with poised spears before the doors. Now the thatch was catching; bright flames surged toward the starry sky. In the midst of that radiance stood a woman, eyes blazing, her golden hair streaming toward the sky. As Bera drew closer, she saw that the woman was chained.

Are you Gullveig? her heart cried. *What are you doing here?* Unwilled, her lips began to move, giving voice to the goddess' reply—

"Enslaved I stand within your hall—three times you have burned me, three times speared me, yet I endure . . ."

From the darkness beyond her vision she heard a woman's choked sob, then Olvir spoke again.

"What do you mean? Where is my son?"

Bera tried to block out the image of the burning woman, but found herself being drawn closer.

"While your chains bind me, I cannot see beyond the circle of fire . . ."

The flames grew brighter; heat seared her skin.

"Set me free!" Did those words come from without or within?

Fire exploded around her and she screamed.

When Bera came to herself, she was lying in the boxbed. Her skin felt hot, and she ached in every bone. She flinched as something cool touched her forehead. A woman's shape was bending over her; for a moment Bera saw the face of the goddess in her vision, then she blinked and it was only the thrall-woman Achtlan.

"Thank you . . ."

Achtlan lifted the cloth from her brow, dipped it in water, and laid it back again.

"What happened?"

"Chieftain says you should not try to do seidh when you have fever." It was the longest sentence Bera had yet heard from her.

She started to explain about the vision, to say that she had not been fevered when she began the ritual, but let her lips close upon the words. Better to let them think she had misjudged her fitness for working magic than her ability. No one must know how badly she had failed.

Bera closed her eyes, hoping that the other woman would assume the tears that were sliding from beneath her eyelids were only moisture from the cloth. She made herself breathe deep and slow, as if she were falling into sleep. After a few moments she heard the bench creak and sensed that Achtlan was leaving her.

Now she felt cold. Perhaps she was ill after all. Bera peeled the cloth from her brow and pulled the blankets up around her. Sleep was a good idea. Tomorrow, perhaps, she would feel well enough to understand, or else she would be worse and it would not matter. She shut her eyes again, but oblivion was long in coming, and when it did, the image of the burning woman filled her dreams.

Bera kept to her bed all of the net day, putting off the moment when she must read confirmation of her failure in men's eyes. But when the hall wakened the next morning, she knew she could lie still no longer, and taking a heel of bread and a skin of thin ale, she slipped out of the hall.

As soon as she passed the wall of the garth, she began to feel better. She stopped, turning her face to the sun, and took a deep breath. As the energy in the air tingled through her body, other senses suddenly awakened. Power throbbed in the earth beneath her; she could tell that beyond the birch wood ran a stream; spirits sang in the wind that stirred her hair. This was how a man blinded might feel if his vision was returned. Bera began to weep, understanding only now how she had feared that the skills by which she had lived since she was fifteen years old had forever gone.

But why had they deserted her even for a little while? Frowning, she turned, and retraced her steps to the gate in the wall. There was no visible difference, but as she went through she felt a tremor and the air went dead.

All around her, the folk of the farmstead were going about their tasks. Bera could see and hear them perfectly, but she realized now that she could not touch their spirits at all. Skin prickling, she slipped back through the gate and stood gasping until she felt warm once more.

The garth was warded, and within its circle the invisible energies that supported life could not be sensed at all. How could she not have noticed it when she first arrived? Fear of the raiders and the fatigue of her journey must have dulled her senses, and after Olvir refused her first offer, she had been too polite to try her skills.

She had to leave this place as soon as possible. But her failure in the seidh seat still rankled, even if, as she now suspected, it was no fault of her own. She extended her awareness toward the woodland, seeking a place where she would be able to hear the spirits as she had not been able to do in the hall.

In the midst of the birch-wood the ground rose abruptly into a small mound, its sides overgrown with brambles and young trees. It was old, thought Bera, a relic of the howe-age before men began to burn their dead, surrounded by an oval kerb of stones. This was not one of Olvir's ancestors, or he would have tended it; but perhaps that would make the wight all the more grateful for her attention. She unstoppered her skin bag and poured out the rest of the ale in offering.

"Old one, hear me—I come seeking wisdom. Lend power to my journeying and let me see truly."

A wind sighed through the birches as if in answer, and she felt a subtle warming in the atmosphere that told her she had been heard. She kirtled up her skirts and began to climb the mound.

The top was slightly hollowed, as if the place had been used for sitting out before. Bera wrapped her cloak around her and lay down, gazing through the fringe of grasses at the sky. She could feel earth and wind, sun and forest, as one feels the presence of other folk in a hall. She hailed them as old friends whom she had not met for far too long, then closed her eyes and released her breath and slid into the singing silence within.

How could she have mistaken the dead darkness she had encountered in the hall for this shimmer of sensation? She had not even needed to summon the spirits—they were already here.

Brunbjorn, guard me, wise ones, show me— she articulated her prayer. *Will King Hakon win his war? Will Asmund Olvirsson come safely home?*

A confusion of images flickered around her; laughing, she rode the flow of vision, fixing her attention with the discipline of long experience, as if she were keeping a small craft on a steady course across the sea. And then it was the sea she was seeing, speeding over churning waves toward an island where a flat field lay beneath a low ridge.

She saw King Hakon's forces drawn up in a long line, and the army of the Ericssons approaching from the south, from the pass through the hills. But as she watched ten of the King's men crept around behind the ridge, carrying furled standards on poles. In another moment, the Ericssons and their Danish allies were attacking, but the ten men with the standards had split up, and were waving their banners as if ten more squadrons were coming up from the shore to help the King. And the Danes, thinking themselves outnumbered, turned and ran.

The King's forces, pursuing, struck down many. When they reached the ridge, the Ericssons could see how they had been tricked and turned to fight, but the Danes continued to flee. A young man with the bearing of a king was struck down along with many more, but the rest of Eric's sons reached their ships and escaped, leaving King Hakon in command of the field.

Even so deep in trance, Bera found herself smiling. Her first question was answered. It remained only to foresee Asmund's homecoming, and her reputation would be redeemed. She cleared her mind, keeping her intention firm, until vision showed her laden tables and laughing faces, and Asmund sitting in the high seat beside his father, lifting a horn of mead.

"Is it well with you, lady? You are newly recovered, and when they could not find you in the hall, we began to fear—" On Olvir's face, Bera recognized real concern. He was a good man, however ignorant he might be of magic. Or perhaps even that criticism was too harsh, she thought, rubbing at her eyes as if to push the veils that blinded her spirit away. A few days in this place had been enough to deaden her own perceptions, and this was his home.

"The walk did me good." Even though she now knew the exact point at which vision ended, with every moment her memories of what had happened beyond it were dimming. But she had to tell him her news.

"Sometimes the outlands hold wisdom that those who stay within the garth cannot know. I sat out on the mound in the birchwood, and the wights have shown me that the king has won a great battle on an island, and your son Asmund will soon be home. "Nay—" she continued as he began to look skeptical. "I do not ask you to believe me now. Time will surely prove the truth of my words."

As she turned away, a murmur of speculation swept through the hall. Where before there had been only pity, folk looked at her now with hope or skepticism in their eyes. Only Achtlan, stirring the boiling meat in the cauldron, continued her work with no expression at all.

As Bera met the other woman's dark gaze, her memories of the afternoon seemed suddenly as empty as a child's day-dream. But she had neither expected nor imagined that moment of transformation at the garth wall. She moved toward the Irishwoman, frowning.

"When I first came here, Olvir told me that you, too, were a wisewoman," she said quietly. "Why have you not sought the answers he needed? Especially when I . . . failed . . ."

For several moments Achtlan continued to stir, her reflected features fragmented as Bera's lost vision as the ripples swirled. Bera waited, patient and unrelenting.

"To believe in such things is self-deception." Achtlan said finally.

Bera stared at her. "It was *you*!" she exclaimed softly. "You cursed me that night! You have used your power to deny all magic!"

"There are no powers . . . The only reality is what is here and now!" retorted the Irishwoman, stung for the first time to some show of emotion.

"The reality here is what *you* have chosen to believe!" Bera answered her. "In this hall the only vision I could see was the goddess Gullveig, chained among the flames. But in the old story, she refused to believe that steel or fire had power to harm her, and so she went free!"

Achtlan looked up, and Bera flinched from the black despair in the thrall's eyes. "*My* goddess betrayed me . . ." she said flatly. "This is the only protection I have, and I will not allow you to take it away!"

Bera waited, spending most of the hours of light outside the garth. On the second day her patience was rewarded, and just as dusk was falling, Asmund Olvirsson came home. He and his men were laden with blood-stained Danish armor and tales of glory, boasting of their exploits and praising the king.

"Look at them! You cannot deny my knowledge now!" said Bera to Achtlan, who was supervising the thralls as they set up tables and benches beside the long hearth.

"All I know is I have two dozen mouths to feed, and it is dark soon."

"You could have been getting ready for them if you had listened to me—" muttered Bera as the Irishwoman turned away to give orders about the ale. Then she rolled up her sleeves and went out to help tend the cauldrons.

It was a memorable evening. Bera, smiling as she fondled the silver arm ring with which Olvir had rewarded her, allowed herself to drink more deeply than usual. By the time she crawled into her cupboard bed, her head was spinning, and she fell swiftly into oblivion.

The world is burning. Screaming silently, the goddess struggles against her chains. Smoke billows above her, its harsh reek catching in her lungs. Fighting for breath, she twists in her bonds—

Bera coughed, heaving convulsively, and something gave way. With a gasp she sat up. Where was the fire? Her staring eyes saw only darkness, and she realized now that the bindings against which she had been fighting were only the tangled bedclothes. A *nightmare* . . . she thought, kicking the blanket aside, *left over from my vision* . . . Swiftly the images faded from her memory.

But the smell of smoke was stronger now.

Bera yanked open the bed-curtains and peered into the shadows of the hall. The hearthfire had been banked for the night—in the long trench only a few coals yet glowed. Achtlan would not have left green wood smoldering, and yet the acrid scent that had awakened her still hung in the air.

The darkness resonated with the familiar wheeze and snore of sleeping men. But there was something else—Bera tensed, certain now that she heard men talking in hushed voices, and then, unmistakeably, the crackle of flames. She reached out to the log wall beside her and found it warm, looked up and glimpsed a sparkle of light in the thatching above her, and scrambled from the box-bed, shouting "Fire! Fire!"

Like an echo, from outside the hall came the bray of a horn.

The hall erupted in confusion as men still drunk from the celebration stumbled about, groping for their weapons. Bera dressed hurriedly, fumbling in the dark.

"Warriors, to me!" Olvir's bellow rose above the din as someone thrust a torch into the coals and held it high. She glimpsed Asmund shrugging into his hauberk, half-naked men clutching spears and swords.

"Olvir!" came a shout from outside. "Are you awake, old man? Are you warm enough? Soon you will be warmer still!"

"Havard Arnasson . . ." said Asmund, swearing. "He'll have fire set all around the hall, and men waiting outside the door."

Bera swallowed, realizing that she had foreseen this in her first vision, and thought it only an image, like the goddess in chains. Heated air rushed in as the door was opened. In the dancing firelight she glimpsed the glint of steel.

Spears came darting through the smoke, and Asmund's men picked them up and cast them back again. Outside, someone cried out in pain, and the housecarls laughed.

"What is it you want, Havard?" called Olvir. "Let us settle the old feud now, for when the king hears of this, you will suffer for it!"

"The matter will be settled, all right," snarled the man outside, "but the Danes will get the blame. Will you come out fighting or stay to be burned?"

"First, let the women and thralls go free—" answered Olvir. By now the roof was well alight, and the beams were beginning to burn. A trail of sparks dropped from the thatch above him, and he stepped backward.

"Very well—but no tricks—"

The women and slaves were crowding toward the door, clutching their possessions and weeping. To one side she glimpsed Atchlan, her face, even now, as unmoving as if it had been carved from stone.

Bera tried to remember the old rune against burnings—

> *"That seventh I know, if o'er sleepers' heads*
> *I behold a hall on fire . . ."*

But she could not recall the rest of the spell.

She grabbed her carved staff and moved forward with the others. The first group of women ran out through the door, sparks sprinkling their shawls like rain. She saw Haki among the thralls that followed, and sighed with relief that at least he would be safe now.

Achtlan was behind them. As Bera started after her, the roofbeam groaned; she looked up and saw that it was burning furiously. Without thinking, she grabbed for the other woman's arm and jerked her backward just as the roof fell in.

"I do not thank you—" said the Irishwoman. "Now I die slow, from smoke, instead of fast in the fire."

Bera stared at her. "If it were not for you, we would not be dying at all! I would have given Olvir forewarning, and I would not be fettered by your mind-spells now, so that I cannot even reach out to the gods! The walls that protected you have become your prison—" she shouted as Achtlan shook her head in denial. "'The goddess is burning, set her free!"

The Irishwoman was still shaking her head, but she

was weeping now, coughing as the smoke grew thicker. Bera dragged her back, forcing her down to the dirt floor where the air was still relatively clear.

"I cannot . . ." Achtlan said hoarsely. "I served Brigid—I cannot call her while I am slave—"

No time now to argue whether it was she or the goddess that had made that law. Bera cast an exasperated look from Achtlan to Olvir, who was waiting for death in his high seat, the sword he could no longer swing unsheathed across his knees.

"This woman has given you good service, lord—will you let her die free?"

Olvir stared at them, then gave a short laugh. "Be it so—before the gods you shall stand witness—I am only sorry it will be so soon!" His gaze went back to the door, where two of his men had tried to break out and fallen back into the flames, transfixed by enemy spears.

Achtlan sagged back against one of the houseposts, her face working. Bera shook her head, feeling the barriers that had dulled her inner senses crumbling, wincing as the anguish of the dying and the fury of the men who still stood at bay in the hall struck her suddenly unshielded soul.

To die will not be so terrible now that I have my soul again, she told herself, fighting for control. *At least I know the way to the Otherworld. . . .*

Achtlan was weeping, her pain striking raw on Bera's nerves.

"Tell me about Brigid," she said, hoping to distract her.

"She is one and three, the daughter of the Dagda, the daughter of a king," murmured the Irishwoman. "She has skills of healing, of bardcraft, of the forge . . . she hangs her cloak on a sunbeam, she—"

But Bera was no longer listening, her inner vision seized suddenly by the memory of a goddess in flames.

"Gullveig is bound in the midst of the fire!" she seized Achtlan's arm. "Call upon your Brigid to break those chains"

She focused her energies, reached out to the other woman's spirit and slammed the image toward her. Achtlan jerked beneath her hand, and in the next moment Bera lost awareness of her own body. She knew only that she and the Irishwoman were together, falling inward toward the bright circle where Gullveig danced in the flames.

And suddenly she *was* Gullveig, holding out her bound hands to a bright figure who approached, red cloak billowing around her, upon her fair head a crown of candles, and a hammer in her hand.

I cast off my chains . . . both voices rang out together. *I command the fire* . . .

The hammer flashed down, and the goddesses disappeared in an explosion of light.

Someone was shaking her shoulder.

Bera opened her eyes and saw that Achtlan was pointing toward the front of the hall. The blazing beam, in falling, had shattered, and the two halves had rolled apart. The walls were smoldering, but between the pieces lay a clear path, barred only by a scattering of glowing coals. They got to their feet, eyes wide with wonder.

Bera turned to Olvir. "If you have the courage to take it, there lies the way to freedom—"

The chieftain shook his head. "I would rather die in my own hall than on Havard's spears."

Bera smiled, seeing, with doubled vision, the two goddesses beckoning. "I will deal with *him*. Achtlan, lead Olvir and the others out after me."

She moved forward, sweeping the larger chunks of glowing wood aside with her staff, and the heat of the fallen beams seemed no more than the warmth of a hearthfire as she passed. Then it was behind her, and she was emerging into the firelit night.

For a moment, Havard and his men stood staring. Whatever they saw, it was twice as tall as she was, and the light that flickered on their shocked faces was brighter than could be accounted for by the fire. Then, falling over each other in their terror, and gabbling, they ran away.

Bera stood aside as Olvir and the others pushed through the door after her, feeling the power that had filled her fade. Haki hurried toward her, the joy in his old face changing to concern as he saw her sway. As if their enemies' hate had fueled it, the fire was dying, too. She took a deep breath, awareness touching the sleeping earth, its energies even now beginning to awaken as the eastern sky lightened with the approach of day.

Bera drew a deep breath, and sighed, finding no scent on the wind but the sweetness of new-mown hay and the resinous tang of sunlit pine. It was their clothes that retained the taint of the burning—before they left Olvirsstead they had washed and aired them, but that smell would take a long time to go away.

She might say the same, she thought as she surveyed her companions, for the memories. Perhaps Haki, swaying to the motion of the wagon and shaking the reins from time to time across the horse's back to keep it going, was least affected. He had seen so much in his long life; what was one danger more?

For Achtlan, gazing at the forest through which they were passing with the delight of a child just learning to see, the four years she had spent as Olvir's thrall were a nightmare that the coming of daylight drove away. It was Bera herself, who remembered only too vividly what it had been like to lose her contact with the spirits of this land, who had most reason to fear the future, for she had promised to see the other woman back to Ireland.

Olvir had not been ungrateful. The gold he had given them would buy passage on some trader bound for the kingdom of Dublin. Wherever the Norse had settled, there should be work for a Voelva, and in Ireland, perhaps new skills to be learned from the people of Brigid as well.

Bera realized that the feeling that glowed in her belly was anticipation, not fear, and she began to smile.

THE TEARS OF THE MOON

by Cynthia Ward

Cynthia Ward was born in Oklahoma and has lived in Maine, Spain, Germany, and the San Francisco Bay Area. After attending Clarion West '92, she moved to Seattle with her husband. She has sold stories to *Sword and Sorceress* (Vols. VIII, IX, XI, XIV, and XV), *Marion Zimmer Bradley's Fantasy Worlds, Bending the Landscape: Horror, The Ultimate Dragon, Asimov's, Galaxy, Tomorrow, Absolute Magnitude,* and many other magazines and anthologies. She writes the monthly "Market Maven" market-news column for *Speculations* writing magazine. She is working on an SF mystery novel.

Tamra had come to the forbidden pond with Khylom to see who they were going to marry. An old tale said that anyone who circled the Moonpool three times, praying all the while to the Moon Goddess and the Earth Goddess, would see in its waters the image of his future wife or her future husband. So Tamra followed her friend around the Moonpool, whispering prayers and glancing down frequently at the uneven ground to make sure she didn't stumble and fall into the water.

At the conclusion of his triple circuit of the pond, Khylom flung himself down on his hands and knees at the very edge of the rocky bank, and leaned forward recklessly far. He scanned the smooth water eagerly.

"I see her, Tamra!" He looked up, his dark eyes

glowing with delight, and pointed at the water. "There! See?"

Tamra knelt more carefully, mindful of the sharp gray stones and even more mindful of the water. She scanned the still surface of the perfectly round pond.

"I don't see anyone," she said, which wasn't true. She saw herself and Khylom. She also saw the moon, full and silver, though surely the sun was alone in the sky, sinking toward the western mountains. Tamra glanced up, confirming that Atanata, the Moon Goddess, was nowhere to be seen. When Tamra looked down again, the moon was no longer reflected in the pond. Tamra shook her head. She had seen something that wasn't there. Again.

Sometimes when Tamra was working in the drought-stricken wheat fields, pulling weeds or emptying water buckets, her sight would shimmer with a silver light that blotted out the world around her, replacing it with images of her village in flames and of the Othoni Barbarians killing her neighbors.

"Oh, Tamra!" Khylom sighed in exasperation. "How can you not see *anyone*?" He laid a hand on the back of Tamra's head and turned it so that she was looking at his reflection. "Surely you see Chesza's reflection there beside mine!"

"I do," Tamra said, lying. She saw no sign of the wine-maker's beautiful daughter beside Khylom's reflection. But Tamra didn't need to see Chesza's image to worry that Chesza would marry Khylom. Khylom was a poor farmer's son, but he was as handsome as the idol of the Sun God that stood in the city of Halarion. And Tamra had seen Chesza's father taking his carriage to the tiny cottage of Khylom's parents, and Khylom's parents walking to the wine-maker's elegant villa.

Tamra looked at her own reflection. The Moonpool showed her beside Khylom, but she feared this image showed only the present, not the future. She feared Khylom would never be her husband.

To hide her anguished expression, she raised her waterskin and took a long drink. The water tasted warm and sour, but Tamra was not tempted to drink from the pond. The pond water looked cool and inviting, and smelled sweet in the drought-parched air. But the pond was sacred to the Moon Goddess, and so its waters were dangerous to mortals. No fish swam in the pond; no fly flickered on its surface. No animal trail was beaten through the lilies that surrounded the uncannily circular pond. Indeed, the night-black lilies that grew around the pond grew nowhere else. The Moon Goddess, hunting deer long ago with a beloved mortal woman, had slain Her lover by accident with one of Her silver-tipped arrows. No mortal flesh may survive the touch of Atanata's arrows, so She turned her beloved to lilies, that the woman would not perish utterly; and the pool was formed by the tears the Moon Goddess wept for Her lost love.

Tamra preferred to stay away from Atanata's sacred pool, and not because of its hazardous waters, or the stern injunctions of the village elders. She had sneaked to the Moonpool once in childhood, and had seen the moon when the moon wasn't in the sky. It had looked big and close, like it was falling out of the sky to crush little Tamra. After that, she had stayed away, until last year, when Khylom had started slipping away to the Moonpool to look for Chesza's image in its waters. Tamra had always come to the pond with him.

"How beautiful she is," Khylom sighed, staring dreamily at the image of Chesza only he could see.

How rich she is, thought Tamra. Chesza was the only child of the wine-maker, the richest man in the village of Sorion. But Tamra knew Khylom was more interested in Chesza's looks than her father's money, and so Tamra kept her mouth shut.

"How I want to marry her," Khylom continued in a hoarse whisper, and Tamra tensed, knowing what was next. "To be her first and only love," he murmured, and turned Tamra's head so that he was gazing deeply into the eyes. "I must be worthy of the honor," Khylom said, and kissed Tamra on the lips.

This was what Tamra had been waiting for. Khylom liked to practice kissing and touching, making himself "worthy," as he put it, of the lovely Chesza. That was fine with Tamra. For her, it wasn't practice. She wanted to marry Khylom. She and Khylom had grown up together, as neighbors and constant companions. It had never occurred to her that Khylom would consider marrying anyone else, until the day he took her to the Moonpool to seek a glimpse of their future mates, and chattered all the way about his hopes of seeing Chesza's image.

Tamra refused to think about Khylom and Chesza together. If she ignored Khylom's talk and kept herself always available to him, she was sure he would realize which girl really loved him. And if she ignored her strange dreams of barbarians she'd never seen in her life, the dreams would surely go away. She saw the dreams sometimes even when awake, but they weren't visions, of that she was sure. A woman's visions were a gift from the Moon Goddess, and a sign that the woman had been chosen by Atanata to serve Her. But most women chosen by Atanata were women-lovers, like the Goddess Herself. Tamra was not in love with another girl, so she couldn't be having visions.

She had certainly never wanted visions. Chosen girls were sent far away, to the island of Eisana, for initiation and training at the Great Temple of the Moon. Once she was a priestess, a woman was assigned to another temple; but all temples were in cities. Tamra had never wanted to leave her village. She didn't want to leave the boy she loved.

As the sun set, Tamra and Khylom stayed hidden in the tall lilies beside the forbidden pond. They removed each other's tunics so they could kiss and touch each other everywhere. Tamra would have let Khylom do even more, but he would not risk getting her with child. He knew he'd have to marry her then.

Afterward, Khylom fell asleep, but Tamra lay awake, admiring him in the moonlight (the moon had risen, but she wouldn't look at that silver disk, lest she think about being chosen by Atanata for Her priestess-order). Tamra twisted a curl of Khylom's night-black hair around her fingers. He had long glossy locks that flowed past his shoulders, where Tamra's hair, like that of most villagers, clung close to her scalp in tiny, wiry curls. Khylom was tall and dark and lean-muscled, a man at sixteen, and gorgeous as the Sun God. Tamra too was sixteen, but she wasn't a beautiful woman. She was too thin, and her pallid skin betrayed some brutish barbarian ancestor. She was dark only in the depths of the dry season.

This summer, she was dark as Khylom himself, for the sun was scorching the kingdom of Theszonisha and all neighboring lands with a terrible drought. Tamra and the other villagers prayed daily that the rains would return before the wheat died and the grape vines and olive trees shriveled to naught. The streams ran dry in the mountains, and Sorion's wells were low. And the villagers dared not draw water from the ever-full Moonpool even for their crops.

Tamra turned her eyes to the pond, which shone silver now, like Atanata's great chariot-wheel fallen to earth. Tamra had heard of years so dry that the heat and dust turned the world as brown as leather. Years so dry that thirst-maddened villagers tried to drink the sacred waters. Tamra shuddered, remembering the description of what had happened to those villagers, and she laid her arm across her sleeping love's shoulders, as if to protect Khylom from the drought.

Sometimes a drought had no chance to drive the villagers mad enough to drink from the Moonpool. Sometimes the Othoni Barbarians came over the mountains first.

Tamra closed her eyes against the very idea of the barbarians.

That was a mistake. Against the darkness of her eyelids they appeared, striding through her village with skin as pale as dust and long hair the color of flame, or the color of dry grass, or the color of their bronze blades. Sorion burned around them, providing light enough for them to see the fleeing villagers. They captured the women. They killed the men and children as readily as a villager would swat a mosquito. And one of the men they killed was Khylom.

Tamra gasped, and woke up. The hideous scene vanished.

Thank the gods! It had only been one of her dreams.

She no longer felt Khylom under her arm. In the light of the full moon, she saw Khylom was gone. He often slipped away from the pond while she slept, so eager was he to avoid his parents' wrath. His disappearances always made Tamra feel like she'd been punched in the chest, but she couldn't blame him. His father had a nasty temper, and would beat Khylom if he found out Khylom had gone to the forbidden pond. Tamra's own parents would be upset if they ever discovered where she went so many nights, but they would never strike her for going to the Moonpool. But Khylom didn't believe Tamra's parents were kinder than his own, so Tamra didn't understand why he never paused to wake her up when he fled the forbidden pond.

Her tunic was still faintly warm from where Khylom

had lain upon it. Dressing, she smelled a trace of his sweat. She knew her beloved was probably already home in bed, but still she sat up and looked over the nodding lilies, hoping to see Khylom walking back to Sorion. Instead, she saw a large group of men silently approaching the village with drawn swords.

The Othoni Barbarians had come, like something out of dark legend, driven by fate and drought over the high gray mountains that guarded the northwestern border of Theszonisha. In their desperation, the barbarians must have overwhelmed the Theszonishan garrison in one of the passes, slaughtering the soldiers despite their superior iron breastplates and swords and their high stone walls and towers. Then the Othoni must have descended the pass and slipped around whatever city lay at its base, avoiding its troops, which would be numerous enough to stop the barbarians no matter how desperate their hunger. So the barbarians had come into the cultivated, defenseless foothills of Theszonisha—and found the village of Sorion.

The invaders were numerous—there were at least a hundred—and they didn't know Tamra existed. If she kept quiet, they might never know they'd passed by one of the women they intended to violate.

Tamra had never seen herself in her visions of the barbarian attack. This, she realized, was because she would survive. The barbarians would never see her!

But they would burn her village. They would rape her mother and sisters. They would slay her father and brothers—and Khylom. Khylom would not escape their swords. Tamra had seen his death in her visions.

She closed her eyes. "O Goddesses of Earth and Moon, as you love the Theszonishans," she said silently, "I pray you will save the village and people of Sorion from the brutal Othoni."

The darkness behind her eyes turned suddenly to brilliant silver, sparkling like water, and the silver gave

way to the familiar, terrifying vision of the Othoni
Barbarians ravaging Sorion. And Tamra knew her
prayers, however heartfelt, would have no effect. The
Moon Goddess had sent Tamra visions so that she
might warn the village, and she had not done so.
Clearly Atanata deemed the visions sufficient; She
would do no more.

Tamra stood up. "Ho, foolish barbarians!" she
cried. "Do you think to find anyone in that village?"

The barbarians wheeled as one. When they saw her,
they raced silently toward her, raising their swords.
Then one man spoke, in a low but carrying voice. A
commanding voice. It said one word, and the barbarians halted. They all looked to the same man, who
strode forward among them, to glare at Tamra with
eyes as colorless as the thin ice that formed over pud-
dles on the coldest days of the rainy season.

The man spoke again, addressing Tamra in her own
language, barbarously accented, but understandable:
"Theszonishan girl, what do you there, calling insults
upon us?"

"A priestess' vision warned us you were coming, so
my people have run away," Tamra lied. "But we are
not far away, so I knew you would find us. Swear by
your gods that you will not harm me, and I will show
you where my people are hidden."

The Othoni began to murmur, glaring at her, and
she didn't need to understand their harsh tongue to
know they mocked and threatened her. Then the ice-
eyed man spoke a word, and his followers went silent
as hunting wolves.

The ice-eyed man switched to Theszonishan. "I
swear by Thuvan Wargod and by His Lady Fraysa the
Fair, no harm will come to you, farm girl, if you show
us where your people are hiding."

"This way." Tamra pointed. "Just across the water."

The Othoni looked at each other, and many spoke

a word; the same word, Tamra thought, for all that she knew nothing of their language. She saw several of the barbarians licking their lips and looking past her, and she knew the word must be "water."

She turned, and froze, a sick feeling shivering through her. The Moonpool was a pond no more, but a great broad lake that stretched as far as she could see.

Vision, or illusion? Tamra dared not touch the water, so she could not test whether she was hallucinating with fear, or experiencing a vision so powerful she saw it with open eyes.

A barbarian seized her arm, and terror slammed her heart against her ribs with such force that she thought the bone would shatter; her whole body would shatter and fall in pieces at the barbarian chief's bare feet. But she had no such easy escape from his crushing grip. He laid the edge of his bronze sword against her throat. His narrow ice-pale eyes bored into her wide dark eyes like daggers.

"No trickery, farm girl!" the huge chief snarled. He wore hammered-bronze ornaments and an ill-cured wolfskin. Tamra choked on the stinks of the hide and his dusty, sweaty body. "Lead us to your people," he rasped, "or die a painful death."

As he fell silent, she heard the sounds of men stepping into the water, or splashing their faces, or drinking from the pond. The sounds immediately gave way to screams that ended in mid-breath.

The barbarian chief cast a startled look around, his blade drifting away from Tamra's throat. His astonished expression transformed into a snarling mask of pure rage, and he screamed "Treachery!" in Tamra's tongue and drew back his sword for a blow that would sever her head from her shoulders.

Tamra had known that the barbarians, sweaty and dusty and thirsty, would not be able to resist the cool, alluring appearance of the Moonpool. It would be just another farm pond to them. She had known that some of the barbarians would discover the secret of the water by seeing it kill their comrades, and had known that these survivors would slay her. She had hoped only to kill as many barbarians as she could before she died, and upset the rest so much that their wrathful shouts would alert her fellow villagers to the presence of the enemy. She hoped her people would have time to flee to safety, or to take up their hunting bows, woodcutters' axes, hoes, and mattocks, and defend themselves.

Many of the barbarians were dead. But many still lived, and one was the chief, his sword speeding for Tamra's neck.

Tamra leaped backward, toward the water. She was going to die, but she wouldn't let it be at the barbarian's hand if she could help it. The chief held onto her arm for a second, but, overbalanced by her jump and his own sword-swing, he let go. He flailed his arms, trying to keep his balance. It didn't work. He, too, fell into the Moonpool.

The water closed over Tamra's head. The moonlight shimmered on the receding surface. She was surprised she could still see the light. Shouldn't she already be dead? Perhaps the sacred water did not bring instant death, as the villagers thought. But surely no one could survive being turned into—

She struck the bottom, her back settling into soft mud that rose up in clouds to hide the silver shimmer above. The loss of light frightened her, as did the growing ache in her lungs. She knew it would be impossible, but she tried to swim. Her arms swept through the water. Goddess be praised, she could *move*! The discovery filled Tamra with energy, and she arrowed upward, to break the surface of the pond.

The lake, rather. The Moonpool had truly become

a lake—one that had continued to widen as she'd sunk to the bottom. The waters had spread to touch every barbarian. Tamra knew this because every barbarian was motionless, standing or crouching or lying in the water. Or frozen in flight. Those barbarians who had tried to run away from the spreading water stood with their backs to her, their legs raised in mid-step, their long hair flung straight out behind them with the speed of their flight.

The waters of the Moonpool were not poison, but they were deadly. They turned all living things, save the night-black lilies, to stone.

All living things save the lilies and, miraculously, Tamra. She swam, her skin still soft and supple, her limbs still moving freely; and when her hand struck bottom, she stood up and walked.

Villagers were running toward her, shouting in horror at the sight of the Othoni invaders, turned into so many gray statues, and exclaiming in wonder at Tamra's continued movement.

"Stay back!" Tamra shouted, terrified that the villagers might run unknowing into the newly expanded margins of the pond. "The water will kill you!" she cried, though she didn't know. Perhaps the water's curse was temporarily lifted for all villagers—but she doubted it. *"No*, mother!" she screamed, seeing her mother had not stopped with the other villagers, far from the moonlit water, but came onward, reaching out to embrace her daughter. *"Stay where you are!"* Tamra cried. "I survive only because the Moon Goddess has chosen me!"

Tamra's mother stopped. She stared at her dripping daughter as if she couldn't believe what she'd heard. And Tamra's father, and all the other villagers, seemed equally stunned.

"Don't touch me until I've washed in safe waters," Tamra said, stepping from the Moonpool and leaving behind the ranks of stone barbarians. "It's true," she said. "The Moon Goddess has chosen me. I had a vision that barbarians would attack our village, but I didn't believe it. Even after I had the vision several times, I told myself it was just a dream, born of fears roused by the drought, and so I didn't warn you of the coming attack. The Moonpool has shown me how I deluded myself and almost killed you all. I could not have survived these waters had Atanata Herself not preserved me."

The villagers murmured in awe, but made no attempt to touch Tamra. And Khylom would not even meet her eyes. She felt suddenly as if her heart had turned to stone in her breast. But she told herself Khylom was only surprised to learn the Moon Goddess had chosen her.

She turned and walked away from the village. She left the terraced foothills behind and, as the sun rose, she found a stream that had once flowed to flat land, but now died on a mountainside in its own rocky bed. She used this failing source of water to clean herself. She rinsed her hair and her tunic many times, and she scrubbed her entire body repeatedly. When at last she felt clean, she rubbed herself dry with handfuls of living leaves from a gnarled old oak. The leaves did not turn to stone.

When her tunic had dried, Tamra dressed and returned to the village. She saw that the Moonpool had shrunk back within its original shore. She saw no gray stone figures, so she knew the waters had retreated quickly, and the villagers had cast ropes over the stone-struck barbarians and dragged them with mules until the uncanny statues fell into the depths of the Moonpool.

Tamra's mother waited beside the pond. She ran to embrace Tamra, laughing with joy at her daughter's survival, and weeping with sorrow because her daughter must soon go to the island of Eisana, for initiation into the order of the Moon Goddess. Tamra would not return to the village, not to stay, for the priestesses were assigned to temples all around the Great Inner Sea, and temples were found only in cities.

Despite the drought, the villagers held a great feast in Tamra's honor, because she had saved them, and because mortals chosen by the gods were rare, especially in a tiny village. And no one had ever heard of a mortal chosen as Tamra had been.

All the villagers came up to Tamra to thank her and wish her a safe journey—all save Khylom. He avoided her. But when the feast was done, and deep darkness and silence had fallen at last upon Sorion, Tamra walked down the village's lone street to the window of Khylom's room. She knocked upon the wood shutter (for Khylom's family was too poor for glass windows). Khylom, as firstborn, had the privilege of sleeping under the window of the room he shared with his brothers. Tamra rapped many times before the shutter opened, and Khylom peered out.

"I leave for the city of Halarion on the morrow, to present myself to the moon priestess for the journey to Eisana," Tamra said, speaking low so she would not wake Khylom's brothers. "Already I am lonely. Already I miss you more than I would my own life. Will you not give me a farewell kiss?"

"You'd turn me to stone!" Khylom said.

"You know better than that," Tamra said, astonished. "You saw me kiss my family with no harm. How can you think I would risk turning them, or you, to stone?"

"Why should I kiss you?" Khylom whispered, eyes narrowing. "If someone saw, they might carry the tale to Chesza, and then she'd never marry me. Go away, Tamra, and *stay* away."

He closed the shutter so quickly he almost struck Tamra's face.

She pressed her hands to her breastbone. Surely her heart had turned to stone, it was so heavy in her breast—and it was shattering. Tears stung her eyes, bitter as the Moonpool waters. By seeking him out for a kiss, by threatening his pursuit of Chesza's heart, she had lost Khylom.

She looked at the closed shutter, and realized she was wrong. She'd never had Khylom to begin with.

Khylom had never loved her. He hadn't even pretended to love her, speaking always of his love for Chesza. Even when he'd used Tamra's body, he had made it clear he wanted only Chesza.

Tamra felt like she was dying.

She had not died in the terrible waters of the Moonpool. She would not die of this.

But she went to the Moonpool and wept there for the loss of her love. She knew the Moon Goddess, Whose tears had formed this pond, would understand her sorrow. She wondered if Atanata had chosen her because the goddess had always known Khylom did not love her.

When the sun rose, Tamra returned to the village, to make ready for her journey to the Great Temple of the Moon.